Praise for *Thank You for Sharing*

"Impossible to put down! A delicious pressure-cooker-style slow burn of a romance, *Thank You for Sharing* contains the greatest 'only one bed' scene I've ever had the pleasure of reading. Not only is the romance delightful, but Rachel Runya Katz handles the complexity of grief and trauma with the tenderest of touches, creating a safe, welcoming space for her characters and readers alike. I have no doubt that readers will fall head over heels for Liyah and Daniel!"
—Alexandria Bellefleur, bestselling and Lambda Award–winning author of *Written in the Stars* and *The Fiancée Farce*

"Rachel Runya Katz's witty, heartfelt debut will transport you back to the lazy days of summer-camp crushes and breathless first kisses. *Thank You for Sharing* combines steamy, electric chemistry with thoughtful social commentary to create an unforgettable love story. This sexy, sweet romance is a delight."
—Regina Black, author of *The Art of Scandal*

"This is a funny, gentle friends-to-lovers story that lingers in the quiet moments and lets the reader bathe in the romance that burns slow—but oh so hot. A perfect read to escape into on a rainy day and be bear-hugged in your feelings places . . . even if you, like hesitantly thawing heroine Liyah, insist you don't have them."
—Jen Comfort, author of *The Astronaut and the Star*

T0038525

"Rachel Runya Katz's *Thank You for Sharing* is a magical love story. This is a poignant, sharp, and sexy romance with the kind of complex, bighearted characters and emotional honesty readers will adore. I loved it!"

—Carley Fortune, *New York Times* bestselling author of *Every Summer After*

"*Thank You for Sharing* is one of those books where someone will get to see themselves reflected on the page for the first time, whether in the complications of being a Jew of color, or the validation of a prickly, proud woman being fully loved for, not in spite of, her prickliness. Daniel and Liyah are both so fully drawn, and their story will stick with me for a long time. I'm so glad it exists."

—Anita Kelly, author of *Love & Other Disasters*

"This book wrapped a fist around my heart and refused to let go. Gorgeously written, with two magnetic leads, an irresistible group of friends, and a warmth that radiates from every page. Rachel Runya Katz is a true talent."

—Rachel Lynn Solomon, *New York Times* bestselling author of *The Ex Talk*

"I can't wait for everyone to fall head over heels for *Thank You for Sharing*. Rachel Runya Katz has a sparkling, singular voice: witty, observant, razor-sharp, and devastatingly tender. I treasured every moment I spent with Daniel, Liyah, and the rest of the vivid, complex supporting cast. This book is a gift."

—Ava Wilder, author of *How to Fake It in Hollywood*

THANK
YOU
for
SHARING

a novel

RACHEL RUNYA KATZ

ST. MARTIN'S
GRIFFIN
NEW YORK

This is a work of fiction. All of the characters, organizations, and events portrayed in this novel are either products of the author's imagination or are used fictitiously.

First published in the United States by St. Martin's Griffin, an imprint of St. Martin's Publishing Group

THANK YOU FOR SHARING. Copyright © 2023 by Rachel Runya Katz. All rights reserved. Printed in the United States of America. For information, address St. Martin's Publishing Group, 120 Broadway, New York, NY 10271.

www.stmartins.com

Designed by Kelly S. Too

The Library of Congress Cataloging-in-Publication Data is available upon request.

ISBN 978-1-250-88829-7 (trade paperback)
ISBN 978-1-250-88830-3 (ebook)

Our books may be purchased in bulk for promotional, educational, or business use. Please contact your local bookseller or the Macmillan Corporate and Premium Sales Department at 1-800-221-7945, extension 5442, or by email at MacmillanSpecialMarkets@macmillan.com.

First Edition: 2023

10 9 8 7 6 5 4 3 2 1

To Patrick. I love you so big.

Some of the thematic content in *Thank You for Sharing* contains discussions of sexual assault and the death of a parent; neither event occurs on the page. For more information, please visit the author's website.

THANK
YOU
for
SHARING

CHAPTER 1

"**COHEN-JACKSON**, huh? That's quite the odd combo."

When Liyah looks up, her airplane seatmate is glancing at her full name in script on the cover of her planner before making eye contact. There's a small smile playing at his lips, as if he finds her surname amusing. This reaction is not new to her, but she is simply Not In The Mood.

Liyah nearly missed her flight this morning. She managed to leave for the airport within a reasonable amount of time, an impressive feat for someone raised at the intersection of the Jewish Standard and Colored People time zones, but the fog had other plans. Karl (Neen informed her that the fog in San Francisco has a *name*) usually burns off around mid-morning but was thicker and slower to dissipate today. So she, Neen, and Ringo Starr (her best friend's beloved VW Beetle convertible also has a name) found themselves trapped behind a seven-car pileup, Neen anxiously sticking their head out the window every forty-five seconds to assess the nonexistent movement of traffic.

At the departures' lane, Neen spared Liyah their usual teary goodbye speech. Instead, they wordlessly offered Liyah their right ear, which she met halfway, bumping together the matching star studs in their earlobes. Such had been the pair's secret handshake since a drunken evening in Alien Piercing & Tattoo nearly seven years prior. Liyah wound up sprinting to her gate and, suffice it to say, she skipped out on the bagel she'd planned to purchase before boarding.

She'd heaved a sigh of relief (she was not out of breath; her body just hated running) when she arrived at her assigned seat and found that her neighbor was someone her age. With her luck, she'd pictured a shrieking toddler or, God forbid, a chatty old man. She thought his presence meant a few hours of peace as she attempted to subsist off a free bag of pretzel mix and ginger ale.

Apparently, she thought wrong.

She gives him a long look, eyes skating over his high cheekbones, the slight bend in the bridge of his nose, burnt honey-colored almond eyes. *He's white and East Asian. Korean*, she guesses, before mentally kicking herself for playing ethnicity detective. She realizes he's just done the same to her, and mentally kicks herself yet again for feeling guilty. Her metaphorical shins are starting to bruise.

Where is he from? Someplace that would give him enough cultural literacy to spot a truth in her last name (Cohen being decidedly Jewish, Jackson being decidedly not) but not enough to remain unfazed or to know he should stifle his shock. Or, at the very least, not to say something to the effect of, "You're quite obviously Black *and* apparently Jewish? How strange!" Never mind that a man his age has probably committed the bulk of Drake's discography to memory.

She checks her watch. They're not due to land at O'Hare for another hour and fifteen minutes. *Maybe he grew up in the Bay Area. Maybe he went to a high school that was majority East Asian where nobody said a damn thing about his name or his parents or so much as looked at him sideways. A* pang of jealousy accompanies the thought. Regardless, he of all people should know better.

"What an original comment," Liyah starts, voice saccharine. She pointedly looks down at the redwood tree sticker on his laptop before meeting his eyes. "Stanford must be proud to have such an observant alumnus."

The man's smile abruptly falls, and he makes a waving motion with his hands as if to erase his words as he opens his mouth. Liyah, still Not In The Mood, declines his attempt to backtrack.

She purses her lips. "Tell me, then, what is the right way to be biracial? You're normal, but everybody else is a total freak?" He looks down at his hands, stunned. Liyah's lips stretch into a smug smile, pleased that she's hit her mark.

"That's not—" He sighs strongly enough to sag both shoulders, apparently thinking better of what he was about to say. "I'm sorry," he mutters, cheeks deeply flushed.

Liyah nods curtly and slips her planner back into her tote bag. She can no longer remember why she withdrew it in the first place. She turns away from him, the warmth of her anger creeping up her neck. As the minutes pass, her heartbeat slows, and her outburst settles around them. The anger shifts toward shame. She pulls up the shade at the window and looks out. The plane is suspended in a soup of fog, thick and white, all depth and dimension indiscernible. She closes her eyes and imagines herself floating out there, disembodied from her grumbling stomach.

This is so like her. Bored out of her goddamn mind (yet somehow still incomprehensibly busy) at work, she spent the last three weeks counting down the seconds until she could leave for Fourth of July weekend. She isn't even off the flight home, and she's already miserable again. Must be a new record.

Maybe she should say something. Not because she's in the wrong (she isn't, although her general grumpiness hasn't helped) but because the discomfort in the air is bordering on suffocating. She ventures her gaze over to him. His focus is buried in a *GQ* magazine, a gentle crease formed at his brow. His jaw (sharp, freshly shaven) clenches and releases as he turns the page. The movement causes Liyah's eyes to trail down his arms toward his hands. She spies a bit of ink peeking out from under his rolled sleeves. His fingers are long and sturdy, the littlest one on his left hand adorned with a silver ring.

She averts her eyes before he catches her staring. He's undeniably good-looking. If only he'd waited until they were deplaning to make an asinine comment, she might've been able to spend this final hour of her prison sentence appreciating the way his tongue swipes over his bottom lip as he reads instead of contemplating making use of one of the four emergency exits.

Maybe she should nap. The coffee and ginger ale sloshing in her stomach disagree. At this point, she's not sure whether her need for food or fresh air will win out upon landing. It's quite possible she'll take a later shuttle to economy parking just to pay two dollars more than she should for a caprese sandwich.

She nearly shudders at the thought. Something feels so intrinsically wrong with buying food on the way out of the airport. No, she'll stick it out, and hope her stomach doesn't autocannibalize before she makes it to her apartment.

CONTEXT, DANIEL. CONTEXT.

He wants to stick his head in one of the overhead bins and shut it. Repeatedly. The second she narrowed her eyes, the whites around her black irises all but disappearing, he realized his mistake. Had they been several other places—a synagogue for the High Holidays, say, or a conference where his neck would be adorned with a name tag reading DANIEL

Rosenberg in bold lettering—she would have at least had a chance to take his attempt at flirting for what it was. As is, he came off as a hypocritical jackass. Which is leagues below a regular jackass.

Staring down at the GQ issue he swiped from his college roommate this morning, he tries desperately to ignore the way her eyes periodically bore holes in the side of his head. Momentarily, he wishes he were religious enough to be wearing a yarmulke and tzitzit on this flight. Maybe even some awkwardly straight payes instead of his neatly trimmed sideburns. The desire is fleeting. He'd scarfed down a bacon, egg, and cheese sandwich immediately after takeoff and fully intends a repeat performance at a neighborhood café this evening—for Daniel, unkosher breakfast sandwiches are not reserved for any particular time of day.

He had been looking for a conversation starter since the moment he shuffled into the aisle to let her take her seat. Her mass of long, tightly wound curls was pinned back on the side closest to him, revealing her delicate nose and double piercings in her earlobe that seemed to match the set of moles situated high on her cheek. Once seated, she'd looked up at him through dark eyelashes and offered a small smile before turning to look out the window. He was no longer annoyed by the small plane; the lower ceilings also meant two-person rows, and he got his precious aisle seat with no third party between them.

He's not enough of a lech to know how to go about flirting with a random woman on an airplane, so when she pulled out the notebook, his heart hammered in his chest. He couldn't believe his luck: Jews of color aren't exactly commonplace where he grew up—him, his mother, and his sister being the only ones at his shul in Madison—and there is no non-Jew on the planet with the last name Cohen. Here was a way to establish camaraderie presented on a silver platter, or rather embossed on a leather notebook. He could maybe even find an excuse to see her again.

Now, his luck has run out. He's grateful that he at least shoved his foot in his mouth closer to landing than takeoff. He considers introducing himself—first and last name—or just explaining bluntly that he's a Korean Jew and is excited to have a kindred spirit. That might have worked as an immediate follow-up to his gaffe, but when she looked at him the way his cat, Sweet Potato, stares at a bug she plans to devour, he chickened out. Now, he's waited about thirty minutes too long, and he resigns himself to never entering her number into his phone.

It's probably better this way. Daniel's love life has been dormant for so long that it might be dead. Besides, she might live in San Francisco. He was only in town for the long weekend, successful in his single-minded mission to board his Sunday flight home thoroughly hungover and equally sick of his college suitemates. Aliyah's number would likely never do more than burn a hole in his contacts list. He feels a little odd thinking her name, since she hadn't offered it, but he is unlikely to forget it anytime soon.

When he no longer feels the heat of her gaze—or deathly glare, really—on the side of his face, Daniel risks a glance. Her eyes are closed, eyelashes nearly grazing the moles on her cheek.

Wait, he thinks, panic rising as a scratchy lump in his throat, *I've seen those before.*

No, it couldn't be. Her name was Leah.

He blinks slowly, swallows, feels his blood thicken. Her name was *Liyah,* as in Aliyah. Which means he's officially gone from mildly idiotic to perhaps the unluckiest moron alive. All those years of summer camp, he never saw her name written out.

His memory of her, age thirteen, crystallizes: features softer and less defined, hair in cornrows that reached her collarbone, face lit only by a camping lantern Daniel's father packed him. That look of total trust in her dark eyes. Which morphed into naked contempt the very next day.

She doesn't recognize him, he's sure of it. A touch of insult sinks his stomach. He's a good six inches taller than he had been, and the braces on his teeth and baby fat in his cheeks are long gone, but is he really that forgettable? Then again, every time she looks at him, he gets the sense that it's more about shooting daggers than cataloging his features.

The universe must be conspiring against him. There's no other explanation. Accidentally making a beautiful girl hate you once is one thing—but twice, a decade and a half apart? He's cursed.

A flight attendant stops at their row, offering a chance to give up their trash. Daniel holds his breath as Liyah awkwardly reaches over him to deposit her can-pretzel-bag-cup sandwich into the extended plastic bag. When she pulls back, her eyes flit across him, irritation plain as ever. But this time, they snag, widening slightly before she whips her head toward the window.

Widening, he decides, in recognition.

Liyah says nothing. But the soft *tap, tap, tap* of her forehead against the windowpane tells Daniel all he needs to know.

Mercifully, the plane lands, the FASTEN SEAT BELT light dinging off a few minutes later. He is a little too quick to his feet, half stumbling out into the aisle, but the past four hours of sitting in a cramped airplane row have rendered his knees nearly as sore as his ego. He opens the overhead bin and slings the strap of his duffel bag over his chest, rushing to make room for Liyah to stretch her legs while the first half of the airplane empties.

She leans up on her tiptoes to get to her small roller suitcase. He tries not to let his gaze linger on the bit of midriff her sweatshirt exposes as it lifts over her olive-green leggings. The suitcase appears to have shifted to the back of the bin, and she grapples with the wheels as she tries to pull it out.

Daniel steps forward and pulls it down for her with ease, depressing the button to raise the handlebar before passing it off to her. He smiles sheepishly, hoping that the convenience of his height has redeemed him slightly.

"I could have gotten it, Rosenberg," she says, making eye contact with him for the first time in the better part of an hour, her murderous look only intensified.

His stomach, along with his smile, plummets. Daniel can almost hear the cartoon whistle and crash as it lands somewhere near his lower intestine. There were three Daniels in their cohort at camp—each mononymously known as Rosenberg, Schwartz, and Gross. But Liyah had always called him by his first name. Like if *she* said "Daniel," any listener should know prima facie that she was talking about him. On anybody else's lips, "Rosenberg" is a term of familiarity, even endearment. On hers, it means *I know exactly who you are, and you are nothing to me.* Maybe it was better when she didn't remember him. "Liyah—"

"Thank you," she mutters—compulsively, it seems, because she frowns around the words like they're bitter in her mouth. Daniel decides not to risk speaking and nods. The wave of moving passengers reaches them, and she turns to walk away without a second glance.

Daniel waits, motioning for the man in the row across from him to move first. A buffer between them, he finally exits this wretched flight.

"Neen!" Liyah shouts, elongating the single syllable as she swipes to answer the FaceTime. She bursts with excitement and relief at the sight of them on the patio of their favorite café, almost (but not quite, make no mistake) forgetting about her empty stomach. A cheese quesadilla sizzles in her cast-iron pan, and she props her phone against her kitchen utensils jar so she can tend to it with both hands.

"C-J," they croon back, a clinking sound accompanying the turn of their head. Today, Neen wears hollow plugs in their quarter-inch gauges, hoop earrings threaded through the holes. "I hadn't heard from you since your *I didn't have time to eat before boarding* text. Wanted to make sure you were still alive."

"I am, but barely." Liyah slides the quesadilla onto a plate, nearly moaning at the smell of butter and melted cheese as she lifts it toward her lips to blow it cool. She taps gingerly with an exploratory finger, then hurriedly sinks her teeth into the crisp tortilla, feeling the warm cheese ooze between her lips. This time, she actually moans.

Neen peers over their vintage 1970s sunglasses at the screen, letting out a laugh. "I don't think I've ever gotten that noise out of someone who was fully clothed."

Liyah goes bug-eyed in mock offense, unable to keep from smiling around her half-full mouth. "Do you have any idea how long four hours feels on an empty stomach? With dead headphones, no less. I was ready to keel over." She stops her tirade to take another bite, which she only mostly chews before swallowing.

"The flight was that bad, huh?"

Liyah blinks her eyes open before she even realizes she closed them. She starts to wonder what gave her away, but she stops herself. Their friendship is counted in decades, plural, despite neither of them having hit thirty. What they have isn't quite telepathy, but it's about as close as it gets. "I don't even know where to start. The person sitting next to me"— she heaves a sigh—"saw my name on something and, y'know, expressed surprise." She catches Neen's wince. She's grown now, so she usually handles it better, but it's always been a bit of a sore spot. "I went off on him, and he was completely terrified. And then I calmed down and spent like thirty minutes wondering if it was overkill. Maybe I was just a bit hangry, it was harmless and came off the wrong way, but then—"

"You? Hangry? Never," Neen interrupts, giggling in response to Liyah's glare.

"As I was saying, I spent the rest of the flight feeling supremely guilty. And hungry—"

"You mentioned that."

Liyah rolls her eyes. "Yes, well. We've established that it's a determining factor of my mood."

"If you're so sure he meant no wrong, why'd it nettle you so much? I'm having trouble imagining that you were enjoying friendly banter up until this point, your extenuating circumstances and all." They pause, lowering their sunglasses and arching a brow as if scanning Liyah's face through the phone. "Ah, he was cute!"

"NO!" Liyah is treated to Neen's expert side-eye. "Well, I mean, yes, but no. That's not why. He was mixed, so he should've known it was a dumb thing to say." Neen is clearly still incredulous. "This isn't even the good part of the story! So, I'm feeling guilty, hungry, etcetera, and then I get this niggling feeling. And maybe it's the way he looked at me, but I'm like *I know this guy from somewhere.*" She takes a deep breath, followed by another bite of quesadilla.

"And?" Neen demands.

Liyah swallows. "And I realized that it was Daniel Rosenberg."

Neen's already round doe eyes widen. When the initial wave of shock rolls over them, they laugh. "Wow, he's Jewish! You must have really done a number on him if he didn't introduce himself right away. I mean, just how hungry . . ." As Neen trails off, their eyes practically bulge out of their head.

"Wait. *Thee* Daniel Rosenberg? Of Jewish sleepaway camp fame?"

"The very one," Liyah affirms tightly.

"Oh, you *are* angry. I thought this"—they circle their hand, palm open, at her—"might have been some sort of sexual frustration. Do you want me to fly to Chicago and punch him for you? I'll do it. He's been on my shit list for fourteen years."

"I don't need you getting an assault charge over something that happened in middle school." Neen gives her a look like *I think we know it's more than that* mixed with *you've done it for me.* Which, to be fair, it is, and she has. But when you're twelve and precocious, you can talk your way out of a suspension. She's not sure her Student of the Month record would help her post their bail. "Besides"—Liyah takes another bite, so she doesn't have to say her next words with any real conviction—"we barely remember each other."

They bring one hand to their chest. "I mean this with my whole heart, C-J: you're a moron. You remember each other perfectly well, or he wouldn't have been so terrified, and you wouldn't have gotten so worked up."

"I am not worked up," she says, and watches Neen's eyes slide to about where her shoulders should be on their screen. Liyah releases them, hoping it passes as a shrug. "And it took me a long time to recognize him. When we were thirteen, he was less . . . I don't know. He has a tattoo and went to Stanford, apparently."

"Wait, what?" Neen says, jostling the phone as they sit up so straight Liyah thinks they'll shoot out of their chair. "What was the tattoo?"

"I couldn't tell, honestly. It was just the ends of it on his forearm, a bunch of abstract lines, maybe."

They shake their head. "Tentacles. They're jellyfish tentacles. C-J, I *met* him!"

Liyah stops mid-chew. "When? How? Why do you know that?"

"You would, too, if you loved me enough to take off work to get here in time for the pool party!"

"A First of July party is not a real thing, Neen. It did not warrant using my precious time off."

"It is! It definitely is, because Dan—you know, Daniel Tran, my work husband, total lightweight—had his roommate from Stanford staying with him. And the roommate was a half-Asian guy with a jellyfish tattoo who he called Rosenberg. Which would make sense since his name is also Daniel. Because I *met Daniel Rosenberg*." They bring their phone closer to their face, brow furrowing as though searching for something. "C-J, no wonder you didn't recognize him at first. That man did not grow up to be cute. He is *sexy*."

Liyah swallows thickly. She described him with that exact word in a diary that probably still exists in her parents' attic somewhere. And that was when he was barely her height and had braces with rubber bands that required removal before eating and a mop of wavy hair he had no idea what to do with.

"It's him!" Neen says, just as Liyah's phone pings with a screenshot of Daniel Tran's Instagram post. Neen stands in the center of the photo, head thrown back in laughter, the russet tones in their deep brown skin set aglow by the sun. To their left is Dan, red-faced and grinning, jet-black hair tucked behind his ears. And on their right is Daniel Rosenberg, his smile slightly crooked and bright, his full lips a muted pink. Just as Liyah remembers it. He's shirtless, his arm slung around Neen's shoulders, his tattoo on full display. The body of the jellyfish starts where his right shoulder meets his chest, the opening of the bowl shape rippling over his deltoid muscle as if in mid-swim. Its ruffled arms wrap around his bicep, thinner tentacles cascading around them, their ends reaching his forearms. The strokes of ink tangle with his veins, and she is forced to notice the lean muscle beneath his skin. His shape looks earned rather than worked for, like he's an athlete and not a gym rat.

"He's definitely . . . tall," she says.

"Tall? That's how you'd describe him?" Neen's jaw hangs slightly ajar. Liyah nods, stubborn. "Fine. But I'm sure he knew it was you immediately. You were a hot child."

"Okay, one: that is an incredibly weird thing to say. And two: it's not even true. He didn't say a word about it. Doesn't exactly seem like the memory is keeping him up at night." Probably because it never meant anything to him in the first place, and we tend to do better at remembering those who've wronged us than those who we've wronged. The thought makes her feel stomach-churningly silly. Here she is, fingernails still hooked into anger at someone to whom she is barely a footnote. Like always.

Neen blows a raspberry. "Tall. I can't believe you said he's tall. He's *fine*, C-J. I'm talking speeding-ticket-in-construction-zone fine."

"Newfound attraction to men?"

"Never. I was under the impression that you had one, though. Did you damage it in the wash?" Neen laughs at their own joke. Liyah rolls her eyes. "Why don't I get his number from Dan? Thirty more minutes in his presence and I bet you'll be having hate sex in the nearest bathroom."

"*What?*" Liyah sputters.

"It's really the perfect plan," they continue. "Get your rocks off and avenge your thirteen-year-old self! Unless he violates some part of your dating rulebook that I can't manage to keep track of?"

Liyah shakes her head. "The rules are so I can *avoid* dating."

"Okay, and? It doesn't get more casual than hooking up with an insanely hot person you dislike."

"Ha ha. I don't want to talk about this anymore." Neen

seems to sense that Liyah means it, so they move on to complaining about their new manager at their very West Coast tech company who doesn't even understand the product they're selling.

Liyah sits on the couch with the remainder of her quesadilla as she listens, feeling her blood sugar slowly climb back to a healthy level. She sighs. This time yesterday, she was cuddled up to her best friend on a picnic blanket in the middle of Mission Dolores Park, and it was the best she'd felt in weeks. There, she could almost pretend that she's satisfied spending eight hours a day making minor updates to old exhibitions that barely require her bachelor's degree. That her last friends-with-benefits situation didn't implode the second the girl sent a text beginning with *I'm v drunk and I've been thinking about us.* That Neen was probably only bothering her about every cute person who walked past them (and now, Daniel Rosenberg) because she shut down when they tried to talk to her about said implosion. None of that mattered when her favorite person in the world was wrapped around her and the sun was warming her face. But now, she's home. And as comfortable as her couch is, as much as she's proud of the life she created in this city, she finds herself dreading the week ahead.

DANIEL UNLOCKS HIS door to a quiet apartment. The low hum of the dishwasher tells him he just missed Alex, his bartender roommate and the part owner of a speakeasy in River North, leaving for work. Sweet Potato trots over to him, purring almost violently as she walks figure eights around his ankles. "Missed you, too," he murmurs as he bends down to scratch her ears. The purring continues, the cat practically gluing herself to his calf, like she senses his bad mood.

He deposits his duffel in his bedroom, thoughts racing. Daniel spent more nights of eighth grade than he could count imagining what he was going to say to Liyah when he had the chance—half apology, half demand for an explanation—only for her not to show up the next summer. The Julys of his childhood had been blurs of bug bites and sunburns and her braids with star-shaped beads on the ends, and then she was just gone. It's not like he thinks about her often now, but it's not *never*. Especially considering his recent increase in sleepless nights with a highlight reel of his worst memories playing on repeat.

Murphy's Law, right? He finally decides that he's ready to be a half-functioning adult with a social life again and look where it gets him.

Maybe he should google her. How many Aliyah Cohen-Jacksons could there be in Chicago? He'll find her email or her Instagram and draft a message—begin with the apology he knows he owes her, ask to get coffee and explain himself. If it goes well enough, they can catch up and reminisce and then maybe do it the next week. They'll be friends again, and he'll have one less clip for his insomnia shame montage.

Or she'll delete the message unread, and he'll feel even more guilty and embarrassed than he already does.

He thinks back to the look of absolute vitriol she gave him in the airplane aisle as he handed her the suitcase. The latter outcome seems the likely—or perhaps definite—one.

So, he goes about the rest of his evening, unpacking and making dinner and petting his cat, trying not to replay every moment of the flight this afternoon and the end of that summer fourteen years ago in his mind. And when he fails, his watch reading 2:33 a.m., his only solace is that he'll probably never see Liyah again.

CHAPTER 2

LIYAH feels like she's in a deodorant commercial as she grips the edges of her office bathroom's sink. *You got this. You got this. You got this.* She tugs at her blouse, making sure its hem covers the ruffled waist of her ill-fitting slacks.

She doesn't exactly hate her body, not anymore. Her teenage years (and a good bit of her early twenties) were spent full-throat sobbing in dressing rooms every time she went pants shopping. Since then, a few clothing brands have developed "curvy" denim cuts, where the waist is true to size but there's a good bit of extra fabric in the hips, butt, and thighs. The first pair Liyah tried on had inspired not only happy tears, but also an unparalleled level of brand loyalty. The Field Museum's exhibition employee dress code allows for jeans, but today, Liyah is pitching an entire exhibit, and it feels like something that requires more elevated attire.

This twenty-minute meeting cost her approximately three *I'm writing to follow up*s and five almond milk lattes (the former to her boss, Jeff, and the latter for his assistant, Becca). When the exhibitions staff had their department-wide meeting the week after the Fourth of July, the head curator had announced the acquisition of several rare early hominid skeletons. Liyah had never so excitedly recorded her notes. This is her first chance since graduation to do the work she'd had a taste of while writing her master's thesis, the work she's dreamt of doing since the moment she first set foot in the Burke Museum, her father's hand dwarfing her inexplicably sticky four-year-old fingers.

During the weeks since, this project has been the lead player in Liyah's brain, and she has clocked an extra seven hours a week compiling sources and coming up with a plan. Come to think of it, she also bought lunch a few times for Siobhan, one of the department's graphic designers, to secure her talents. Siobhan said she didn't need it, but Liyah rambled on about unpaid labor and Siobhan eventually relented. This meeting is the most expensive of Liyah's life. If Jeff goes for it, though, it'll all pay off.

She checks in the mirror for sweat stains, life imitating corporate art. Lifting her arms reveals how scrunched the fabric is under her much-needed belt. She makes a mental note to find a tailor this weekend.

Liyah takes a deep breath and heads out to the conference room. The laptop is already connected to the projector, a presentation made complete by Siobhan's graphics queued. She drums her fingers on the tabletop. *Deep breaths.* Jeff is usually running behind, but she can't help but worry he's forgotten about the meeting or decided it's not worth his trouble. She doesn't want to think about how many more almond trees it would cost to reschedule. But then the door to the room creaks open, interrupting her thought spiral.

"Liyah!" Jeff, always a smidgeon too loud for the room he's in, arrives with Becca in tow. They've technically been co-workers for three years, but Becca keeps to herself, and prior to the coffee bribery, she'd hardly spoken four words to Liyah. Jeff takes a seat, notepad and pen at the ready. "Sorry to keep you waiting. Let's hear it!"

"Thank you for meeting with me." Liyah clears her throat. Jeff's expression is blank, and likely to stay that way. She mentally morphs him into Neen's smiling face and, with a deep intake of breath, starts the PowerPoint. "When I heard that we had a chance to bring the hyoid bones of early hominids to the Field, my first thought was how they weave into the story of the evolution of speech."

"Yes, yes, the lack of space for the laryngeal air sack differentiates us from nonverbal apes." Jeff gestures his hand as if to say *I know all this, get to the point.*

A quick press of the mouse changes the slide. "Right, the hyoid bone can give us an idea of the origin of language, but what if we used the open exhibit space on the second floor to tell a broader story of human evolution? Not just the nuts and bolts of natural selection, but the greater intricacies of the development of traits that we view as especially key to our humanity." Liyah moves from slide to slide, going through the presentation exactly as she practiced with Neen. She stumbles a bit at first, but eventually hits her stride. By the time she reaches the end, make-believe Neen has long since disappeared, but the smile on Jeff's face remains.

"This is . . . good. This is really good," Jeff says, nodding. Liyah bites the inside of her cheek to keep from grinning. "It would complement our exhibit on the evolution of Earth. You know, how our home came to be, and then across the atrium, how we came to be."

It's quite possible that no amount of cheek biting is going to stop Liyah's ear-to-ear grin. "Right!" she says. "Blurring the lines between the biological study and the social scientific study of, well, us."

Jeff clucks his tongue. "This will require a lot more than the handful of skeletal remains and tools I already have secured. Even I can't sign off on this without asking the higher-ups. How do you think it fits into our goal of attracting more young adults? We've got the kid market cornered, and re-tirees love museums, but we're struggling with people your age."

Liyah pauses, considering. She vaguely remembers Jeff talking about marketing at their last meeting, but she zoned out after the acquisition was announced. "Well, surely a new exhibition will bring people in."

He leans forward, placing his hands palms-down on the table. "If you want to be bumped up to curator next year, you're going to need to think beyond that."

"Next year?" Liyah blurts. Curator by thirty, *that* was her goal. Her college advisor had looked down his nose when she told him (*ambitious, aren't you?*) and Neen said they would print the website update the moment it went live and mail it to his house. Her mind spins. Curator by twenty-eight? If that's on the table, it changes everything.

"Look," Jeff continues, "you know what the board wants—better membership numbers. No matter how much you and I may wish it would come from a new exhibition, it proba-bly won't. Unless it's all mirrors and colored lights for social media." Liyah restrains her eye roll. Last year, she worked on one of those, and despite the Field's admirable efforts to incorporate genuinely educational content, a little bit of her died every day she spent designing it. "If you work with the marketing guy they hired, I'll pitch them your idea. Together, that would be a pretty convincing promotion package."

"What exactly would working with him entail?"

"Meet with him, come up with events that will attract a millennial audience, and send me a proposal. You're young, and you know this museum well. I'm sure you'll make some-thing great."

Spending time away from her exhibitions sounds like a monumental waste. But *curator* rings in her ears. She grits her teeth into a smile. "I could do that."

Jeff claps his hands. "Great! I'll send you the details. Forward me your slides and I'll pitch it to the board. I can let you know what they say by end-of-week."

"Thank you. If it works out, I would love Siobhan to be the graphic designer for the project. She did a wonderful job helping with this presentation." She's not sure if this is an appropriate request to make, but she would feel immensely guilty if she said nothing.

Jeff nods to Becca. "I'll keep that in mind." He pauses, as if remembering something. "You studied evolutionary anthropology, right?"

"Yes. Or, actually, it was called biological anthropology at Northwestern, but yes—" She wills herself to stop midsentence. Excitedly spewing unnecessary information is a habit she's never been able to kick.

"Okay, then. You'll need someone to help with the cultural side of things. No promises, but it might be worth asking around." He gives a pointed look. It seems her clandestine rivalry with Emiliano (cultural anthropologist, colossal priss) is not as clandestine as she thought.

Even so, Liyah full-on beams as she thanks Jeff and Becca. She barely manages to wait until they leave the room to do her victory dance and pull out her phone.

Liyah

It went well. He's gonna bring it up the ladder, and all I have to do is meet with a marketing guy about appealing to a millennial crowd. Which, gross, but Jeff said it would be, and I quote, "a pretty convincing promotion package." AH!!!!

Neen's reply is almost immediate.

Neen

ahhhhhhhhhhhhhhhhhh
hhhh curator C-J! kicking
bones and takin species'
names

Liyah

God you're corny. And
getting ahead of yourself.
But thanks I love you!!!

Neen

sent u $$ for celebratory
lunch! knock yourself out
and don't even think about
sending it back. it'll start a
vicious cycle greater than the
venmo wars of 2014

Liyah

Ugh love you miss you!!

Neen

love you miss you too xo

Liyah all but sprints to her office and swings open the door. "I'm taking you to lunch!"

Siobhan startles, her fair, freckled skin turning beet red as she pulls out one earbud. "Jesus, Liyah. Scared me half to death."

"Jeff liked it! He's gonna let us know if it's a go by Friday."

"No shit, huh? Congrats, love."

"Your graphics took it to the next level. I couldn't have done it without you. Hence, lunch."

"I don't believe that for a second. Also I will physically fight you if you try to buy me food again." She holds up a finger. "And if you start on about wage theft, I won't even go to lunch with you. Doing favors for friends is *not* the leading cause of underpaid workers."

Liyah shoots a playful glare over her shoulder as she sits. "Alright, noted. But I told Jeff that you should do the graphics."

"If it gets me off this stupid newsletter revamp, I might have to buy *you* lunch." Siobhan sighs. "Speaking of, can you proofread this?"

Liyah, too drained from the meeting to stand up, scoots her chair across the small room until she can read Siobhan's screen. As much as she hates doing the work, she does a good job of it. The design would inspire at least a quick read-through instead of an instant delete. "There's no *u* in *favorite*," she says, pointing.

Siobhan groans. "It's murder keeping up with American spellings. You know, the English started this damn language, shouldn't we defer to their rules?"

Liyah places her hand over her heart. "Not Siobhan Gallagher saying something positive about the English. Must be below *zero Celsius* in hell."

"Don't go getting used to it. And get back to work." She punctuates this with a kick to the base of Liyah's chair. It rolls halfway back across the room, and Liyah finishes the journey, Siobhan's laughter tangling with the stuttered sound of Liyah's awkward scooting.

As she clicks through her in-box, archiving, deleting, and replying as needed, the details for tomorrow's meeting appear in a message from Jeff. She'll be having coffee with Brett (ew) at a little place in the Loop on Wednesday, nine sharp. Annoyance nips at her.

"Siobhan, what're the odds of me getting through a ninety-minute meeting with a marketing specialist named Brett without rolling my eyes?"

"Nil," she replies. Liyah snort-laughs.

Aliyah Cohen-Jackson, Curator. Fine, she can tolerate a few meetings with a corporate hack. Maybe he'll be dumb enough to fall for feigned feminine incompetence and do all the work.

"How's the pharma account going?" A new route was put up at their bouldering gym, and Jordan spots Daniel from ten feet below.

Jordan was the one who discovered Chicago Rocks two years prior. Before that, they had worked at the same marketing firm for a year and a half without ever interacting. They were aware of each other, especially as the rest of their company is nothing if not incredibly white, but they were hired at different times and had never been on the same project.

One day, Jordan showed up at his office at 5:05 p.m., leaned on the doorframe with the kind of twinkling smile that Daniel previously thought only existed on film, and asked Daniel how he felt about rocks. They've been climbing together three days a week since. Daniel is eternally grateful that Jordan chose him to ask that day, and not only because it gave him a good reason to cancel his overpriced gym membership.

Daniel reaches for the next hold. His hand is too sweaty for a solid grip, so he dips it in the bag of chalk hanging from his hip. *Much better.* "I might be transitioning away from it, finally." He hoists himself up another several inches, his feet finding security on new holds. "If we get CTA, I'm pulling out all the stops to be lead. Brett also emailed me about an account I might want, but he did it after five, so I refused to open it on principle."

Jordan's laugh echoes up at him. "If anybody at Kinley would be more excited to post about trains than cutting-edge medicine, then I guess it would be you."

"Hey, the L has never failed me."

Jordan snorts. "I can probably name five times off the top of my head that you've been late this month *specifically* because of the Chicago Transit Authority."

"We have a complex relationship." Also, he hates big pharma. When he was assigned the account, there were many envious eyes on him. He pretended to be excited; it was a big account for someone so junior at the firm, but he's wanted off since the beginning. As anybody with a basic—let alone intimate—knowledge of the industry's standard practices would. Daniel reaches the top of the wall, so he releases his legs and does a few pull-ups on the last two climbing holds.

"*Cough,* show-off, *cough,*" Jordan calls.

"Did you inhale some chalk there?" Daniel asks, and he doesn't need to look down to know that Jordan is giving him the finger. He starts his descent, the path down easier than the path up now that he's built some muscle memory. When his feet land softly on solid ground, he grabs his towel to wipe the sweat from his brow and sees that Jordan has already gathered his things. "Wanna grab a drink?"

Jordan shakes his head. "I would, man, but I told Nisha that I'd watch some crime documentary with her. I don't know why women love that shit. It's nightmare fuel."

"Aite, another time," Daniel replies, following Jordan outside. The air is warm but breezy, a perfect August night.

"Whatever happened to that woman from the airplane?"

Daniel regretted telling him about Liyah approximately three seconds after he let it slip. He should've known that

Jordan, a true romantic, would never let him hear the end of it. The inquiries came every day at first, only recently decreasing to about once per week. He shakes his head. "Why won't you let this go? It's been over a month."

"Because you haven't mentioned a girl—*woman*—to me since, well, before, you know . . ." Jordan trails off. Daniel could throw him a rope, but he doesn't. Let Jordan dig himself out of his own hole. "You haven't mentioned a woman to me in over a year."

"Jordan, I mentioned that I ran into someone I used to know and that she absolutely *hated* me. Somehow, you've forgotten the second part."

"You also said she was hot." Daniel gives him a flat look, and Jordan holds up his hands. "Okay, I'll let it go. I just wanna see you happy. It's been a minute."

"I live with Alex; I've already got enough unsolicited dating advice." Daniel's roommate frequently reminds him that he has a standing offer to woo a lady with never-ending free drinks. Alex's words, not Daniel's. His six-month dry spell maybe hasn't been ideal, but it's not *that* bad. Between Jordan's serial monogamy and Alex's serial ghosting, neither of Daniel's closest friends in the city have ever learned how to spend two weekends in a row with an empty bed.

"Whatever you say, man. I'll see you at the gala on Friday."

Daniel groans. "Don't remind me." He can think of near infinite ways he'd rather spend his Friday night than at a museum celebrating his firm's twentieth birthday. Clipping Sweet Potato's front claws, say, even at the risk of another scar between his forefinger and thumb. His only solace is the possibility of an open bar. He extends his hand and they part ways with a sweaty dap and twin *see ya later*s.

On the L, he swipes through his phone until he reaches the app store. Six months isn't that bad, but it's starting to get to him. His thumb is hovering over the little cloud-shaped redownload button next to the Tinder icon when he thinks better of it. The situation is not so dire that he's willing to subject himself to overly forward questions about which side of his family he got his dick size from—gross—or white women who are creepily obsessed with Korean popular culture—somehow grosser. For now, his hand works perfectly fine.

When he finally gets to his apartment door, he finds it already unlocked. Alex must be off tonight. Sweet Potato saunters over to him and weaves between his ankles: her customary welcome home the greatest consistency in his life. He bends down and scoops her up. Despite her impatient meows, she doesn't squirm, and instead softly pats his jaw with a front paw. It took her weeks to warm up to him after he'd adopted her, and he still savors every bit of her affections. Just then, a thud comes from Alex's room, and Sweet Potato thrashes to jump out of Daniel's arms.

The thud is followed by a low-pitched moan, and Daniel surmises that the lack of light coming from Alex's door is not because he's napping. They live in a building with decently thick walls, but their bedroom doors are perpetually propped open so that Sweet Potato can roam freely without ever losing access to her litter box. It's great to have a roommate who loves his cat, but not if it means that Daniel is the audience to this particular concert of groans.

He thinks about shutting the door, but he doesn't want to make their houseguest feel awkward, and he certainly doesn't want an accidental view of Alex's bare ass mid-thrust. Instead, he empties his gym bag and tosses his work clothes into the laundry hamper. The groans and thumping continue until the rush of water from Daniel's showerhead drowns out the noise.

He slips into the shower, letting the hot water soothe the muscles in his shoulders. They always ache by nighttime, the cycle of underuse at his desk and overuse on a rock wall catching up to him. As he lathers, he hears a door slam shut. At least he won't have an unfortunate soundtrack to his dinner. It's like the world is conspiring to make him keenly aware of exactly how long it's been since someone else touched him. Maybe he'll take Alex up on a complimentary bar tab this Friday; the guy must be doing something right if he's managed a one-night stand on a Monday.

Shit, the company party. Daniel groans, turning off the shower. Endless drinks and wooing will have to wait until next week.

CHAPTER 3

LIYAH pushes open the door to the coffee shop five minutes prior to her meeting, surveying the crowd with a deep frown. She may not value the work she's here to do, but she *does* value Jeff's opinion of her, and she doesn't want Brett to complain that she's made him wait her usual seven-to-twelve-minute delay.

Punctuality does not come naturally to Liyah, and her timeliness cost her her morning coffee. Which means her caffeine headache is minutes away, and Brett had to pick the coffee shop with the longest line in the known universe. She's faced with equally unappealing choices: take the required fifteen minutes to order and receive her drink (and risk upsetting Brett by being late) or figure out which suit-clad guy buried in his phone is hers for the next hour and a half (and risk upsetting Brett by being herself, sans coffee).

After a moment of indecision, she goes with the latter.

It's damn near impossible. Every guy here looks *exactly* like his name is Brett. There should be a law against this many MacBook Pros and navy suits in one room.

Liyah makes a sharp turn, bypassing the pastry case, and there: the guy in the back corner has two coffees in front of his MacBook and an empty chair across from him. If it's him, she'll have to buy a lottery ticket on her way home. She waves, but his head is down, so she crosses her fingers and makes her approach.

Back Corner is distinctly different from the rest of the navy suit species because his blazer is removed, sleeves rolled to his elbows. At least she can confirm that he's warm-blooded. He lifts his arm to brush his fingers through his hair, displaying tendrils of black ink peeking out from his rolled shirtsleeve. She freezes.

What are the fucking chances?

Liyah steps back gingerly, as though moving too suddenly will destroy the fabric of whatever alternate universe she's stumbled into. Even frazzled, she's sufficiently quiet, but the navy suit at the table to her left knocks over his cup, cursing loudly as he tries desperately to save his MacBook from death by drowning.

That's when Daniel Rosenberg looks up.

His face travels from blank to surprised to something like smug. Which is when she realizes that from his perspective, she's just been standing there, staring at him. She sails past frazzled, docking at horrified. "Hey, Liyah," he says tentatively, as though he's not sure whether he's supposed to acknowledge her. Maybe *smug* is the wrong word, but whatever his expression, she doesn't like it.

"God, why are you even here?" she asks, not really meaning to say it aloud.

His smile falls away. "I'm meeting someone for work," he replies, gaze traveling down Liyah's arm to where she white-knuckles the handles of her tote bag. She forces her fingers to relax, and his eyes snap back to hers.

"*I'm* meeting someone for work," Liyah parrots.

Daniel holds her gaze, nodding slowly. "Both can be true. I, um, wanted to—"

"I haven't had coffee today and I'm about to be late for my meeting," Liyah interrupts. "I really can't do this right now."

He gestures at the untouched mug across from him. "If you want this, it's yours. My guy hasn't showed yet."

Liyah frowns. "Is this your atonement for what you said on the flight?"

He lets out a short laugh through his nose. "I was just trying to be friendly, and you had to go and bite my head off. That was atonement enough."

She folds her arms across her chest. "That is a gross exaggeration."

"You sure?" He tilts his chin up, revealing his neck. "There might still be teeth marks."

"Alright, well. This has been exactly as nice as I would've expected it to be. Positively *lovely*." She drawls the word, making sure Daniel knows she means anything but, and turns, ready to begin her search for Brett once more.

"You sure you don't want the coffee?" he says, looking at her expectantly.

Liyah hesitates. She would very much like to stalk off without another word. But now she's genuinely late, and talking to Brett in this state could very well lead to a complaint in Jeff's in-box. "Your fellow . . ." She looks him up and down, grimacing. Even seated, it's obvious that unlike Liyah, Daniel has a tailor. An expert one. Slacks can't possibly fit like that off the rack. She hates how they emphasize the long line of his leg, hates even more that she notices. "Foreign acquisitions manager, I'm guessing, won't mind?"

"Digital marketing strategist."

Liyah gasps, hand on cheek. "I can't believe I assumed you had a boring, corporate job. That sounds *riveting*."

Daniel brings his right hand to his heart. Liyah looks at the edges of his tattoo, reminded of the photo Neen sent her, chlorinated water-slicked skin glistening in the sun. "You wound me," he says. His voice is pained, but the look of amusement he wears, while subtle, reaches his eyes. Like he thinks she's making fun of him, rather than saying *fuck off forever, please and thank you.* "It's fine, I promise."

"Okay, well," she says, picking up the mug, pleasantly surprised to find it still warm to the touch. "I'm going to go find Brett. There's gotta be one—or five—in here," she mumbles.

He laughs, and there's a pang of familiarity in her gut. It's a little throatier, sure, but that sound hasn't changed much in fourteen years. Liyah presses her lips together. "Looks like the coffee was yours all along. I'm guessing the name Jeff means something to you?"

There's a blinking moment before an intense surge of nausea. *Oh.* Brett pawned this meeting off on his underling like Jeff did to her, which means . . .

"Absolutely not."

Daniel furrows his brow. "You don't know a Jeff?"

"Oh, I do. One who failed to give me some very important information when I agreed to do this." Liyah thinks back to her morning commute. Does she remember getting on the L? Is there any chance that she fell to her death on the tracks and this is her personal hell?

Daniel frowns. "Look, I didn't know it was you, either. I see that you're unhappy with this development—" Liyah cough-laughs. Daniel's frown deepens. "But can you sit down and play nice for a little bit? I need this account to go well."

"*You* need this to go well? *I* need to play nice?" Liyah sputters.

"Liyah, come on." He sighs. "Have some coffee, and we'll get to work." And then the left corner of his mouth tugs upward.

God, she could combust on the spot. She could yell, stomp, storm out, tell Jeff she's sorry, but she cannot do this, her promotion be damned. But that would mean letting Daniel Rosenberg ruin this, too.

So, Liyah inhales deeply, pulls out the chair, takes her seat, and brings the mug to her lips. The first sip of coffee is nothing short of divine on her tongue, but it lands like pure acid in her stomach. "I assume you've read Jeff's email?" He nods. "I'm going to level with you, I don't really see the use of my being here instead of working on my exhibition. I was hoping I could show up and give Brett a doe-eyed damsel in distress look until he did everything for me, but I'm guessing that won't work on you."

Daniel shakes his head. "It would not. I have a sister."

Liyah nods, making eye contact with her coffee mug. Kayla, if she remembers correctly. A few years older, loud, beautiful. "I can't believe I'm saying this, but I wish I were sitting with a Brett right now." He brings his fist over his mouth as he laughs, like she's shocked it out of him. "I'm not joking," she says.

"I know," he replies. "Still funny."

Play nice, she tells herself, and takes another sip of coffee. "I know nothing about marketing, but I have basically an encyclopedic knowledge of the Field, so that's what I'll contribute."

"Encyclopedic, huh?" he challenges. Liyah nods. "How big is the building?"

She smirks, folding her arms across her chest. "There's over 480,000 square feet of exhibition space on the original three floors, with an additional 186,000 added in 2005 on the two underground levels. In case you're behind on your arithmetic, that adds up to 666,000, which is probably why the team who did the website decided to report it as two separate numbers. Ask me something difficult, Rosenberg."

The corner of his mouth quirks again, an almost-smile. "Okay, Liyah. You are the Field Museum's Britannica. Is there anything off the top of your head that might draw in a crowd that doesn't usually go to museums?"

Liyah taps her bottom lip. "Oh! SUE—our *T. rex*—is both the physically largest and most complete skeleton of one ever found! Ninety percent of her was recovered. We've even got her furcula."

"Her what?"

"Wishbone."

Daniel shakes his head, half laughing through his nose again. "This is your idea of something that would attract millennials who don't care about museums?"

"If it doesn't, there's no hope for our future." He looks at her blankly. "What, Rosenberg? If you have anything better, I'm all ears." She traces the handle of the mug, willing herself not to say the words forming on her tongue. A losing battle. "I'm shocked you won't go along with whatever I say, seeing that you've always been so fond of stealing my ideas."

"Are you serious, Liyah? We're doing this?" He sounds exasperated, maybe even a little angry. It's satisfying, knowing that she can disturb his calm.

Liyah purses her lips demurely. "I don't think we're doing anything."

"We're not going to get a single thing done if all you do is swipe at me. You want to talk about color wars?" She watches Daniel clench his jaw, the line of his brow lowering.

The fifth night they snuck out of their cabins, they met in the observatory at midnight. He always had this little camping lantern with him, and they had turned it off so that they could better see the stars. He pointed to Ursa Major. She showed him Cassiopeia, Draco, Hercules, and Capricorn. When they flicked the light back on, he was looking at her just like that. More serious, more resolute than she'd ever seen him. She swore she would memorize that moment, imprint it behind her eyelids for the rest of her life. Two days later, she promised herself she would scrub it from her consciousness completely.

Another beat. Liyah considers letting him stew, but the words tumble out: "It was never just about Maccabiah."

"THEN WHAT WAS it about, Liyah?" Daniel looks up at her. "The closing ceremony was the last time you spoke to me that summer. And then you didn't come back."

She blinks slowly, inhales like she's trying to hold herself together. "Fine. Yes, let's talk about it."

"Great." He leans back in his chair, absently turning his coffee cup with his left hand. "I'll start: I'm sorry I didn't warn you about the closing ceremony. I found out pretty last minute, but it was still shitty. Now, do you think you could tell me what it is I did that made you hate me?"

Liyah scoffs, her head tilting as if physically taken aback. "I'm sorry, what?" Her voice comes out with a slight tremor, and Daniel thinks it might be the sound of her blood boiling. "You want me to tell you *what you did*?"

"Yes. We knew each other for years, Liyah. That summer, we snuck out of our cabins every night for a week, and we would talk for hours. We"—*don't look at her lips, Daniel*—"kissed, and while I know it was awkward since we were children and had no idea what we were doing, it was also the most thrilling moment of my early teenage life. And then you completely disappeared. Over a stupid sports competition. You don't think that begs an explanation?"

If someone opened the door to the coffee shop right now, that tiny gust of wind would be enough to sway Liyah's jaw. For a moment, they just look at each other, and Daniel can hear his pulse in his ears.

"Do you even remember what happened that year?" she asks on an exhale.

They were in the oldest cohort of campers who still participated in color wars, on opposing teams—Liyah on Adom, red, and Daniel on Kachol, blue. They were supposed to meet behind the pool house the night after closing ceremonies, but Liyah never showed. "I know there were a lot of . . . similarities between Kachol's closing ceremony performance and Adom's."

"Similarities?" Liyah balks. "It started with three people decked out in the opposing teams' colors, who were then tagged by blue flashlights, only to shed their red, green, and white T-shirts and be resurrected as Team Kachol. Which is *identical* to what I had planned with Adom. You stole our thunder and won the trophy, betraying me in the process," Liyah says. She clenches her jaw, raises her chin, challenging him to defy her.

"I told you that I wasn't planning the closing ceremonies—"

"That doesn't mean you couldn't have used me for intel."

Daniel sighs, shoulders relaxing. "You stormed out after that, didn't you?"

"What does that matter?"

"It matters because if you hadn't, you would have heard Eli and Gross bragging about running an amateur sting operation to spy on your practices. They told everyone who would listen."

Liyah's face softens a fraction. "But why wouldn't you have just told me that?"

Daniel shakes his head, smiling. "I don't know. I was an insecure idiot, mostly. A girl stood me up, and my first thought was *she thinks I'm ugly and told her whole cabin I'm a bad kisser,* not *she thinks I masterminded a courtship to better my chances at being first in line for an ice cream party.*"

"There were also bragging rights," she says.

"Right. *That's* why I confessed my crippling arachnophobia." Finally, she smiles. It's brief but fucking dazzling. He runs his fingers through his hair, resisting the urge to avoid eye contact. "I'm sorry, Liyah. It took a few days for it to occur to me what it looked like to you, but it shouldn't have. And I should have found you and told you."

Her eyebrows lift. "About Maccabiah?"

"Yes, about Maccabiah," he reiterates, holding her gaze, feeling his pulse in his throat.

Liyah sighs. "I probably wouldn't have let you. I was pretty angry." He looks at her like *ya think?* and she wrinkles her nose at him.

"You didn't—you didn't stop going to camp because of that, did you?" He's wondered over the years, even before he ran into her on the flight. It's not a good feeling, to think that you might be the reason someone lost something they loved. Certainly not when it's 3 a.m. on a Tuesday and you still haven't fallen asleep.

"No, I didn't stop going to camp because of Maccabiah," she says carefully. Daniel's body sags with relief. "I did a program at the Burke Museum the next summer."

Daniel smiles. "Well, it's good to know that it wasn't because I was a bad kisser. You've really worked wonders on my teenage ego."

The glint in Liyah's eye turns devilish. "He deserves it. Putting your hand on someone's stomach and leaving it totally limp while you kiss is an underrated move."

His whole face blushes. Neck and chest, probably, too. He busies himself by rotating his laptop to show her his open document. "We should probably do some brainstorming, while we're here. In case advertising SUE's enormous furcula isn't enough."

"I don't see why it wouldn't be," she grumbles.

"Liyah."

"Fine, what've you got?" She leans forward, gently nudging his laptop so she can see the screen better. Her forearm hovers an inch above his, and he swears he can feel the hairs there stand on end. After a moment of scanning, she says, "This looks like a Pinterest board. Why are there so many pictures of people drinking wine? And sleeping bags?"

"A lot of museums in New York do cute events to appeal to the millennial crowd. Sleep-ins, wine nights, themed parties, that kind of thing."

"We already do a sleepover for parents and young children."

"But what about an adults-only version? Real-life *Night at the Museum*."

Liyah props her elbow on the table and rests her chin in the palm of her hand, seemingly unaware that she's pushing the invisible line that bisects their space. "The board wants us to get more young *members*. How is one night going to do that?"

"We do a raffle for a free membership at the end of the night for anyone who signs up for the newsletter. Then, you hook the rest via email with promises of SUE's furcula."

"Men only want one thing." She shakes her head. "SUE is more than just her furcula, Rosenberg."

Over time, the coffee in their cups dwindles and the document on his screen grows. Daniel leans back in his seat, readjusting his legs under the table. They're solidly on her half, but she sits with her legs crossed and close to her chair, her upper body spilling over into his space as she gesticulates or leans over the laptop. His exact opposite.

Miracle of miracles, by the time Liyah packs her things, they have an actionable proposal and a few decent backup ideas.

"Well, I've gotta go, but thank you for the coffee," she says.

"Are we good?" he blurts. "I mean, it seems like we're

going to be working together a lot, and it would be easier if you liked me." Liyah fiddles with the strap of her bag, looking away. Not the response he needs. "Look," he says. "Kinley is doing its twentieth-anniversary party at the Field on Friday. How about you stay after work, and I sneak you in for some food? A peace offering."

Liyah glances to the ceiling then back at him, clucking her tongue. "You're determined, aren't you?"

"When I need to be."

"I'll consider it. I really have to go, though. Have a . . . good rest of your week, Rosenberg."

"You, too, Cohen-Jackson," he replies. She exits the coffee shop, not looking back. He watches the sway of her hips as she goes, unable to shake a sinking feeling that something has been left unsaid.

CHAPTER 4

SIOBHAN grabs Liyah's arm, stopping her from stepping out into the lobby. "We have an explicit invite," Liyah reminds her. "It's fine."

"*You* have an explicit invite," Siobhan insists. "I'm a stow-away."

"I doubt they'll mind. They've all had chances for seconds, and there's still enough food to feed the entire crowd twice more. They'll probably toss most of it anyway."

Siobhan chuckles. "I see, so this is about saving the planet. Here I was thinking you were just looking out for your belly."

Liyah makes her best innocent face, clasping her hands and batting her eyelashes. "Whatever do you mean? Food waste is a serious problem in the U.S., and stealing this food is the *only* way to stop it. It's a public service. Your good deed for the year." Siobhan tries and fails to bite back a laugh. "Listen, there's like six women here. If we stick out that badly, that's on them. They should be embarrassed to even question us." Siobhan nods hesitantly, still unconvinced. Liyah sighs. "If they do, I'll say we're Daniel Rosenberg's plus-two. He won't care."

"I thought you said you weren't planning on talking to him," Siobhan says, brow raised.

"I'm not," Liyah insists. "I'm planning on using him as an excuse to take the food and run."

"I'll let you do the talking."

"Works for me," Liyah replies, and walks toward the buffet with all the self-assuredness of someone who belongs at the party, Siobhan at her heels.

The spread is truly expansive. It's like they expected a crowd three times the size. Two guys are chatting at the other end, and from where Siobhan and Liyah first grab their plates, they can't even eavesdrop. She is curious in a way she wouldn't usually be about the goings-on of two suit-clad men in their late twenties. One guy has his back to her, but the other seems to be the only other Black person in the building. She wants to ask him what kind of Olympic-level code switching he employs to get through a week at Kinley. He holds himself with such understated confidence; maybe he has the right affect to pull off weaving between AAVE and standard English mid-sentence. If so, Liyah is envious. Sometimes it feels like she talks one way with her dad's family and another with the rest of the world.

They've inched their way toward the end of the long table (seriously long, this company must pay well) and Liyah's trying to figure out how to wedge a miniature baguette between some mashed potatoes and sautéed asparagus when she feels someone approach in her periphery.

"You came," Daniel says as she turns toward him. He balances his plate (equally overfilled) in one hand with ease. The suit he wears is navy, but nicer than the one from Wednesday. She really should ask for the name of his tailor; lapels should not lie so cleanly against someone's chest. She loses her train of thought somewhere around his pocket square, only regaining it when she passes the bridge of his nose and sees his eyes flick up to hers, as if they'd been somewhere around her lips. "Were you not going to say hello?"

"I would have gotten around to it," Liyah says.

"She would not have," Siobhan stage-whispers across the table, making Daniel laugh and abruptly reminding Liyah that there are other people in the room.

"I brought a friend. Hope that's okay," she mumbles.

The guy Liyah was watching at the end of the buffet saunters over, clapping a hand on Daniel's shoulder. "I guess I did, too," Daniel says.

The guy clears his throat. "You gone introduce me?"

Daniel laughs. "Jordan, this is Liyah. Liyah, Jordan."

"Daniel forgets his manners sometimes. It's nice to meet you." Jordan flashes a smile. His teeth look brilliantly white against the deep brown of his lips. The lineup on his fade is perfect, too, done to accentuate the masculine squareness of his face. Jordan is handsome. Almost too handsome, in a way that screams trouble. It figures, though—attractive men tend to be friends with other attractive men. Not that she's *attracted* to Daniel. She's just, you know, seen him. Jordan extends his hand, and Liyah accepts it.

"Don't I know it. This is Siobhan." Rather than reach across the buffet, Siobhan offers a wave.

"Nice to meet you," they say at the same time.

"Are you a market operations specialist, too?" Liyah asks.

"Digital marketing strategist," Daniel corrects.

"My mistake, I'm still working on my proficiency in capitalism mumbo jumbo. No offense, Jordan."

Daniel's eyes cut to her. "What if I'm offended?"

"I truly do not care." Maybe Liyah should pause to think before snapping at him, especially given their working relationship, but her limited self-control borders on nonexistent in Daniel's presence.

"What do y'all do?" Jordan asks.

"We work here at the Field. I'm a graphic designer," Siobhan offers, stealing Liyah's chance at what she's sure could have been several more rounds of witty retorts.

"I'm an exhibition developer-slash-designer. The slash is an important part of my job title, it's even there next to my picture on the website."

Jordan quirks his eyebrow. "And for those of us not fluent in museum mumbo-jumbo?"

"I'm probably whatever you'd think a junior curator would be." She looks down at the buffet table, grabbing a small butter packet and balancing it precariously on the edge of her plate. "Also, if I'm being honest, sometimes my job amounts to colonialism mumbo-jumbo."

"So where can you work?" Daniel asks. "Without the mumbo-jumbo."

Liyah shrugs noncommittally. "I don't know. The world is terrible."

Siobhan snorts. "Please don't get her started." Then, in response to Liyah's glare, "What? I'm not saying you're wrong, I'm saying that it's Friday night, and some of us want to steal food and go home to wine and Netflix in peace."

"Wasn't your grandfather in the IRA?"

"I'm saving my car bomb for when the English invade Chicago. Which, by my measure, is not going to be in the next three hours."

Liyah laughs, then glances at Jordan and Daniel, mildly concerned that Siobhan's pitch-black humor might've scandalized their company. "Well, we're off to scarf this down in a corner. Nice to meet you, Jordan," she says, turning away.

"Wait—" Daniel grabs her arm. His touch is gentle, undercut by rough calluses on the pads of his fingers, and it falls away so quickly she might've thought she imagined it if it weren't for the lingering heat on her skin and apologetic look on his face. "Do you, um, wanna sit with us?" Daniel asks.

Siobhan turns bright red. This exchange probably hasn't helped with her nervousness about seeming out of place. Liyah, in her stead, says, "We're not really dressed the part. Don't want to draw too much attention."

"I promise you, nobody cares."

"Also, we've been looking for an excuse to head out for a drink," Jordan chimes in, glancing at his watch. "I'd say we need twenty more minutes of face time before we escape, but y'all are welcome to join."

"Well, that sounds about thirty times more exciting than my original plans," Siobhan agrees, without consulting Liyah.

If she'd been up front with Siobhan about how she really knew Daniel, she might not be in this predicament. But it's too late now, and by nine thirty, Liyah finds herself in a basement in River North. When they arrived at the bar (Daniel's suggestion, apparently his roommate works there), Liyah and Siobhan were wary of the unmarked door in a dark alley. Siobhan even went so far as to warn their companions that she carried pepper spray. But really, Liyah should have expected this when Jordan referred to the bar as a *speakeasy*. She'd just assumed he meant that the bar was dimly lit with a few velvet chairs, but after they entered and passed through an unassuming dining area, she was floored.

The place is truly committed to capturing Prohibition-era Chicago. The walls are papered in a vintage print and lined with framed photos from the 1920s. There must be significant soundproofing, because the live jazz didn't hit until they were down the stairs and through yet another set of doors. Liyah nurses an old-fashioned (infused with cigar smoke by Alex, the roommate apparently) and looks around. The concept sounds like true yuppie nonsense, but in practice, it works.

"Thanks for joining us," Jordan says, and Liyah peels her eyes away from a four-foot-tall photograph of a Black flapper girl smoking a six-inch cigarette.

"We should be thanking you, for the drinks and all," Siobhan says. Liyah nods her agreement.

Daniel waves them off. "It's nothing, Alex always gives us the first round on the house. Perks of rooming with a mixologist."

Liyah nearly chokes on her whiskey. "Mixologist?"

"He'd kill me if he heard me say that, but he does actually have a certification."

Liyah, having gulped a few sips of water, lifts her tumbler. "It was well-earned. This is delicious."

"Mine, too," Siobhan adds between sips of a drink as red as her cheeks.

Jordan takes a healthy swig of his scotch. "Whose idea was it to have the party on a Friday night? It's been a long enough week as it is."

"I'll drink to that." Daniel taps his glass against Jordan's.

Liyah rolls her eyes. "Yes, I truly pity the two of you. Free gourmet food as far as the eye can see. Tragic."

"The best we ever get at the Field is free pizza. And not even, like, Malnati's or anything." This is not the first time Siobhan has complained that Jeff never caters deep dish. Siobhan likes it so much that Liyah's half convinced it's the reason she chose Chicago when she graduated from Trinity College Dublin.

"Nah, the food is great. It's more working the room full of very, very white guys when I'm supposed to be off the clock."

Liyah winces, the feeling all too familiar. She spent all of undergrad being confused for the only other Black woman in her major. The Field isn't a paragon of diversity by any means, but it's just about gender balanced and she's not the lone person of color in her department.

Daniel groans. "Remember last Christmas party? The photographer practically chased us around with his camera."

"They still call it a Christmas party?" Liyah cringes.

Jordan nods. "Yup. And they out their damn minds if they think another picture of us'll convince anybody. Having the same three people of color on the website more than once is worse than nobody at all."

Liyah laughs. "They should teach a class on how to deal with tokenism in college. It would have been more useful than most of my general education requirements. I don't do any math, like, ever."

"I hope it's not rude to ask, but why do you work there, then?" Siobhan says. If she's uncomfortable with the topic of race, she doesn't show it. But, then again, she's shared an office with Liyah for three years, so she might have been acclimated by immersion.

"It pays," they say at the same time.

"To be honest, I genuinely like it," Daniel adds. "Not all of it, but I do get to be pretty creative."

"I like the people part." Jordan flashes a smile. "Gotta put this charm to good use, right?"

Siobhan nods, perhaps a touch too vigorously. Liyah stuffs down a laugh, lest she cause a full-chest blush. She is thankful her own skin doesn't show her emotions quite so plainly. Siobhan finishes the last of her drink. "I have to use the toilet. Liyah?"

They're barely out of earshot when Siobhan grips Liyah's arm and leans toward her ear. "Are you going to explain why you knew those two fine things and didn't think to share them with me until now?"

Liyah laughs loudly enough to startle the table they pass by. "I met Jordan tonight, same as you."

"But you met Daniel on Wednesday! And all you told me is that he was 'some corporate guy who barely had one functioning brain cell.'"

"I said he probably shared a single brain cell with the rest of his office."

Siobhan pushes open the door to the restroom. "He seems perfectly intelligent. You just don't want to be doing the marketing thing."

"You're right, I don't. And I especially don't want to be spending my Friday night with him! This project might go for months, Siobhan. I'll see him plenty during work hours."

"Hear me out," she says. "What if you saw him plenty outside of work hours, too? And you brought me? And he brought Jordan?"

"Siobhan—"

"Please, Liyah." She presses her palms flat together, holding them in front of her pouting lips. "Only a few times, until I work up the courage to ask Jordan to drinks myself."

"I don't think you realize what you're asking of me. It's hard enough to tolerate him in a professional context, I'm not going to make it to the first event if I see him more than that."

"He can't really be that bad, can he?"

Liyah shakes her head. "You don't know the half of it." An understatement. After their conversation on Wednesday, it seems like *Daniel* doesn't even know the half of it. In some ways, Liyah feels like she doesn't, either. That summer was more than half her life ago, and it was never Daniel himself being unkind. Before running into him, she thought she had let it go. But when she looks at him and sees glimpses of the boy he used to be, it's hard not to feel a hot thread of shame and disappointment needle through her chest. "What happened to needing to use the toilet?"

"I wanted to talk to you!" Siobhan says, confirming Liyah's fear that she was never going to disappear into the stall and forget about it. "Will you consider it?"

"I don't know if I'm even capable of being nice to him."

Siobhan snorts, folding her arms across her chest. "You haven't been tonight, and he doesn't seem to mind." Liyah opens her mouth to protest, but Siobhan continues: "Think of it as practice! Or like a vaccine. You'll inoculate yourself to Daniel on the weekends, and then working with him won't be quite so difficult."

Someone swings the door open, and Liyah presses back against the wall to let them through. "I don't think it works like that," she grits out.

Siobhan pouts again, making her eyes go round. In the dim light of the bathroom, they're the same pale blue as the eyes of the husky who lives in the apartment above Liyah. Literal puppy-dog eyes. "Liyah, I did all those graphics for you. Over many lunch breaks. Unpaid, I may add, so—"

"God, fine! Okay! I'll help you see Jordan again." She holds up a finger. "But only until your wings are strong enough. Then I'm pushing you out of the fucking nest."

Siobhan wraps her in a warm hug (one of her best talents—she smells delicious and applies just the right amount of pressure) and whispers *thank you* repeatedly into Liyah's ear.

"You're too good at guilt-tripping," Liyah says after she pulls back.

"Well, I was raised Catholic." Siobhan winks. "Let's go get them another round. We've been in here so long they'll think we've got the shits!"

"So THAT'S LIYAH. Holy shit, man." Jordan gives Daniel a long look.

Daniel takes a swig of his gin and tonic. Last he checked, Jordan was with Nisha, but sometimes his flings are as short as they are intense, and he'd been grumpier than usual at the office today. Also, Jordan wasn't lying about his charm—if he decides he wants to go for it, it's usually a done deal. For about three months, that is. "Yeah, from the plane."

"Yeah, I got that. You're telling me you didn't get her number?" Daniel shakes his head. "Not even her Instagram?"

"Dude, I told you already, no." Daniel tips his head back to drain the rest of his glass. He has a feeling he knows where this conversation is going, and he doesn't particularly want to be sober for it.

"You're fucking hopeless."

Daniel stares down at his empty glass. "Wow, thanks."

"No, I mean, look at you! If a girl who looked like that was flirting with me . . ." He shakes his head, pursing his lips.

"Antagonizing," he corrects. He thinks about that moment she realized who he was—how her eyes widened a fraction before she turned away, how the air on the plane seemed to go from stale to positively stifling in milliseconds—more than he'd like to admit. "Not flirting with me." Jordan sucks his teeth disapprovingly. Daniel exhales. "Seriously, man, she genuinely dislikes me. There's a lot of glaring involved."

"She's probably imagining you naked. Which is very clearly what you're doing to her."

"I can't take you anywhere. You watch too many romantic comedies. And too much porn."

"Hey, it's gotten me this far." Jordan punctuates this with a dazzling grin.

"Yeah? How's Nisha?"

The grin falters. "I ain't getting into all that. This is about you and your total lack of game. You need a wingman."

Daniel shakes his head adamantly. "Dude, I told you, we're working together! I do not need a wingman."

"You absolutely do. Lucky for you, I'm at your service tonight. I can distract her friend and y'all can make a quick getaway."

"You and Alex are too much alike. I don't need your help getting laid. And, again, if I did, it wouldn't be with a *client*."

"Oh, so you want a date? Aite, then by the end of the night, I'll have made sure you have a reason to see her again." He pats Daniel's arm. "I got you, man."

"I'm on thin enough ice with her as it is. Please don't—" Daniel starts to protest, but Liyah and Siobhan are back, carrying a new round of drinks.

Siobhan passes one to Jordan, and Liyah sets Daniel's down in front of him, making a show of looking him up and down. "You know, I read somewhere that liking gin and tonics is linked to psychopathy." Daniel shoots a look at Jordan as if to say *see, genuine dislike*. His eyes, unfortunately, are met with a subtle wink.

"It must've been an old study—we also like bourbon now," he replies, surprising a smile out of Liyah as she takes her seat.

The four of them fall back into easy conversation, even with the constant fear of Jordan playing a modern reimagining of Yente, sans babushka. It's fun being here, hanging out with people other than Jordan, Alex, or, let's be honest, Sweet Potato. Somewhere in the din of the music and conversation, it hits him how much of a homebody he's been as of late. Months of his sister Kayla's incessant nagging to go out more, and it's the soulful timbre of a jazz singer in a tasseled dress that sinks it in. He won't tell Kayla. She's already taken on too much of his happiness as her personal responsibility as elder sibling, especially since last year. Plus, she can be insufferably bossy. Liyah would love her.

"Liyah, check your email!" Siobhan all but shrieks.

Liyah groans. "Please, no, it's a Friday night. I'll look tomorrow."

Siobhan digs into Liyah's purse herself and thrusts the phone at her. "No, now."

"God, okay! Sorry, Jordan," she says before unlocking her phone. She taps a bit, then her jaw slackens. She looks up at Siobhan, as if to check that she read it right. When she nods, Liyah's face lights up. "Oh. My. Fucking. God. We got it."

"*You* got it."

"What did y'all get?" Jordan interjects. Daniel would have asked, had he not been busy absorbing the sheer joy radiating off Liyah.

"My exhibit—Jeff got the board—he, wow . . ." Speechless is not a look Daniel expected to see on her.

"Liyah here pitched an entire exhibit based off a few skeletons we're acquiring." Siobhan fills the men in. "Our boss's bosses green-lit it. And I'll get to be lead on graphics, so it's a pretty big deal."

"Wow. Mazel tov," Daniel congratulates her.

Liyah's eyes meet Daniel's, and she smiles at him. A teeth-baring, eye-crinkling smile. *Holy shit.* "Thank you. I'm beyond stoked. I'd try to be modest but right now I'm honestly too excited."

Jordan raises his glass. "To no modesty." Daniel sighs, the only one here who truly appreciates how much Jordan lives up to his toast. They all clink glasses and sip their drinks. To Daniel's delight, Liyah has yet to wipe the smile off her face.

"Now you'll just have to convince Jeff on the land acknowledgment."

"Ugh, Siobhan. Don't remind me," Liyah says. Then, by way of explanation, she adds, "It's for the colonialism mumbo-jumbo. As you can probably imagine, basically all artifacts exhumed prior to this millennium—and some after, honestly—were taken without the permission of the indigenous peoples who occupied the land. There's a paragraph about it on the website but I want something below every case in the exhibit."

Daniel frowns. "And you don't think that's gonna be an easy sell?"

Liyah shakes her head. "Jeff can be . . . traditional."

Jordan laughs. "We deserve extra benefits for dealing with 'traditional' bosses, among other things."

Liyah nods. "They should pay for therapy. Or at the very least, our bar tabs."

"If you lot know of any good support groups, we're all ears."

Jordan perks up at Siobhan's words. *Oh no.* There's a familiar glint in his eye, an expression Daniel recognizes from watching him pitch ad campaigns to clients. He doesn't need to say anything for Daniel to know in his bones that Jordan has thought of an opportunity to shove him and Liyah together, likely dooming their new working relationship—and therefore his freedom to pick his own accounts—from the start. "Why don't we start one? We can meet here and drink away our sorrows."

Daniel is surprised. From Jordan, he expected much worse.

"Half of our sorrows are caused by dealing with the middle-aged men in our department." Liyah uses the little black straw from her drink to point between him and Jordan. "You two won't get offended?"

Daniel leans forward, holding eye contact for a beat. "I thought you didn't care whether you offended me?"

"I don't." She looks from him to Jordan. "My concern is for group morale. It's meant to be therapeutic, after all."

"Ah. Well, I think our masculinity will survive," Daniel says.

Liyah's gaze drifts down his face, then back up. "Shame," she says, smile wicked.

Their sparring is cut short, yet again, because Daniel laughs too hard to source a rapid-fire comeback.

"So, what?" Siobhan says from her side. "We form a support group?"

Daniel clucks his tongue, thinking. "No, too tame. It's dire stuff, surviving our late twenties." After receiving agreement from the group—with much less fight from Liyah than expected—he draws up a contract on a napkin:

HOUSE RULES

1. Meet: Friday nights, ~~10~~ 9 (Siobhan wakes up early), at Prohibition
2. Anything said here stays here
3. No toxic masculinity

Jordan Ames

Aliyah Cohen-Jackson

Siobhan Gallagher

Daniel Rosenberg

And thus, the Speakeasy Survival Club is born.

CHAPTER 5

LIYAH balances her phone on the windowsill so that both hands are free to mist and wipe the dust off her large-leafed plants. This is how she spends virtually every Sunday: on a video call with Neen and doing chores around her apartment.

"Anyway, I think I maybe hate my job," Neen says, pulling their foot close to their face to blow on freshly painted toenails.

"Show me! And you don't, you love coding." Neen angles their phone so that their feet are in full view. There are little cactuses on their big toes, and the rest are painted a terracotta brown.

"I didn't say I hated coding, I said I hated my job. Do you think everybody feels this way?"

"What way?"

They sigh. "I don't know. Restless?"

"To varying degrees, probably." Restless is exactly how Liyah felt before she started this new exhibition. Now her work feels interesting, maybe even meaningful, but sometimes she worries that if she slows down for a moment, that feeling will set in again. Liyah sighs. "If they're still happening when you visit in October, you can join one of our Survival Club meetings. Complaining is the ultimate cure for millennial ennui."

Neen's ears perk up. "Will Daniel Rosenberg be there?"

"Unfortunately, yes. He is a founding member."

Neen side-eyes Liyah through their front-facing camera. "What do you mean 'unfortunately'? I know you, and you would *not* have agreed to the whole thing if you weren't warming up to him."

"I only agreed as a favor to Siobhan." This is her fault, really, for telling Neen about Daniel's apology. It completely flipped their opinion of him (*A man admitting he was wrong? In this economy? I'm in love*) and somehow convinced them it had flipped Liyah's, too. Maybe it did, but only in that she logically knows he's not truly a terrible person. It hasn't done much to soothe the shameful unease that nestles in her gut whenever she remembers that summer.

"Right." They raise their eyebrows. "I bet he'd tell me his birth time if I asked."

Liyah shakes her head. "You're relentless." Neen, who believes in astrology in a way that's only endearing when it's not weaponized against you, has repeatedly reminded Liyah to ask for Daniel's time of birth. They claim it's only to determine whether Liyah and Daniel were destined to meet again, but they also asked Liyah how she'd thought he looked in a suit. Liyah was not fully comfortable answering that for herself, let alone for somebody else. Instead, she rolled her eyes, which got Neen off the subject of wayward attractions but also onto another mysticism rant (*You randomly met two times after a fourteen-year estrangement. Twice! And yet you still insist there is no fate to govern your life*). Liyah would have noted that the key word was "randomly," but then there would have been no peace to be had.

"I have to look after you! If left to your own devices,

you'd hang out with like two people ever. You don't even have a real roommate!"

Neen's not wrong. Liyah answered an admittedly odd-sounding Craigslist posting after a disastrous postgrad rooming situation, and now she has a two-bedroom in a neighborhood she loves to herself. The utilities are entirely Liyah's responsibility, but she splits the rent with a girl who uses the apartment twice a year to convince her conservative parents that she doesn't live with her boyfriend. Liyah's still not sure if her roommate's name is Lara or Laura. A multiyear relationship sounds like a nightmare if it requires lying to your entire family about it. Actually, a multiyear relationship is a nightmare, period. Neen is the only person outside of her family that Liyah has managed to never get sick of or drift away from.

"I have friends from Northwestern," Liyah argues.

"Yeah, but do you see them?"

Liyah doesn't respond, because Neen already knows the answer. She grabs lunch or goes out with friends from college every now and then, but she's never been great at keeping in touch with people who aren't right in front of her. And she's been even more absorbed in her job than usual, hence mostly spending time with Siobhan. It works out though, as Siobhan is incredibly introverted and latched on to Liyah almost immediately after moving stateside. Neen, on the other hand, hosts house parties regularly and hates hanging out in a group of fewer than four people. Unless they're with Liyah, of course. "Well, I have an active sex life, at least," she tries.

Neen snorts. "One, you hardly speak to the people you sleep with, so that doesn't count. And two, no, you don't. Not anymore. I'm pretty sure the last person was what's-her-face who you ghosted after she said she liked you. And that was months ago!"

"I didn't *ghost* Ivy, and it wasn't *months* . . ." Liyah

pauses, realizing that it's practically September. Which makes it months, plural. "I've been busy with the exhibit."

"Yeah, and it's stressing me out vicariously. You need to socialize more, and you need to send me Daniel's time of birth. You said he was born in Madison?"

"Neen! I am not asking him for that."

"Oh, come on," they pout. "It's hard to vet people from a distance, and I want to make sure you aren't falling in with any unsavory types."

"What, so if you find out he's a Taurus rising or whatever you're going to block his number from my phone and sabotage my promotion?"

"No!" They replace the cap on a bottle of topcoat. "I'll only do that if he has more than one Scorpio placement in his big three. Okay, babe. I've got to get some work done. Talk to you soon?"

Liyah nods. "Love you," she says, blowing a kiss. Neen returns both and exits the call. Maybe she should head to the Field and try to be productive, too. She still hasn't unpacked the delivery from Friday.

She drops her phone on the sofa and heads to the kitchen to pack up her laptop. As she's about to close the screen, a new message appears. If Jeff were more thoughtful, or perhaps a decade younger, he would keep the new exhibition emails in an easy-to-follow thread. Instead, he emails sporadically and often neglects to include a subject line. Sometime last week, Liyah had gotten fed up and set up a filter that searched for keywords and delivered everything to a specific folder. This one escaped, as it contains barely a sentence fragment: *use second-century Chinese paper?*

Fossilized bones are more her wheelhouse, but her mind is already jumping to the importance of a section on the written word, and she knew her limits when she proposed the exhibition. She'll reluctantly ask Emiliano (his unendurable personality has proven to be undercut slightly by his expertise) to make sense of it tomorrow.

Her phone vibrates from the couch cushion, and Liyah's eyes slide to the clock on her wall. Two hours have gone by since she told herself she'd go deal with the delivery. Liyah unfolds her legs and stands up to go check it.

Daniel
hey liyah! it's daniel
rosenberg. weird q: feel like
an afternoon coffee?

She rolls her eyes. Does he think she didn't save his number? Even if they weren't working together, the SSC group chat is already so active that she cannot distinguish his and Jordan's texts from context clues alone.

Liyah
Full name over text? Did I
miss your 80th birthday?

Daniel
we know a lot of daniels

Liyah
I haven't seen Gross or
Schwartz in fourteen years.

Daniel
jordan bailed on our usual
time and i can't be trusted to
actually work in a coffee shop
by myself
i was about to start on the
field account

Liyah

You need a babysitter?
Figures, you're rather
childlike.

Daniel

clearly this was a bad idea

Liyah

I do have a babysitting
certificate. I'm not going to
a coffee shop, but you can
come with me to the Field
to scope it out and ask any
questions you want

And unpack and photograph several boxes of plaques for her exhibit. But he doesn't need to know that yet.

DANIEL MEETS LIYAH at a side entrance to the Field Museum, pastry bag in hand. His stomach does a nervous flip at the sight of her leaning on the door to hold it open and the sudden realization that this is the first time she's intentionally spent time with him outside of business hours. Technically speaking, he's still here for work, but he's also keenly aware that they could have saved this for the middle of the week when he'd be in a suit and she'd be wearing—well, not quite business casual, but also not summer weekend clothes. Namely, an olive-green tank top—probably her favorite color, she wears it a lot—and a pair of tattered denim shorts that look like they were designed specifically with her in mind. She doesn't smile as he approaches, but she doesn't scowl, either. He'll take the win.

"For you," he says, offering the waxy brown paper sleeve.

She peers into the pastry bag. "A croissant?" She scans his face, her eyes narrowing slightly. "You didn't have to get me this."

He shrugs. "You need the fuel if you're going to be developing-slash-designing on a weekend."

She tears off a generous piece and points it at him. "This better not be your way of softening the blow that Brett rejected all our proposals. I can't do another brainstorming session at Planet Navy Suit. The atmosphere is too different from Earth's; I'll suffocate."

Daniel chuckles. "Always so suspicious."

Liyah sucks her teeth. "I often have reason to be."

"Not this time. The wine night, sleep-in, and holiday party are all a go," he says. "Sometimes a croissant is just a croissant."

"Okay, then. Thank you." She stuffs the piece in her mouth. Her eyelids flutter shut, the same blissed-out look she had at her first sip of coffee during their Wednesday meeting taking over. He considers cracking a joke, but he'll hate himself if some offhanded gibe makes her stop doing that around him.

Instead, he slips through the door, waits for her to take the lead, and watches her bound up the steps in front of him. Those shorts are even better from behind, white frays brushing against the smooth brown of her thighs.

"Do you want to see my babysitting certificate?" she asks as they reach the top landing and begin weaving through a narrow hallway.

"What exactly does it certify?"

"Mostly that I know rescue breathing for infants and toddlers and that I won't give you shaken baby syndrome." Liyah pushes through a slit in floor-to-ceiling plastic sheeting, gesturing for Daniel to go in ahead of her.

The room is cavernous in shape and atmosphere, boxes

strewn about. Five diffuse spots of warm light hit the floor in the center of the room; several more illuminate seemingly random swaths of white wall. Liyah strides toward one box, picks up the stack of papers that rests atop it, and drops to a cross-legged seat on the floor.

Unsure what to do with himself, Daniel joins her on the ground, propping his elbows on his bent knees. "This is where you wanted to do the wine night?"

"No, this is part of my exhibit. But we can *plan* the wine night while we unpack these." She tosses him a—thankfully closed—box cutter.

"Why do I feel like you invited me here to do manual labor?" he jokes, disappointment swirling through his stomach. Liyah's invitation is not proving to be the step forward he'd hoped.

"Because I did. Here, this one should be the smaller placards. Can you unwrap them and lay them out over there? Then I'll do the printouts of the corresponding artifacts and you can photograph them."

Daniel rubs his hand over his chin, trying not to laugh. "Oh, I *can* photograph them? How kind of you."

This earns an eye roll. *Eye roll* is a misnomer, actually: Liyah rolls her head, too, her shoulders even aiding the action. It seems to require her entire upper body. "Listen, Rosenberg. This needs to get done. So I am going to do this while we talk about the wine event supposedly so magical that previously uninterested adults will be begging to give us their money and attention. You can help me, or you can stand in the corner facing the wall while I work."

"Well, when you put it that way . . ." He slices open the first box. "I thought *you* needed this to go well," Daniel mutters.

She sighs, shoulders sagging. "I do need it to go well. That doesn't mean I believe it will."

"We'll figure it out. I need this to work, too," he says.

Liyah furrows her brow. "No, like, Jeff said that I need the numbers of young adult members to go up if I want to make curator. Which I really, really do. I'm sure you'd survive one bad performance review."

"It's not just about my job performance." He lays out a card that reads *Gravettian Venus Figurine, Calcite, 24,000–22,000 B.C.E.* "I had to persuade Brett to let me pick my two main accounts, so if I don't deliver, I'm going to end up working with the worst of the worst for the foreseeable future."

She tilts her head. "I didn't realize you chose this."

Daniel blushes. "I mean, Brett seemed happy to pawn it off on me."

Liyah thumbs through her stack of papers, placing one with a sculpture of a woman with large breasts, belly, and hips above the placard. "What's the other account?"

"You know the CTA?" He unwraps another Venus placard for one made from limestone.

"Do I, a Chicago resident, know about the Chicago Transit Authority? Yeah, I think I've heard of it," Liyah deadpans.

"Well, looks like my job is obsolete. Digital strategy: marketed." Liyah laughs. It's quick, and she tries to conceal it, but Daniel's chest inflates a little with pride. "It's not as exciting for the firm as, like, pharma, but I enjoy it."

Liyah props her elbow on the box next to her and rests her chin in the palm of her hand. "Why do you say *pharma* like that?"

"Like what?" he mumbles, even though he's likely already given himself away.

She drums her fingers along her cheekbone, squinting at him. "Like you're allergic to it."

Daniel shrugs, averting his eyes. "Maybe I am."

"Or do you just like trains better?"

Liyah's guess is what Daniel had let everyone at the firm think—he finds medicine boring. If he doesn't want to go down this rabbit hole, he'll let her think the same.

His mouth, betraying his mind, says, "I'm not so into the ethics of it. There's a lot of making small changes to the same drug to maximize patents and price gouging on medicine that people literally need to survive." His throat tightens. "Did you know that there's the manufacturing capacity to supply more than enough chemo to the U.S., but there's a shortage almost every other year? It's only about profit margins." He holds his breath, fighting the urge to put his head in his hands.

Liyah's gaze is steady, as if she's studying him carefully. He prays that she doesn't ask why he knows all that; something tells him his treacherous vocal cords aren't going to give his usual canned response about a *New Yorker* article.

She doesn't press him. Instead, she drops her hand from her face, leans back, and quirks the corners of her mouth. "Who knew there was a bleeding-heart leftist under that suit of yours?"

His shoulders relax, relief washing over him. He constructs a smile. "There's more to me than meets the eye."

Liyah snorts. "Like what? A collection of secret L train tattoos?"

He gestures down at his exposed skin—Daniel runs hot, temperatures over sixty-five mean shorts and as many undone buttons as he can get away with. He thought he was clever when he got the jellyfish done, that it would be *easily* hidden under clothing. As it turns out, it's on full display for half the year. More, when you consider how many buildings in Chicago abuse their central heating in the winter. "I don't know how I would've kept them from you." Liyah's eyes trail down the line of his legs, assessing him, and he finds himself looking back at her. Those shorts seem to hug her narrow waist perfectly, emphasizing the fullness of her hips and thighs . . .

He blinks, snapping himself out of it before he does something embarrassing while she sits a foot away. When he focuses back on her face, there's an unexpected subtle pinkness in her cheeks. Does she flush like that when . . .

For fuck's sake, Daniel. Get it together.

"I didn't really peg you as an ass tattoo type of guy," she says. "But I guess you never really know someone." The second part comes out tightly, and he can't help but read into the subtext. They were doing okay, he thought.

He decides to go for levity, gasping and covering his mouth. "Rats! I've been found out. Detective Cohen-Jackson has done it again."

Liyah does another full-torso eye roll, handing him a printout of a figurine and pointing to its place in the row of placards. The next placard reads *Self-Portrait of a Pregnant Venus, Photograph, 2022.* "What's this one?" he asks, showing Liyah the description.

Her eyes light up, and she sifts through the pages with a loud rustle until she finds the sheet she's looking for. "Here! For a long time, historians assumed that these Venus figurines were made by men, and that the secondary sex characteristics were exaggerated to cater to their gaze. They typically have minimal facial detail or no head at all. But recently, there's been a movement to consider another option: that these were self-portraits. If you look at a Venus from the top down, it closely resembles the view a pregnant person might have when looking down at their naked body."

Daniel looks at the side-by-side, and a strange feeling spreads through him. Something so ancient and a picture of someone growing new life so recently are one and the same. "Wow," is all he says.

Their gazes meet, and she bites her lip and averts her eyes. "For the wine night, what if we made the pairings related to the exhibitions somehow? Like each one was theme-based on the country of origin or the label."

Daniel nods. "That's a great idea. We could have 'tasting notes,' both for the food and drink and for the exhibition. Cabernet Sauvignon, vintage 2018 with notes of cherry. Pairs well with Inside Ancient Egypt, vintage, um . . ."

"Twenty-four hundred B.C.E." Liyah smiles. "With notes of natron. That's the salt they used to dry out bodies for mummification."

"I'll contact a few local wine bars this week and see what we can do. See?" Daniel says. "We make a good team."

"Let's wait until we pull this off before we jump to any wild conclusions. I still hate this, but it's better than being forced to turn Evolving Planet into an Instagram trap. Like half of that exhibit is about mass extinction events. I don't think anyone can make that sexy."

"What's wrong with people wanting to take nice pictures?"

"I'm not even gonna touch that statement, Rosenberg. Start the photographs," she says, passing over a mid-2000s-era digital camera. Just then, her phone screen lights up. She looks down and smiles.

Shit. If he were interested in her—which he isn't, that's such a horrible idea he's not sure how it managed to cross his mind—it would be a bad sign.

Daniel waggles his eyebrows. "Texting somebody special?"

"No. Or yes, I suppose. It's my best friend, Neen." She pauses, as if debating whether to continue. "You met them, actually. At Dan's pool party."

He furrows his brow. "Your best friend is Neen Khatri? Tran's Neen?" *More importantly,* he thinks, *you talked to your best friend about me?*

"Neen is their own person. But if they had to be somebody's, I'd like to think they're *my* Neen, not Tran's."

"Well, *your* Neen is awful at beer pong," Daniel says.

"They convinced you to let them do a celeb shot and lost you the game, didn't they?" He nods, and Liyah grins. "A classic move. They are . . . not a coordinated person."

"Tell them I say hi."

Liyah shakes her head. "God, no. At least not until after you leave, otherwise they'll call and demand that you recite your exact time and coordinates of birth for your zodiac chart."

"You say *zodiac* the way I say *pharma.*"

"Well, that's because I had to listen to Neen prattle on about it this morning." She swipes the box cutter from his side and starts on the next package. "The idea of destiny is stupid. I'm sitting here with you in an empty exhibition room because I want to, not because Saturn told me so."

Daniel beams. It's a good thing he texted Liyah when Jordan canceled; he wants to be right here, too. "I was under the impression that you only wanted me for my labor."

"Aw, you're short-selling. You also brought me a croissant."

CHAPTER 6

SIOBHAN pushes the drunken noodles around on her plate. "What if we casually ask everyone to give their relationship status?"

Liyah blinks slowly, *mm-hmm*ing to stave off the laughter in her throat. Nothing about Siobhan taking three sips of her drink and blurting something like, *Tell me, lads, any lasses waiting for you at home?* would come off as casual. As sweet as the strawberry-shaped barrette that clips back her bangs? Sure. But not casual. Liyah bites her tongue, though, because even she isn't that insensitive. "I'm not sure that would work." She catches the stricken look in Siobhan's eyes. "I mean, as far as looking casual. Honestly, you should just outright ask. Own it, you know?"

"Easy for you to say. You're always so bold. I would turn red as a fire engine. You know sometimes I blush so hard it hurts?"

Liyah hides her snort behind her water glass, dropping her fork to pat Siobhan's hand. "I don't mean to be dismissive. I get it's nerve-racking. I'd throw up if I had to admit having feelings for someone."

Siobhan frowns. "Bollocks, I've seen you do it with my own two eyes."

Liyah shakes her head. "You've seen me select hookups. It's easy to tell if someone wants to fuck you. *Especially* cis men, but everyone shows it plainly if you know what to look for. It's not the same as asking for a date."

"I don't think I could be bold doing that, either." Siobhan sighs and taps her phone to check the time. They've got another fifteen minutes before they need to head to Prohibition.

"I know it sucks, but being direct is the best I can come up with."

"Maybe I could bring up dating in general? Do you think that's a good idea?"

Liyah nods hesitantly. "I mean yeah, that could work. You're not guaranteed to find out whether he's currently single, but it's a start." Liyah isn't fond of the idea, but Siobhan is prone to a type of social nervousness that Liyah can't fully empathize with. Insisting on doing things her way might lead the poor woman astray. Still, she is a god-awful liar, so Liyah makes a swift change of subject. Once she gets Siobhan talking about the merits of various HGTV shows, Liyah shovels some basil fried rice into her mouth.

By the time they pay their bill, Liyah is a touch too full. She's thankful that the walk to the bar grants ten minutes for her stomach to settle. From the look on Siobhan's face, it hasn't done the same for her.

When they get to the alleyway, Liyah gives Siobhan's hands a squeeze. "I see the gears grinding in there. You're going to be fine."

"How do you know?" Siobhan bites her lip, looking toward the door.

Liyah gives a smile. "You already thought he was cute last time. So cute that you blackmailed me into helping you see him again."

Siobhan frowns. "I didn't blackmail you, I guilt-tripped you. And you weren't even the one who came up with the Survival Club."

"I agreed to it! That's more than enough," Liyah says. "Anyway, my point is that you were already attracted to him, right?" Siobhan nods. "See! You spent a few hours with him, and he still wanted to hang out more. You did great."

Siobhan nods again, this time a little more energetically. "I guess that makes sense."

"Also, you're hot." Liyah doesn't have to dig deep to find this reassurance; it's plainly true. Beyond her endearing freckles and bright eyes, Siobhan is soft and wide everywhere, body curved with the elegant lines of a renaissance painting (though the swell of her hips and belly far surpass what fifteenth-century Europeans imagined for Aphrodite). Had she not been Liyah's coworker and ostensibly heterosexual, Liyah may have harbored a crush of her own. "Everybody loves an accent," she adds. This earns Liyah the laugh she intended. Satisfied, they start toward the bar.

They were running what Liyah would consider to be on time (fewer than twelve minutes late) prior to the pep talk. As such, they find that Daniel and Jordan have already snagged a table and their first round of drinks.

Siobhan inhales deeply, her line of sight snapping straight to Jordan. Liyah is surprised at his casual dress, though she supposes in the absence of a mandatory work party, he had time to go home and change. He wears a very plain (but muscle-accentuating) gray T-shirt and blue jeans that are cuffed to reveal a truly incredible pair of Nike high-tops. Her sixteen-year-old brother, Avi, would love them. Not that he needs more shoes. His collection is already spilling over into the closet of Liyah's childhood bedroom.

Daniel looks dressed for an entirely different event in a button-down that seems to be Frankenstein'd from two separate shirts, an oversized pocket once belonging to the white half sewed onto forest green. It's the kind of shirt that needs to be seen in broad daylight to determine whether it's a work of art or better suited as tinder for a bonfire. She wants to bet the latter, but there's something about how it sits on his shoulders under the low incandescent lights. When Daniel catches her eye and waves, she sees that his shirtsleeves are rolled up to his elbows.

"Tell me, have you heard of short-sleeved shirts?" Liyah says once they reach the table.

Daniel pauses before answering, rightfully wary. "As a matter of fact, I have."

"Pro tip: if you wear one, you don't have to wrinkle your cuffs trying to prove to the world that you have forearms."

"Hello to you, too." Daniel chuckles and slides two drinks across the table. "Old-fashioned for you, cranberry dawn for you."

Liyah plucks the stem off the cherry from her drink and sets it on her napkin. As she chews, the rest of the group exchanges much less snarky greetings.

"So." Jordan cracks his knuckles. "What's on the agenda for therapy tonight?"

"Hey! We haven't started our drinks yet. The benefit of holding our sessions here is that we're not required to be stone-cold sober," Siobhan argues. Flirtatiously. It seems so effortless that Liyah is confused as to what she had been so worried about on the walk over.

Jordan holds up his hands. "Fine, fine. No Survival Club talk until y'all give us the signal."

"You know, you'd be at least halfway through your drink if you got here on time," Daniel says.

Liyah rolls her eyes. "Half this group runs on JST; I assumed the start time was more of a suggestion."

"JST?"

"Jewish Standard Time," Daniel and Liyah answer Siobhan simultaneously.

Daniel continues. "Some of us have managed to transcend our ethnic stereotypes in favor of punctuality."

"You were late to work yesterday, man."

Liyah snort-laughs.

"That's 'cause I'm a CTA patron, not 'cause I'm Jewish," Daniel protests.

Liyah reaches over to pat his exposed forearm. "Whatever you need to tell yourself, *Daniel Rosenberg*."

THEY'RE ON THE topic of dating. Somehow, it's not even Jordan's fault. This was bound to come up eventually, but that doesn't make it any more pleasant. Siobhan bemoans not knowing how to get back into the scene after breaking up with her boyfriend back in Ireland a year ago. Which means they're treated to Jordan's sage dating advice, including how once you figure out which app to use for what, it's *easy* to find a girl you like. Daniel's about to explain how wrong Jordan is, but Liyah beats him to the punch.

"That's because you're a straight Black man. For better and definitely for worse, racial stereotypes can work in your favor on dating apps." She takes a healthy swig of her third old-fashioned. Daniel wonders if she orders them for the cherry; each time Alex fixes her a new one, she pops the fruit in her mouth first. There's a growing pile of stems on the napkin in front of her. "Daniel and I, on the other hand, get the short end of the stick. Statistically speaking."

Daniel laughs. "Ah, so I could've been blaming it on statistics this whole time."

She nods. "You could and you should." She pauses, considering. "I mean, we do benefit from colorism and the fact that being mixed is, like, a trend now, but still. I'd bet good money that women make opposite assumptions about your guys' respective endowments." It's a good thing Daniel had paused before taking another drink, or he'd be choking right now.

Siobhan turns a shade of crimson. "Liyah!"

"What? There have literally been studies on this." She gestures to Daniel and Jordan with her straw. "Tell me I'm wrong."

Daniel blushes as Jordan gives a smug smile. *Asshole.* "You're not wrong."

"Case in point. I have a million and one horror stories. I'm sure Siobhan does, too. I don't think any woman survives unscathed."

Siobhan shakes her head. "I've never used the apps, to be honest."

"Ah. Well, don't listen to Jordan, I don't recommend it. And don't get me started on gold star–obsessed lesbians."

Daniel pauses. *She's gay.* This catches Daniel off guard, disappointment tumbling through his chest. Misplaced disappointment. Since when do the sexualities of his quasi-coworkers-slash-reluctant-drinking-buddies matter to him?

"Lesbians give star ratings for hookups?" Jordan asks, giving Daniel an unwanted mental picture of what he types into the Pornhub search bar.

"What? No, Jordan. Gross. It's a, like, purity thing. You're only a gold star if you've never had sex with a man, which cuts out bi women for obvious reasons. Most people aren't like that, but y'know, it still sucks."

Okay, not a lesbian. Misplaced relief, this time. But just because she's interested in men in general does not mean she's interested in him. And, again, he reminds himself, *it shouldn't matter.* "I have to agree. Not that I've ever been asked about my star rating. But I've heard 'I don't usually find Asian men attractive, but . . .' a lot." Also, the dick size stuff, but he is *really* not keen on rehashing that part of the conversation. He's never had any complaints, which is something he might feel compelled to share if they keep harping on the idea of small penises. Something tells him that would break House Rule #3.

"See! Dating is all on apps now, and apps are terrible. Ergo, dating is terrible." Liyah purses her lips.

"Well, aren't you a ray of sunshine," Jordan says.

She frowns. "You need to liberate yourself, Jordan. Stop subscribing to the lie constructed by Godiva or whoever to convince you to spend thirty bucks on chocolate every February."

"I'm learning so much about your worldview," Daniel says, enjoying the jolt in his belly at having Liyah's full attention shift toward him. "Were puppies invented by landlords so that they could charge you an extra deposit? Is salt the brainchild of hypertension?"

Her eyes narrow at him. "Salt and puppies are real, tangible things."

"What, and love isn't?" Jordan asks.

Liyah rolls her eyes, leaning back in her chair. "I think I've said enough. I don't want to give poor Jordan a heart attack."

"You're seriously going to say that love isn't real?" Jordan repeats.

"Not love, per se. Romance. Romantic love, I don't know." She waves her hands around. "My point is that dating is shitty, often made shittier by factors out of your control. This is an observable fact, I'm not just grouchy."

Siobhan laughs. "You're usually grouchy about something."

"No! I'm realistic."

Daniel takes the opportunity to reach over and pat Liyah's arm. "Whatever you need to tell yourself, *Oscar*." This garners a light chuckle from Jordan, hysterical laughter from Siobhan, and a flesh-penetrating glare from Liyah.

"Alright." She slaps her hands down on the table, standing

up. "I need a tequila shot if we're going to be doing any more of this therapy. Any takers?" There's a chorus of agreement, and she stalks off to the bar. More pairs of eyes than just Daniel's follow the oscillation of her hips as she moves. She doesn't seem to notice, and he imagines there would be a lot of tellings-off if she did. He laughs softly at the thought.

Soon, Liyah returns, clutching a saltshaker and four small glasses adorned with limes. Together, they complete the salt-tequila-lime ritual, resulting in varying grimaces.

Liyah, face returning to neutral after she squeezes her eyes shut at the bitterness, says "L'chaim," and slams the glass down on the table. This begets House Rule #4 on the napkin contract:

4. Liyah and Daniel will explain Hebrew and Yiddish
   phrases for the uninitiated

"I'm surprised you like tequila. I was beginning to think you only drink for the fruit." Daniel gestures to her stash of cherry stems.

"Tequila comes with a lime," Siobhan points out.

"You can't do this with a lime, though." Liyah plucks a cherry stem from her pile and places it on her outstretched tongue. As she pulls it into her mouth, the rest of the Survival Club watches, rapt. Her cheeks suck in and out, her tongue bobbing around for several seconds before she pinches the end of the stem between her middle finger and thumb. She withdraws it slowly, holding it up for the group. When Daniel drags his gaze away from her lips, he sees a tight knot at the center of the stem. He would not trust himself to stand up right now. She grins wickedly.

Daniel coughs. "You certainly can't."

"Wait, how do you do that? I've always wanted to know!" Liyah launches into an explanation for Siobhan, going back and forth between open and closed-mouth demonstrations. Thankfully, this looks sillier and less . . .

"You might wanna rehinge your jaw, man," Jordan whispers to Daniel.

"Shut the fuck up," Daniel says, more tightly than intended. Sure, the girls are distracted, but Jordan has a bit of a hubris problem.

Jordan lifts his hands in surrender, laughing. "Just playing."

Daniel shakes his head. "I'm going to get another round." He takes his leave and Jordan reinserts himself by asking for a demonstration of his own. Surprisingly, Liyah guides him with the patience of a preschool teacher.

"One sec, Daniel," Alex says by way of greeting as he approaches the bar. He watches his roommate rapidly skin a grapefruit and drop perfectly curled peels into four champagne flutes. Alex sprays what must be edible glitter into each glass before sending them on their way with the server. "Alright, roomie. What can I do you for?"

"Same drinks for everyone, I think."

"Next time, convince your friends to try something new. I didn't develop this whole cocktail menu for nothing, you know."

Daniel smiles. "When what you've given us is already so good, it's hard to venture out."

"What are you buttering me up for?" Alex clucks his tongue. "Did you clog the sink shaving again?"

"No. Speaking of . . . I never asked, but who was over last week?"

Alex leans back, a few curls falling away from his forehead. "How is that speaking of shaving?"

Daniel shrugs. "It's not, but I didn't have a better segue."

Alex shakes his head. "That was *Marc,* with a *c,*" he says.

"Will Marc with a *c* be coming around again, or have you broken another heart?" Daniel asks.

Alex laughs. "Only time will tell, my friend."

They stay until nearly one in the morning, and Siobhan yawns uncontrollably. She laments that she's likely to fall asleep on her bus, so Jordan offers to split an Uber with her. Liyah is weirdly encouraging of this idea, and Daniel can't tell if she's eager to ensure her friend has a way home safe or if maybe . . .

Better not to get his hopes up. Regardless, Daniel and Liyah end up next to each other, knees just barely touching— which is in no way intentional on his part—in a completely empty blue-line car.

Liyah releases a small laugh. "What?" Daniel asks.

"It's just . . . it's Friday night. We're spending Shabbat together again. But with tequila."

Daniel smiles. "Do you think Rabbi Joe would be disappointed in us?"

"Oh, *immensely,*" she says.

"When was the last time you did Shabbat for real?"

Liyah tilts her head, squinting. "I honestly don't know. I'm more of a twice-a-year Jew, you know?"

He does know. Daniel can't remember the last time he was in shul outside of the High Holidays since his youngest cousin's bar mitzvah. "Passover seders and shul for Yom Kippur?"

She nods. "I usually make it in for Rosh Hashanah, too, so I guess technically thrice. I also light candles on Chanukah, but I don't really think that counts."

"You're better than me. I don't usually make it in for Rosh Hashanah, but I do have dinner with my family."

"I don't think God has done any smiting lately, so you're probably good."

"I thought you didn't believe in God?" he asks, making eye contact with Liyah's reflection in the opposite window.

"I don't. I'm in it for the tradition. I like knowing that I'm doing the same thing Jews across the world have been doing for centuries."

Daniel thinks of Havdalah at camp, everybody standing arm in arm around the circle, feeling the warmth of fire from a braided candle, the smell of spices and the blend of voices in song, and Liyah tucked at his side. He hasn't done it since, but it was always his favorite ritual. "I get that. I still haven't decided what I believe. The world is a very big place."

"Yeah," she says. "What's your stop?" Liyah turns her head to look up at Daniel, and he's happy to have an excuse to look back. They're sitting close enough for him to see the faint sunspots scattered across her cheeks.

He swallows. "Damen. You?"

Her eyes widen. "Wait, where do you live? Mine's Division."

"I'm in Wicker Park."

She lets out a whistle. "I'm on the border of East Village and Noble Square. That's crazy, we've been neighbors this whole time and met again on a flight from San Francisco."

Daniel wants to comment on how friendly she's being, but it'll ruin the moment. Instead, he says, "Small world, I guess."

"Ah, contradictory evidence! Does this tip you more toward faith or atheism?"

Daniel thinks for a moment, then grins. "If I knew the answer to that, I might have made up my mind already."

The LED display flashes DIVISION all too soon. Daniel hesitates but decides to stand up and offer Liyah a hug goodbye. She looks at him blankly, feet rooted to the floor of the car. His arms are almost back at his sides when Liyah tucks perfectly into him, her curls tickling the underside of his chin, warmth spreading from every point where their bodies connect. She smells faintly of tequila, but also of lavender and something he can't quite put his finger on. Before he has time to debate what it might be, she's gone.

SSC #3 MEETING NOTES

Secretary: Jordan

- Talking to bosses
  - From Siobhan: not sure how to end casual conversation w/ boss
    - Liyah: say you're excited to get back to work
    - Daniel+Jordan second this
  - Jordan: personal questions you don't want to answer?
    - Siobhan: subject change
- Dating
  - From Liyah: "literally all you have to do to get a guy to sleep with you is touch his arm"
    - Siobhan: that can't be true
    - Daniel+Jordan can neither confirm nor deny
- General adult life
  - Siobhan doesn't understand American tax system
    - Explanation too difficult over drinks, will return to it in spring
  - Everyone: Daniel+Alex need renter's insurance
    - Dumbass
- Rule addition: 5. Siobhan must explain Gaelic words and Irish slang

CHAPTER 7

WINDY City Wine and Cheese is a converted warehouse space just beyond the Fulton Market District neon sign (designed with a combination of horizontal and vertical text that has launched Siobhan into a rant about legibility in typography on more than one occasion). The décor is apropos to the area, with exposed brick, high ceilings, wood beams, and brass finishes. But Peter, the owner, looks more like he's been plucked straight from the Pacific Northwest: a plush (mostly silver) mustache, curls escaping the back of his beanie (suggesting a mullet of the tattooed lefty rather than the hair metal variety), and a Pendleton crewneck (despite this early September evening being altogether too warm for wool). His skin is smooth save for delicately defined wrinkles at the corners of his eyes. Liyah can't decide whether he's in his late thirties and spent his twenties on the kinds of adventures that earn you smile lines and gray hairs, or in his late forties with a diligent diet of wheatgrass and green smoothies, fine wine as his only indulgence.

Peter twirls the end of his mustache as he reads over the list of the five select exhibitions and their accompanying synopses.

He frowns, which very well could be a facial tic that means he's concentrating, but has Liyah nervously shifting on her stool nonetheless. "I know that some of these aren't actual wine-tasting notes. Like, I'm pretty sure 'earthy' is? But we'd probably have to get creative for the one about mummification salt. Which is okay, of course," tumbles out before she can stop herself. Daniel rubs his hand over his mouth, as if trying not to laugh. Liyah clasps her hands together, trying not to smack him.

"Salinity is a very important characteristic of wine, tasted along the outer edge of the tongue," Peter says.

"Wine is salty?" Liyah laughs. She can feel Daniel's glare. Mentally, she returns it twofold.

Peter chuckles. "Not all wine, no."

"As you can see, we're not wine experts," Daniel says. "That's where you come in. Per our proposal, we have the budget to do five exhibition pairings, with one of your bartenders—"

"Connoisseurs," Peter corrects, straight-faced.

Both Liyah and Daniel stare at him blankly for a moment, and Liyah feels the gentle press of Daniel's sneaker over the toe of her mule before he continues. "Right, one of your connoisseurs at each exhibition."

"Aw, I'm just yanking your chain!" Peter slaps his thigh, and Liyah decides that despite initial appearances, he's in his early forties and *very* Minnesotan. "Shoulda seen the look on your faces! This all sounds like a good deal to me. I'm not much of a museum guy myself—they're too boring for words—but that's nothing a little wine can't fix."

"Then you're exactly our target audience," Liyah says, plastering a smile over her irritation. The pressure of Daniel's foot increases sharply.

Peter is back to mustache twirling. "I've got some ideas for you. Okay if I grab a couple bottles from 'round back and do a tasting? I can talk you through the notes and we can pick the ones you guys like."

"Perfect," Daniel replies, and doesn't release Liyah's foot until Peter disappears through the door behind the bar.

"Ow," she hisses. "I would have behaved."

"I don't believe that for a second," he says with a shake of his head.

"He knows where I work! That was such an unnecessary comment."

"Right. Because you're so good at keeping your opinions to yourself."

Liyah folds her arms across her chest. "In a professional context, I can be."

Daniel scans her face, the left corner of his lips tugging upward. "I have three solid weeks of evidence to the contrary."

"You are a special exception, Rosenberg."

"He's not wrong, you know," he says. Liyah's eyes widen. "No! Not about museums being boring. About people's boredom being fixed with wine."

"If you have to drink to enjoy something, then you shouldn't be doing it," Liyah argues.

"Says the woman who takes a shot every time Jordan tries to get her to talk about dating."

"You're exactly right," she retorts. "I have no business talking about my feelings."

When Peter returns, he's pushing a cart that clarifies that the *some* part of *some ideas* loosely translates to *a fuck ton*. There are at least twenty bottles of various red, white, and pink wines. Single-ounce pours add up much faster than Liyah would have guessed, and she soon finds herself tipsy and giggling all too easily at whatever Peter says.

Peter starts on an explanation of the taste map (which Liyah is almost certain is pseudoscientific) and instructs them to hold out their tongues and stroke the different regions he describes. Liyah turns to Daniel, expecting to laugh. The image of him slowly running his index finger along the outline of his tongue is ridiculous, yes, but Liyah is also completely unprepared for how her breath hitches, her own taste buds feeling the phantom roughness of his calluses as he adds his middle finger, too. Intensely erotic, undeservedly so.

She swallows her entire pour of a grenache and feels its acidity not on the inner sides of her tongue but in her whole mouth, coating her esophagus. Liyah coughs, and Peter jokes that if she didn't like that one, she could have said so. She mumbles a response about how it's fine, good, even. Something like that. Her mind is too cloudy, and her cheeks are too warm to know exactly. All she knows is that she's hurtling toward dangerous territory, and she desperately needs to change course.

THANKS TO THEIR newly sacred Friday nights, Daniel has seen Liyah tipsy a few times. It's different here, somehow, without Siobhan's deeply macabre sense of humor or Jordan's—what's the opposite of self-effacement?—to buffer. When she laughs, bright-eyed, it's all for him. Or *at* him, but still.

There's an extra intensity to Liyah's attention when she has had a bit to drink. When it's pointed at Daniel, he feels not like he is the only man in the room, but like he is the only thing that exists in the universe. That if he were to look around, he'd find himself transported to a blank void with naught but the two of them.

He was in that void with her most of the night, but a switch flipped, and now it's like she'll pay attention to anything *but* him. He feels a touch of relief as they agree on their top five wines and exchange handshakes and goodbyes with Peter. They spill out onto the street, making their way toward the

Grand L station, and Daniel is thankful for the night breeze cooling his neck and forearms.

"You know," he says, looking down at Liyah as she strides beside him. She's a fast walker, easily keeping pace with his long stride. "There's nothing wrong with meeting people where they are with these events."

Liyah looks up at him, that laser focus of hers warming his face. "I know you think that. You're most comfortable when you're loudly wrong."

She doesn't seem like she's joking. Daniel's shoulders sag. "Right, yeah. I'm an idiot, untrustworthy, yada yada. Whatever, Liyah."

Liyah laughs through her nose. "Glad you're self-aware."

Daniel's chest tightens. "Sometimes I can't—I mean, are you really that much of an ideological purist about this? People should either care about natural history as much as you or they shouldn't bother at all?" he asks.

"No, of course not! This just feels so *pointless*."

"It's not pointless, Liyah. It's a good way to get people to the museum."

"For the events!" Her gaze cuts up to him. "It's a good way to get people to the museum *for the events*, not for the museum. So, what will that leave us? Some extra patrons for the night? That's not what my boss is looking for. And it's not what my boss's bosses are looking for. They want sustained membership. Despite my many misgivings about Jeff, he does actually care about the Field. The board—or at least some people on it—only care about the numbers. And they think we have to be *trendy* to do that. Like, sorry, not everything looks perfect on your social media feed! But sometimes it's interesting anyway."

"Why not do the eye-catching exhibits and fun events to get people in the door? Won't they stay for the rest of it?"

"Sure, why not?" She gives a sarcastic shrug.

Daniel ignores the bait. "Well, regardless, the wine night is gonna be good. Trust me," he says, to which Liyah scoffs. He stops in his tracks. It takes her a half second to realize, so she pauses just ahead of him.

"What?" she demands.

"You're seriously still mad about Maccabiah?" Her lips press into a harsh line. "You are, aren't you? Come on, Liyah, we already went over this—it wasn't me who took your idea! And honestly, even if it was, that was a decade and a half ago. Isn't that a little long to hold a grudge about color wars?"

He watches Liyah press her hands into her thighs, as if restraining herself. "It wasn't only about color wars," she says. "You *told* people."

Daniel shakes his head. "I told people what, exactly?"

"I asked you not to tell anybody that we were hooking up! You gave me your word, and yet somehow your whole cabin knew enough to steal my bras off the clothesline and sharpie *Property of Rosenberg* on every single one. And that's probably the nicest thing anybody said to me about it."

Daniel furrows his brow. "Liyah—" he starts.

"No!" she interrupts. "You don't get it. It was different for girls in middle school. I mean, honestly it still is, in subtler ways, but that's beside the point! We weren't officially together, and we made out, which made you hot shit and me a slut in training."

The first thought he has is *I would have made us official in a heartbeat,* but even as his heart slams against his rib cage, he can tell how unhelpful that would be. Instead, he fires back with his second: "I never told anybody! Gross slept on the bunk below me, and he knew I was sneaking out. I denied it every single time he asked, but he had the biggest mouth in the boys' shetach, you know that."

"Even if that were true, Rosenberg, you didn't warn me," she spits out. "I had to bear the brunt of it completely on my own."

"You ran away after closing ceremonies and refused to talk to me for the rest of the summer. How was I supposed to warn you? Carrier pigeon? What do you want from me?" He waves his arms. Liyah's eyes follow the movement and her frown deepens. "Sorry I didn't understand the intricacies of misogyny when I was in *middle school.*"

"Yeah, well. It's not like that was even the last time who I was or wasn't with became a topic of controversy. People spin whatever narratives they want, and if you do the slightest thing to confirm it, then that's who you are forever. If there's a boy and a girl involved—or a man and a woman, for that matter—the boy always comes out smelling like roses. When you're the unlucky girl, you're on your fucking own. Whether it's assholes at summer camp, or assholes in high school, or assholes in college. It's all the same. Whether what happened was your fault or his or neither or both, it's all the fucking same! Over and over again. You got congratulated. I lost whatever few friends I had. So yeah, maybe you weren't the one pointing fingers and calling names, but you were supposed to be my friend. You were supposed to be my friend, and you didn't stick up for me. *Nobody* stuck up for me back then. I might as well do it now." Her chin tilts up as she says this, jaw clenching. Always the picture of tough, but his heart breaks a little. He runs the string of words through his head again, and it feels even sadder.

"Oh," he whispers.

She holds up her hands. "Please, I don't want your pity."

"That's not pity, Liyah! It's sympathy, and a healthy dose of guilt." Daniel rubs the back of his neck. "I know I said this already, but I really meant it. I was an insecure idiot. You were—" He struggles to find the words. "I knew some of that was happening—the, um, bra thing, at least—but you always just blazed onward like it wasn't affecting you. I thought you were the coolest person I had ever met, and I felt rejected and caught up in my own shit when you ignored me, so I didn't see what was right there. Of course it was affecting you. I should have known. I'm so sorry."

Liyah's features soften, and Daniel is reminded of that night in the observatory. That look of trust. It's much rougher around the edges than it had been, less consuming. But the echo of it is there. "Thank you," she says.

"I'm sorry for what I said earlier, too. The thing about not understanding misogyny in middle school. It was a really fucked-up thing to say, since you had to actually experience it." Liyah's eyes go glassy. Daniel steps toward her, hesitant. She doesn't move away. "Can I hug you?"

"Sure." She moves forward. "But only to make you feel better."

"Okay, Liyah," he says into the hair that pushes against his face. He inhales as he wraps his arms around her, breathing her in. *Wine and lavender, a hint of cocoa,* he thinks. This is the third time they've hugged—not that he's counting—and he can't deny that his body loves the feel of her against him, how she tucks so neatly under his chin. His skin tingles, blood thrums in his veins.

"You really didn't tell anybody?" she murmurs into his chest.

"I didn't, I promise," he replies softly. Another second passes, and then they separate, Daniel clearing his throat. "Are we good, Cohen-Jackson?"

"Yes, Daniel," she says. "We're good."

SSC #4 MEETING NOTES

Secretary: Daniel

- Work/life balance
  - Liyah made a "what's that" joke. Everyone is concerned
    - She insists it is just a joke. Still concerned
  - Jordan & Daniel suggest rock climbing
    - Siobhan suggests spin class
    - Liyah suggests yoga
    - Jordan has violated rule #3 by complaining that yoga is too girly
- Dating
  - Jordan needs to spend some time single holy shit
    - Jordan insists he is not a serial monogamist. Nobody buys it
- General adult life
  - Jordan is a grown man with disposable income and therefore he needs a bed frame
    - Dumbass
- Jordan feels that he has spent most of the night under attack. Everyone disagrees
- Rule addition: 6. Jordan may reference his charm no more than once per meeting
  - Jordan claims this is proof of previous note. Everyone disagrees

CHAPTER 8

LIYAH is drunk. Not four-drinks-over-four-hours buzzed the way she usually is at Survival Club meetings, but properly drunk. Which explains why she cannot, for the life of her, stop stealing glances at Daniel's chest. His eyes are on Siobhan now, laughing at something she says, so Liyah's gaze slides over. The top two buttons of his shirt are undone, and any time Daniel leans back or turns to the side, the fabric falls open a bit. His skin is lightly flushed and a mole on the left side of his sternum is playing an exceedingly frustrating game of peek-a-boo. This is his fault, really, for deciding that his button-down needed to show off his chest instead of just the standard forearm display.

She is *definitely* drunk, because during this particular glance, she fails to pull her eyes away fast enough and Daniel catches her staring.

He smirks, bringing his hand up to rub his chin. The ring on his pinky glints in the low light. "Avid interest in my shirt choice, Liyah?"

"I'm just wondering where you find these. Is there a boutique somewhere in Wicker Park that specializes in casual button-downs with headache-inducing prints?" This one is covered in watercolored oranges. It's not bad, especially since it matches the orange and green accents on his sneakers, but some have been truly awful. Last week he wore something that could have been scraped off a bus seat from the eighties.

"Oh, you're looking for a wardrobe makeover." His eyes run up and down her slowly. She knows he's doing this to emphasize his point, but goose bumps erupt across her skin. "I can see why. I don't know anywhere that's open this late, though, so you'll have to hold your excitement in until tomorrow."

"I'll take your fashion advice over my dead body," Liyah fires back.

"I'll make sure to bring a good outfit selection to your shiva house."

"House Rule number four!" Siobhan and Jordan say in unison, not for the first time.

Liyah looks at Daniel expectantly. As per their tacit agreement, it's his turn to explain. He takes a sip of his drink and says, "It's what you call the home of the mourning family for the week after the funeral."

"Shiva means seven, for seven days," Liyah adds.

Jordan shakes his head in response. "Y'all are fucking dark."

"I don't know, I think it was a good one," Siobhan says, much to Liyah's chagrin. As it happens, her displeasure seems to be synonymous with Daniel's delight.

Liyah takes a drink from her glass, some surprise cocktail that Alex insisted they all try. It's ginger-heavy and probably sugary enough to give her a headache tomorrow, if the tequila shots haven't already ensured one. She decides to change the subject. "Daniel just wants to avoid giving away his trade secrets."

Siobhan claps her hands together. "Right, back to Emailing Like a Man 101. Don't you try to get out of your Survival Club duties—we had to explain why you need a bed frame when you're flush and over twenty-two last week."

"Thanks for that, by the way," Jordan says. "You set me back a couple hundred bucks."

"Well, I already had a bed frame," Daniel interjects.

"Good for you, man. Nobody ever complained before."

Liyah laughs. "Maybe not to your face." She makes a *get on with it* gesture. "The email workshop. I would like it on record that I'm listening out of curiosity, not because I believe I should change my behavior. Not a big fan of *leaning in*."

A chorus of groans greets her. "Okay, Liyah," Jordan says. "You got an example? Hand it over."

Siobhan scrolls around her in-box before passing her phone off to Jordan. He and Daniel huddle around the screen with concerned expressions on their faces.

"Okay, first of all, you need fewer exclamation points." Daniel backtracks when he sees Siobhan's frown. "Sorry, it's not terrible. It's just that every other sentence is kind of a lot."

"See," Liyah says. "I told you a good rule of thumb is three to five." Jordan laughs, and now it's Liyah's turn to frown.

"No, try one. Max."

DANIEL IS THANKFUL for the collective decision to forgo their usual few rounds in favor of several. He's spent the entire week dreading the upcoming holidays. Sure, it'll be nice to see Kayla and his mother for Rosh Hashanah. It'll also be nice to see the food, as Kayla sweetens her challah to ring in the new year with chocolate chips instead of the traditional raisins. But he can't help but feel like the table will be painfully empty with only the three of them. And since he doesn't plan to make the two-hour drive out to Madison next Wednesday for Yom Kippur, he's going to be totally alone for services. He's heard grief gets harder around Christmastime, and he supposes that this is the Jewish equivalent.

The quantity of alcohol Daniel's consumed has prevented him from thinking about it, or at least helped him let the thoughts pass by instead of dwelling. He's struggled the whole week trying to work around the knot in his chest, but it appears that the knot is no match for bourbon. The only downside of his drunkenness is that he's even more aware than usual of his attraction to Liyah. Her lips are painted a very distracting color of red, and he's only managing to look at her eyes half the time she talks. Thank God Alex got her off her usual old-fashioned; Daniel wouldn't survive watching her tie a cherry stem right now.

Liyah kicks him under the table. "Pay attention, dummy," she stage-whispers.

"I was!" He was not.

"Oh yeah? What's Jordan talking about?"

He ventures a guess. "Love?"

Liyah scans his face as if trying to determine if it was a lucky guess. Daniel blinks. Eventually, she huffs and turns her focus to the rest of the group. Daniel does the same.

"Wait, so you're saying you had your first kiss and then lost your virginity in the same night?" Siobhan's eyes are wide, aghast. Daniel hasn't heard this particular Jordan story before, and it piques his interest.

Jordan wears a cheeky smile, the type that makes Daniel appreciate the extent of his friend's charm. "It was a passionate moment."

"No. You can't leave it at that. Go on," Liyah demands.

"I may have implied that I was more experienced than I was. But what was I gone do? She was popular."

"You weren't?" Siobhan seems truly astonished by this. She tries to cover it quickly, but Daniel knows a woman enamored with Jordan when he sees one. His eyes flick to Liyah. If she knows, she doesn't let on.

Jordan smirks. "I did okay. But she was dating-the-starting-point-guard-type popular. He cheated with most of the cheerleading team, and I offered my shoulder to cry on."

Daniel smiles. Typical. "While spitting as big a game as you could, I'm guessing."

"You know how I do. She never found out I was a virgin, and we dated for a whole year."

"Very J. Cole of you." Liyah lifts her glass. "I'm impressed." Jordan clinks his cup against hers and knocks his drink all the way back.

"Okay, now that I've told my embarrassing story"—Liyah and Siobhan exchange a look at Jordan's effort to play off his brag—"someone else has to tell theirs."

"First time for sex or a kiss?" Daniel asks, half joking.

Jordan takes the question on its face. "Either. Both if you want."

"Okay, I'll go first. Then we'll go around the table," Siobhan says.

Daniel's eyes slide to Liyah, waiting for her to protest. She knows full well that they'll tell the same story. But she nods her agreement, never meeting his gaze, wearing that same alcohol-brightened smile, like she truly couldn't care less. Daniel mimics her nod, dazed.

"Alright, I was in sixth class," Siobhan says.

"I hope this is the kiss story," Liyah says.

"It is! It was the bloke who grew up next to me. We went cycling around the neighborhood together, and then I told him I liked him. He full-on snogged me. It was kind of gross. Tongues are weird if you think too hard about them, right?" Everyone nods.

When she doesn't continue, Jordan asks, "And the other story?"

"Eh, less interesting. Took someone home from a pub on my eighteenth birthday. The utterly horrible beginning and end of my one-night-stand career."

Liyah furrows her brow. "Wait, so you've only had sex with three people?" Siobhan turns an impressively deep shade of red. "Oh God, I'm sorry. I didn't mean to . . . fuck." Liyah reaches for her cocktail as if looking for a way to busy herself, but the glass is empty.

"It's okay, I know it's not that many."

Liyah shakes her head. "No, no! I sometimes forget that me and Neen both have kinda high body counts. I'm a dumbass. You're normal. I mean, any number is normal. Because there's no right way to . . . Daniel, can you go before I bury myself deeper in this hole?"

"Um, first kiss . . . I was thirteen? I think." Daniel gulps, trying his best at an easy tone. It's one thing for Liyah to agree to do this, but another to push him to share. He looks down at his drink, at the print of a 1920s mobster, at the mercury glass mirror—really, anywhere but Liyah—feeling like his every movement might give him away. "It was at Jewish sleepaway camp. We snuck out of our cabins and made out on the archery field."

"Arrows are very romantic," Jordan says.

"It was the middle of the night, so Cupid didn't make an appearance. I'm sorry to disappoint."

"Daniel and I went to the same camp," Liyah says.

"Wait, *what*?" Siobhan says. "You guys were childhood friends?"

Liyah fiddles with her straw, waving Siobhan off. "That's beside the point. They would leave seventeen-to-nineteen-year-old counselors in charge of thirteen-year-olds and it was practically the Wild West." Daniel looks at her, directly now, his heart in his throat. Her lips curve into a smug smile. "I didn't have to sneak out, though. She slept in the bunk above me. They really forget about gay people when they make gendered cabins."

His stomach drops. *I wasn't her first kiss?*

"I'm stuck on the fact that you lot knew each other and said nothing," Siobhan says, looking at Liyah. "I was under the impression that your issue with him began and ended with the marketing project you didn't want to do." Liyah wilts slightly under her gaze.

"Well, I hadn't seen her in fourteen years," Daniel tries.

"And we weren't, like, close friends," Liyah adds, her words spreading like venom through his veins.

"Is that where you lost your virginity, too?" Jordan asks.

"No, not everybody's a speed demon like you, sir," Liyah shoots back. Jordan smirks. "Stop smirking, Jordan."

"Can't, my face is just like that. So, what's the story?"

Liyah makes a face as though the drink she's sipping is long expired. "Hard pass."

Jordan doesn't seem to take the hint because he's about to press on. Daniel stops him before he can start. "Mine's a good story. It was my senior year of high school, and my parents were gone for the weekend, so I invited my girlfriend over. To set the scene: candles, lava lamp, the works."

Siobhan snorts. "Lava lamp?"

"I said the *works*. And then, my sister walked in. She didn't even knock, just pulled the door right open. Apparently, she didn't know that my parents were out of town and when the house seemed empty, she thought we'd all been murdered. She went back downstairs and got in her car and drove back to her dorm without saying a single thing to me."

Jordan laughs and Siobhan gasps at the punch line, but Liyah just looks relieved. He doesn't realize just how relieved until half an hour later when they're waiting on the L platform.

"Thanks for doing that. Telling your embarrassing story," she says, staring intently at her shoes.

"Who said I was embarrassed? It might be one of my proudest moments; I still managed to get us both to the finish line after Kayla interrupted." It was so embarrassing that he couldn't look Kayla in the eyes for almost a month afterward, but he wants to give Liyah an out.

She doesn't take it. Instead, she looks straight up at him, holding his gaze for a long moment. "Thank you."

Daniel swallows. "You're welcome." The train comes, and they board in comfortable silence. He feels impossibly tired now, and he leans his head on the probably filthy pole that he and Liyah hold on to. His hand grips the bar just above hers, so they're millimeters from touching. In his drunken, sleepy state, he's tempted to close the gap.

"I'm drunker than I've been in a while," she says.

"Me too. You know," Daniel starts, looking down at the fluorescent lights dancing in her irises. "That summer, you told me that I was your first kiss."

Liyah grins. "No, I didn't."

He shakes his head, and his hand slips lower, the underside of his pinky pressing along the line of her thumb. "You did. I remember asking you."

She rakes her teeth over her bottom lip slowly, and when she's done, her smile spreads even wider. "You asked me if I'd ever kissed a boy before, and I said no. Which was the truth."

Daniel squeezes his eyes shut, pressing his free hand to his forehead. "Oh, God."

Liyah pulls his hand away, her laughter ricocheting in the sparsely populated car. "Weird Q," she says, then pauses, as if making sure that Daniel realizes she's making fun of his text message that one time. "What are you doing for Yom Kippur?"

He shrugs. "Going to services and trying not to think about how hungry I am, I guess."

"Want to go with me?"

"Really?"

She stumbles into him as the train lurches to a halt at the Chicago Avenue stop. He's surprised at how easily his hand finds her lower back to steady her, even more surprised at how she seems to melt into his touch. Must be the liquor. The train starts again, and he pulls away.

"Yes, really. I don't know any practicing Jews my age here, on account of the whole thrice a year thing. And . . ." She trails off.

"You get stared at when you walk into a mostly white synagogue?"

She grins. "Might as well really give them something to look at."

He matches her smile. "Might as well."

Before they part ways at Division, Daniel tries to convince Liyah to let him walk her home. She insists she's fine and makes a big show of lifting her leg so he can see that the heels of her shoes are thick and stable. He begs her to stop, given that she's wearing a skirt, which results in an "I've got spandex shorts under this, you prude" and Daniel feeling like his entire body is blushing. Eventually, she agrees to text him when she gets to her apartment. It may only be because the doors are about to close, but it appeases Daniel all the same. The message comes as he's walking down from the platform at Damen.

Liyah

Home safe, worrywart.

Daniel

glad to hear it. not a
worrywart

Liyah

Sure, and I'm not grouchy!

Daniel

she admits it!

Liyah

Which means, in turn, that
you admit it.

Daniel

touché.

He smiles to himself the entire walk home, humming one of the jazz tunes the band had played earlier in the night. As soon as he's locked the apartment door behind him, he scoops Sweet Potato into his arms. She purrs loudly, and he wonders if she knows that he's intoxicated and that's why she gets so cuddly. Maybe it's that he's a little extra affectionate and she is meeting him where he is. Either way, he's always happy to come home to her after a night out.

The next morning, he wakes up with Sweet Potato sitting on his chest, his head pounding. He must have forgotten that hangovers exist last night; there's no other explanation for voluntarily doing this to himself. And now, despite his brief respite, he still has the next two weeks to face. His phone lights up with a notification:

Liyah

Please add "No more than
one round of tequila shots"
as number 7 on the list
of rules. Or at least make
whoever suggests them buy
the Tylenol.

SSC #6 MEETING NOTES

Secretary: Siobhan

- Work projects
  - Siobhan wants to know if anybody actually reads newsletters
    - Mostly no, but the examples she's given are quite eye-catching
  - Daniel would like to know what everyone's favorite thing about the CTA is
    - Jordan says nothing
    - Siobhan says that the L is mostly aboveground—unpopular opinion but she loves how the tracks look weaving through the city
    - Liyah says the places it takes her
  - Liyah and Jordan would not like to talk about their work, thank you very much
    - Liyah would like to specify in all caps: "I ALREADY HAVE TO WORK WITH DANIEL. I WOULD LIKE NOT TO THEN HAVE TO TALK ABOUT SAID WORK WITH DANIEL ON FRIDAY EVENINGS WITH DANIEL"

- Dating
  - Liyah is still adamant that romantic love is not real, or is "back on her bullshit," in Jordan's words
    - Siobhan and Jordan say this makes her a right grouch
    - Daniel is more agnostic, but leans toward its existence
      - Liyah says this is because Daniel's agnostic about everything, and if he were capable of making up his mind, he'd see the light
      - Jordan says that it's more darkness than light
      - Liyah insists that we move on

- Daniel's sister made delicious challah
  - "Siobhan, you don't need to take notes on that"
  - Liyah asks that he have Kayla email her the recipe
    - See, taking notes was quite helpful

- Yom Kippur is next week and Liyah is already grouchy about fasting
  - Daniel says it's not that bad
  - Liyah requests that Siobhan stops writing that she is grouchy
    - Seriously, she is not that grouchy
    - "Please stop"

- No rule additions this week

CHAPTER 9

THE morning of Yom Kippur, Daniel and Liyah meet at the L stop on Division. Last night, Liyah had made them late (even by JST) to Kol Nidre, the single most attended Jewish service, and they were relegated to the folding chairs set up in the back of the shul to accommodate the overflow. The makeshift pews were not spaced appropriately for Daniel's legs, and Liyah kept having to stifle laughter as he tried to fit himself in diagonally. A consultation with Google Maps revealed that he had a shorter walk to her stop than she did to his, so they adjusted accordingly.

Liyah feels out of sorts sitting on the train in fancy clothing, the silk bag with her bat mitzvah tallis on her lap. It's also quite strange to be next to Daniel like this in the daylight. She's accustomed to a quiet car, Daniel's face yellowed by the plastic overlay on the harsh overhead lights. This morning, it's full and bright and noisy in a way that doesn't sit well given that she skipped food and coffee in observance of the fast. She hardly says anything the whole way there. He doesn't seem to be in a chatty mood, either, and she hopes there's a shared understanding that no eating means no lengthy conversations. Besides, as Neen loves pointing out, Liyah's natural snark edges toward outright rudeness when she's hungry.

When they push open the doors to the synagogue foyer, a few pairs of eyes flicker their way. Liyah looks at Daniel, and he raises his eyebrows at her, amused. They stop to put on their tallisim and kippot (Liyah brought several bobby pins to affix her kippah to the crown of her head, otherwise she'd spend the services picking it up off the floor) before heading toward the doors to the main sanctuary. A greeter stands by a table with stacks of machzorim. He hands one of the prayer books to an elderly woman and points her to the door.

When Daniel and Liyah approach, he eyes them curiously. "Are you two in the right place?" he asks.

Liyah swallows, taking the man's question about as well as a punch to the gut. *This is not your first rodeo,* she reminds herself. Despite her empty stomach, she's ready to vomit.

Daniel must feel her tense up because he reaches for her hand. "Oh, this isn't the Baptist church's Yom Kippur service?" he jokes, trying to lighten the mood. But Liyah is already fuming.

The greeter belatedly clocks their religious garb and starts to apologize. Liyah doesn't hear a single word he says. She takes a deep breath to make sure that her voice is low and level so no bystanders can overhear.

"I hope you add 'I have sinned against you with racism' to your vidui this year, you brainless prick." She yanks two of the machzorim directly off the table. She wants to say more, but Daniel squeezes her hand and pulls her away before she gets the chance.

He doesn't let go until they're tucked away in a hallway that must lead to the rabbi's and cantor's offices. Her skin tingles at the loss of touch, but then his hands are on her shoulders and he's looking into her eyes. He takes exaggeratedly deep breaths as if she's meant to follow, and when she does, she realizes that she was hyperventilating.

"I. Am. So. Mad," she bites out.

"I see that," Daniel whispers. Now his hands are running up and down her upper arms. It's soothing. And immensely irritating. He's so calm. She's falling apart, and he's perfectly serene, unruffled.

"This doesn't get to you?" she manages.

He swallows. "It does. Maybe not quite as much, but you're right, that guy was a brainless dick." His irises flick back and forth, as if he's checking each of her eyes individually for signs of an impending explosion. "Are you doing a little bit better?"

Her pulse no longer feels fast enough for her heart to give out, so she nods. "Prick."

He moves back an inch. His breath no longer fans over Liyah's cheeks. "What?"

"I said *prick,* not *dick.* Blame Siobhan." Liyah smiles, and Daniel's entire body seems to relax. "Did you cheat and have breakfast?" she asks.

He shakes his head. "I haven't eaten since five yesterday, same as you."

"Then why do you seem so . . . fine? And how were you patient enough to figure out how to calm me down?"

"I'm plenty hungry, I just have willpower." She frowns, and he chuckles. "My sister Kayla's a therapist, but even before that she was good at this kind of thing. She taught me some tricks of the trade."

Liyah sighs. "Ah, well. Tell her I say thanks."

"Do you want to go back in?" Daniel asks.

Liyah can tell he means it. She has the option to stay or go. Because this is not the first time someone has said this to him, just like it's not the first time for her. She wonders if he ever talks to his father about it, and how he reacts. Her mother has never been great at fielding her and Avi's experiences with white-assimilated Jews. They'll repeat one of several common invalidations, and her mom freezes up completely, tears welling. As if Liyah communicating the reality of her experience is a personal attack.

The first time in her adult life that she walked into a Jewish space without her very short, very Ashkenazi-looking mother to contextualize her existence was Rosh Hashanah her sophomore year of college. It took one step in the door for someone to tell her she must be lost. She turned on her heels and left the Northwestern University Hillel, stewing in her dorm room for the next two days. It was the only year of her life she didn't observe the High Holidays. She told her mother, and they fought so badly that they didn't speak directly until winter break. And the thing is, as much as she wishes her mom could have better understood the pain that led to her making that choice, not observing didn't feel right, either. Like it was letting them win. Like it was saying, *you're right, I don't belong,* even though Liyah is Jewish to her very core. Even though her Blackness and her Jewishness are inextricably linked because she's never been one without the other.

She takes another deep breath and nods. "Ready."

"Okay." He drops his hands from her shoulders. "I can't believe you told that guy to repent."

"He deserved it!" Liyah protests.

Daniel shakes his head. "I'm not judging, I'm admiring. You're quick on your feet."

She follows him back to the foyer, where the offending greeter waves them into the sanctuary, avoiding eye contact. Fortunately, they caught the L early enough that Liyah's meltdown hasn't cost them good seats. They snag a spot toward an aisle (for optimal sneaking out) and Daniel makes an audible *phew* when he fits his legs into the row. Liyah bites her lip to avoid laughing. Yom Kippur isn't really a laughing holiday, and she certainly doesn't need to draw any more attention to herself.

When the services make it to Al Cheyt, the part of vidui where the English translation of each confession begins "We have sinned against you with," they keep making eye contact. Just when Liyah thinks she's got ahold of herself, Daniel winks, and she has to cover her snort with a cough. The woman to her left shifts away slightly. *Well, at least I was convincing,* she thinks.

The rest of the morning goes by smoothly, if very slowly. Liyah can't remember the last time that she enjoyed shul this much. Even when the rabbi drags her sermon on a little too long, she doesn't get agitated. Instead, she nudges Daniel and whispers, "Since she can't have any water today, you'd think it would be in her best interest to wrap it up before she makes herself hoarse." He keeps his face as still as possible and rubs his lips together, but she can see the laughter in his eyes.

At the end of the Torah service, Liyah's patience wears thin, even with Daniel by her side. The rabbi announces that it's time for Yizkor, and Liyah enthusiastically shoves her tallis back in its bag and gets ready to go. Daniel steps back to allow her to pass.

"You go first," she says impatiently.

He shakes his head. "I'm gonna stay for a bit."

"It's Yizkor, you don't—"

Oh. *Oh.* You don't traditionally stay for the memorial service unless you've lost a parent, sibling, or spouse, which means . . .

"I'll be right outside," Liyah says gently, pushing past the bruising shame of her thoughtlessness.

She walks to the foyer, kicking herself. She'd tried to correct him, to rush him out. God, even for her, this is bad.

Throngs of other lucky people who don't qualify for Yizkor mill about. Liyah wishes tradition didn't require her to leave Daniel behind. He's so young. Everyone else is likely too absorbed in their own mourning to worry about him, but she's never been to Yizkor, so she can't be sure. Thankfully, the movement of dispersing congregants disguises her anxious pacing.

The next half hour is the slowest of the day. The crowd mostly dissipates, and Liyah is forced to switch from pacing to picking at her fingernails. When Daniel emerges from the sanctuary, her cuticles are destroyed and his eyes are rimmed red.

"THE WAY I see it, you've got four options," Liyah says as they exit the building.

Daniel expected that she would greet him with a hug or ask how he was feeling. Maybe he should have expected this, though. It's much more Liyah. The breeze and fresh air are the closest second to the drink of water he really needs. He rolls up his sleeves. She doesn't go on, and he realizes that she's waiting for his signal. "What are the options?"

Liyah takes a deep breath. "One: we can talk about it. Two: you can tell me what you want to do for the rest of the day, and we'll go do just that. I won't break my fast early, but if that's what you need, I'll sit there and try not to glare while you eat." He searches her face. It seems she means it. "Three: you can come along with me to do what I usually do on Yom Kippur. And finally, four: say 'Liyah, fuck off' and I'll leave you to your own devices."

Daniel tries to smile. He's not sure he does a good job of it. "I wouldn't say that."

"I promise I won't be offended if you choose option four." She elbows him. Daniel wants to grab her hand, but she hasn't offered it, and he worries it would be unwelcome. "So, which'll it be?"

He could talk about his dad. About thumb wrestling during High Holiday services well into his teenage years, his mom discreetly kicking his dad's shins, desperate to get them to stop. Maybe he should; he knows that's what Kayla would do. But he barely made it through his first Yizkor and he doesn't think he has the energy. "Let's do the third one."

Liyah nods enthusiastically. "Excellent choice." It makes him smile, even though she probably would have said it regardless of what he picked. She fishes around in her tallis bag and extends her arm as if to hand him something, but there's nothing between her fingers. "Since you didn't choose option one, I'm giving you this ticket. It's good for one 'I want to talk about it' at a later date."

Daniel takes the imaginary token and tucks it into the pocket of his slacks. "So, what are we doing?"

"We're going to go home, where we will watch a depressing documentary about something wrong with the world. I know it's technically no electronics today but please remember that I've watched you eat bacon."

He laughs. "You've seen me use my phone already."

She nods. "Right, and I've seen you use your phone already, so don't say anything about how my traditions are against the rules."

"I think it makes a lot of sense. It's in the spirit of reflection," he says, looking straight ahead. Even so, he feels Liyah's gaze on the side of his face.

"Exactly!" she says. "Please tell my mother that."

After a train change and some walking, they approach an old redbrick building that looks like it was built immediately after the Great Chicago Fire. Liyah's apartment is on the second floor, and it's cozy and colorful and very lived-in. There are three large windows in the living room, mostly obstructed by enormous houseplants in mismatched pots. Daniel follows her in removing shoes at the door and unceremoniously flopping down on the couch. It's green—no surprise there—but it's darker than the color she usually wears and made of velvet. The cushions are soft but supportive and it even has a chaise attachment long enough for him to stretch his legs.

"This is an excellent sofa."

"It'd better be for what a pain in the ass it was to get up that staircase," she replies.

He strokes one of the throw pillows. It's charcoal gray, furry, and impossibly soft. "I like this, too."

Liyah makes a noise of disgust. "Of course you do."

"You don't like your own pillows?"

"It's my 'roommate'"—she makes air quotes with her fingers—"Lara's. Or Laura? You know what, I'm pretty sure it's Lara."

"And where is this fabled roommate?" Daniel asks.

"At her boyfriend's, where she actually lives." Liyah points to the only closed door in the apartment. "That's hers. It looks like a Michaels store caught a stomach bug and vomited it into existence. I keep it sectioned off so that it doesn't infect the rest of the place."

"Except for the throw pillows." Daniel smiles.

Liyah frowns. "Yes, except for the throw pillows. Are you more in the mood for climate crisis or the prison industrial complex?" She points the clicker at the screen.

"Each fun in its own right, but today is a climate crisis kind of day, don't you think?"

She hums in agreement. "Climate crisis it is." She puts the movie on and promptly curls up in the fetal position, her head on one of the throw pillows. She's several inches away from him, but her curly hair fans out, spilling over onto his lap.

They watch in total silence, their empty stomachs having

prematurely depleted their daily word stores. When the film finishes, Daniel twists his torso, using the back of the couch as leverage to crack his back. Liyah flinches at the noise.

"Sorry," he murmurs. "So, what's next on the agenda for Liyah Cohen-Jackson's Yom Kippur?"

She smiles. "It's the most important part: the afternoon nap." Liyah stands up, smooths out her skirt, and pads her way to the bedroom. Daniel supposes he's meant to follow. She lies down on top of her comforter and pulls the throw blanket up to her shoulders. "No outside clothes in the bed," she explains.

Daniel nods. As much as he loves the CTA, he wouldn't want pants that had touched a train seat on his sheets, either. "Do you mind?" he asks, motioning to his dress shirt. Liyah shakes her head, so he unbuttons it the rest of the way and removes it, along with his belt. In a thin T-shirt and with his slacks riding low on his hips, he climbs onto the most inviting bed he's ever seen. Maybe it's the fasting-induced lethargy, but it seems like he and Liyah have identical taste in furniture. His head hits the pillow, and he sighs. *Lovely.*

"Glad you like it," Liyah whispers, and it's the last thing either of them say before dozing off.

Daniel wakes up to Liyah rubbing his forearm. He blinks a few times, dazed. It seems to him that no time has passed, but the angle of the light seeping through his—not his, Liyah's— bedroom window says otherwise.

"You gotta wake up, we're gonna be late for Mincha."

"I don't know if I want to go back for the afternoon and evening services. I mean, I usually do, but . . ." Daniel's tongue tastes of sleep and his throat is dry on account of not having had any water since yesterday, and his voice comes out low and gravelly even after his attempts to clear his throat. "Is that okay?"

Liyah nods. Without thinking, he reaches for her hand. Her entire body stills. He's about to withdraw it and apologize, but she laces her fingers through his. "Yeah, that's okay." A pause. She holds eye contact so long that it's almost unnerving, like she's seeing right into the depths of him. Even though the blinds cast a strip of sunlight across her eyes, her irises are so black that it's impossible to distinguish them from her pupils. "What do you want to do with the last hour and a half?"

He wants to stay in bed, exactly like this. But he knows that's the wrong answer. "Got anything to read?"

Liyah jumps up and strides toward the living room, motioning for him to follow. He regrets saying something before remembering that her couch is equally comfortable. She thumbs through the wide bookcase that's under her TV and extracts two thin hardcovers. "Is poetry okay? It's about all I have the attention span for." Daniel nods. "These are by Edward Hirsch."

"Jewish?"

"Yep. And a Chicagoan. Thought it would be fitting." She holds up one of the books. "This one is an extended eulogy for his child. So, depending on the type of person you are, it's either perfect or the worst possible thing."

He considers. "I'll read that one." She nods and extends it toward him. When he takes it, she curls up the way she had during the documentary and cracks the spine on her own.

Daniel hasn't read poetry since his last high school English class. Ten pages in, he can't imagine why he'd given it up. He reads hungrily, forgetting the world around him. For a while, he thinks he might cry, but the tears never come. Instead, he wells up with so much emotion that he's frozen in place. The great sorrow, the great love on each page is staggering and familiar. And yet, beautiful. What a feat, to turn so much pain into so much beauty. Daniel is filled with simultaneous envy and empathy.

He doesn't return to reality until he reaches the final phrase. The book snaps shut, and both he and Liyah startle at the sound. She waits for him to speak first for the second time today. "Can I borrow this for a little bit?" he asks.

"You can keep it if you like, I've already read it five times."

"Thank you." Daniel rubs the back of his head. Back in this world, he can feel his stomach rumble. "How much time left?"

"Negative five minutes."

He sits up straight. "What? And you haven't eaten yet?"

"I had to let you finish! Go pour us cups of water and I'll get the bagels toasting." He does as she asks, and she rummages through her freezer. "Pumpernickel, everything, or poppy?"

"Pumpernickel."

"Good choice. Brownstein's makes the best pumpernickel bagels in all of Chicago."

Daniel hands her a glass of water and waits for her to take a sip before he gulps his down and goes to refill it. "Have you checked?" he jokes.

"Actually, yes."

"Really?"

"It took a few months of careful research, but it was well worth it."

Daniel laughs and shakes his head. Of course she did. She fixes them both bagels with a healthy dose of shmear and lox. Apparently too hungry to make the four-foot trip to the table, Liyah takes an enormous bite as soon as she's handed one of the bagels off to Daniel. He's starving, but he waits and watches Liyah. Her eyelids flutter shut as she chews, her entire face relaxing, the corners of her lips turning upward, and a sound somewhat like *yum* escapes her mouth.

Worth the wait. When he finally tastes his bagel, he has to restrain himself from demolishing it in two bites. He may not have been privy to her studies, but he believes Liyah's review. It's the best damn bagel he's ever eaten.

SSC #7 MEETING NOTES

Secretary: Liyah

- Work
  - Liyah wants everyone to understand how exciting it is that they have a prepubescent *Homo erectus* skeleton
    - Seriously! Do these people not understand how rare they are?
  - Siobhan's working on the website, which is better than the newsletter
    - She respectfully requests that we all look at the web page to ooh and aah
    - (I'm kidding, it looks so good!)

- Dating
  - Liyah would like to note both vocally and in writing that talking about this every week is like an extended root canal
  - Group dating app profile workshop for Siobhan
    - Jordan and Daniel graciously wait while Liyah embarrasses Siobhan, taking a hundred pictures of her holding an Alex special cocktail
    - (What do you want from me? She looks great!)

- Rule addition: 8. Daniel and Jordan may not talk about any sports team's chances prior to the start of the season. This includes all Chicago teams. Liyah will engage in basketball talk after the season starts, but it must be limited for Siobhan's sake.

SSC #8 MEETING NOTES

Secretary: Daniel

- Forgot to take notes during work section. Sorry
  - Liyah said, "You should be."
- Alex joined us for an illicit round on his break
  - Would like to say that he and Marc with a *c* are exclusive. Everyone cheered
- Liyah only made fun of Daniel once tonight. It was for being late due to "JST," when very clearly it was due to L train delay
  - When asked if she would like an award, she said yes

- No rule additions

CHAPTER 10

LIYAH reclines in the guest armchair of Maria's office, waiting for her therapist to return with tea. The décor has changed since she was last here. It was Maria's first week in the new building, and the walls felt hauntingly empty. Nothing to stare at when she needed to avoid eye contact.

Maria quietly enters the room and deposits a steaming mug on the table next to Liyah before taking her seat beneath a wire sculpture. Its radial lines hover above her side-parted Afro like sunrays. "It's good to see you, Liyah. You look well."

"It's good to see you, too." Gesturing to the various paintings, she adds, "I like what you've done with the place."

"Thank you. It's mostly the same as before I moved, but a new space changes everything, doesn't it?" Liyah nods. "So, how have you been these past few months?"

"Pretty good. I was unhappy at work, which I guess you know because that's like sixty percent of what I talked about last time. But I pitched an exhibit that weaves together biological and cultural anthropology, and it was green-lit, so I've been working on that."

"Congratulations. That sounds like a lot of responsibility. Which is what you wanted, right?"

Liyah blows on the tea before taking a sip. "Yeah, it is. It's a lot of work, though. Half of my social life is spent working with Daniel on the marketing project I got saddled with. And that's still technically work."

Maria nods. "I'm not sure you've mentioned Daniel to me before."

"Oh, right. I hadn't run into him yet, I guess." During the first few months of seeing her, Liyah met with Maria twice a week. When she was no longer in crisis, they dropped down to weekly, then biweekly. Now, even though it's been two years since they switched to checking in every three months, Liyah still forgets that the relative infrequency means Maria is often missing the kind of context she used to always have. "I knew him as a kid, but that's a long story." One she's told Maria, but only in the broadest of strokes—she felt betrayed by a camp friend, didn't go back the next summer, one drop in an ocean of reasons to mistrust those who romantically pursue her. "He's one of the members of this thing I do on Fridays—the Speakeasy Survival Club. It's basically just drinking buddies, but we also complain about work and adulthood and take meeting minutes for fun. There's four of us—Siobhan, and Daniel's coworker Jordan. That's the other half of my social life. It's kind of dumb, I know . . ."

The large hoop earrings Maria wears sway as she shakes her head. "That doesn't sound dumb. It sounds like a good support network."

"We joke that it's group therapy but with liquor."

Maria smiles, nodding. "That seems nice. And how have you been otherwise? Did you end up resolving that issue with Ivy?"

Liyah swallows, embarrassed. She knows Maria isn't here to judge her, but she's also seen this scenario play out a good number of times, and it never sounds great when she says it out loud. "I haven't spoken to her since I sent that last text message. I haven't been sleeping with anybody else, though. Between work and SSC, I haven't had any time."

"That's the only reason? A busy schedule hasn't ever stopped you before."

She takes another sip of her tea. "Yeah, that's it. I mean, I only ever see Siobhan and Jordan and Daniel, and I don't sleep with my friends, so."

Maria holds her gaze. "Right. We can move on, I'm just checking in since there seems to have been a change in your behavior. If everything is alright and you don't want to talk about it, I get that, but this is why we're here. Are you sure there's nothing that's been coming up for you?"

"Nope, all good," Liyah replies, hoping the levity in her tone will ward off Maria's suspicious eye.

The rest of the session passes without event, and Liyah returns to her office feeling triumphant, another quarterly appointment where she's generally been doing well on the books. Her elation only extends so far, the colony of messages in her in-box having doubled in size since this morning. She clicks, skims, and deletes what she can, until a particular message catches her eye: *Delivery Confirmation.*

Liyah opens it and only makes it a few lines before she jumps up, leaving her desk chair spinning as she races down to the mail room. Two boxes are waiting for her: one small, presumably the samples from the wine bar they've partnered with, and one large enough she'll need a dolly, presumably the signs explaining the exhibition pairings. She rips the bigger one open, and the top sign is the one for Inside Ancient Egypt. Peter suggested they pair it with a French Chablis that has "a strong character of salinity." Daniel and Liyah had nodded along, making eye contact as soon as he looked away and biting the insides of their cheeks to avoid laughing.

She takes a picture of herself with the sign, loads up a dolly (not even minding the squeaky back wheel), and pushes her way to the freight elevator. It's ancient and exceedingly slow, so she spends the ride typing out an email with the photo attached.

To: Daniel Rosenberg <dwrosenberg@kinley.com>
From: Aliyah Cohen-Jackson <a.cohen.jackson@fieldmuseum.org>
RE: T-MINUS 8 DAYS UNTIL THE WINE MOMS DESCEND UPON US . . .

Look what arrived! So excited to experience the saline. #salty

Liyah

P.S. I can't remember, is it supposed to be on the tip of the tongue or the inner sides? Or is that acidity . . .

To: Aliyah Cohen-Jackson <a.cohen.jackson@fieldmuseum.org>
From: Daniel Rosenberg <dwrosenberg@kinley.com>
RE: T-MINUS 8 DAYS UNTIL THE WINE MOMS DESCEND UPON US . . .

Is the hashtag about you or the wine?

Daniel

P.S. Tip of the tongue is sweetness, inner sides is acidity, outer edge is salinity. Did you not pay any attention in the meeting? Peter would be ashamed.

To: Daniel Rosenberg <dwrosenberg@kinley.com>
From: Aliyah Cohen-Jackson <a.cohen.jackson@fieldmuseum.org>
RE: T-MINUS 8 DAYS UNTIL THE WINE MOMS DESCEND UPON
US . . .

🙄

Liyah

P.S. Guess I'll have to return my sommelier license.

Liyah pushes open the door to her office with her elbow, dragging in the dolly and nearly dropping her phone before Siobhan jumps to her rescue. "Thank you, sorry," she says.

"It would help if you weren't trying to do three things at once. What's got you smiling at your phone? Have the pinky toes come in?" Siobhan asks.

"What? Oh, no. Stuff for the wine-tasting night. I was emailing Daniel about it."

"So, are you ready to tell me what happened on Yom Kippur?"

Liyah's face heats. How would she even begin to explain why such a simple question set off a nuclear warhead in her chest? But Siobhan can't know about the greeter, can she? There's no reason for Daniel to have mentioned it. "What do you mean?" she asks. "You want me to run through the order of the service?"

"I want you to explain how you went from finding Daniel—what was it you said, 'tolerable'?—to *smiling at his work emails*. Don't try to deny it, there's been two Survival Club meetings since then, I've seen you two."

Liyah shakes her head. "He's funny, sometimes. And I still make fun of him plenty."

"Yeah, but you're never outright mean."

"Thanks." Liyah scowls. "What a high bar."

"You're the one who set it, love." Siobhan winks. Liyah rolls her eyes.

"You and Neen are both so dramatic. I'm not that bad. Yom Kippur was . . ." Intimate, somehow. She knows the dynamic has shifted; between their conversation after wine tasting and Yom Kippur spent together, they might be actual friends again. Neen's bad enough (*He admitted he was wrong* twice? *I mean honestly, C-J, between that and his face you should've shown up at his place in lingerie and a trench coat by now*); she doesn't want Siobhan to ruin it by getting any ideas. "We had each other's backs, you know? So we wouldn't feel like the odd one out."

Siobhan stares her down. "Is that what you used to do for each other at summer camp?"

Always too perceptive for her own good. Or rather, for Liyah's good. "I already told you, camp was a long time ago. I hardly remember it. Yom Kippur was practically an extension of Survival Club duties."

Siobhan sighs. "So that's how you're going to play it?"

"I'm not playing anything. Besides, we should be worrying about what's happening outside of SSC with you and Jordan."

"There's nothing to worry about anymore. He has a woman that 'it's complicated' with, so that's that."

Liyah nods, then furrows her brow. "Wait, how do you know that?"

"I, em, I asked him on the way home last week." Siobhan flushes a deep red.

"Oh my God, Siobhan!" Liyah squeals. "That's great, I'm so proud of you."

"Thank you." Siobhan spins her chair so she's once again facing her desktop monitor. "I'll go back to this nonsense and pretend I didn't notice your oh-so-smooth change of subject."

Liyah removes the boxes from the dolly and opens the

large one again. She pulls out the Inside Ancient Egypt sign to reveal another Inside Ancient Egypt sign. She groans. They better not have charged her for the duplicate; she doesn't want to have to explain it to Jeff. She moves the second sign, revealing a third. And fourth, and fifth. Every single sign advertises the salty Chablis. *Fuck*. She ducks into the hallway and presses call.

"We're absolutely fucked," Liyah says as soon as Daniel answers the phone.

His laugh filters through the receiver. "Congrats? Or, I'm sorry? I need more information."

"They're all Chablis! All the signs are Chablis!"

"Wait, what? Do you have the receipt?"

"Yes!" Liyah all but shouts. "I checked the confirmation. I uploaded five separate files, like I thought. These took two weeks to get here. And we used the full budget allotment. Even if I could reorder them, they won't be here in time!"

He exhales. "Two weeks? Have you tried going in person so they can print in front of you?"

"That was my first choice! The mounting thing at the FedEx near here is broken, and they said they could only give me the flimsy paper posters. And we're out of time to place a new order online!"

"Liyah, take a deep breath. Forward me the confirmation and I'll get a refund. Go print the paper ones. I'll pick up some posterboard tomorrow and we'll mount them ourselves. You're not above a bit of arts and crafts, are you?"

"Daniel, I'm not going to be able to take a deep breath until the signs are fixed!"

"And they will be—" Daniel starts, but Liyah cuts him off.

"If you say 'trust me,' I swear to fucking God—"

"I gotta go. Send me the confirmation, Liyah. See you tomorrow!" And then he's gone, and Liyah is left, alone in the hallway, telling herself not to hyperventilate.

• • •

DANIEL DECIDES TO continue the email exchange after his
lunch:

> To: Aliyah Cohen-Jackson <a.cohen.jackson@fieldmuseum.org>
> From: Daniel Rosenberg <dwrosenberg@kinley.com>
> RE: T-MINUS 8 DAYS UNTIL THE WINE MOMS DESCEND UPON
> US . . .
>
> Okay, definitely about you.
>
> Daniel
>
> P.S. Where did you get it, wish.com?

> To: Daniel Rosenberg <dwrosenberg@kinley.com>
> From: Aliyah Cohen-Jackson <a.cohen.jackson@fieldmuseum.org>
> RE: T-MINUS 8 DAYS UNTIL THE WINE MOMS DESCEND UPON
> US . . .
>
> Don't you have something better to do, DW? A marketing strategy
> to digitize? Posterboard you promised to purchase?
>
> Liyah
>
> P.S. I looked it up. Turns out it's complete bullshit. The difference
> in sensitivity to flavor on different areas of the tongue is minute at
> best!!

And before his coffee meeting with Ella Hill, who'd
started a boutique hiking gear store kitschily called Hill &
Mountain:

To: Aliyah Cohen-Jackson <a.cohen.jackson@fieldmuseum.org>
From: Daniel Rosenberg <dwrosenberg@kinley.com>
RE: T-MINUS 8 DAYS UNTIL THE WINE MOMS DESCEND UPON
US . . .

It was a mistake letting you have my work email. You can't give me
the same name as an animated five-year-old girl. I'm getting them
tomorrow, like I said.

Daniel

P.S. Don't tell Peter. It'll ruin his day.

To: Daniel Rosenberg <dwrosenberg@kinley.com>
From: Aliyah Cohen-Jackson <a.cohen.jackson@fieldmuseum.org>
RE: T-MINUS 8 DAYS UNTIL THE WINE MOMS DESCEND UPON
US . . .

Daniel Wilfred,

Your problem is that she's a girl, not an aardvark? House Rule #3!

Liyah

To: Aliyah Cohen-Jackson <a.cohen.jackson@fieldmuseum.org>
From: Daniel Rosenberg <dwrosenberg@kinley.com>
RE: T-MINUS 8 DAYS UNTIL THE WINE MOMS DESCEND UPON
US . . .

Do the rules still apply via email? And no, my problem is that she's
in kindergarten.

Daniel Definitely Not Wilfred Rosenberg

And when he's back at work, his proposals all approved
and no redrafting to do:

To: Daniel Rosenberg <dwrosenberg@kinley.com>
From: Aliyah Cohen-Jackson <a.cohen.jackson@fieldmuseum.org>
RE: T-MINUS 8 DAYS UNTIL THE WINE MOMS DESCEND UPON
US . . .

Obviously. William. Walt. Wistopher. Wimothy. Getting warmer?

Liyah

To: Aliyah Cohen-Jackson <a.cohen.jackson@fieldmuseum.org>
From: Daniel Rosenberg <dwrosenberg@kinley.com>
RE: T-MINUS 8 DAYS UNTIL THE WINE MOMS DESCEND UPON
US . . .

Ice cold. Woo-jin. It means "treasure of the family."

Daniel

P.S. Sometimes romanized as U-jin, before you go getting any
terrible pronunciation ideas.

To: Daniel Rosenberg <dwrosenberg@kinley.com>
From: Aliyah Cohen-Jackson <a.cohen.jackson@fieldmuseum.org>
RE: T-MINUS 8 DAYS UNTIL THE WINE MOMS DESCEND UPON
US . . .

Ah, how very youngest child.

Liyah

P.S. Because I'm not elderly, I managed to google the
pronunciation. I like it. Suits you.

Daniel stares at his screen for a few minutes, trying and
failing to come up with a response. He jiggles his leg under the
desk, impatient with the slowly ticking clock. He refreshes his
in-box, but still no feedback about his campaign for the CTA.
It would look bad to head home before five, so he forces himself to do the mindless work of sorting through his emails.
Unfortunately, this means his mind wanders.

Daniel has not spent a lot of time thinking about his dad in the last ten months. At first there was the funeral, and the shiva, and the calls and texts and emails and Facebook messages. It all made him think about his dad constantly, an infinite slideshow of memories playing through his mind. But then, after about a month, the outpouring of condolences stopped. He forced the slideshow to stop, too. It was the only way he could get himself un-stopped.

Lately, the memories are coming back. Ever since Yom Kippur. It's a slow drip rather than a fire hose, thankfully, but the water never runs out. Maybe it'll always be running around this time of year. He should probably ask Kayla, but he doesn't.

When he gets home, he heads straight for his bedroom, trading his suit for a long-sleeved shirt and some soccer shorts. *Exercise, Daniel. That'll fix this.* He rummages through his closet for his running shoes, gives Sweet Potato a few scratches behind her ears, and he's off.

The music coming from his headphones is as loud as it can be without drowning out the noise of oncoming cars, so he can't hear the slap of his rubber soles on the pavement. He first heads to Wicker Park, but when he sees a man pushing his kid on a swing, Daniel promptly turns away. Instead, he runs through the neighborhood, rows of brick buildings passing him by, along with the occasional stroller or leashed dog or kid on a bicycle. An image of his dad, teaching him how to ride a bike. He runs faster. His dad, grinning when he got the puppy to roll over. He runs faster. His dad, teaching him and Kayla how to change a tire. He runs faster.

By the time Daniel ends up back at his apartment, it's pitch-black outside and every muscle in his legs quivers with overuse. He makes it up the stairs with great effort and winces as he crouches to scoop Sweet Potato off the ground. She nuzzles her face against his neck, and he smiles.

"Thanks, Sweet P." If he doesn't get in the shower soon, his whole body will shut down and it might never happen. He tosses his cat forward and she lands gracefully, meowing and trotting toward her favorite perch on the couch.

Hot water pelts his back, and he feels his muscles already becoming sore. It's a welcome ache, easy to focus on. He stands still for a while after he's clean, letting the water wash over him. Eventually, it runs cold. Daniel swears, fumbling to turn it off as quickly as he can and towel himself off. Alex is already at Prohibition, so he just wraps the towel around his waist and heads to the kitchen.

He settles on the couch with some leftover pasta and a basketball game he couldn't care less about on the TV. Sweet Potato keeps trying to lick the rim of his beer bottle, and eventually he gives up on shooing her away and just refuses to set it down. At the commercial break, he checks his phone. He's got two messages: one in the Survival Club chat and one from Kayla.

Liyah to SSC

Compatriots: is there room for one more to join our ranks next week? Neen will be in town and they're an absolute blast. Daniel can confirm.

Neen's visit is by no means news to Daniel; Liyah mentions it every time they meet to plan events. When Liyah's that excited, it's hard not to be excited for her, as evidenced by Daniel's current emotional investment in the acquisition of hundred-thousand-year-old pinky toe bones. He sends off a response:

Daniel to SSC

if by "blast" you mean that they'll probably get as much of a kick out of liyah bullying me as she does, then sure, they're a blast

Jordan to SSC

Definitely sounds like a blast. Good by me

Siobhan to SSC

So excited to see them again!!! Mate of a club member is a mate of the club :) That should be House Rule #9.

Daniel to SSC

aite, on it.

Daniel doesn't feel like getting up to find the growing napkin contract, but he'll get around to it later and send a picture for proof to the group. He thumbs over to the thread of messages with his sister.

Kayla

Danny, does your place still work? I know you don't want to talk about it, but it's coming up, so I want to make sure everything's set. Love you.

Daniel
yeah, i'll talk to alex about it.
love you.

He rubs his hand over his mouth, clenching and releasing his jaw. His whole body must tense, because Sweet Potato stretches and climbs down from his lap, leaving a circle of ginger hair in her wake. So much for not thinking about his dad.

SSC #9 MEETING NOTES

Secretary: Siobhan

- Jordan is wondering where Neen is
- Liyah reminds him that she said "next week" in the group chat, and claims that straight men have bad text message reading comprehension
  - Jordan says this is borderline offensive
  - Daniel admits that his sister told him something similar, would not like to give further comment
- Arts & Crafts
  - Liyah and Daniel fully made us help mount posters for their wine night in the middle of a bar. The things we do for friendship
- Work
  - Daniel's campaign ideas were approved by the CTA
    - He would like to thank Siobhan and Liyah for their helpful brainstorming, and further wants it on record that Jordan is a dick
  - Jordan's supervisor has done a few things that could be construed as hitting on him
    - He uses his Rule #6 charm allowance on this story
    - Liyah and Siobhan advise reporting to HR
      - Daniel is concerned that he will get shit about this from their very bro-y office mates, but also says "fuck em, do what is right for you"
    - Jordan decides he's going to first talk to her about it, and bring HR on later if this doesn't work
  - Liyah spent several minutes trying to explain the evidence of right- and left-handedness in ancient tools, none of us are listening
- Dating
  - Siobhan would like to report that the dating profile workshop from last week has resulted in a date for this weekend!

- General adult life
  - Daniel: has anybody been to therapy?
    - Liyah and Jordan, but not Siobhan
      - Both recommend
    - Kinley's insurance covers mental health care well

- Upon review of a picture of Jordan in uni, Siobhan would like Jordan never to wear a "Kiss me, I'm Irish" T-shirt
  - That's not what "Black Irish" means

- Rule addition: 10. Liyah must explain anthropological terms so that the rest of us can follow along with her work updates

CHAPTER 11

LIYAH refreshes the weather page of the local news website, desperate for it to contradict what she can see through the Field's glass front doors: it's snowing. Hard.

She is not going to panic. There's only a dusting on the ground so far, and Neen's flight delay could be construed as a silver lining, since Liyah no longer has to worry about leaving the wine night early. She'll personally make sure it goes off without a hitch. Patrons have been filtering in for the last half hour, collecting tiny plastic cups and filling the museum with happy chatter.

"It's going to be alright," Daniel says from where he leans against the pillar across from Máximo, the *Titanosaurus* who takes up a significant portion of the half-acre Stanley Field Hall.

"I agree. I am choosing to be optimistic." Liyah grips her now empty cup of Sangiovese (earthy, pairs well with Underground Adventure) so tightly that the flimsy plastic deforms with a soft crackle. Daniel looks at her hand and raises his eyebrows. "I know, flying swine, snow in hell, etcetera," she says. "But I am *trying*."

"Should I be *trying* to get you more wine? Xanax? Maybe horse tranquilizer?"

She glares. "Not funny."

"I'm gonna go with the wine," he says, and saunters away.

Liyah takes a deep breath, looking around the hall. From her vantage point, she can see up and across the atrium to the walled-off section of the second floor that will one day house Evolving Us. Smiles and laughter abound from passersby on their way to see SUE, and she imagines what it would be like to see that with her exhibition as the backdrop.

Eventually, she can't help herself, and she checks the web page again. The words *largest October snowfall on record* stare back at her. The powdered-sugar dusting outside begins to look more like a buttercream.

Liyah's phone vibrates, a call from Neen flashing across the screen. She wants to believe that it's to say they've finally boarded, but a pit in her stomach tells her otherwise.

"C-J," Neen starts, pausing to take a deep breath.

"No. Please don't tell me—"

"My flight's canceled. I'm sorry, babe."

The disappointment washes over Liyah in a bone-crushing tidal wave. Neen's visit is what's gotten her through the last week, nay, last *several* weeks of more work than she'd bargained for. Certainly more work than the Field had bargained for based on her utterly mediocre salary. Daniel approaches with two cups of pinot noir, his features puckered with concern.

"I can hear you sighing, C-J. They're rebooking me for next week, so you just gotta survive without me until then, K?"

Gripping the phone tightly, Liyah uses the heel of her other hand to massage the wrinkle in her forehead, squeezing her eyes shut. "I'm not sure I can."

Neen laughs, the sound slightly distorted, their mouth too

close to the receiver. "You can and you will. I gotta go get Ringo out of economy parking, but I'm gonna see you so soon."

"Not soon enough!"

"At least try to have a good weekend. Go enjoy your winter wonderland."

"It's fucking October. I'm suing."

Neen giggles. "Who, the Weather Channel? Or God?"

Despite herself, Liyah smiles. "I'll let you know when I figure it out. Love you, miss you."

"Love you, miss you, too. See ya, C-J." With a click, they're gone.

"Are you okay?" Daniel asks, handing her a cup. A look out the window confirms that the snow on the ground is steadily piling up and the flurries in the air have dramatically reduced visible distance. Liyah swallows half the wine in one gulp. "I'm going to take that as a *no*," he says.

Liyah looks at the floor. "Neen's flight's been canceled."

Daniel steps in front of her, his tall frame shielding her from the crop of millennial museumgoers, who are beginning to seem less like an achievement and more like a liability. He touches her upper arm, his hold warm and gentle. "I'm so sorry. I know you were looking forward to it."

"I realize I said I was trying to be optimistic, but look," she says, showing him the news.

He swallows, runs his hand through his hair. "Shit, okay. Do we need to call it?" Liyah closes her eyes, takes a deep breath, and nods. "Okay, what do you need from me?"

"Can you tell the Windy City people? I'll handle the rest and you can head out."

"I'm gonna help you, Liyah. This is my event, too."

"You don't have to—"

He's already turning away. "It's nonnegotiable."

Liyah makes it over to the PA system in a daze. She announces the early closure, wishes everyone a safe route home, stumbles through apologies and promises to reschedule. Outside, the storm clouds darken the sky, and she feels a rush of midnight tiredness at barely six o'clock.

Her phone vibrates incessantly in her pocket.

Siobhan to SSC

Not trying to be the killjoy,
but can we cancel? I'm quite
cozy here and I really can't be
arsed to put on thermals.

Jordan to SSC

Thermals?

Siobhan to SSC

You know, long johns. I'm
sure you have a pair.

Jordan to SSC

Not a pair, only one ;)

Daniel to SSC

asshole
but yeah, let's cancel. me
and liyah are still at the field
trying to get everyone home

Jordan to SSC

Shit, good luck. Maybe if the
snow melts we could see
Neen tomorrow?

Liyah almost doesn't want to respond, like pinging it across cell towers is what will make it real. Avoidance won't help, though. She'll just have to figure out a text that makes her sound less dejected than she feels. Broadcasting her mopiness would only add insult to injury. After a moment of consideration, she fires off the best she can come up with.

> **Liyah to SSC**
> Neen's flight was canceled
> :(next week, tho!

They respond about as expected: a thumbs-down reaction from Jordan and a long message that begins with *Sorry, love!* from Siobhan. A separate message appears:

Daniel
heard your announcement.
you're right, we'll reschedule.
it'll be okay. WCW+C has
been notified

> **Liyah**
> Thank you, heading to help
> with coat check. Then figure
> out how to get home.

Daniel
may i suggest the CTA? you
take the 146 from museum
campus to washington, then
hop on the blue line from
there

> **Liyah**
> Yes, thank you SO MUCH
> for explaining my daily
> commute. I was gonna leave
> early to get Neen, so I drove

Daniel

oh. may i suggest driving
yourself home?

She knows exactly what expression he made as he typed the message: lips rolling against one another so that he doesn't laugh before the words land, the corners of his eyes crinkling. *Oh my God,* she could throttle him. And she would, if she weren't already running toward the STAFF ONLY door that leads to the employee side of coat check.

Liyah

Again, SO helpful. What
would I do without a man
like you to tell me things my
tiny woman brain couldn't
figure out on its own?

I can't drive in the snow, you
dolt.

When she picks up Daniel's call, she gives a particularly dramatic eye roll in the hopes that he can hear it through the phone. "Can I help you?"

"Yes. I need someone to explain how a twenty-seven-year-old woman can't drive in the snow," Daniel says, ignoring the irritated tone she's doing her best to put on.

"I grew up in Seattle!" Liyah protests. "It's hilly and the city practically shuts down whenever there's more than an inch on the ground. We just didn't drive anywhere."

"And you've lived in Chicago for how long?"

She sighs. "Since I started college."

"So, you've lived in Chicago, Illinois for an entire decade, and you haven't learned to drive in the snow?" he demands. She rolls her eyes. "Don't roll your eyes at me," he says.

"Ah! He *can* hear it. I use the CTA when it snows. I thought you of all people would appreciate that."

"I take the L for the pleasure and convenience, not because I should've failed my driver's test."

"Shut up." Liyah huffs. "I'm an excellent driver."

"Want me to drive you? I actually know how to drive—"

"I know how to drive!"

"—and I can walk home from your place."

Liyah pauses, considering. A large part of her wants to tell Daniel exactly where he can shove his precious Midwestern license, but she also isn't too keen on leaving her car overnight and risking a ticket or a tow. The only other option is to brave the road. She looks out the window in the hallway. There must be four inches on the ground already. Liyah groans, mostly to indicate her reluctance to Daniel. "Maybe I'll sleep here."

"Alone, in your office?" he asks.

"I'm not alone, I've got Martha," she says, pushing the back door to the coat check open.

"Who's Martha?" His voice is incredulous. Liyah can practically see his eyebrow quirk.

"Our newest acquisition," she says. "She's estimated to be about two hundred thousand years old."

"Why the hell is your skeleton called Martha?"

"Well, what would you want me to name her?"

"Never mind. Liyah, I'm driving you."

She weaves her way through the room, brushing past what must be metric tons of wool and down. "I don't have time for this. I'm hanging up."

Toby, eyes wide, hair sticking up at all angles, breathes a sigh of relief when he spots Liyah. "It's a madhouse."

"I know, I'm sorry. I'm here to help." He gives her a quick rundown, and she's off, retrieving peacoat after puffy jacket after belted trench and trying to smile as she hands them over to frantic patrons.

She's making a run for ticket #178 when she crashes directly into Daniel. His hands find her waist, preventing her from teetering over, and she can feel his breath on her forehead. Even through her sweater, his fingers burn into her skin, warming her blood, accelerating her pulse. "What are you doing here?"

"Like I said, I'm gonna help you."

"This is employees only."

Daniel laughs. "I think we're past that point." He spins her out of his way, jogging toward Toby, and she goes back to her quest for #178.

It takes forty-five minutes to get the last of the wine night attendees on their way home, and at the end of it, Liyah is a frazzled, heaving mess. Wordlessly, Daniel follows her out of coat check and down the winding network of hallways toward the east employee exit. She knows he intends to drive her home, but she is emotionally depleted, completely beyond arguing.

Outside, the wind whips snowflakes into her face, blurring her vision. She squints toward the parking lot, and an image of the sole remaining vehicle takes shape. Her car, completely covered in snow, only the tops of her tires visible.

Total and utter defeat. She slumps against the side of the building.

"It's okay, Liyah. We'll dig it out," Daniel says.

She looks up at him, feeling the walls of her throat thicken. "I don't have a shovel. Maybe we could use our hands around the tires, but look at the lot. How would we drive out of that?"

Daniel frowns. "What do you mean you don't have a shovel?"

"I mean I don't have a shovel! It's October. It *never* snows this much in October."

"Well, shit." He shoves his hands in his pockets, joining her against the icy Georgia marble. "We'll have to leave it. I'm not sure if the bus is going to come, but we can walk to the L."

Liyah closes her eyes for a moment. When she opens them, she looks down at her shoes. There's already a layer of white sprinkled over the brown leather. "They check at four, and any car left gets a ticket or a tow. I'm staying."

"I thought you couldn't drive in the snow."

"The city'll have sent plows out by then. I've already got my air mattress for the sleep-in next week. I'll set an alarm for three thirty and figure it out."

She makes eye contact with Daniel now, and it's amazing how bright the amber of his eyes looks with only one orange-hued streetlamp to illuminate them. His tongue sweeps out over his bottom lip, and she knows he wants her to forget about the car and head home. He doesn't tell her, though. Maybe he realizes the futility. Instead, he says, "Alright, then. Let's go inside. ID card?" He holds out his hand expectantly.

"Go home, Rosenberg."

"Absolutely not. ID card, please." He taps his fingers against his palm twice, reaching it toward her.

She looks at his hand, back up at his eyes. "Daniel, this isn't your responsibility. I'm the one who decided to drive—"

He interrupts her with a loud exhale. "Liyah, I am not leaving you here, and I'm getting cold. Swipe us in yourself, or give me the ID."

EVENTUALLY, LIYAH OBLIGES, and he smiles like he won a prize. "Got anything to eat?" he asks when they reach the top of the stairs.

"There's leftover shitty pizza from today's staff meeting," Liyah grumbles, doing an about-face, presumably toward the pizza.

Daniel follows at her heels. "Perfect, I was planning on pizza for dinner tonight, anyway."

"Frozen?"

"Nope, I made the dough last night."

"Ah," she says. "The dichotomy of Daniel Woo-jin Rosenberg. Digital marketing strategy in the front, tattoos and artisanal pizza in the back."

He laughs. "I'm a complex individual. Do you still have those wine samples in your office? Want me to grab some?"

"Yes *please*. Third door on your right." He turns to leave, but Liyah calls after him. "Wait—where do you want to eat? We can access anywhere in the main three floors from here."

Daniel grins. "Well, ever since you mentioned it, I've been dying to see SUE's massive furcula."

They meet there fifteen minutes later—Liyah with a box of microwaved pizza, paper plates, plastic cups, and her laptop, Daniel with a small crate of wine and Liyah's overnight bag. Finding that neither of them have a corkscrew, Daniel slips off his left shoe and tucks a bottle of Chablis in its heel before pounding it against the floor. The sound echoes off the walls of the empty exhibition room, tangling with the din of the inflating air mattress. Beads of sweat collect on Daniel's forehead, and by the time he gets the cork to pop, Liyah sits cross-legged on the already made bed, two plates of pizza in front of her.

"Where'd you learn that?" she asks.

"My dad," he says, busying himself by filling their cups. The moment he joins her, Liyah stuffs a bite of pizza in her mouth and does a not-quite-moan, not-quite-groan. Daniel feels it in his core.

The overhead lights have been turned off for the night,

the only light in the room provided by the spotlights on SUE and the LEDs that line her platform. As they eat, eerie quiet hollows the space around them.

"It's weird being here without other people," Liyah says before taking her second bite.

"Yeah, it is. I think *Night at the Museum* instilled a certain fear in me." She nods. "Do you want to put on some music?" He opens his Spotify app and passes her his phone.

"Oh my God." Liyah gasps, turning the screen to him. "Madcon's *Conquest* is your most recent search?"

"Before you make fun of me, I need you to know that I have a very strong emotional attachment to that album."

"I would never make fun of you for liking Norway's greatest export." She's already scrolling, jumping to her feet. "And this album! I played it so much in high school I thought my dad was going to throw out my iPod Nano." Daniel watches as she heads to one of the interactive tables in front of SUE, bending at the waist to prop the phone up against a model bone.

Tshawe Baqwa's version of Frankie Valli's classic lyrics comes through the tiny speakers, and Liyah twists around to face Daniel, doing a spot-on lip-sync rendition. *"Ooh, put your loving hand out, baby, I'm beggin' you,"* Liyah mouths as though the smoky timbre comes from her throat. Daniel almost believes it.

Then, the beat drops. And Liyah *moves*.

It's obvious that she's an incredible dancer. Not because she's showing off—it's clear from her theatric hair flips and microphone miming that she's being silly—but because even in her fun, she's hitting every goddamn note with her hips. It's rare that Daniel has the opportunity to look at her like this, to unabashedly stare without risk of seeming creepy or enduring snide comments, so he takes full advantage. She does a little spin, and that spark of attraction he'd felt when she first sat next to him on the plane lights a flame in his stomach.

The second chorus hits, and Liyah sings along, loudly and very poorly, motioning for him to put his hands out. He laughs and accepts, and she drags him to his feet and toward the makeshift dance floor that was once an exhibition hall.

Daniel has never been a dancer. He volunteers to lift the chair at weddings and b'nai mitzvah on his dad's side of the family just to avoid crushing toes in his terrible attempt at the Hora. But here, in front of this dinosaur, alternating between the snorkel and the sprinkler while Liyah giggles and maddeningly twists her hips, he's not above a career change.

"I can't keep up with you." He shakes his head, but he's smiling so hard it hurts.

"Sure you can," Liyah says, and then her hands are on his hips and she's guiding them back and forth. He steps closer to her, heart racing. "Just relax."

An impossible task with her looking at him like that, but he nods and steals a breath and does his best to follow along.

Without thinking, Daniel places his hands over Liyah's. "Your fingers are still cold," he murmurs.

"Sorry," she says, but doesn't remove them. Instead, every motion brings them closer, as though there's a magnet right between his hip bones and it's pulling on something behind her belly button. Liyah's breath tickles his throat. Her irises are pools of black, barely catching the ambient light from SUE's display. A lot about her has changed, but her eyes look exactly as they did in the camp observatory, lit up by his dad's lantern. *I want to kiss her,* he thinks, and he swallows the thought whole.

The song ends, forcing them back apart. He flexes his fingers, trying to calm the nerves still reeling from Liyah's touch.

"Want to watch something?" she asks.

"Not before you show me SUE's furcula," he replies.

"It's right there, joining her coracoids," she says.

"Right." Daniel sweeps the hair off his forehead with his left hand. "I obviously know what coracoids are. But in case some of our audience members don't . . ."

Liyah lets out a sparkling laugh, pointing toward SUE's chest. "Those flat pieces that look like shoulder blades. The furcula is the swoopy thing above them."

He looks at the bone, shaped more like a boomerang than the enormous Operation board-game wishbone he'd pictured. "It's smaller than I expected."

Liyah clucks her tongue. "Yet another unrealistic beauty standard for women." Daniel laughs, and she flashes a smile up at him. "Satisfied? Can I set up my laptop now?"

They end up watching a reality dating show that—despite yelling at her computer screen—Liyah insists she has no personal investment in. At some point, shoes are kicked off, cardigans removed, shirts untucked, blankets pulled up. It's not comfortable, per se, lying on this mattress that depresses more than it should under Daniel's weight. It's maybe even uncomfortable, but in this moment, Daniel is the happiest he's been all year.

WHEN THE SHOW ends, Liyah puts on *Mean Girls,* in part daring Daniel to comment on her choice in media. He doesn't, and she spends the one-hour-thirty-seven-minute run-time pretending not to notice that whenever one of them moves, they sink toward the center of the mattress. Toward each other. It's sheer luck that they've yet to collide.

The credits roll, and Daniel yawns, stretching his arms over his head. She shuts her computer, sliding it into its sleeve.

It's almost midnight, and they have to be up in three and a half hours. She's reminded of their long nights sneaking out at camp, followed by days spent napping in the sun while their friends gossiped and played Egyptian Rat Screw. Liyah has been remembering a lot more of those details lately, memories she thought were long lost to shame and embarrassment. The bad things are still there, too. There's just room for more. "Bedtime," she says.

"Is it okay if I take my shirt off?" Daniel asks, his voice shy. "I, um, sleep kinda hot."

Liyah swallows and nods, burrowing beneath the covers. She stares ahead at SUE as he partially undresses, keeping her focus fixed even as he rocks the entire mattress when climbing in. She sees his half-clothed form in her periphery anyway, everything about him a sharp reminder that they're no longer thirteen.

They exchange *good night*s and Liyah curls up, facing away from him. She struggles to make herself comfortable, not wanting to bother him. As she makes minuscule adjustments, she wishes she had pushed him on letting her stay here alone. She typically doesn't even sleep with the people she hooks up with, and she fears that she'll spend the entire night wide awake, hyperaware of Daniel's every move. With a third leg shift, she's about halfway to where she wants to be.

As she's starting to settle, Daniel pokes her side. "Liyah?"

"What?" She rolls over, wasting an especially outstanding glare in the low light of the room.

"Gimme your hand." Daniel fumbles around the floor on his side of the mattress, apparently finding what he was looking for and placing it in her palm. He uses his callused fingers to close her fist around . . . nothing. "This is the ticket you gave me. Can I use it now?"

Any trace of irritation vanishes, and Liyah turns her hand

over so that she can hold his. "I told you it was good for whenever you want," she says softly.

"About a year ago, my dad died." A deep inhale. Liyah squeezes his hand as her heart squeezes in her chest. "Lung cancer," Daniel says.

CHAPTER 12

DANIEL takes another deep breath. He's glad for the dim room. "Are you gonna ask?"

"Ask what?"

Daniel swallows. "If he smoked."

"Oh. No, I wasn't going to," she says carefully. "Doesn't really matter, does it? Either way, he was your dad." She says it like it's easy, like it's obvious.

That's new to him. "Most people ask. And it makes me so goddamn angry. He quit smoking decades ago and the doctors said that we can't really know if that's what caused it. He used to joke that giving up cigars ruined his pensive professor shtick, but Eomma always would respond that no one bought it in the first place . . ." He lets his voice trail off, then inhales to regain his composure. "So, maybe it was the tobacco, and maybe not. But who fucking cares? Is it better if he played some role in it? From where I'm sitting, I can tell you it isn't. Not one bit." Daniel goes silent, and Liyah reaches for his other hand. His breathing is shaky. He should probably turn back, tell her to forget it and go to sleep. He's not going to make her sit through this.

But Liyah runs her thumbs over the backs of his hands, and his resolve crumbles. He knows right then that he'll tell her anything she wants to know. Maybe more.

"I stayed in Madison for the funeral and shiva, and I managed to function through it. Then when I got back here, I just . . . shut down. Kayla took an extra week off work so she could watch me. It was like she thought I would starve without her." He lets out a dry laugh. "I don't really remember eating much during that time, so maybe she was right. I couldn't wrap my head around it, around him being gone. Which is silly and childish because it's not like it was sudden. He was sick for years, on and off, and in the end . . ."

He pauses to gulp for air. Liyah takes the opportunity to say, "It's not silly or childish, Daniel."

He has no idea how to respond to that. She gives his hands another squeeze. "In the end, he was so tired. It was a relief in some ways, to know he was no longer in pain. But mostly, I just want him here. It feels like . . . I don't know. A hole in the floor maybe? Like he died, and then this giant pothole appeared, and for a while all I could do was stare at it, because I didn't know how to fill it in. I'm not sure if Kayla told them or they just realized how much of a mess I was, but Alex and Jordan kept checking on me. I think I was scaring them. It's kind of a blur. They helped a lot, though. More than I can hope to repay. And then there was my cat, Sweet Potato."

"You got Sweet Potato last year?"

"Yeah. I was passing by the animal rescue and saw her in the window. An hour later I was three hundred dollars poorer thanks to an adoption fee and an opportunistic PetSmart employee. I thought Kayla would say it was rash, but she approved of the idea. Said it was good for me to be responsible for something other than myself." He pauses, losing his train of thought.

"She's your phone background, isn't she?" He nods,

surprised that Liyah noticed. "Sweet Potato helped with the hole in the floor?"

He considers it. "Not really. But she helped in other ways. I just decided to pretend the hole wasn't there. But now it's biting me in the ass, because I can't pretend forever, and I still don't know how to patch it."

It's a while before Liyah speaks, like she's waiting to see if Daniel has more to say. He doesn't. "The pharma account?" she whispers.

And there it is: that tumbleweed of anger balled into sadness that likes to roll around the desert of Daniel's chest cavity. "During his second time through chemo, there was a shortage, and he delayed one of his rounds so it could go to the pediatric unit. It probably didn't make a difference, but I can't help but—" The words catch in his throat.

Without hesitation, Liyah crosses the small distance between them and wraps him in a hug. Her fingers run up and down his spine, and he tucks his head into the crook of her neck, inhaling the scent of her. Lavender, cocoa, spice. All he can think is how much he needs her closer, so he pulls her in tightly, feeling her torso melt against his, legs threading together. Tears prick the backs of his eyes, and he can't bring himself to care if Liyah notices.

"Thank you for telling me," she murmurs, her lips brushing against his ear.

"Thank you for listening," he says into her neck.

"Do you want to tell me about him?"

Daniel shakes his head, nuzzling his nose farther into her shoulder. "But . . . another time, maybe?"

Liyah nods, her jaw scraping against his cheek. He pulls back a little, enough that he can just barely make out the planes of her face.

"God, I'm sorry, I'm dumping all of this on you. I didn't mean to—"

"No, Daniel. Don't apologize. We're friends, and I'm happy to listen." *Friends*. The word fills him up, and he lets it. He thought she felt that way, but it's nice to hear her say it.

"Do you want to tell me something?" he asks. The hand running across his shoulder blades stills. "I mean, I've already proven that I'm very good at carrying around your baggage."

Liyah giggles, playfully slapping his back. "I told you multiple times that I could get it from the overhead bin myself."

"Still, I did a great job, didn't I?"

"Sure you did." A pause. "What do you want to know?"

"Whatever you want to tell me. Worst breakup?"

Liyah shrugs. "I haven't dated anybody seriously since high school, so there hasn't really been anything to break."

"Really? But what about the dating app misadventures?" Daniel doesn't hide his surprise. The Liyah in his mind always had a slew of admirers, and he'd thought for sure that at least one would have had the sense to try to tie her down.

"I only do very casual."

Come to think of it, she's the only SSC member who hasn't mentioned an ex. Daniel had chalked it up to a desire for privacy, like with her first-time story. Maybe there's more to it. "Oh. Why?" he asks.

Liyah's laugh is unmistakably sardonic, melodic but hollow. "I think there's been enough emotional turmoil for the night. Another time, maybe."

"Okay." Daniel tightens the hug one last time, then releases her to her side of the air mattress. "Good night, Liyah."

"Good night, Daniel," Liyah whispers, and he allows his eyelids to fall heavy.

AFTER WHAT FEELS like thirty seconds of sleep, the alarm blares loudly. The only sign that time has passed is the deflation of the air mattress, which has forced Liyah half on top of Daniel, his elbow poking her squarely in the sternum. It's far from the least comfortable part of waking up in this position.

They scramble to their feet, dress, pack up the mattress and bedding, and make it to her office in record time. They stow the crate of wine and sleep-in materials under her desk, and then they're off, racing to the east museum lot before the meter maid can beat them.

Liyah, hyperventilating, swings open the door with such force that it bangs against the side of the building. Then she checks her phone, sees that it's only 3:45, and stops to catch her breath. "We did it." She wheezes.

"And the streets are plowed," Daniel says. She turns to him, and the look on her face must really be something, because he releases a raucous laugh between heavy breaths. "I'll still drive you, don't worry."

She bites her lip, fixated on the snow-blanketed pavement below. Even plowed, there's still a lot. "But I don't want to make you walk from my place in this."

"How about I drive you to mine to get you through downtown, and then you can drive the rest of the way? You can take side streets and go as slowly as you want. We still have a few minutes, I could run back in and print you a 'student driver' sign."

"I'm pretty sure you're joking, but don't you *dare*."

Daniel shakes his head, his sleep-crumpled hair brushing across his forehead. Then he leans his head down until his eyes are level with hers. "Liyah," he whispers. He's so close, the white wisps of her shaky exhale graze his face. "Please let me drive?"

"Alright, fine. To your place only," she says, and starts down the steps.

As Daniel walks with her to the parking lot, he's got a big smile plastered on his lips and a rosy flush in his cheeks.

Liyah, on the other hand, shivers violently, her grimace deepening with every shudder. Her fall coat usually doesn't fail her, but it's no match for a surprise blizzard. She tosses Daniel her keys and shoves her icy hands into her pockets.

"You're in a good mood," she says as he fiddles with nobs to push the driver's seat several inches back. They spend most of their time together seated, so Liyah often forgets about Daniel's height, but then he does something like this, and she finds herself fighting the impulse to let her eyes crawl up and down his long frame.

"It's the first snow of the season!"

"The wrong season. And it's four in the morning. We slept like two hours," Liyah grumbles, but Daniel's still sporting a million-watt smile. As he pulls out of the parking lot and toward the densely gridded streets of downtown Chicago, he's all ease and confidence, one hand loosely gripping the steering wheel where Liyah would be white-knuckling it. The playlist Liyah had been listening to before the wine night seeps through the speakers, and she reaches over to spin the dial for the volume. Music roaring, she matches Daniel's reclined posture and closes her eyes.

Daniel wakes her when they reach his place, and Liyah rubs her face, squinting. The flakes in the air are slower, but still falling. She isn't sure if the plows haven't made it here yet or if the ground covering has replenished that quickly.

"Liyah, it's not plowed yet. Just let me—"

"It's only a few blocks, Daniel. I'll be fine." She tries to hold in her yawn, not wanting to undermine her point. It's a losing game.

After they say their goodbyes (and earnest, if begrudging, thanks), Liyah climbs into the driver's seat. As she adjusts it forward, she can see Daniel watching her. He's standing there, arms folded, easy smile, as she psyches herself up to drive the rest of the way home.

She rakes her fingers into the roots of her hair. "You can do this, Liyah," she mutters aloud. Despite the rolled-up window, she can *feel* Daniel trying not to laugh. Does he really need to be standing there? She checks her rearview and side mirrors once, twice. He's actually laughing now. *Fuck him,* she's leaving.

Liyah turns the steering wheel to pull onto the street, gently depressing the gas pedal, but nothing happens. Which is probably because she hasn't started the engine.

Fuck, fuck, fuck.

Liyah startles at the rap of Daniel's knuckles on the driver's window but obliges when he motions for her to roll it down. "You sure you don't want me to drive you home? Offer's still good."

She glares. "You'll get frostbite walking back in your dress shoes, and I don't want that on my conscience."

Daniel exhales heavily through his nose, fisting his hands into his coat pockets. "Fine, I won't drive. But you're tired, it's snowing, and this is a wreck waiting to happen. Stay here and get some rest. It'll be plowed by daylight, and then you can drive yourself home, okay?"

He's offering to have her spend what's left of the night? Liyah hasn't even seen the inside of his apartment before. She parts her lips, ready to say she doesn't need help, but that's clearly untrue. Also, she's suddenly painfully curious about the color of his bedspread, whether he has any art on his walls, how well-stocked he keeps his spice cabinet. "Alex won't mind?" she asks, still hesitating to step out of the car. "I don't want to intrude."

DANIEL SIGHS, LOOKING up at the large, lazily falling snowflakes. Liyah is being about as difficult as he expected, and it's doing nothing to dampen his mood. The coldest days of winter, he'd happily abandon, but he'd be lying if he said his years in California hadn't made him miss the snow. He pulls on the car door handle, swinging it open. "You are not intruding, and Alex is weathering the storm at Marc with a *c*'s."

"Alright," she relents, exiting the vehicle at last, crunching the fresh snow under her heeled boots. She silently follows him up to his apartment, slipping off her shoes and coat at the door. He does the same, and rolls up his shirtsleeves for good measure, wondering how long it'll take for Liyah to notice and poke fun.

But Liyah is too occupied with the fluffy, purring animal in her arms to take stock of him. "Sweet baby," Liyah coos, bending her neck to plant a kiss between Sweet Potato's ears. The cat shuts her eyes and lets it happen, tufts of orange hair obscuring Liyah's nose. Apparently remembering Daniel's presence, Liyah turns and says, "I can't believe you haven't introduced us before."

He shrugs. "Don't think she'd do too well in a crowded bar. Sweet Potato, this is Liyah. Liyah, Sweet Potato."

"Sweet Potato!" Liyah echoes, planting another kiss.

Daniel grins. "Wow, she loves you."

Liyah looks up at him, eyes bright. It's not just him, it seems: Sweet Potato can cure all ills. "Jealous?" She smirks.

"I am. After I adopted her, it was a few weeks and several tuna bribes before she let me pet her without hissing."

Liyah laughs. "Guess I've got the magic touch. Alright, where are your sheets? I can take the couch."

Daniel swallows. "Liyah, we've already shared an air mattress." *And I learned what it felt like to wake up with you on top of me, which I definitely will not be replaying in my mind for the rest of my life.*

"You know what?" she says. "I'm too tired to argue."

Daniel smiles. "A rare treasure. Want a change of clothes? I can grab some sweats and a T-shirt."

"Yes, please." She bites her lip, her eyes traveling down his legs. "Wait," she says. "Could you just grab me the largest T-shirt you've got?"

"Sure." Daniel does just that, then shows her to the bathroom, pointing out which face wash and lotion are his and directing her to the drawer full of spare toothbrushes.

Back in his room, he undresses hurriedly, switching into the plaid pajama bottoms his mom got him that he never wears. Considering he usually sleeps stark naked, this'll have to do. Thank God he changed his sheets earlier.

"Daniel?" Liyah calls from the bathroom. He darts out of his room, thinking that he forgot to get her toothpaste. When he arrives, Liyah asks, "Is this a one-night-stand kit?"

His cheeks burn. "Blame Alex."

She turns toward him, smug smile on her face and hand on her hip. "Alex's hookups regularly use silk hair scrunchies and tampons? I mean, maybe some do, but a whole drawer? That seems unlikely."

Daniel blushes deeper, shaking his head. "No, but he insisted I keep them. I figure I should listen, he's the hookup pro. Not that we're . . ."

"Well, Alex, orientation aside, sure knows how to please a lady. I might 'accidentally' forget to return this scrunchie. I'm always losing mine."

Daniel laughs. "Take as many as you want, they're not getting much use."

"Sure they aren't," Liyah says, patting his bare chest and sliding past him to disappear into his bedroom.

MAYBE SHE SHOULD have asked for the sweatpants, but Liyah's seen Daniel's legs, and she's also seen her own. It's possible that the height difference would have compensated for his lack of hips, but it's not the kind of day where she could handle the emotional blow of his pants failing to pull up over her thighs. Now she's looking in his mirrored closet door and hoping that the mid-thigh reach of his T-shirt isn't too indecent.

Then again, there's nothing decent about Daniel's naked torso, let alone the trail of dark hair that disappears under his flannel pajamas (or the way his tan skin stretches over his gently defined stomach, or how his tattoo perfectly accentuates the muscles in his arms).

She shakes her head vigorously, trying to dislodge her thoughts. *You're a grown woman; you can share a bed without going there.*

Footsteps approach the door, and Liyah does a quick survey of his nightstands. His book and phone charger are on the left one, but Sweet Potato is curled up asleep on the right side of the terra-cotta-colored duvet, and Liyah doesn't have the heart to move her.

During her moment of indecision, there's a knock. "You decent?" Daniel asks.

"Yeah." *I hope.* "Trying to figure out how to get in the bed without disturbing your cat. Come in."

"Slide her toward the middle, she won't mind." Liyah does as he says, and Sweet Potato barely stirs. "Shirt work out okay?"

"Yes, I am now a proud Wisconsin Badgers fan," Liyah says, sitting down on the bed. Great. From this angle, she's got a view of his V-lines to contend with. She quickly draws the covers up over her goose bump–studded skin. His covers. Because she's in his bed. Not an air mattress they're sharing out of desperation—his *bed.* Only now does she realize she could have left her car and walked home, or told him to grab his snow boots before he drove her.

Daniel smiles, sitting down on his side of the bed to remove his socks. "As you should be," he says.

Liyah lies back, pulling the sheets up to her nose. Daniel's sheets. She's telling herself not to panic, but then he lifts the blanket on his side and slides under the covers with a sigh that makes her stomach flip. *I am in Daniel's bed. I am in Daniel Rosenberg's bed. What the fuck am I doing here?*

"Liyah, I need you to stop freaking out."

She turns to face him, frowning. "I am not freaking out."

"We'll deal with Jeff and Brett come Monday. For now, let's get some rest." Liyah swallows and nods, even though the wine night could not be further from her mind. "Good night, Liyah. Thanks for showing me SUE's furcula."

"Stop objectifying her, you perv."

Daniel's laugh fades into a yawn, and with a twist of a knob, he casts them into darkness. Liyah doesn't even remember her head hitting the pillow.

A fact Liyah thought she'd never know: Daniel Rosenberg cuddles in his sleep. So does his cat. She distinctly remembers settling under the sheets with a good foot of mattress between her and Daniel, Sweet Potato curled up at the foot of the bed. Now, Liyah finds herself in a Rosenberg sandwich. Sweet Potato is situated in the right angle formed by her thighs and torso; Liyah, in turn, rests against the same place on Daniel. His arm drapes loosely over her waist and his heavy breath (or maybe snore, but that seems too strong a word for the sound he's making) tickles the back of her neck.

Liyah is surprised not only that she slept through the night, but also at how comfortable she finds herself in this bed that smells like Old Spice and clean sheets and *Daniel.* That is, until her stomach grumbles. Contemplating how to extract herself without waking her bedmates, Liyah tilts forward slightly. The Rosenbergs (or is it Rosensberg, like passersby?) remain where they are, chests rising and falling in somnolent rhythm. A wiggle. Still nothing. Feeling bolder, Liyah rocks forward.

Disaster. The motion causes the already curled UW Madison shirt to ride up farther and Daniel's hand to fall from her waist to the bare skin just above the seam of her panties. His touch sends a current through her entire body, causing her every hair to stand on end and her to shoot bolt upright in the bed.

"S'everything alright?" Daniel mumbles. His morning voice is deep and gravelly but between rubbing his eyes and slurring his words, he gives the impression of an enormous, disoriented toddler.

"Yes, um, go back to sleep. I'm going to make breakfast." Liyah stumbles out of the bed as fast as humanly possible, a now very awake Sweet Potato meowing at her heels.

Safely in the kitchen, Liyah grips the edge of the counter and heaves out the breath she's been desperately holding. *What. The fuck. Was that.* Ending up in bed on a Friday with someone beautiful is Liyah's forte (at least, before the new exhibition and the marketing project got in the way), but waking up next to them? Feeling an innocent brush of their fingers on her stomach in guilty places? She's miles out of her element.

Oh, God. Liyah, of all people, understands how precious a gift trust is. How much that kind of friendship can mean. Hell, she was seconds away from dragging him into the worst of her own issues. She probably would have if he had pressed her. Which is why she needs to stop reliving the drag of his calloused fingertips across her skin.

Daniel's body was warm and firm against hers when she woke, bent around her like she was meant to fit there.

Stop, Liyah. She should never have listened to Neen, always egging her on.

She should call Neen.

But she can't exactly pick up the phone and say, "I shared an air mattress followed by a real mattress with Daniel

Rosenberg and now I think I'm attracted to him; do you have a horoscope for this?" when Daniel's in the next room.

Right, breakfast.

Liyah rummages in his fridge, extracting eggs, cheese, and a bell pepper. It occurs to her that he might want some form of breakfast meat, but he doesn't have any in his fridge, so she pulls open the freezer drawer. Underneath a package of bacon is a familiarly stamped brown paper bag, now encased in a freezer-safe Ziploc. Brownstein's Bagel Bakery, while good enough to forgive the alliteration, is a train ride and two buses away from here.

There's a pang in Liyah's chest, something like flattery but sharper. She slides two pumpernickels into the toaster oven and busies herself chopping an onion and heating oil in a pan.

Liyah is pouring beaten eggs over the browned vegetables when she hears Daniel emerge from his bedroom. "The coffee's ready, but I hope you like your bacon burnt," she says. "I have many talents, but cooking dead animals is not one of them."

Daniel chuckles. "Thank you. We'll just call it extra crispy." His voice is still rough and low, in the way it only can be when you've run it raw or haven't used it in a while.

She turns to face him. Mentally, she knew that he wouldn't be wearing a shirt. Before was bad enough, but the sight of him now is catastrophic. His dark hair is messy, a loose wave falling in front of his face. Those tartan pajama pants hang low on his hips, and the entire left side of his body glows from the snow-reflected sunlight streaming through his window.

Liyah's teeth sink deeply into her bottom lip, and she returns to scrambling the eggs. "Yeah, let's call it that."

"Liyah?"

"Yes?" she says, voice a little too high-pitched, not looking up as she scrapes the egg scramble onto plates with the toasted bagels.

"Do you feel weird about our conversation last night? Because you're not making eye contact."

Well, maybe you should get a new physical form, or if you insist on this one, at least have the decency to keep it covered. She pushes his plate toward him, looking him directly in his amber-colored eyes. "I don't feel weird about it at all. I'm just hungry."

He smiles. "Ah, yes. I'll let you get something in your tummy before the claws come out."

She rolls her eyes before emphatically taking a large bite of eggs. They're delicious. She sighs, contented. Maybe her reaction to him this morning was just an unusual brand of Liyah's normal hunger-induced emotional dysregulation.

They eat in silence, and when Liyah finishes, Daniel rises to clear the plates and load them into the dishwasher. Sweet Potato curls up on Liyah's lap and purrs at her head scratches while Daniel scrubs at the pans.

"Weird Q," Daniel says while drying one with a dish towel. "You doing anything on Thursday night?"

"I don't think so, why?"

"It's my dad's Yahrzeit. We're going to be doing some of the traditions for Jesa, which is the Korean memorial for the anniversary of a death. My mom did it for her grandparents when she still lived with our family in Busan. Would you want to come?"

"Oh, um. Are you sure? Won't it be a family thing?"

He nods. "I'm sure. We're not going to be doing the full tradition on either side, just lighting a Yahrzeit candle and eating his favorite foods. And it'll be here, because Jesa are held at the firstborn son's house, so you don't have to schlepp out to Madison or anything."

"That sounds nice. I'll be there." Even with her response, Daniel looks hesitant, so Liyah smiles warmly to reassure him. Eventually, he returns the gesture.

CHAPTER 13

DR. ESPINOSA'S office stands in stark contrast to her clothing, which plainly exists only in shades of brown and off-white. Plants dot every surface, all in what look to be handmade ceramic pots. An aromatherapy diffuser on a reclaimed wood side table infuses the room with eucalyptus-scented vapor. The Moroccan rug below his feet matches the yellows and oranges in the Native American blanket that lies across the leather sofa. It should feel cluttered, but it's pleasantly full and cozy. He wonders what Kayla's office looks like. If he had to guess, he'd say fewer plants but even more color.

They've gone through the pleasantries, and now Daniel's sitting across from her silently, drumming his fingers on his knees.

"What made you decide to make this appointment?" she asks after a minute passes.

"Kayla—my sister—says that everybody should go to therapy, and I've got insurance."

Dr. Espinosa smiles, the wrinkles next to her eyes becoming more pronounced. Daniel places her age somewhere slightly north of halfway between him and his mother. "Smart woman."

"She's a therapist, too."

She nods. "I see. Well, what made you pick up the phone now?"

Daniel swallows. It feels weird to say this to someone you've known for all of fifteen minutes. Then again, she probably hears about much worse every day. Should he really be here? Everyone expects to lose their parents. Maybe not in their twenties, but still.

He decides it's worse to sit there in silence, wasting both of their time. "The anniversary of my dad's death is on Thursday. I think I should talk about it?"

"I'm sorry to hear that, Daniel. I'm glad you came in."

It takes him a little while, and a few more leading questions from Dr. Espinosa, but eventually he starts to talk. He recognizes some of her techniques from Kayla and smiles to himself because he's never been more certain that his sister is great at her job.

The hour is up before he knows it, and it's jarring to go from that indoor forest where all his secrets flow freely to the busy street below. He's got about twenty more minutes if he doesn't want to invent a fake client lunch to appease a prying colleague, and he intends to spend it with a bacon, egg, and cheese on a bagel. He's chasing the everything seasoning with black coffee when he gets a message from his sister.

Kayla
So????

Daniel
i am miraculously cured.

Kayla
Hilarious.

Daniel

it was good. said more than
i thought i would. how do
therapists get us to do that?
witchcraft

Kayla

If I told you, I'd be out of a
job! Love you, Danny.

Daniel

love you too

He pockets the phone and finishes his sandwich. When did he get here? In college, when Lily cheated on him with her differential equations TA, he moped around for a bit before spending an entire weekend cross-faded and party hopping with Tran and Evan. The weekend after he told his parents that he wasn't going to apply to medical school and his dad yelled at him for an hour, their antics earned him a hangover that can still churn his stomach if he thinks too hard about it. And even though the bender was less extreme when he and Emily, his first post-college girlfriend, parted ways, he weathered the heartbreak more or less the same. It's not that any of it quite compares to his dad's death, it's more that he's always handled everything in his life like he's Teflon, letting it all roll off his back. This must be adulthood, then: going to therapy and *talking* about it instead of pretending it isn't there.

He remembers the moment when he was dancing with Liyah, how badly he wanted to kiss her. That's completely different, though. She's finally his friend, one of the closest ones he has. He's not going to mess that up. She's too important, and there're other beautiful women in this city he can kiss.

He decides that'll be his next move in therapy, working up the nerve to start dating. Or, at very least, redownload Tinder. Baby steps, and all.

LIYAH FINISHES READING her email, filling with an overwhelming urge to slam her computer shut. It's her desktop, not her laptop, so instead she says, "I swear to fucking God!"

"If God's fucking, she's a wee bit too busy to hear you swearing," Siobhan calls, not looking away from the open Photoshop file on her monitor.

"Ha ha. Jeff is mad at me about the wine night ending early."

Siobhan spins her special-order ergonomic desk chair around to face Liyah. "What? I just thought Jeff had sent another email where the entire message is in the subject line."

Liyah shakes her head. "Much worse. *Dear Aliyah,*" she reads from her in-box. "I mean, first of all, when has he ever called me by my government name? I feel like I'm getting first-name-middle-named by a parent."

"Go on."

"*I have reviewed the numbers after your little wine shindig*"—she pauses for Siobhan's disgusted groan—"*and we saw no appreciable difference in the membership sign-up rates. Now, I understand that there may have been some extenuating circumstances—*"

"Yes, like a *fecking blizzard.* Does he think you have a weather machine?"

"It gets worse. *There may have been some extenuating circumstances, but the proposals that you and Kinley brought are all quite costly. If we're going to shell out for a local winery, or a DJ for the costume party this weekend, the board and I expect results. Need I remind you that—*"

Siobhan holds up her hand. "Christ. Never mind, I've

heard enough. If he weren't our boss, I'd say tell him to eff off. It goes on like this?"

"Basically. He's dangling curator in front of me, acting like this is some personal moral failing. Yeah, I would've liked for the night to go long enough to do the membership raffle. I would have also liked not to work coat check with Toby and Daniel, or spend half the night on an air mattress in front of SUE while I waited for the snowplows to come."

"You stayed here alone? Oh, I'm so sorry, love. I didn't realize. I know you're petrified of driving in the snow."

"I wasn't technically alone." Liyah fidgets with a pad of sticky notes. "Daniel stayed with me. Still, less than ideal."

Siobhan sucks her bottom lip into her mouth, brow furrowed. "I see. And you drove yourself home after that?"

She shakes her head. "Well, no. He drove us." Siobhan stares, nodding. "What?" Liyah asks.

"Nothing. It's almost five—why don't you send Jeff something like 'I understand, I'll do better next time' and delete it? Then we can bunk off."

Liyah laughs, looking up. "I'm gonna have to use context clues for that one and guess you're offering to leave early."

Siobhan smiles, the worried look melting away from her freckled face. "Come on, let's head out."

As Siobhan gathers her belongings, Liyah replies to Jeff with unearned kindness. She hits send, then moves to delete, but another message pops up what feels like seconds later:

To: Aliyah Cohen-Jackson <a.cohen.jackson@fieldmuseum.org>
From: Jeff Chapman <jeff.chapman@fieldmuseum.org>
RE: Wine Membership #s

Also, I heard from security something about you sleeping in an exhibition. Was this for the sleepover or the snow? Regardless, you should have slept in your office.

Since we didn't see improvements, I'm going to say no to the photo booth this Saturday. We can't afford extraneous expenses.

Sent from my iPhone

God, she hasn't felt this chastised since she punched Corey Packton in the cheek in seventh grade. And even then, she mostly got herself out of it when she told the principal what he'd said to Neen, slurs uncensored. Liyah folds her arms on the desk, resting her forehead on her wrists. The photo booth was a *major* component of the event—they needed it so that attendees could vote on the costume contest. This whole marketing thing is absolutely fucked, cursed from the beginning.

Wait . . . "Siobhan, you have a DSLR, right?"

"Oh no, did Jeff nix the photo booth?" Liyah grunts in affirmation. "Yeah, I've got one. Also, I have an eighty-square-foot piece of black fabric we could use as backing—don't ask. No lighting, though, but I reckon we could rent?"

Liyah lifts her head. "You are a lifesaver," she says, but her stomach still turns. The way this marketing effort has gone, she's half convinced she's going to be out of a job and designing polka-dotted pop-up Instagram traps for the rest of her career.

Siobhan walks over, placing her hand on Liyah's shoulder. "Delete the email. And then hot chocolate, my treat."

Liyah nods, but her mouse slides from the trash icon to the arrow. She types out a quick message and hits forward before getting ready to go.

The response comes an hour later, when she's almost successfully forgotten about the email in the first place:

To: Aliyah Cohen-Jackson <a.cohen.jackson@fieldmuseum.org>
From: Daniel Rosenberg <dwrosenberg@kinley.com>
RE: Message from a Fan

Yikes. You're right, we can do it ourselves. Want me to show you my worst from Brett? The typos alone will keep you laughing for days.

Daniel

P.S. I got my costume together last night. Every millennial in Chicago is gonna be a member after Saturday, I can feel it.

CHAPTER 14

AFTER Liyah texted Daniel to inquire about his dad's favorite dessert, he imagined that she would show up with a box from the bakery down the street. Instead, he answers the door to her holding two enormous trays of homemade carrot cupcakes.

He smiles. "I told you it was just my mom and Kayla, right?"

Liyah rolls her eyes. "Listen, I did not make two batches of cream cheese frosting just to get sassed. You gonna let me in or not? I'm sure whoever's in 3B would love to take these off my hands."

"Did I sass you? I meant to thank you." He steps back, holding the door open wide and gesturing inside. "Your majesty."

She wrinkles her nose at him in a way that is supposed to be angry but is mostly very cute, thrusting one of the trays at his free arm and waltzing into his apartment.

"You must be Liyah," Kayla says after Daniel slides the dead bolt on the door. "I'm Kayla. It's nice to finally meet you in your adult form." She takes the remaining tray from Liyah and sets it on the dining table.

Liyah smiles. "Guilty as charged. But whatever Daniel's told you about what a bully I am, I swear it's only half true." Kayla grins, warming to her instantly. "It's nice to see you again, too," Liyah finishes. She removes her coat and shoes, rounding the corner to the kitchen.

"Hey, Liyah!" Alex calls from where he's undoubtedly been sweet-talking Daniel's mother.

"Hello! No shift tonight?"

"Nah, still working. Just had to say hi to my favorite Rosenberg before I left," he says, kissing Daniel's mother on the cheek. She swats his arm in response, but her expression reads incredibly charmed.

"You must be Dr. Rosenberg," Liyah says, facing Daniel's mother, who is standing over the stove frying scallion pancakes.

She lifts the spatula to wave. "Please, call me Minji."

"Nice to meet you, Minji. Thank you for having me."

"Oh, it's our pleasure, honey. Now, would you mind helping to set up?"

Kayla appears helpful by directing Liyah in setting the table without lifting a finger herself, a tactic she spent years perfecting on her brother. Daniel doesn't realize he's been standing in their apartment's tiny foyer, useless, for several minutes until Alex approaches him on his way out.

"I'm really sorry I can't be here, man," he says, placing a comforting palm on Daniel's shoulder.

"It's okay, you can't help that your job is nocturnal. Thank you for helping cook."

Alex nods, slipping his arms into his leather jacket. "Yeah, of course. If you need to call me afterward, don't hesitate, okay?"

"Yeah."

"I'm serious. I can always slip outside for a break, and I can probably get someone to cover the end of my shift. And I can definitely cancel on Marc with a *c*."

Daniel swallows, his throat suddenly feeling thick. "I really appreciate it. I'm gonna try to get through it on my own, though." Not really on his own, though. He's got his mom and sister here with him. And Liyah.

Alex flashes a smile. "Okay. Just remember that you don't have to."

Daniel's heart swells a little as he hugs his roommate good-bye and wishes him a good night at work. As the door swings shut, he feels a poke in his left side and turns to find Liyah with her hands on her hips.

"Are you going to make yourself useful or just let the women do the work?" she demands, eyes narrowing. Kayla laughs from behind her. The seam of Liyah's lips is a neutral line, but with too much tension around it. Daniel has gained enough proficiency in Nonverbal Liyah to understand that this is a carefully concealed smile.

"Why do you think I invited you instead of Jordan?" he retorts.

She rolls her eyes and Daniel follows her to the kitchen to bring several serving dishes of food to the dining table. The spread is everything his dad loved to eat, to the point where none of it seems like it should be on the same plate. There're his mom's scallion pancakes, but also sautéed rapini, all the fixings for build-your-own veggie tacos, Buffalo chicken wings, sour beers, carrot cupcakes. He surveys the incongruous feast before him, the extra place setting for his dad, the Yahrzeit candle in a tray on his ottoman, and wonders how he's going to get through the night without crying.

The light outside his living room window fades into a

swirl of rust and magenta, denoting both sundown and the time to light the candle. His family and Liyah stand around the ottoman, his mother's arms wrapped around his waist, his fingers interwoven with Kayla's. Even though they're six Jewish adults short of a minyan, they recite the Mourner's Kaddish. His dad would have loved it, them simultaneously honoring tradition and flouting the rules. Liyah joins in on the line meant for non-mourners, her voice warm and soft. He takes his eyes off the flame to meet hers and shocks Liyah and himself by smiling.

The prayer finishes, and Kayla and his mother squeeze and release the parts of Daniel they're holding. The air in Daniel's apartment feels different, almost charged, as they take their places at the dinner table.

Minji Rosenberg, not for the first time at a family dinner, is the one to break the silence. "I hope you all aren't waiting for Aaron to start, because if you are, I fear we'll be here quite a while."

Laughter erupts around the table, and it's a moment before Daniel realizes that some of it is bubbling out of him. He moves through the dinner in a daze, smiling and nodding along to the anecdotes that his mother and sister share, laughing as they give Liyah the third degree. The food is delicious, as his mother's always is, and he carefully finishes each dish before moving on to the next to avoid any unwanted flavor combinations.

Liyah taps his foot with hers while Kayla argues with their mom about the year they went to Disneyland. "You doing okay?" she says under her breath, eyes still fixed on the women of his family.

He nods. "Yeah. Thank you."

Kayla throws a balled-up cupcake wrapper at Daniel's head. "Noona!" he whines at the same time as his mom says "Kayla!"

She ignores them both. "You've been quiet the whole night. Care to share with the class?"

Their mom gives her a cold look. "If Daniel doesn't want to speak, he does not have to. Stop pushing him."

Daniel shakes his head. "No, no. It's okay." He takes a swig of his sour. "God, these are disgusting."

"I like them," Liyah says from his side.

Kayla chuckles. "That makes one of us. You would've won Dad over with that alone."

Liyah laughs hesitantly, looking to Daniel. "It's true. He loved funky beers. He even tried to brew some himself. He wanted to start a—what did he call it?"

"Nano-brewery," his mom says fondly.

"Yeah, but the beer he made was somehow both flavorless and bitter."

"Truly disgusting," Kayla joins, shooting an encouraging smile his way.

"He, um . . ." Daniel quiets as he feels three pairs of eyes on him. He knows conceptually that he and his mother and sister are experiencing the same loss, but sometimes he feels so alone in it. He steels himself. If there's anybody to talk about his dad with, it's the other two people who loved Aaron Rosenberg most. And Liyah, who nudges his foot. "He made a batch right before he sent me off to college and left three full growlers under my bed without telling Eomma." Daniel glances her way. She looks momentarily scandalized, but her face softens, and she shakes her head nostalgically. "He thought it would make me a hit with the other freshmen on my floor. And it did, because we bonded over how bad it was. An RA caught us with it and when I explained that it was homemade and gross and I was trying to appease my father, she let us slide with a warning. At winter break, he asked how everyone liked it, and I didn't have the heart to tell him. Which turns out was a mistake because he gave me more to bring back in January." Daniel feels tears welling up in his eyes, but he's smiling.

His mom reaches over to take his hand, and Liyah reaches under the table to squeeze his thigh. He looks up from his plate, and there's Kayla: her usual broad smile adorned with tears streaming down her face. She rises from her seat and strides over to Daniel, wrapping her arms around him. His mom follows suit.

"We love you so much, Danny. Understand?" Daniel nods. "Good. Liyah, get in here." And she does. Suddenly, Daniel realizes what made the air change: his entire apartment feels almost exactly like this hug.

They stay like this until his mom declares that it's time to leave the room so Aaron may accept the offering. They pile some food onto the empty place setting and begin the work of clearing the rest of the table.

"So, she's Black and Jewish," his mom says as they wash and dry dishes, assembly-line style. Daniel looks around but finds that Liyah is engrossed in conversation with his sister.

"Yeah. Her dad didn't convert like you, but she and her brother were raised Jewish."

His mom nods. "Interesting."

Daniel stops working on the dish he was buffing dry. If his mom has a problem with that, it's immensely hypocritical. But she wouldn't be the first hypocrite in an intermarriage. He tenses, squares his jaw. In Korean, he asks, "Why is that interesting?"

His mom hums, attempting to seem aloof. "You must have a lot in common with her," she replies. His shoulders relax, and he goes back to the task at hand. "She's very pretty," she says, this time in English.

"Eomma!" he protests.

"She's all the way over there with Kayla, she can't hear

me." She uses a soapy, gloved hand to wave him off. "Are you going to tell me you don't think she's pretty?"

"She's gorgeous, Mom, that's not—"

She silences him with a knowing look. "Whenever you want to let your eomma in on your life, you just let me know. You know, Kayla calls me every week."

Daniel groans. "Laying it on a little thick, don't you think?"

"Are you leaving?" his mom says loudly instead of responding to Daniel. He turns to see Liyah hugging Kayla goodbye.

"Yes, unfortunately I have to be up rather early for work. Thank you so much for having me here, though. It was lovely to meet you both."

"Yes, of course. We loved having you," his mom says.

"Did you walk here?" Daniel asks.

"No, I drove. Didn't want to drop the cupcakes."

"Okay. I'll walk you to your car?" He says it like a question, and Liyah gives him a smile of assurance.

They make the entire trip down the stairs and around the corner in silence. When they reach her car, she stops and turns toward him, looking him dead in the eyes. Her expression is like it has been the whole night, warm and comforting, and he's so thankful that she's here. More than he can put into words.

"Liyah," he begins, but his voice gets stuck in the back of his throat.

She reaches up to cup his left cheek in her hand. He involuntarily presses into it, and her thumb glides over his cheekbone. "I was honored to be here," she says.

The words have only barely left her mouth when his lips are on hers.

If he'd intended anything at all, it would have been for a

chaste kiss, lips just barely parted to fit together. That's how he's imagined kissing her since that moment in front of SUE. Tentatively. But he did this without thinking, so that's not what it is. He crashes into her, and Liyah's hand moves from his cheek to the hairs at the back of his head. She tugs, and he groans, rolling his hips into her stomach, feeling her body pressed along his as he pins her to the car. His body knows how it wants to touch her, not even muscle memory from all those years ago, but bare instinct.

As his hands find purchase in her hair, her tongue swipes across his bottom lip, and his mouth opens and welcomes her into him. He is aware of every subtle repositioning, each movement creating a new cause-and-effect map in his mind. If she scrapes her nails against his scalp, he'll tighten his grip on her hip; if he sighs into her mouth, she'll pull his lip between her teeth. Her tongue, tracing his, is electrifying. He's a live wire, seconds from sparking, and still all he can think of is how she tastes like cream cheese frosting and home.

Then, he feels a firm pressure on his chest, Liyah's hand pushing him away.

LIYAH'S PALM ON Daniel's sternum tells her that his breathing is just as ragged and labored as hers. What it doesn't tell her, and what she really wants to know, is if he also feels every inch of his skin on fire. Her knees are weak, and she's thankful that she has the side of the car to keep her upright.

"Daniel."

"I'm sorry," he says, and the apology confirms what she feared, or rather knew, to be true. That this was a mistake.

Which, it had to be, because she can't remember the last time she was kissed that *intently*. Certainly not when fully clothed. And she was stupid enough to lose herself in the moment, to be someone who could be kissed like that. By Daniel. A friend, presumably a person who gives a shit about her beyond how expertly she can use her tongue.

"You're grieving. I don't"—she struggles to catch her breath—"I don't want you to kiss me for comfort."

"No, Liyah, that's not it. I'm not using you as my support blanket, or anything like that."

"Emotions are running high, then. You can't know what you want in this moment. And that's okay. But we have to *work* together. Through January, at least."

Daniel gives her a long look, long enough for her to take in the flush in his cheeks and his kiss-swollen lips, the bob of his Adam's apple as he swallows. "Okay, then. Should we . . . just forget about it?"

She nods, slowly. "Already forgotten." She lies through her teeth, still breathing heavily.

"See you and Neen at Survival Club tomorrow?" he asks.

"Right, yeah." His hair is mussed (her fault), so she reaches up and does her best to arrange it.

"Thanks," he says, regarding her carefully. "I'd better get back. Good night, Liyah."

"Good night, Daniel," she responds, and climbs into the driver's seat of her car, willing her heart rate to slow. She doesn't start the ignition until he disappears around the corner.

Last week, when his hand on her bare belly sent her spiraling, she'd chalked her reaction up to her empty stomach. Now, though, her stomach is too full in the way it always is after a special occasion with a Jewish family. So why could she feel his kiss in her *toes*?

The second she closes the door to her apartment, she picks up her phone to call Neen.

"C-J, as I've told you via text, my flight has not been canceled and there is no forecasted inclement weather."

Liyah presses her knuckle into her forehead, trying to relax her brow. "Neen, that's not why I'm calling."

"Are you okay? You sound like you just ran a marathon."

Liyah grimaces. "No, much worse. I kissed Daniel Rosenberg. Or he kissed me." She waves her hands around, even though Neen can't see her. "I don't know, we kissed."

Neen laughs. "Oh, finally. How was it?"

"Finally? What do you mean *finally*?! It's the anniversary of his dad's death. He was looking for comfort."

"Are you sure that's all it was?"

Liyah sighs. "Well, he suggested that we pretend it never happened, so I'm pretty sure."

"Hmm. Interesting."

"Why is that interesting?" she asks, rubbing at her chest, convinced she has cardiac arrhythmia. Like, medically speaking. This cannot be normal.

"Just is. Did you like the kiss?"

Liyah balks. "What does that have to do with anything?"

Neen whistles. "That good, huh? So, when are you gonna fuck him?"

"Neen!" Liyah nearly shouts into the phone. Clearly, they do not appreciate the gravity of this particular freak-out.

"Babe, you sound like you need a glass of wine and some sleep. I'll be sharing a bed with you for the weekend, so we can hold off on deciding who'll be in it next for a few days, okay?"

"Neen, how am I supposed to go to Survival Club meetings now? Do the sleep-in? Or the holiday party? Or any of it? Have I ruined everything?"

"*Aliyah Rivka*. You made it through an entire class that was TA'd by a one-night stand from the previous semester. I think you can handle one little kiss just fine."

Liyah wants to argue, but no good reason comes to mind. "Okay, okay. You're probably right."

"Of course I am. See you tomorrow!"

"See ya, Neen." The call ends.

Standing in front of her refrigerator, Liyah decides to heed some of Neen's advice after all, and swigs directly from a mostly empty bottle of sauvignon blanc. Maybe it'll submerge the butterflies in her stomach until they asphyxiate. One can only hope.

CHAPTER 15

WHEN Daniel told Kayla there was a Survival Club meeting tonight, she complained that if she'd known, she wouldn't have booked a morning flight back to New York. He apologized profusely for the oversight, but secretly, he's relieved. Usually, he'd love a chance to watch her let loose, as a lot of their closeness in their adult years has been brought on by shared drunken nights and hungover mornings. But Kayla is the most observant person he knows, and he only got through yesterday without her figuring out he'd kissed Liyah by the skin of his teeth.

He shouldn't be thinking about the kiss. When she pushed him away, her face scrunched so tightly, he was sure she hadn't wanted it, even if she'd kissed him back at first. Must have been an unconscious reaction, like how she always melts into his hand when he places it on the small of her back, or how she'd curled up into him and whimpered in her sleep when he tried to take his arm off her. So, he suggested that they forget about it, because he's sure that's what she wants to do. *Already forgotten,* she said.

He hasn't forgotten. In fact, he's replayed it approximately one hundred times today. He can still feel her fingers in his hair, her tongue tangled with his, her hand on his chest as he watched her heave labored breaths.

Get ahold of yourself, Daniel.

So here he is, half an hour early to the tenth iteration of the Speakeasy Survival Club, nursing a gin and tonic and trying to do just that. As Alex poured his drink, the sole upside of his father's death was revealed: if Daniel's acting weirdly, everyone in his life will chalk it up to grief and ask no further questions.

Siobhan arrives first, followed shortly by Jordan and then, fashionably late as usual, Liyah. There's a light in her eyes and a flush in her cheeks and she seems to have chosen jeans that accentuate her hips and waist and a tight shirt specifically to torture him, though he suspects he'd feel this way no matter what she wore. He's so caught up in Liyah as she approaches that he almost misses Neen walking by her side.

"Daniel," she says, wrapping him up in a hug that makes his heart race, before moving on to Siobhan, casual as ever. Maybe she has truly forgotten. "Siobhan. You both remember Neen. Jordan, this is Neen, quite possibly the best person who has ever lived on the face of this earth. Neen, this is Jordan, the answer to the question 'What if A$AP Rocky had an MBA?'" Everyone laughs, but no one quite as hard as Jordan, who gives his most dazzling smile as he shakes Neen's hand. Daniel and Liyah exchange a look that says *this should be interesting*.

It becomes increasingly clear as the night goes on that Jordan is totally enamored with Neen. Unfortunately, his attraction to them apparently acts as horse blinders for their equally obvious attraction to Siobhan. The third time Daniel catches Jordan winking, he can no longer contain himself. He elbows Liyah and says out of the side of his mouth, "Quite the show, to watch Jordan openly lusting after Neen—"

"Who in turn is openly lusting after Siobhan," Liyah finishes under her breath, a coy smile playing at her lips.

"Who in turn is openly lusting after Jordan. The circle of life."

At this, Liyah gives up on pretending to pay attention to Jordan's story and looks directly at Daniel, eyes wide. "You know?"

Daniel chuckles. "It doesn't take a brain surgeon to figure out. Can't blame her though, he's charming. Like you said, Pretty Boy Flacko in a suit."

She bites her lip. "Does he know?"

"I mean, he's probably gathered that she finds him attractive, but I don't think he's aware of the crush, if that's what you mean."

Liyah lets out a breath. "Okay, good. Please don't tell him. She'd be mortified and I'd feel awful for confirming it for you."

"I wouldn't do that, Liyah. I can keep a secret." Daniel doesn't mean the subtext, but it's clear that's how Liyah takes it. She swallows, reaching for her drink.

Already forgotten, my ass, Daniel thinks, and rides that high all the way back to the rooftop of Liyah's building. They all lean on the brick lip, buzzed and chatty, looking up at the starry sky, and Daniel is struck with an intense wave of déjà vu. Except, as attracted as he remembers being to Liyah in that camp observatory, it's about twenty times worse now. She's standing sandwiched between him and Neen and their arms keep brushing, Daniel hyperaware of each touch even through many layers of fabric.

Neen withdraws a robust joint from the depths of their jacket. "Anybody care to partake?"

"Neen!" Liyah exclaims, aghast. "You brought a pre-roll all the way from SF?"

"It's legal here, isn't it?"

"Yes, which is why you didn't need to risk a felony charge to smoke tonight!"

Neen shrugs, wearing a charming smirk that Daniel realizes is not unlike Jordan's. "Weed's better in California, though. If you're so appalled, don't have any."

Liyah rolls her eyes. "I didn't say I was *that* appalled." She glares daggers at the laughter, which turns out to be the general direction of everybody. Daniel hopes he's not imagining that her eyes linger a little bit longer on him.

JUNIOR YEAR OF college, Liyah went through a two-month period when she smoked weed nearly every day. Not at all coincidentally, Arielle, the girl she was sleeping with at the time, was their dormitory's plug. Since then, Liyah's sessions have become fewer and farther between, but one thing has stuck with her: she finds watching people smoke sexy. Maybe it's something about drawing attention to the lips, or maybe it's Pavlovian conditioning, but if someone she already thinks is good-looking lights up in front of her, it never fails to make her skin feel hot.

Daniel places the joint between his lips and begins the process of relighting it on a Chicago rooftop in October. That is, after a few attempts, he's forced to carefully cup his free hand around the flame to keep it from going out, the light illuminating his palm. The end glowing red orange, he takes a deep inhale and pauses, closing his eyes before passing the joint and the lighter off to Jordan. When he exhales, finally, the thick curls of smoke hardly leave his lips before he circles them back through his nose. Liyah is transfixed.

"French inhale," Neen says, rolling their eyes. "Nice," they drawl.

Daniel, face and shoulders already relaxing, blows the rest of the smoke out with an easy grin. He doesn't seem to mind Neen's ribbing. "I did go to college in California, you know."

"You learned this at Stanford? Here I was thinking a school like that had nothing to offer," Liyah jokes, trying to ignore her tingling nerves.

Daniel shakes his head, still smiling. Though that could be the weed. "Quick as ever, even high."

It's not quite true, because if Liyah were sober, she'd be able to shoot him a glare, or at the very least conceal her smile. Instead, she wears her pleasure at the compliment on her entire face and does a pathetic shrug to try and play it off. It feels like everyone's eyes are on her.

Until they aren't. The recycling symbol of unrequited lust returns as Neen's contraband makes it the rest of the way around the circle. Daniel and Liyah lean back and watch, amused, exchanging the occasional look. Liyah is happy standing here on the rooftop, not saying a word, quieted by the night air and the smoke.

No, not happy. *Content.* Daniel's got those half-lidded eyes and that slightly crooked smile and she'd bet anything that he's feeling her emotions right along with her.

"Does it get exhausting, being so on all the time? Don't you ever just wanna, like, relax?" Daniel's voice is deep and coarse, the way it is when he wakes up in the morning. This thought distracts her, and she stares at him blankly for a moment as she processes the question once again.

"Poking fun at you is relaxing for me," Liyah eventually responds.

Daniel elbows her gently in the ribs. "Of course it is."

He looks at her, and she watches his tongue sweep over his bottom lip, and she is struck by how much she wants to replace his tongue with hers. The desire hits her like a freight train, and if they were alone, she'd be unable to restrain herself from pressing up against him right then and there.

But they're not alone, and she'd sooner throw herself off this rooftop than kiss anyone, let alone Daniel, in front of her friends. The inconvenience of their presence will save her from rejection and the ensuing embarrassment she'd wake up with in the morning. Imagine that, having him push her away and then doing the museum sleep-in tomorrow. She's seen the words *I'm sorry* forming on his kiss-bruised lips every time she blinked today, heard *should we just forget about it?* beneath everything Daniel's said. Being brushed off by the same person twice would be bad on its own, but Liyah has to *work* with him. She shudders.

Jordan holds the pre-roll out to Neen, and instead of taking it, they lean in and toke from between his fingertips, exhaling smoke into the moonlight with a blithe smile. Liyah wonders if the boundaries of gender and sexuality are even flimsier than they appear. She looks to Daniel, and he seems to be thinking the same.

Then Neen laughs, insouciant as always, plucking the joint from Jordan's hand and taking another long drag. If people are like magnets, Neen is every pole. Anyone can get drawn in if they find the right alignment. This fact is something of which they remain woefully unaware.

Daniel's low whisper interrupts Liyah's train of thought. "We're good, right? I know we said . . ."

Liyah holds her gaze steadily forward, telling herself that the shiver zipping down her spine is from the chilly air. "We're good, Rosenberg." She turns to look up at him, but he's already leaning in to whisper something else and her nose nearly brushes his. Daniel's eyes flick back and forth, searching hers like they had on Yom Kippur.

And he pulls back.

DANIEL IS PLAYING with fire, and he knows it. When he's not high and it's not the middle of the night, he's going to work on getting his thoughts in check. As it is, he spends his walk home replaying every look Liyah gave him tonight and wondering what would've happened if he hadn't pulled away from her at the last moment.

She would have shoved you away and told you off, and she would be right to do it, dumbass.

He wants to call Kayla, which is an impulse he wishes he was rid of. He's approaching thirty, for fuck's sake. He can't always be calling Noona to make it better.

Considering that Liyah turns him into a sixth grader poking the girl who sits in front of him until he gets her attention, even if it's just a stuck-out tongue and a muttered *jerkhead* before the teacher notices, it's kind of fitting. Maybe he does need his big sister to explain all the funny feelings in his chest.

It's two thirty in New York, but Kayla's always been a night owl and her body should still be on Central Time, so Daniel picks up his phone anyway.

"How was the Doomsday Preparation Cult, Danny?" she says by way of hello. He smiles.

"Speakeasy Survival Club. Good, actually. I wish you could come," he says, only now realizing how silly the name sounds, and how true the last part is.

"And whose fault is that?"

"Sor-ry," he singsongs.

"God, you're stoned, aren't you?" she says.

Daniel pouts. "It's within my rights as an Illinois resident."

"Yes, and I am very jealous. However, as both your sister and a licensed therapist, I have to ask if this is a good idea given yesterday. Are you alone?"

"Walking home by myself, yes. But it's not like that. Liyah's best friend is visiting, and they brought some."

"Okay, well. I've had most of a bottle of pinot so I'm not sure why I'm lecturing." She chuckles wryly.

Oh. It always seems like she's handling things better than

he is, but maybe she's just . . . handling them differently. "You okay?"

"No. And neither are you and neither is Eomma, but that's normal, because Dad died relatively young and it was a really fucked up thing of him to do, if you ask me."

"It was, wasn't it? Wasn't the thought of some future kiddos calling him *Zeydie* supposed to keep him going for another ten years?"

Kayla laughs, more earnestly. "Ten? We are both *very* single, and it's not like they can speak right out of the womb. I'd say twenty for good measure."

Daniel's grinning now, a block and a half away from home. "What's getting called *Zeydie* if they can't walk yet? I'm thinking imaginary grandchildren should've given him another thirty, at least."

"Thirty-five at the absolute minimum," Kayla agrees.

"Right. It's not like fighting cancer for another forty years is too much to ask."

"Simple, really." She pauses, and he can hear her pouring another glass of wine. "I'm glad you called."

"Me too."

CHAPTER 16

ON the steps outside the Field Museum, Neen's ring gets stuck in Liyah's hair. "C-J, hold still!"

"Just take it off, we'll detangle or cut it out after," Liyah says.

"I *can't*," they huff. "Do you have any butter?"

"Why would I have brought butter on the train? And where do you think I would keep it?" She gestures down at her outfit. No bag because Angela Davis did not have one in her interview from California state prison. No pockets, either.

Neen tries a new angle, and Liyah yelps, jerking her head toward their hand to avoid a rip. "I'm sorry!" they shout.

Liyah, fed up, grabs Neen's arm and twirls them in a distorted ballroom dance, slowly unwinding her picked-out 'fro from one of their many rings. "I don't know why you insisted on wearing those. They don't go with your outfit," she says. Since the sleep-in was on Halloween, Liyah and Daniel decided to make it a costume party. The decades theme was Liyah's idea. She wanted *some* semblance of a connection to the general concept of history. Neen and Liyah are the 1970s from different corners of the world: Liyah in the iconic orange turtleneck, brown tweed skirt, and orange tights of Dr. Davis's 1972 interview, Neen looking like they've stepped directly out of an early '70s Bollywood film. Except for their collection of modern rings, of course.

"It's my signature!"

"You know, it's a wonder you haven't lost one of those inside of someone yet."

Neen laughs. "Oh, I didn't tell you that story?"

Liyah shudders. "Please tell me you're joking."

Inside, they make a beeline for the taxidermy African elephants in the lobby, the agreed meeting spot. The others are already there, in full costume.

"Glad you finally showed up," Siobhan says as they approach. "Since I got here, I've learned that Jordan is not, in fact, dressed as Aladdin, and received a lecture on eighties pop rap."

"Liyah couldn't be on time if her life depended on it," Daniel says.

"This is an obvious MC Hammer costume. Come on, the gold jacket!"

"It's not even my fault this time, I had to detach Neen from my hair!" Liyah protests.

"Why is Jordan shirtless?" Neen asks.

"I'm MC Hammer!"

Daniel laughs. "It's a little cold out for that."

Jordan crosses his arms over his bare chest. "There's central heating here, man. Y'all are mean."

"I see Daniel is serving Danny Zuko realness," Neen says. "And Siobhan is a *wonderful* Bubbles."

Siobhan curtsies. "Thank you."

Yes, wonderful heterosexual *Bubbles,* Liyah wishes she could remind Neen. "Gorgeous. Also, not on theme."

"*The Powerpuff Girls* premiered in 1998. I'm the nineties."

"And Liyah, you're a . . . go-go girl?" Jordan asks.

The entire group gawks at Jordan. "You're an idiot," Daniel says. "She's obviously Angela Davis."

"My bad, she's wearing tall boots!"

"They're era appropriate." Liyah holds up her hands, pausing. "You know what? I give up. Daniel, photo booth?"

He looks down at her, pulling the unlit cigarette from the side of his mouth and tucking it into the leather jacket he probably borrowed from Alex. "I'm afraid to leave these three unsupervised."

"As you should be. But leave them, we must."

Liyah isn't sure if the event idea was really that good, or if she's just overdue for some good karma, but there are three times the attendees of the failed wine night. Almost all are dressed to theme, and the line at the photo booth seems never-ending. Liyah would regret the decision to run it herself (thanks be to Jeff) if she weren't feeling the high of the merriment around her.

She holds Siobhan's DSLR while Daniel uploads each photograph to the appropriate decade category. QR codes pepper the exhibits, advertising the voting period, after which the annual membership winners will be announced. By nine, there are 1,534 pictures up, and even though the way Liyah's 'fro partially obscures her eyesight is driving her crazy (her cut is most definitely not designed to be picked out) and Daniel's pompadour is slightly deflated, they're both smiling from ear to ear.

Before they pack up the station, they send a summons in the SSC group chat. The others are tipsy from visits to the bar set up under the hanging *Pterosaur,* and getting a picture with all of them in frame proves a nearly insurmountable challenge. But they get one, eventually. Jordan lies on the floor in front with his head propped up on his hand, a knee pointed skyward to emphasize the low crotch of his harem pants. Siobhan is behind his head, bent at the knees and blowing a kiss to the camera (which has the added benefit of revealing some truly excellent cleavage). Neen stands at Jordan's feet, arms outstretched mid-dance. And Daniel and Liyah are sandwiched between them, Liyah doing her best to imitate Angela Davis's inquisitive head tilt while staring down the camera, Daniel's elbow on her shoulder as he withdraws a cigarette from parted lips.

Liyah runs back after the timer-triggered shutter clicks, looking down at the display. She grins, hugging the camera to her chest.

Neen prances toward her, demanding to see. Liyah releases her grip to show them, and they wolf whistle before shouting, "We are *so* hot!"

Jordan and Siobhan huddle around them, pointing and laughing at details on the tiny screen. A giddy warmth spreads through Liyah's chest; she's already drunk on the old-fashioned she's yet to order. Daniel looks at her from behind their friends, and the corner of his mouth tugs upward. She holds his gaze, and that feeling spreads further, until she's bursting with it.

Daniel's eyes dip to her mouth. He absently pinches his bottom lip between his forefinger and thumb, and she can *feel* it, just as she had felt his fingers along her tongue at Windy City. Her pulse quickens. She looks away. Jordan and Siobhan are still absorbed in the camera, but Neen's head is up, eyes pointed directly at her.

"I'm going to the bathroom," Liyah announces. "See you guys downstairs." She hurries away, Neen undoubtedly at her heels.

Inside the bathroom, they follow her, stomping, into a stall. "Neen," she complains. "I do actually have to pee."

They fold their arms across their chest. "Okay then, drop

your tights. It's not anything I haven't seen before." Liyah's ass is barely on the toilet seat when they say, "Please don't kill me, but this is the part where I bring up Daniel."

"What, find something you liked in his birth chart?" Liyah smirks, desperately trying to maintain control of the conversation. Which is difficult, given that she's actively urinating.

"It feels like, speaking as a completely objective third-party observer with absolutely no personal interest in the matter," they say, quoting *She's the Man*, the pair's favorite sleepover film, "there might be something there beyond a mistaken grieving kiss."

Liyah scowls. "Doubt it."

"C-J, come on. You flirt with each other like it's breathing. And those brooding looks—you could cut the tension with a knife. I don't know how Jordan and Siobhan put up with it every week."

"I think they're busy with other things," Liyah mutters.

"A friend with benefits would be a nice change for you."

"I only ever have friends with benefits," Liyah protests, reaching for the toilet paper.

"No, you only ever have benefits with benefits. Besides, he's like, stupidly good-looking. Heterosexual Nico Kim with better taste in clothes and a considerably boring-er job." Liyah would say that the jury's still out on Daniel's clothing taste, but Neen is also no stranger to a wildly printed button-down.

"I literally have no idea who you're talking about."

Neen's eyes go wide as if Liyah's confusion is unimaginable, pulling out their phone. "The hot orthopedic surgeon on *Grey's*!"

Liyah rolls her eyes. "If this is all an elaborate ruse to get me to watch your medical dramas, it's not going to work."

"You'll want to watch every episode when you see Dr. Kim."

They waggle their eyebrows, shoving the phone in front of Liyah's face.

The man on the screen makes royal-blue scrubs look much better than they ought to. His hair is straight, smile too symmetrical, and there's no bend in his nose, but Liyah begrudgingly admits that there's more than a passing resemblance in his eyes and jaw. "Fine, whatever. I can sorta see it."

"See! Stupidly good-looking."

"If you think so, then why don't you sleep with him?" Liyah retorts.

"A whole list of reasons, starting with *he's a man* and ending with *he'd probably slip up and moan your name and then I'd be traumatized for life.*" Despite herself, Liyah laughs. "Look, at this point, it's bound to happen. And if it doesn't, it's a missed opportunity."

"Yeah, yeah. He's cute, but he's a friend."

Neen clucks their tongue. "You're not seriously gonna keep your hookup rulebook forever, are you? I know it served its purpose for a time, but I think you can let it go now."

A therapist or two has said as much, but Liyah isn't so sure. "It's gotten me this far."

Neen pauses, sucking in their lip. They could point out that Liyah didn't have the healthiest relationship with sex after the end of her freshman year of college, and it only started improving about two years ago. Or, they could say that she *still* has a total aversion to serious relationships. From the way the silence hangs in the air, she knows they're considering it. But then, they sigh, most likely resolving to bring it up another day. "Just consider bending the rules. For her sake"—they look pointedly at Liyah's crotch as she pulls up her tights—"and let me know if it does happen. Wait—don't flush, I have to pee, too!"

"I'm leaving this stall, now." *And never thinking about*

what I may or may not feel toward or do with Daniel ever again, if I can help it.

"Bye, C-J. Get me a drink!" they call after her.

LIYAH HAS BEEN disappearing on Daniel all night. At the photo booth, after the costume contest winners were announced, and now from the screening of *Night at the Museum*. To be fair, she's also disappearing on everyone else, but with him it feels personal. They make eye contact, and then suddenly she has somewhere pressing to be, even though the event is well-staffed and running smoothly.

He's watching her retreating form when Jordan leans over and whispers, "So . . . Neen is fine as shit."

Daniel supposes it's true. But given Neen doesn't exactly give off the vibe that they're attracted to people of his gender, he's never really thought about it. "And?"

"Just making an observation."

Daniel laughs, turning back to the screen. "Good, because if you do more than that you're gonna get that ego of yours badly bruised."

He looks over, and Jordan's frowning. "Y'all are always on me about how you're not supposed to assume people's sexuality, now I'm supposed to?" he hisses. "They're hot, and I might have a chance."

"I'm not assuming, Liyah told me."

"Fuck."

Yeah, *fuck*. For the first time in their friendship, it feels like Daniel and Jordan are somewhere close to the same page in their sex lives. He could commiserate, but that might lead to mentioning the kiss that supposedly never happened, so it's best left alone. "Sorry, man."

"Yeah, me too," Jordan says with an easy laugh.

They watch for a few minutes before Jordan leans in again. "I don't wanna get on you to talk if you're not feeling it, but I want to check in about Thursday."

Daniel stops breathing, wondering momentarily how Jordan found out about him and Liyah, until he realizes that he's talking about his dad. He swallows. "Oh, um. Yeah. It was good to be with my mom and Kayla."

"Did Alex do his whole pretending to hit on Minji thing?"

"Yeah, but at least he wasn't there the whole time."

Jordan whistles. "Can't blame him. If we weren't friends, I'd be happy to be your stepfather."

This cracks Daniel up, and Jordan laughs along with him. "Cucking my dead dad is low, even for you."

Jordan grins. "My bad," he says, but Daniel knows he did it intentionally, to make him laugh. "You good, man?"

"I'm doing better, actually. We talked about him. I haven't really done that much."

"That's big! I'm proud of you." He waits a bit, but Daniel doesn't feel like there's much more he's ready to say. Jordan shrugs, taking another handful of cheddar popcorn from the bag that rests against his bare stomach.

Another twenty minutes, and still no sign of Liyah. "I'm going to go make sure nothing's gone wrong," he says.

Daniel scours the key spaces, but Liyah's not at either bar, by the DJ, or at the bistro. Some staff members have started to set up the air mattresses, but as best he can tell, Liyah is not among them. Maybe she's gone back to the movie in his absence? But as he passes by a STAFF ONLY door, another option occurs to him.

When he pushes through the plastic sheeting, he finds that the room has been completely transformed since he last saw it. Cave paintings line the walls, and tiny Venus sculptures stand encased in glass on podiums in the center of the room. Liyah's leaning against the wall, directly underneath the freshly printed words ART IN THE UPPER PALEOLITHIC ERA, frowning.

"Thought I might find you here," Daniel says, striding toward her.

She doesn't look up until he's right there, and even then, all she says is, "Hi."

"Hi," he replies.

"Hello."

"Howdy."

"Top of the morning."

That one makes him laugh. "This place looks great. It's really coming together." She nods, bites her lip, then looks to the sky, blinking. "Hey," he whispers, stepping closer. "What's wrong?"

"You're right, it does look great. And my favorite parts are on their way, too. But what if it's not enough? I spearheaded an entire exhibit myself, even put up with Emiliano trying to hold the cave drawing analysis hostage so I would consider including the invention of fireworks—which would be ridiculous, like is this one exhibit supposed to cover literally everything humans have ever done? That's impossible." She exhales. "I'm doing all this work that I'm proud of, and I might not make curator because of membership numbers that aren't even really in my control. I mean, for people who truly hate museums, aren't these events just like wrapping shit in cellophane and putting a bow on it?"

Dance music pulses softly through the walls, bass line vanishing as they speak but distinct when they're quiet. "There are so many people here, Liyah," he tries. "I know the wine night didn't go well, but we've got a do-over in January. And we still have the holiday party before then. The numbers'll go up."

"You don't know that!"

"You're right, I don't. But you just have to trust in the process." Liyah snorts. "What?"

"Nothing," she says.

He steps forward and places his palm flat against the wall next to her Afro. He's so singularly focused on her that he *knows* he's not imagining the way she arches toward him. She doesn't meet his eyes. "There is something you're not telling me," he says.

Daniel sees her breath hitch as she finally looks up at him, feels his heart skip in exact time. "I don't know how you do that, Daniel," Liyah says. "Always expect things to go well, give yourself to the world and hope it doesn't break you. As much as I want to say it's because of everything that's happened since, you were like that when we were kids, too, and I'm not sure I ever was." Her eyes dip lower, she bites her lip. Daniel watches as the white brackets her teeth leave on the brownish pink disappear.

He leans down, heart in his throat. She tilts her chin up. A brief exchange of breath.

"Don't do that!" she spits out, frustrated. Daniel drops his arm, putting a foot of distance between them. "You know we can't go there. It's too risky. What if it's . . . There's too much to lose."

Daniel runs his fingers through the hairs at the back of his head, the only part of his hair that hasn't been gelled to oblivion. "Yeah, okay. That's probably smart." She nods, closing her eyes. "I know this might be . . . but do you want—can I give you a hug?" She nods again, and he wraps his arms around her, her body molding to his. Her arms snake inside his jacket, linking around his lower abdomen, and she relaxes entirely, perfectly conforming against his every plane like a liquid taking the shape of its container. She feels so fucking good in his arms, but he can do it. He can push those thoughts away because he knows what this job means to her and what she means to him. "I really think it's gonna be okay," he whispers. He unclasps his hands, using one to rub her shoulder, the other to trace the indent of her spine.

"Optimism is hard for me," she says into his chest.

Daniel laughs softly. "You don't say?"

"Shut up, Rosenberg." Liyah steps back, reshaping her hair from where his chin deformed it.

"You ready for our sleepover at the museum, round two?" he asks.

"Ready as I'll ever be," she replies.

SSC #11 MEETING NOTES:

Secretary: Jordan

- Basketball
  - From Daniel: the Bulls are going to suck this season due to new-ish draft pick rules
    - Jordan confirms
    - Liyah accuses Jordan+Daniel of fair-weather fandom
      - This is offensive
    - Siobhan uses House Rule #8 to call time
- Work
  - Nobody feels like talking about it this week
    - Liyah: "Amen" (pronounced Jewishly like Ah-main)
    - Liyah+Daniel object to the phrase "pronounced Jewishly"
- Dating
  - Jordan+Liyah+Daniel: no comment
  - From Siobhan: so far, Liyah is more right about dating apps than Jordan
    - Several "luck of the Irish jokes"
    - One "does the carpet match the drapes" question despite her being blond and not ginger
    - SSC will select two matches for her to ask out next, Siobhan will report back
- Chanukah Party at Liyah's for next SSC
  - No, two from now. My bad

- No rule additions

SSC #12 MEETING NOTES

Secretary: Daniel

- Work
  - Jeff is an enormous asshole
    - Siobhan backs up Liyah on his assholery, but suggests Liyah ask for help in the future
      - Daniel seconds this. Liyah didn't tell him or Siobhan that he was still sending rude emails about membership numbers
      - Jordan didn't know about them at all
      - Liyah says everybody has to take a tequila shot with her if they insist on going through her character flaws
      - "Yes, even in light of Rule #7"
- Dating
  - Jordan has successfully been single for a month. Cheers.
  - Siobhan's most recent date, picked by Jordan, was not awful, but would probably get along better with Jordan than her
    - "Still progress!"—Liyah
  - Daniel and Liyah think we shouldn't have to talk about this every week.
- For some reason, a Rule #11 cap on Liyah making fun of Daniel is vetoed by the group
  - "Ha!"—Liyah
  - Siobhan and Jordan clarify that it's only because it would be a bitch and a half to enforce
    - "Ha your face!"—Daniel
    - Liyah does signature eye roll
      - She claims this is not her signature. Everyone disagrees

- No rule additions

CHAPTER 17

"**HEAR** me out: kimchi latkes," is the first thing Daniel says when Liyah opens the door. He sets a five-pound bag of russet potatoes and three liter-sized mason jars of bubbling fermented cabbage on Liyah's counter.

"I told you it's just Siobhan and Jordan, right?" Liyah smirks, tearing open the mesh sack and depositing the potatoes into a colander for washing.

Daniel laughs. "Well played. Are you going to hear me out?"

"You're suggesting that we slice some kimchi, mix it with grated potatoes and flour and egg, and then fry it?"

Daniel hesitates. "Yes?"

Liyah lets him stew for a moment before relinquishing her urge to grin. "In what world would that not be delicious?"

He chuckles, shaking his head and relaxing his shoulders. "You had me worried for a minute there," he says, and gets to work.

Liyah is more than happy to play sous-chef and be saved from dodging the splattering oil from the hot pan. If she's being honest, it's also a joy to watch Daniel cook. He's so lost in the ritual of it that she doesn't have to pretend she's not staring. The sleeves of his menorah-printed button-down are rolled up (naturally), the rounded ends of jellyfish tentacles on his forearms on display. She only teases him for it once. He furrows his brow and sweeps his tongue over his bottom lip in concentration and a stray lock of hair keeps falling in front of his face.

"This is how my parents met," Liyah says absently as she places another tray of latkes in the oven to keep warm.

"Your goyishe dad made your Jewish mom latkes?"

Liyah frowns. "First of all, if that is supposed to imply that you are making me latkes, as opposed to this being a team effort, you're an ass." Daniel laughs. *Typical.* "Second, no. I meant Chanukah in general. He saw her lighting the menorah in her dorm room window at U-dub and demanded to know who this white girl celebrating Kwanzaa alone was. So she told him the story of Chanukah. Not the miracle of the oil—she explained how that's the sanitized version for children and that the original miracle was how three hundred Jews were able to fight off their occupiers, but celebrating war and death isn't in line with Jewish values so we do the light thing instead. And, you know, every religion has a winter festival of lights so it's just universal human spirituality. Safe to say, he was enamored."

Daniel laughs. "Now that you've told me, I can't really imagine the people who made you meeting any other way."

"Good story, huh? He grew up in Clarke County, Alabama. Not a lot of Jews out there. Not that he grew up celebrating Kwanzaa, either, but he had heard of it."

They fall into silence, and Liyah watches that bit of hair come loose once again. After the third failed attempt to shake it out of his eyes, Liyah takes pity and washes the eggy mess from her hands. "Come here," she says, and Daniel does a half-squat to bring himself to her level. She brushes the offending strands up, her fingers ghosting against his forehead, and does her best to tuck them into place. She's focusing solely on his hair, but she can feel his eyes on her, and her heart pumps harder in her chest.

"Thanks," he says, barely audible over the sizzle of the pancakes, and she makes eye contact at last.

Here's the thing: Daniel is beautiful. She remembers the first time she noticed it: the summer she turned eleven, during Sechiah. They, along with Gross and Michal, were competing to see who could hold their breath the longest. Liyah and Daniel were the last two underwater, but she surfaced seconds before he did. And when he popped up, hair slicked to his forehead, droplets dangling from his impossibly thick eyelashes, Liyah forgot how to tread for a moment and swallowed a bunch of water trying to come back up for air. She was so embarrassed, she wouldn't talk to him for the rest of the day, and he assumed it was because she was a sore loser. Right now, his gaze flickering down to her lips, she's taking in those eyelashes and the cut of his jaw and the softness in his eyes and the golden undertones of his skin all at once and it's exactly how it was that first time. Too much.

And yet she can't look away. If he were the sun, she'd readily burn her retinas.

"Liyah." Daniel's voice comes out strained, and she loses her breath.

There's a knock at the door, and Liyah jumps back, scrambling to answer it.

"We come bearing drinks!" Siobhan and Jordan hold up their respective bottles of whiskey and gin.

"Perfect, come on in."

Siobhan pulls Liyah aside as Jordan calls a "Hey man, want a gin and tonic?" and saunters over to the kitchen.

She presses the back of her hand to Liyah's forehead. "You feeling okay, love? You're a bit red in the cheeks."

"I've been standing over a hot stove, it's to be expected," Liyah lies.

Daniel whips around, waving the spatula at Liyah. "I've been doing the frying, don't try to take credit."

"Well, I've been by the heat mixing the batter. By hand, might I add," Liyah retorts.

"That's nothing. I'm doing all the hard work, and I've got the oil burns to prove it."

Liyah rolls her eyes. "You're such a baby." She makes her way over to her Bluetooth speaker and puts on her Chanukah party playlist, which consists of whatever alternative R&B she's been listening to recently and the only three holiday-specific songs she knows.

And like that, the tension between them dissipates.

BY THE TIME the three candles in the chanukiah are nothing but colorful, waxy stubs, Siobhan is a few decibels louder than usual, having failed to curb her cocktail consumption after finding the kimchi latkes too spicy to eat. Daniel and Jordan had managed to hold in their white people jokes, but Liyah had not, and to her credit, Siobhan seemed genuinely amused.

The North Carolina–bred chivalry in Jordan has yet to be frozen out by the Chicago winters, and he calls an Uber as he helps Siobhan into her furry pink coat. "I'm sorry to leave you two to clean," he says looking back to Siobhan, who is leaning against Liyah's wall for support.

Daniel shakes his head, offering a "You're good, man" as Liyah waves him off.

"I knew what I was getting into when I offered to host." She hugs Jordan goodbye first, then Siobhan. "Text me the moment you're home."

"Well, I'm sure I'll be scarlet about this tomorrow, but I

had a wonderful night. Thanks for hosting, love." She leans in and gives Liyah an audible kiss on the cheek.

"The moment you get home. I mean it."

"Yes, sir!" Siobhan lazily salutes and waltzes out the door, Jordan trailing her and wearing a concerned frown.

Liyah slides the dead bolt into place with a satisfying click, and Daniel is alone with her once again. They silently go about clearing the table, eventually moving on to trade turns scrubbing and drying the pile of dishes in the sink.

This shouldn't feel weird. They've been doing well—at least he thought—since his dad's Yahrzeit. A bit of uncertainty that night on her rooftop, and again on Halloween, sure, but since then they've interacted with ease. Tonight, watching her joke and laugh and poorly sing along to Adam Sandler's "The Chanukah Song" after that moment in the kitchen . . .

It's broken him. It feels like every single hair on his body is standing up, his awareness of her heightened with her every move. She's wearing this stupid baggy sweater with *Let's Get Lit!* emblazoned across her chest above a cartoon menorah, and she's quite possibly the sexiest woman he's ever seen. With each accidental finger touch as a newly cleaned dish is exchanged, the air grows thicker.

Just before he suffocates, Liyah's phone buzzes, slicing through the heady silence.

She abandons the pot and dishrag to check it. "Siobhan is home and has taken some Advil with a lot of water."

"That's good," Daniel mumbles, his words coming out raspy—as if he hasn't spoken in hours or days rather than mere minutes—and he turns to look at her.

Liyah's eyes skate over his features, lingering at his lips, and he thinks—no, he *knows*—that she feels the denseness of the space between them. "Daniel," she says in a voice he's never heard before, and something knotted inside him comes undone.

"Liyah," he starts, pausing to dry his hands on the dish towel and take a deep breath. He steps toward her, tentatively placing his hand at the small of her back. She blinks, inhaling sharply, but doesn't move away from him. There're a million reasons why he shouldn't say what he's about to say, not the least of them being how she reacted last time. After what feels like an eternity, the sheer desire thrumming through his body wins over. "Do you want me to kiss you?"

She exhales, still frozen in place. "We said we weren't going to do this."

Daniel swallows, nodding. "You're right."

"That wasn't a no," Liyah says.

A slow smile spreads across his face. "Alright, then, I'll ask you again: do you want me to kiss you?"

Her lips part, her eyes widening in a way that almost looks pained. "Please," she whimpers, and tilts her chin toward him.

Daniel closes the gap gently, softly pressing his lips to hers as his hand divulges the intensity of his want by roughly drawing her to him. Liyah presses right back, rising to her tiptoes to get better access, the movement causing her body to slide firmly against his. Her teeth graze his bottom lip, and he groans, kissing her back with full force, tongues tangling, hands finding bellies and hips and necks. Her fingernails skate down his spine and *fuck* he's hard already and he can't even be embarrassed because Liyah's making these soft moans that get louder as his lips latch onto her neck, and when he leans back, her eyes are closed, her face relaxed in that familiar, blissfully lost look he loves so much. He lifts her onto the countertop, and she wraps her legs around him, bringing them closer together, heels digging into his hamstrings.

I've never been this turned on before, he thinks. But that can't be true, can it? He's slept with a fair number of women, and yet . . .

One of his greedy hands slides under Liyah's sweater and crawls up her skin until it reaches the lace of her bra. The other hooks under her thigh, pulling her hips into him even though they're already as close as they can possibly be. A hard nipple presses into his palm as he kneads, and Liyah digs her nails into his bicep. The back of his throat emits an unfamiliar sound, almost like a growl, and Liyah's tongue plunges deeply into his mouth as if she's trying to taste it.

Suddenly, she breaks the kiss, and Daniel's entire body stills. Her eyelids squeeze shut, and she opens her mouth to speak, but says nothing.

Daniel searches her face. "Are you okay? Do you want me to stop?" She's still quiet, breathing heavily. He drops his hands and pulls away, but she whines and uses her legs to bring him back against her, shaking her head.

She's just as overwhelmed as I am, he realizes, and laughs softly, lifting his hands to trace gentle circles on her thighs. "Whenever you're ready, let me know what you want from me. Unless you want me to forget we did this, because I don't think there's anything I could do to make that happen."

He's laughing. How is he laughing?

Liyah is unmoored from reality to the point of being unable to form a sentence, and here's Daniel, sanguine, smiling, the only sign of disarray being the state of his hair. She's not even sure why she's like this; she's not exactly a blushing virgin. It can't just be that Daniel's a good kisser (phenomenal, actually), because she's enjoyed many good kissers before. And none of them have made her feel like she's falling apart at the seams.

His fingers are still running over her thighs, and after a few seconds (or maybe minutes, she can't be sure at the moment), Liyah bites out: "I didn't forget the first time."

Daniel laughs, the corners of his eyes crinkling. "Neither did I."

"Oh." Her heart flutters a bit. "You're wearing too much clothing," she says, and finally has a large enough shred of composure to laugh with him.

His calloused fingers find their way back to the bare skin of her stomach. She remembers noticing the roughness against her skin that first time he touched her at Kinley's anniversary party. Now, she knows they're from his evenings at Chicago Rocks. It's the first time she's ever articulated that thought in its entirety, but it makes her see the pads of his fingers differently. They're an emblem of his friendship with Jordan, a sign of a major part of his life.

That's what it is to let someone in, have someone go from a shadowy middle school memory to full-fledged *Daniel*. It's being able to see a bigger picture from a singular puzzle piece. Funny how that goes.

"And what would you like me to do about that?" he asks, his lips stretching into that crooked smile. He reaches his free hand up to her face and brushes his thumb across her cheekbone, pressing gently on each of her moles.

"Think of it as an extension of rolling your cuffs. If you keep going, eventually you'll get there."

He releases her (this is not her intended result) to roll his right sleeve farther. It catches midway up his bicep, and he makes an exaggerated frown. "Looks like I'm stuck."

"I have to do everything myself, don't I?" she complains, and claws at the buttons until his shirt falls open, slipping it off his shoulders to reveal a delicious expanse of chest, a dark trail of hair on his abdomen. Without thinking, she presses a kiss to the body of the jellyfish, then a bite for good measure. She reaches out and traces the tentacles as they wrap around his arm, something she now realizes she has always wanted to do. "Why a jellyfish?"

"Got stung by one on a family vacation when I was little. I thought it was funny."

"Your dad wasn't mad?" The words fall from her lips before she thinks better of it. She's never more desperately wished for a thicker filter between her brain and mouth. If it sways Daniel, though, he doesn't show it.

"A little, at first. He was worried that I was rejecting Judaism. But when he saw I was still doing the major holidays, he got over it. I think it helped that he thought it was funny, too."

She bites her lip, looking up at him, feeling warmth spread across her chest, down to her belly. "I'm glad."

"Me too. Now," Daniel says, his head dipping so that he can move his lips right against her earlobe. "Is it okay if we don't talk about our parents?"

Liyah laughs and grabs his jaw, guiding his face toward hers until she can capture his lips in a kiss. "Fine by me," she says against his mouth, pulling back only so that she can remove the ugly Chanukah sweater she found on a clearance rack.

"God, Liyah," he says, voice gravelly, as he takes in the sight of her topless.

"There was once a time when you saw me in less every single day," she challenges.

Daniel shakes his head, laughing. "One: I can't believe you want to count seeing each other in swimsuits when we were preteens. I think you know this is different." And she does. Even the picture Neen sent of Daniel shirtless at the pool party is nothing compared to seeing him now, when he's in this partial state of undress just for her. She wants to argue, but her skin feels hot under his gaze, and she can't bring herself to do it. "And two: even if I had seen you like this already, I'd still want to stop and look."

Liyah's lips part, releasing only her breath, because she can't begin to formulate a response.

He waits for her to speak, leaning closer until their noses just barely touch.

It's that tiny bit of contact, so small that it's almost nothing, that destroys what's left of her self-control. "I want you," she says before she can hold herself back. The words are throaty and desperate and nothing like her usual voice, and it's not quite sexy, at least not in the way it should be. Because she doesn't append the words *inside me,* nor does she say *to touch me* and it's almost like that isn't even what she means. She just says *you,* not as in his touch but as in *him,* as in Daniel as a whole, as in he found her loose thread and is going to tug until she completely unravels.

It must be the right thing to say, because his eyes darken and they're back to kissing and unzipping and *feeling* until they're out of breath and nearly naked in her kitchen, her bikini-cut underwear the only thing separating her from the countertop. He presses his lips in a trail down her stomach, peppers kisses on the underside of her thighs, moaning as he removes the last barrier between her and the cold quartz. His tongue and fingers move expertly against her until she cries out, wanting more. More touch, more closeness, more of *him.*

Daniel stands and pulls Liyah against him, lifting her up and stumbling over discarded clothes to her bedroom, where he lays her down and points at her bedside table, one eyebrow quirked. She nods, and he rummages through the drawer, extracting a foil square. He tucks it between his teeth as he pulls down his boxer briefs, doing an adorable little hop to spring free of them.

Liyah sharply exhales at the sight of him, standing naked before her, smiling and holding eye contact as he rolls the condom over himself. *Daniel.* He breaks almost every rule she's ever made for herself. But there's not a chance in hell that she's not going to do it.

Her ambivalence (true meaning, not colloquial) must be apparent because he kneels on the bed beside her and takes her hand. "Are you okay?" he says for the second time tonight. "Do you still want to do this?"

Liyah nods fervently. "Yes, and very, very much."

He lines himself up with her, presses a kiss to her forehead, and scoops her hips off the bed with his hand at the small of her back. "Good, because I want you so badly that it hurts."

She doesn't have the chance to return his words, to tell him just how much it hurts, because he presses into her, and her jaw falls open with a silent moan.

As he presses farther, Liyah squeezes her eyes so tightly shut that she sees stars. There's a moment of stillness as Daniel waits for her to adjust. Or maybe for himself, too, judging by the hiss of breath she feels rush past her earlobe. His weight on her is all-consuming. So good. *So, so good.*

It's not just his weight. It's *everything*. Every sense, every thought is a hazy cloud of Daniel. Part of her, even now, even after months of wanting (and wanting not to want), can't believe that it's Daniel Rosenberg she's doing this with. Who she is letting have so much of her, who is giving her so much of himself in return. Her skin is truly on fire now, made up not of cells but of tiny loci of heat. She might disintegrate.

"Daniel," she whispers, voice strained.

"Liyah," he says back. Like he's in a cloud of her, too. She didn't leave her own atmosphere behind to enter his. They switched.

Or maybe blended together, and now they're both learning to breathe in this new composition of air.

He moves slowly, carefully, as though she's made of glass

at first, and she's desperate for more, so she arches and grinds until he hears her plea and meets her where she wants him, quickening the pace, displaying the same urgency she feels.

That's what it's like the whole time, a call and response, a conversation between their bodies as they change positions and bury themselves within one another. *This is how all language should be from now on,* Liyah thinks. Touch. Waiting for equal and opposite reaction.

"Fuck, Liyah," Daniel says through gritted teeth, his breath fanning over the back of her neck from where he spoons her, his fingers moving over her in perfect time with his hips. She reaches back and threads her fingers into his hair, pulling him in, feeling him kiss her neck as the conversation comes to a close, Daniel holding her tightly as their bodies tense and release around one another.

There's a lot that Liyah could say after she goes slack but given that she recently predicted the obsolescence of verbal communication, the "That was . . . wow" she manages is rather impressive.

Daniel sighs into the crook of her neck. "Wow, indeed." A kiss, pressed to her shoulder. "Thank you."

"Some might say I should be thanking you as well."

She can feel his lips stretch into a smile against her skin. "You're welcome. But I more meant thank you for trusting me."

At this, Liyah's chest constricts painfully, trying to contain the thousand emotions threatening to pour out. If she holds still enough, maybe she won't have to feel any of them. Maybe she'll be frozen in this singular moment, and it will consume her until it is the only point in time she knows: past, present, future. Here, wrapped up in someone who holds her with kindness, will be the only way she has ever been touched, the only way she'll ever be touched again. Infinite in either direction. And impossible as it may be, if she told Daniel that was what she wanted, she knows he would try to hold still as long as he could, just to give her that moment of peace. Because he's right, she trusts him. She presses her fist to her sternum, as if that will hold her closed, and is silent for a minute.

Then, Daniel still inside her, Liyah begins to cry.

CHAPTER 18

IN seconds, Daniel pulls back and turns Liyah to face him, wiping at the tears as they spill over her cheeks. "Did I hurt you?" he asks, his chest tightening at the thought.

Liyah shakes her head.

No relief accompanies this revelation, because the second scenario coming to mind is worse than the first. "Okay, then what's wrong?"

She takes a gulp of air, giving a sad smile. "I'm just disappointed that you don't have a train tattooed on your ass after all," she says, tears still falling.

Despite himself, he lets out a short laugh. "As tragic as that is, Liyah, it's not why you're crying." He cups the back of her neck and presses a kiss to her temple. "I'm not going to force you to tell me anything if you don't want to. I just want to be very, very clear that if you do, you can tell me. Anything."

Liyah nods, drying her cheeks with the back of her hand. "Can you give me a minute?"

Daniel hesitates, but releases her, and makes his way to her bathroom to clean himself up. Behind the closed door, his fingernails dig into his palms, and he tries to steady his breathing. If he's right—and God, he hopes he isn't—he's done all that he can do. *Make yourself available as a safe space, but don't push,* Kayla said, when she'd given her very career-specific version of The Talk.

Not knowing how long of a minute she needs, he opens the top drawer below her bathroom sink and is pleased to find a spare toothbrush still in its packaging. He busies himself by brushing his teeth and washing his face, focusing on the feeling of the bristles against his gums and the water splashing on his skin instead of making himself sick speculating. Eventually, there's no more washing up to do, and he makes his way back to Liyah's bed.

"Can I hold you?" he asks as he sits, the mattress sinking below his weight.

"Yes, but let me wash up first," she says, voice small, and he's left alone in her bed.

The minutes she's gone pass slowly, and Daniel wonders how he'll be able to sleep if she decides not to talk to him. Let alone how he'll be able to sleep if she does.

He knows she's returned when the light switch flips and they're cast into darkness. She climbs back into the bed and curls up in front of him and he gingerly drapes his arm over her, not sure if she'll still want his touch. Then her fingers lace through his and pull his arm tightly around her, and he lets out the breath he's been so tightly holding.

Time trudges onward and Liyah's breathing slows. Daniel is sure she's gone to sleep, but finally, she says, "It was my first best friend in college."

Daniel gulps and gives her hand a squeeze.

"You knew, didn't you? You figured it out?" His chest tightens again.

He rubs his thumb over the back of her hand. "I have an

idea, maybe. But if you don't want me to know, I'll assume whatever I think is wrong."

The breath she takes is deep enough to raise and lower his arm with the expansion and contraction of her rib cage. "Tale as old as coed college, I guess. Boy likes girl. Girl doesn't like boy. Boy waits until girl is extremely drunk and takes her back to his dorm room. Bit cliché, no?"

Some people process sexual trauma with humor, Kayla said. It still catches him off guard. He just squeezes her hand again, because even if he tried, he wouldn't be able to laugh.

"Even more cliché is that I didn't want to admit it to myself at first. Because how could that happen to *me*? *I* am a liberated, independent Black woman who can take care of myself." A wry laugh that Daniel fails to return rings out flat. "Stupid joke. Anyway. Chalked up all my queasiness about the night to having *gone there* with such a close friend, never mind that I vaguely remembered asking to stop and not being listened to." Her voice catches. "No, I didn't report it, yes, I pretended to remain friends with him for a few weeks before suddenly ghosting and feeling guilty. Eventually I went to a therapist and did all that 'admitting what happened and learning healthy coping mechanisms so I don't self-harm via hypersexuality' da da da da da. Now I'm in tip-top shape save for the fact that I apparently burst into tears the first time I sleep with a friend, so that's fun." Her voice is monotone, as if she is a mere observer. Daniel has no idea how she does it. "Sorry you had to witness that," Liyah finishes.

His stomach twisting, Daniel shakes his head. "Liyah, thank you for telling me. You have nothing to apologize for."

"Sorry."

"Liyah—"

"For apologizing." She laughs, and this time he laughs, too. She rolls over to face him for the first time since she started crying. "Be honest, is that what you thought was wrong?"

Daniel pauses, unsure of what she wants to hear. Eventually, he goes with the truth. "More or less, yeah."

"How?"

"You know how Kayla's a therapist? Well, working with survivors is one of her specialty areas." He leaves out *why* she ended up doing the work that she does, which probably helped him recognize what was happening quicker than any crash course in dealing with disclosures ever could.

"Ah, more tricks of the trade from Kayla Rosenberg. You really got lucky with that one; some of us pay by the hour."

"It's probably a good idea for me to see someone who doesn't share most of my DNA and life experience," he says, parroting Kayla's perennial pitch that eventually got him into Dr. Espinosa's office. "But, yes, I am very lucky. Do you need anything from me? I can get you a glass of water or listen more if you want to talk." He smooths the baby hairs peeking out from her wrap.

"Nope, I'm good. Too much talking after our enthusiastic rendition of 'Chanukah Oh Chanukah.'"

"Okay." Then, sheepishly: "Is there anything I can do—or avoid doing—in the future? Any ways you don't want to be touched?"

LIYAH'S EYEBROWS RISE, simultaneously shocked and pleased that she hasn't scared him off. If any of her previous hookups had cried in her arms after the first time they'd had sex . . . well, she would be kind in the moment, but she probably would've never seen them again. Maybe Neen's right, and this is the difference between sleeping with people you hardly speak to and having an actual *friend* with benefits. She bites back a grin, unable to pass up an opportunity to poke fun. "What makes you think there's an 'in the future'?"

"God, no, I'm not saying . . . I'm not trying to be presumptive. Just, you know, *if*—"

"Daniel, you're good. I'm teasing." She watches his shoulders relax. "I don't think so. But I'll let you know, okay?"

"Okay," he says.

Liyah wakes up at a pre-daylight hour of the morning with a painfully full bladder and Daniel's more-than-breathless-than-snore against her neck. On her way to the bathroom, she spies her phone, carelessly left by the sink instead of plugged in by her bed. It's on its last dregs of juice, just enough for her to fire off a few messages to Neen:

Liyah

Had sex with Daniel (you told me so)

Neen

congrats!!!!!!!!!!!!!!!!!!!!!! !!!!!!!!!!!!!!!!!!!!!!!!!!!!!!

Liyah

Cried while genitals were still in contact (top 5 most mortifying moments of my life, should you need to know for a future biography)

Told him about what happened freshman year

Phone on 1%, talk tomorrow. Much love

Thankfully, the typing bubble doesn't give way to a message before the screen goes black. She connects it to the charger at her dining table and turns it facedown lest the start-up screen distract her on the way back to her room. In the bathroom, she leaves the light off, not wanting to be confronted with her reflection.

So, this is what it's like, Liyah thinks as she scrubs her hands in the dark, *telling someone who is neither Neen nor an accredited mental health professional.* Weird, numb, and unplanned are not the adjectives she expected. Once the tears fell, telling him became inevitable, if only for the sake of her dignity. What she can't figure out is why she started crying in the first place.

She creeps back into the room and does her best to climb deftly into bed without disturbing Daniel. Just as she makes it under the covers, he opens his eyes and snakes his arms around her, drawing her back flush against his torso.

"Please don't tell me to forget about this tomorrow," he murmurs.

"Daniel." She says his name slowly, carefully, steadying herself over the irregular race of her heart. "You're the one who suggested it last time."

He shrugs. "It seemed like that was what you wanted. And you're the one who said we couldn't go there."

"Well, regardless, it's not what I want now."

"And what is that?"

"To go the fuck to sleep." She pauses, long enough to be playful but not enough to be torturous. "And then, hopefully, to have a lot of exceptionally good sex."

He hums near her ear, his fingers lazily circling her navel. "That sounds nice. I'd like that, too."

"Yeah?"

"Yeah." He kisses the crook of her neck. "Any idea where I could find a partner?"

Liyah laughs. "Well played."

The next time she wakes, her room is filled with full-fledged, ten-in-the-morning daylight, and the bed is empty beside her. She's not disappointed at Daniel's absence, per se. Maybe a little surprised. Nights alone are standard for doing things casually, and Liyah's snuck out of many a hookup's apartment. It just hadn't seemed like Daniel's style.

She undoes her hair wrap and removes the silk scrunchie she stole from Daniel weeks ago. As she climbs out of bed, she relishes the minor muscle aches that accompany a night well spent. Even the mild soreness between her legs—it's been a while since she's had penetrative sex, and Daniel's body is more than proportionate—is a welcome one.

Until she remembers the end of the night, and her cheeks heat with embarrassment.

Not my finest moment, she thinks as she pulls on the Chanukah sweater that's been folded, along with her corduroy skirt and tights, and placed on top of her dresser. This seems much more like the Daniel Rosenberg she knows. She'll shoot him a thank-you text because she appreciates the care. And because she might be able to glean how his opinion of her has changed from his response.

Or rather, Neen will, when Liyah reads it aloud over FaceTime later.

When Liyah rounds the corner, her kitchen comes into view. Along with Daniel's bare back. He's standing over the stove in nothing but Calvin Klein boxer briefs, a steaming mug of coffee in one hand, spatula in the other.

"You're up," he says.

"I thought you'd left," Liyah says at the same time.

His crooked smile falters. "Should I have?"

She surveys the spread: sautéed veggie sausages piled on one plate, several pancakes on another, and a fresh mug of coffee with her name on it (literally—Neen made it during their ceramics phase). "You made me coffee and breakfast, so I'm going to go with no."

The smile returns in full force. "Just returning the favor. Also, you have twenty-three messages from Neen."

Liyah's eyes go wide. "Oh my God."

Daniel laughs, flipping the last pancake onto the stack and turning the dial on the stove to off. "I didn't read them, I promise. I saw the excessive notifications when I went to plug my phone in."

Liyah stares into her coffee as she takes a sip, an action which is in no way related to her need to avoid eye contact.

"Right, right. Liyah rule number one."

This forces her hand, and she meets his gaze. "Which is?"

"Do not approach unless well-fed and appropriately caffeinated."

A catch-22: any of her usual witticisms will only prove his point. Liyah takes this fact as more of a personal affront than the remark itself. "I'd tell you that you're the unkosher end of a cow, but that would only play into your unnecessary and inaccurate rule-making."

Daniel snorts. "Good thing you didn't tell me that, then, or you might have to admit I'm right," he says, stepping closer to her, his hands looping around her hips and pulling her flush against him. She suddenly regrets having partially dressed; she wishes she could feel his *skin*. He smiles, leaning forward, waiting for her to meet him, and then drawing her into a languid kiss.

From the heat that rises to her every surface, it's clear that Daniel's touch isn't a *do it once, it's out of your system* type of drug but rather a *do it once, immediately escalate to intravenous injection*.

She breaks away with a deep inhale. "I'd say that counts as an approach," Liyah notes in a *gotcha* tone and plucks a veggie sausage from the plate. "Breaking your own rules, aren't you?"

"You've already had some coffee, so you're halfway there. I'm still avoiding any sudden movements."

"You'd better watch it, or this"—she gestures with the breakfast sausage—"will be the only thing of its shape you ever see go near my mouth again." She takes an emphatic bite, and Daniel grimaces.

"What a way with words. Eat your pancakes."

And she does, stopping partway to let him know how delicious they are, if her moans of delight aren't indication enough. Then, because Daniel heeds her words and stops comparing her temperament to that of a feral animal, Liyah finds herself climbing onto his lap and sliding her hand into his boxer briefs. She starts the day with him in her mouth (and under her and over her and behind her) and it is the kind of start to the day that she wouldn't mind making a habit.

When they're collapsed on the couch, chests rising and falling with rapid breaths, Liyah surprises herself by asking what he's doing later.

"I've gotta feed Sweet Potato, but other than that, nothing. Why?" he says, fingers resting on her belly.

"Care for a trip to the Field?"

"Developing-slash-designing on a Saturday? Or, no— you've come to the dark side and want to spend your weekends on marketing," he says with a laugh.

"No, I mean like going to the exhibitions. I can get us in for free." She adds the last bit as if the no-cost admission can rid her of her growing embarrassment. This is not something you ask of a casual hookup, is it? Liyah certainly hasn't done it before.

But Daniel is her friend. Which supersedes the benefits,

she tells herself, and she decides that she has no reason to feel weird about it.

"Alright," Daniel says, sitting upright. "I'll go put on a clean change of non-holiday-themed clothes. See you at your stop in two hours?"

That sounds like the length of time Neen's about to keep her on the phone, but if she puts them on speaker while she showers . . . "Perfect."

CHAPTER 19

ALEX whistles as soon as Daniel steps through the door. "Welcome back! I've missed you dearly."

His roommate's cheeky grin gives Daniel pause as he slips out of his shoes and strips off his coat. Sweet Potato sniffs at him curiously before letting him scoop her up. "Missed you, too." He passes a Tupperware container brimming with leftover latkes, and Alex rubs his hands lasciviously before popping the lid.

"Not you, sweet thing. I was talking to your 'I just had sex' face. I was getting worried I'd never see him again."

Daniel laughs. There's no real point in denying it. "That bad, huh?"

Alex vigorously nods, his mop of curly hair bouncing. "You stink of it, too. Even Sweet Potato noticed," he says.

"Thanks for feeding her, by the way." He neglected to tell Liyah that he had already texted Alex when she asked if he was free. Better to keep some cards close to his chest. "Also, please pop those in the toaster oven. Eating them soggy is gross."

Alex shrugs and takes a bite. "Anytime, but especially if

it's going to get you laid. Was it everything you ever hoped for? Is the sun shining brighter? Did birds sing to you on the walk back? A new feeling in the air?"

"I think I got windburn on my cheeks, if that counts." Daniel can feel his lips sliding into a satisfied smirk, though, and it's enough to make Alex slow clap.

"Bravo, dude, bravo. You tell Jordan yet?"

Daniel shoots him a warning look. Alex mimes zipping his lips. "I'd like at least a *chance* at a second time." He chuckles to himself. "Or third, technically."

Alex whoops. "Finally, man! I can't single-handedly be carrying the orgasms for this household."

"I'm going to shower and change. In part because I probably do stink, but mostly because I want this conversation to end."

"Message received," Alex says, and carries the cold latkes back to his room for his midday nap.

Toweling off his freshly cleaned body fifteen minutes later, Daniel notices little red crescent moons on his bicep. He twists to view his back in the mirror, and sure enough, Liyah's nails have left thin red lines bracketing his spine. He remembers her fingers scraping down his back this morning, sinking deeper when he groaned in her ear, but he'd been too focused on the way she tightened around him and fluttered her eyelids shut in pure bliss when he hit the right angle to realize she was leaving marks.

Goddamn.

He surveys himself in the mirror. Alex is right: there's an air of smugness written all over his features, but he can't help it. Touching Liyah is something else. *Being touched by* Liyah is something else.

Back in his room, he sifts through the various button-down shirts in the casual dress side of his closet. He spends a few minutes waffling between a white one with painted oranges and a light-wash denim. The orange pattern seems a bit sunny for November, but the first time he wore it in front of Liyah, she spent half the night sneaking glances at his chest. He pulls it off the hanger and slips it on.

A judgmental meow comes from the ginger loaf on his bed.

Daniel narrows his eyes. "What?"

Sweet Potato makes no additional noise, but her look says *five minutes to pick out a shirt, huh? It's a museum, not New York Fashion Week.*

He digs through his drawers, pulls on his favorite pair of Levi's, then sits next to Sweet Potato on the edge of his bed so he can roll on thick socks. She stirs at the movement, refolding her limbs underneath her belly and giving him that same censorious look. "I'm being cool, I just like taking my time on the weekends. I wear a suit five days a week, you know."

Sure, we'll go with that, she blinks in response. *Are you going to take twenty minutes for the shoes?*

Daniel gently scratches behind her ears. "It's a human thing, you wouldn't understand. Because you're a cat. Who I'm talking to. I've officially started talking to my cat," he realizes aloud.

Yeah, you're totally playing it cool, she stares, and Daniel gets up in search of his high-tops before she can look any other quips his way.

LIYAH ARRIVES AT Division slightly out of breath twenty minutes after the agreed-upon meeting time and finds that Daniel is walking up as well.

"Right on time." He draws her into a hug but doesn't try for a kiss. *A good thing,* she thinks. It means he probably has the right idea about them. He's got on a beanie that's rolled so it only covers the tops of his ears and a matching green scarf that she hasn't seen him wear before. It's a beautiful color against his golden skin.

"I thought I was running late."

He flashes his crooked smile. "I factored in the expected time delay."

"What is that, Liyah rule number two?" she asks as they move through neighboring turnstiles.

"Number five."

She rolls her eyes, laughing.

They're on the train for two minutes before she blurts, "We're—this is a friend thing, right? We're friends?"

Their gazes meet for a painfully long moment. "Yes, Liyah, we're friends. Are you feeling weird about the sex? It doesn't have to . . . it can be a one-time thing if that's what you want."

"No!" Too quick, an octave too high. She clears her throat. "No, that's not what I want." Too quiet now. *Fuck.* She tries again. "I just want to make sure that we're on the same page if we're going to keep doing this. Especially since we've still got a few events left as semi-coworkers."

Daniel cracks a smile, resting his elbow on his knee and dropping his chin to his palm. "Is this the Liyah Cohen-Jackson 'Let's Keep It Casual' speech?"

She flicks his thigh. "No! I don't usually spend enough time with someone for them to get the wrong idea."

"Well, I'm honored to be the first. Could use some work, though. May I suggest rehearsing in the mirror?"

"Shut up."

"Yes, Liyah." He nudges her knee with his own. "We'll just be friends."

At the Field, Daniel tells her that he trusts her expertise and gives her free rein. They don't have time to visit every single exhibit before dinner, so she decides on what she views as the bare essentials. It's been a long time since she's walked through the museum as a visitor, and it takes no more than five minutes for giddy excitement to take over. Walking alongside Daniel is like discovering it anew. He engages with each plaque, asks questions about how the spaces were designed, teases Liyah for wanting to go through all the interactive stations even though she has the inside scoop. At first, she thinks he might be humoring her, but he lets out an *aah* when a digitally rendered radiodont floats across the wall in her favorite part of the Evolving Planet exhibit, and she knows he feels the magic, too.

"I get why you love this place. I feel like . . . I don't know. Trying to come up with all these ways to promote it, I managed to miss the forest for the trees," Daniel says, bumping Liyah's elbow as they exit Inside Ancient Egypt.

"Yeah?"

His tongue sweeps out over his bottom lip, leaving it plump and glistening. Liyah tries not to stare. "I mean, I still don't think we're going to win new patrons with promises of SUE's furcula alone. But I can do more to promote what the museum already has to offer, instead of just the events. You really do something great here."

Liyah goes on her tiptoes, cupping his ear and whispering, "Softy."

"Stop trying to ruin my bad-boy reputation," he whispers back. Then, at normal volume: "Where to next, tour guide?"

Liyah's probably smiling like a lunatic, but she's a kid in a candy shop. "I've saved the best for last. Underground Adventure, here we come."

She's not even sure why it's her favorite (larger-than-life soil-residing microbes weren't exactly the focus of her anthropology degrees), but it always has been. It's also definitely for kids, but she genuinely enjoys walking through the mirrored halls and strange lights that claim to shrink her down to less than the size of a penny. She makes Daniel stand next to the giant "ruler" on the wall and snaps a picture. "Only three quarters of an inch tall! Looks like you're going to need some help with the overhead bins next time."

"The sign said the shrinking experiment would be reversed at the end!" he protests.

Liyah shakes her head. "You didn't read the fine print. It only works 99.9999 percent of the time. You could be that one in a million."

Daniel feigns a gasp and clamps his hand over his mouth. "There's nothing I can do about it?"

"Not a thing."

"Then you'd better show me the exhibit. I don't want those seventy-four missing inches to go to waste."

He beams when she laughs, and all it takes is a gentle elbow tug to guide him to the wondrous underground. She shows him the best bits, like the earthworm that comes up from the floor and disappears into the ceiling, the enormous crayfish popping out of a pocket of water, the earwig protecting her eggs.

They've almost made it to the exit when Daniel yelps and jumps back, nearly knocking Liyah to the floor in the process.

When she sees the animatronic spider before him, she doubles over in laughter. "It's . . . not . . . real," she wheezes.

"I see that *now*." Daniel frowns, but there's laughter in his eyes as he pats his body as if to check that his major limbs and organs are intact. Liyah is still laughing. "Looks like I'm alive, thank you very much."

She wipes at the tears leaking out of her eyes, taking calming breaths to slow her shaking body.

Daniel grins. "That thing scared the living sh—" He registers the two toddlers running by him as their parent glares. "—ish. Living *ish* out of me."

And like that, her giggles bubble to the surface again and she's clutching her stomach in laughter. Soon, Daniel can't help but join her. Liyah's standing in the middle of the doorway, and an annoyed museumgoer jostles past her, forcing her into Daniel. His arms find their way around her, and they stand there like that, mirth rippling through them until finally they can hold it together enough to walk out.

Any worry Liyah might've had that sleeping with Daniel would make things weird between them is long gone. Everything is as it was before.

Except now, when Daniel sweeps his tongue across his bottom lip before asking if she wants pizza, she doesn't wonder what it would feel like running along hers instead. She *knows*.

The moment the door to his apartment shuts behind them (the pizzas balanced precariously in his left hand) she tests that memory for accuracy. Her neural networks have precisely captured the feel of his lips against hers, but *God*, the way heat radiates through her body from every point where they touch? Her own mind can't do it justice.

SSC #14 MEETING NOTES

Secretary: Liyah

- Work
  - Jordan's supervisor has been less of a total sleazeball
    - (My words, not his. This is important to note for some reason)
  - Liyah is still tiptoeing around Jeff
    - No, would not like to elaborate
  - Siobhan got a Hill & Mountain ad on Instagram! Very exciting

- Dating
  - Siobhan had a good date with Will last weekend
    - They kissed!
    - (Will be asking for details offline)
  - Jordan and Nisha are OFFICIALLY officially done
    - This is upsetting because he said that they'd been over for a month two weeks ago, but managed to reunite and part in that time
  - Liyah would appreciate it very much if Jordan would stop asking her to contribute to this portion of the meetings
    - "It's not my thing" is, in fact, a perfectly good explanation
    - A snowball has been thrown in hell because Daniel agrees

- Note: Siobhan is leaving for three weeks in Dublin next Saturday (WHICH MEANS SHE IS DESERTING US FOR THE HOLIDAY PARTY LIKE A TERRIBLE FRIEND, but I digress). Jordan will be in Raleigh from three days before Christmas. Everybody out of town New Year's. Next week will be the last Survival Club of the year
  - It is on record that everyone has agreed to tequila shots, so this does not count as any one person's suggestion for Rule #7

- No rule additions

SSC #15 MEETING NOTES

Secretary: ~~Jordan~~ Liyah

- Jordan had tequila and did not take any notes
  - "Because he is a dumbass"—Daniel

- Siobhan will miss us, and we will miss her, too

CHAPTER 20

EVERYONE knows what a holiday party is: halls decked in glittery red and green, eggnog abounds, a nondenominational gift giver with a suspiciously familiar Coca-Cola–red suit. A Christmas party, with an afterthought of inclusivity haphazardly slapped over the name.

Daniel and Liyah decided to go tongue-in-cheek with this event, though, and created a *holiday* party in true form. The entrance to each exhibit is transformed into a different day of the year with a house drink to match. There're sprigs of fir, holly, and spiked eggnog in Stanley Field Hall, of course—Daniel knew they'd never escape without gaying some Yuletide. But the Ronald and Christina Gidwitz Hall of Birds has chocolate-dipped strawberries and rosé for Valentine's Day, and the Grainger Hall of Gems boasts streamers, champagne, and novelty New Year's glasses. There's Earth Day at the Abbott Hall of Conservation, the Fourth of July, Halloween, etcetera.

They're standing at a cocktail table near the opening of Wild Color, an exhibition that Liyah informed him—with an impressive scowl—had been conceived as an Instagram trap but did at least have a UV-fluorescent platypus. It's St. Patrick's Day–themed, swathed in shamrock, and is the only exhibition with two drinks. The first being ice water with enough food coloring to run as green as the Chicago River on the Saturday before March 17. And the second being Irish coffee, which Liyah is currently staring down with naked lust in her eye.

"You want one, don't you?" Daniel asks.

Liyah's attention snaps to him, her mouth slightly ajar. "I shouldn't have caffeine this late, I'll be jittery and spend the rest of the party worrying about membership sign-ups."

"Ever heard of decaf? We made sure that was available," he challenges.

"I can't order decaf, that's embarrassing."

Daniel leans forward, propping his elbow on the green tablecloth. "Ooh, a new Liyah rule. Do tell."

She rolls her eyes. "I'll get my Pacific Northwesterner Card revoked. We're a proud, overcaffeinated people."

"Get the decaf Irish coffee. I'm sure it's equally delicious."

Liyah frowns. "But people will see me when I order!"

Daniel shakes his head in response, backing away.

"What are you doing?"

"You're ridiculous. I'm getting it for you."

He knows she wants to tell him not to, so he stalks off before she gets the chance.

Dark-wash denim approaches her periphery. "That was fast," Liyah says, hurriedly typing out the rest of her email to Jeff before drawing her eyes away from the phone screen.

"Aliyah! I thought that was you."

Is it possible to feel your own blood drain from your face? If so, Liyah does. Although it's not physiologically likely, she's pretty sure a pint of it has clotted into a pit in her stomach.

She'd know his lilting French accent anywhere. Her eyes slide to the nearest exit as her pulse quickens in her ears and throat, and she tastes metal. Why did she choose to stand tucked in a corner, away from the stairs? She should have listened to Daniel and walked through the party like a normal patron, ability to people watch and panic about membership sign-ups be damned. Even if she were willing to leave her bag behind, she cannot make a run for it without causing a scene. Her chest begins to heat.

After what might have been an entire millennium, she looks up. "Hi." She hears the word but doesn't feel it escape her throat, like a stranger has commandeered her vocal cords.

"It's been a while." Liyah reads his smile as smug, even if it's not meant that way. His eyelashes are still long, so long that the tips are bleached blond by the sun. She once found them endearing, said they made him look like a baby cow. He says something more, but she's not registering it. Her eyes flick to the cup in his left hand. A ring on the fourth finger. Gold. Maybe he ended up with Sara from sophomore year. She wouldn't know, she doesn't have him on any of her socials. Sara had always been nice to her. They lived in the same dorm. Liyah would take the first opportunity to bolt every time they spoke, but Sara was still nice to her. Does she still see him as a baby cow?

"Aliyah?"

"What?"

"I was asking if you ended up doing the museum thing."

"Oh, um. Yeah. I work here." She gulps, trying to think of a way out, but her mind keeps coming up blank. Her breathing shallows.

"Well, I'm in town for a consulting project, but I extended my stay to see some friends from Northwestern. Do you remember Luke and Molly?"

She nods vaguely, eyes darting around until they land on Daniel. He's thanking the bartender as he picks up her drink.

"Anyway, maybe we could grab a drink while I'm here."

Liyah's jaw slackens. When she closes it, she shakes her head vigorously. "No, we couldn't."

His smug smile turns downward. "You're not still upset about freshman year, are you? I regret how we left things after—"

"Who's this?" Daniel interrupts, an unfamiliar edge in his voice. He sets the Irish coffee down on the tall table to Liyah's left. She makes no move to touch it. Instead, she focuses her attention entirely on Daniel. It's easier that way. His Adam's apple bobs as he swallows, a muscle in his jaw tightening.

"I'm Jerome. Aliyah and I went to school together. We were quite close for a time."

Daniel looks from him to Liyah and back. He straightens slowly, as if to emphasize each inch he has on Jerome. "You're blocking my spot."

Jerome raises his free hand. "Hey, I was just trying to make plans with an old friend. I didn't mean to intrude."

Old friend? Liyah reminds herself to breathe. She presses her palms into her thighs. Daniel's fist clenches.

"She *very clearly* does not want to talk to you. Or did you not hear her say no?" Liyah winces. Daniel's gaze rivals Medusa's. There's a long, exquisitely agonizing moment where nobody speaks.

"I guess I'll be going then," Jerome says at last.

"I think that's a good idea," Daniel replies through gritted teeth.

Even after he disappears from her sight line, Liyah's pulse races and her breathing doesn't regulate.

Daniel swoops down so he's at eye level and places his hands on her shoulders. "Liyah?" Does she respond? She's not sure. He exaggerates his inhale and exhale, so close that his breath fans over her cheeks. She follows his movements, five, six, seven times before she can hear the holiday playlist over the thumping of her heart. "Do you need to leave?"

"I . . . the party. We're only halfway through. What if . . ." She's mumbling, unsuccessfully trying to hide the quaver in her voice.

"Fuck the party, Liyah. Jordan's around here somewhere; I'll text him and he can make sure everything's okay. Do you need to leave?"

"Yeah," she says. "I need to leave."

He nods, reaches over her to pick up her bag. She must put her coat on and walk outside, but she doesn't really remember doing so. It only occurs to her that she's in open air when a snowflake catches on her eyelashes.

"Can I hug you?" Daniel asks once he's led her half a block away, to an area with fewer passersby. No sooner than the nod of her head, she feels one of his arms wrap around the waist of her parka, the other hand stroking the back of her hood. "Do you need to talk?" She shakes her head. Talking is the last thing she wants. "Let me take you home?"

"Yes," she murmurs, the sound of her voice muffled into Daniel's insulated chest.

"Okay," he says, but he makes no effort to move, just pulls her closer. It's exactly what she needs.

LIYAH FUMBLES WITH her keys at her apartment door. Her hands tremble, but it seems important to her that she do this herself, so Daniel doesn't interfere. Forty-five seconds pass before she turns the lock.

Inside, Daniel takes Liyah's coat before removing his own. Her face is still completely blank. They rode home in total silence, the hand he didn't have clasped around Liyah's mitten fisted in his pocket, fingernails digging into his palms. She undoes her boots and wanders to the couch, where she curls up, knees to chest, arms wrapped around shins, rocking slightly from side to side.

What do you even say in this situation? "Are you alright?" would be a profoundly stupid question. He wishes he could call Kayla, but getting anything useful would require divulging more than Liyah's explicitly permitted. He sits down on the sofa a foot away from her, not sure if she wants space. After a moment, she pitches sideways, landing her head in Daniel's lap. He runs his fingers up and down her arm.

"Wanna watch a movie?"

Her cheek brushes against his thigh as she nods. "*10 Things I Hate About You,* please."

He scrolls a few streaming applications and tosses the remote on the coffee table as the opening credits dance across the screen.

Halfway through, she reaches for the clicker and hits pause. "Daniel?"

"Yes?"

"I'm not weak. I don't want you to think I'm weak."

How could that be the takeaway from today? He almost laughs. "That's not at all what I think."

She swallows, and her lips part with a deep exhale. "I'm glad you're here, but I would be okay if you weren't."

Daniel nods. He doesn't doubt it. The problem lies in the cost of that okay-ness. "You're allowed not to be, though."

The tears come quietly, and Daniel's gently swiping thumbs turn gray with mascara. "He's *married,*" she whispers. The horror in her voice churns his stomach. Daniel has never thrown a punch in his life, but part of him regrets letting that guy walk away without a few bruises. "I'm getting upset about this a decade later. I haven't—I haven't dated anybody. I mean, anybody. Because, you know, he told me he liked me, during . . ." She pauses, and Daniel winces. "I mean, I learned my lesson. People don't really *like* me. They want something from me. I was too afraid to even sleep with another friend. And he's married? He's fucking *married*."

The injustice slices deeply, and he wishes he could help shoulder her pain. There's a memory in his body of something like this from when Kayla told him all those years ago. Sadness, helplessness, anger. The inability to provide anything sufficient. He blinks away tears. "I'm so sorry, Liyah," is the only thing he can come up with. He thinks now about standing outside Windy City Wine and Cheese, her saying *it's all the same*—was his failure to defend her at summer camp one more data point to prove her hypothesis? Daniel might not have been the worst, but was he the first person to show her that people will take what they want from her and leave? The depth of her anger toward him when they first reconnected makes sense now, and in this moment, he hates himself.

She sits up and climbs into his lap, wrapping herself around him like a koala. He squeezes her tightly and she sighs into his neck. Liyah's taller than average—plus, the size of her personality probably adds another few inches—but right now he's keenly aware of how much smaller than him she is. How much smaller than Jerome she is.

He wants to punch through a wall. Or vomit. Neither will do her any good.

"I'm kinda hungry," Liyah mumbles into his shoulder.

"Do you want me to order a pizza?"

"Sure. But I don't want you to move."

"My phone's over there in my coat."

"Mine's in my back pocket."

"Fair enough." Daniel chuckles and feels around for the brick of glass and metal, careful not to let his fingers linger. "Mushroom and spinach, right?"

The food comes as they're switching from the movie to

old episodes of *The Good Place*. Liyah wordlessly gets up and heads to the kitchen, rising up to pull down two wine-glasses as Daniel gathers plates and paper towels. She pours generously and brings the entire bottle to the couch.

Her glass is empty before the end of the first episode, despite most of her pizza slice remaining. She reaches for another. Daniel's not sure if he should intervene. If this is what she needs in the moment, he can let it go. So, he sits with his arm resting across her shoulders and watches the show.

At the end of the third episode, the bottle's completely gone, despite Daniel's glass never being refilled.

At the end of the fourth, Liyah's hand, which had been resting on Daniel's thigh, trails up to where his leg meets his pelvis and gives a gentle squeeze. In response, Daniel rubs his thumb across her upper arm. He hopes she can find comfort in his touch.

But her fingers run higher and higher until she's swiftly unbuttoning his pants and slipping her hand into his underwear.

"Liyah," he says in what's meant to be a warning tone, but he goes breathless as she palms him. With every ounce of his available will, he grabs her by the wrist and removes her hand from his waistband. "We can't."

She yanks her hand out of his grip and scoots away from him on the couch, folding her arms across her chest. "Why not?"

When he goes to touch her leg, she pulls back farther. *Okay, no touching.* He sits on his hands to avoid doing so unconsciously and inhales deeply, making his voice go tender. "You're upset right now—justifiably—and you've had a lot of wine. It wouldn't be right."

Her teeth sink so deeply into her bottom lip, he worries it might be painful. "Or maybe you don't want me anymore," she spits back.

Daniel closes his eyes, steadying his breath. "No, Liyah. I want you. I want you more every single day. I'm just not going to have sex with you right this moment."

"But I don't want to feel like this anymore!" Liyah yells, slamming her fists into the couch cushions. An anguished noise comes from the back of her throat, and she hides her face in her hands. "Anything else. I just want to feel *anything* else."

Something snaps inside Daniel's chest. He stands, only to go squat in front of her. Slowly, he offers her his hands. As his heart thunders in his rib cage, she drops her arms and gingerly laces her fingers through his. "I want to help, in any way I can. But not by . . . not like that, not tonight." He tilts her chin upward to run his thumb across her bottom lip, and it comes away bloody. "Liyah, can you let me hold you? I understand if not. But just, please?"

She nods, and he gathers her in his arms, pulling her up to standing. He holds her close to him, relieved that she can't see his tears from where her face is pressed into his sternum. As minutes pass, the chest of his sweater dampens against him, and her whole body shakes.

Eventually, she stills. "Can we be naked instead?" she mumbles. "Not for sex, I promise. I just want to feel your skin on mine."

"Yeah, okay. But please forgive me if my body, you know, reacts."

She steps back, wiping at her eyes as she lets out a short laugh. "I thought you were advocating against sex."

Daniel smiles. "My mind is in the right place, but I can't always direct my blood flow accordingly." Especially not where Liyah's body is concerned. Sometimes it feels like she just looks at him and *bam!* there he goes.

"Okay, I'll ignore any blunt objects that poke at me, you have my word."

• • •

LIYAH HAS CRIED a total of three times in the past six months.
All in front of Daniel. Two of them today. Neen has always
been a crier; they say it's a relief when the tears finally come,
but Liyah has never fully understood it. She doesn't feel relief,
only hollowness and exhaustion.

When Liyah returns from the bathroom, having washed
the mess of smeared eyeliner and mascara from her face,
Daniel is waiting for her under the covers. His clothes are
folded in a pile next to the bed.

Her body thrums with nerves as she pulls her sweater over
her head. It doesn't make sense to feel so self-conscious. She's
undressed in front of him regularly for a couple weeks now,
and yet she finds herself turning away as she peels off her
jeans and unhooks her bra.

She climbs into the bed as quickly as she can, pulling the
sheets and comforter up to her nose. Is he going to reach out
to her first? Most days, she would guess yes. Today, probably
not.

He's watching her intently, and then he does that thing
where his tongue swipes so briefly over his bottom lip, and
the whole picture sends a shiver down her spine. Does he
know he does it so often? Or is it in the blind pane of his
Johari window? She hopes so. It makes her feel special to
notice something that might be a secret from himself.

God, I can't believe I asked him to hold me naked. Her
face heats. *That's so fucking weird. Maybe I shouldn't have
had all the wine.* She nuzzles farther under the covers.

But he's here, isn't he? Waiting for me. Daniel Rosenberg,
who up until six months ago might have been the very last
person she would have imagined could comfort her through
this. She probably wouldn't believe it now if he weren't right
in front of her.

But he is. Ready to give her whatever she needs. So, she inches forward. Hesitantly at first, but then the corners of Daniel's lips turn upward (one more than the other, as always), and she crosses the rest of the distance.

Ahhh.

"So warm," Liyah whispers into his ear. She drapes her leg across his hip by way of pulling him closer. "You smell good, too." As promised, the erection growing against her stomach goes unmentioned.

"So do you." Daniel unclasps his hands at her lower back so that he can use one to trace the side of her body from her shoulder to her knee. The skin he touches pinches into goose bumps; he smooths over his reversed route with soft, calming grips. "You always smell good. Like lavender-flavored chocolate."

A warmth spreads behind her ribs from surprise, amusement, something else. "It's cocoa butter lotion and lavender-scented conditioner."

"The secret Liyah recipe has finally been exposed!"

Liyah giggles. "It's not a secret. I would've told you if you asked."

"Okay, then." He leans his head back to look her in the eye, keeping the rest of their bodies in contact as much as possible. "What else do you smell like?"

"My deodorant is supposed to smell like aloe, but really I got it because it doesn't smell like much at all. I don't wear perfume. The rest is just me, I guess."

Daniel hums. "Well, the *just you* bit smells good."

Liyah closes her eyes, letting the cool smoothness of her pillowcase and the heat of Daniel's hand on her lower back consume her. "You smell like Old Spice Fiji."

"You know Old Spice scents that well?"

Her left eye opens first, then her right. The smile on his face looks exactly like it sounded in his voice. She's smiling, too. A delirious, cheek-splitting grin. "Nope, your deodorant is on your bathroom counter."

"That's cheating."

"Maybe. It's not only the deodorant, though. Your *just you* bit smells good, too." She wants to lean in and get a good sniff, but that would be too much, wouldn't it? They're friends. Instead, she wiggles her hips, trying to get even closer. Daniel tightens his hold on her thigh. "This is a weird conversation. I shouldn't be trusted with that much wine."

He shrugs. "Weird is relative. I'm quite enjoying myself, actually."

"Me too. I feel . . . safe, I guess."

Daniel squeezes his eyes shut, then presses his lips to Liyah's temple. "You have no idea how glad I am to hear that."

CHAPTER 21

THE thing about waking up next to Liyah: it's the best way to wake up. Usually, her hair is wrapped—several curls having fought their way out from the perimeter of the silk scarf—but this morning, her mass of hair spills over her pillow and tickles Daniel's throat. She's always tucked into him like she was made to fit there, her hands gripping tightly on his forearm, holding his embrace around her stomach. As he slowly regains consciousness, he inhales the rich cocoa-lavender smell of her and feels a lovely warmth in his chest.

Another thing about waking up next to Liyah: it proves he's absolutely, positively, undeniably done for.

That's not something he could bring up right now, though. Not after yesterday. So instead, he splays his fingers across her belly, pressing her more firmly against his front as she stirs.

"G'morning," he whispers into her neck, hoping his sandpapery voice isn't too unpleasant.

"Morning," Liyah replies with a yawn. The extra rasp in her words makes Daniel's stomach do a flip. If there's even a lick of reciprocation, then she must not mind his morning voice at all. Not one bit. "Oh God," she says as if she's just now remembering, and her body goes rigid.

"Nope."

She rolls over to face him. "Nope what?"

"Nope, you've got nothing to be embarrassed about. You can talk to me, or you can take all the imaginary for-use-at-a-later-date tokens in the world and we can have breakfast."

"Breakfast sounds good."

"And coffee, of course."

Liyah moans—a sound he'll never get used to, in the best way—and leans forward to kiss him on the nose.

Daniel scrunches the skin her lips touched. "What was that for?"

"It's like you were made in a lab. Too good, I don't trust it."

"How do you mean?" He's fishing, sure, but they're in the very short-lived Morning Liyah Stage 1 where she is sleepy, slow-speaking, and agreeable—a combination that exists at no other time of day—and he can't resist.

She hums. "I just feel like I don't have to explain myself to you. Lots of shared lived experience, sure, but it's also your instincts, or something. I'll be freaking out and you'll remain completely cool, and you don't make me feel judged. Complementary colors. You're a really good friend."

She had him until the end, there. Daniel gulps. *Good friend.* It shouldn't sting; he agreed to these terms in December.

"Your mouth and your dick don't hurt, either," she says.

Instead of dwelling on his disappointment, Daniel kisses the slow smile that spreads across Liyah's lips. "Is that so?" he asks, moving to sink his teeth into the skin above her collarbone, earning a gasp. He trails his fingers up her stomach to cup her breast in the way he knows she likes, brushing his thumb ever so gently over her nipple before pinching it between his index and middle fingers.

Liyah sighs. "And your hands. How could I forget your hands? Please give them my apologies." And then she giggles.

His heart swells. *Perfect.*

Not the feel of her breast under his fingers, not her naked body against his. That fucking laugh.

Completely. Done. For.

"Come on." He presses a kiss to the moles on her cheek before sitting up and swinging his legs over the side of the bed. "Let's get some food and caffeine in you before Morning Liyah Stage 2 hits."

"I hate you."

"No, you don't, you think I'm so good I must've been made in a lab."

"I regret saying that already."

Daniel shakes his head and clucks his tongue. "No takesie-backsies." An eye roll instead of a chuckle; Stage 2 is approaching more quickly than he thought.

"God, the party," she says. When Daniel looks, he sees that she's staring down at her phone. "The sign-up rate is lower than expected."

"It'll be okay, Liyah. We still have the wine night."

"You can't know that."

"You're right," Daniel says. "I can't. It might not work, but we just have to run the events and hope for the best."

They're solidly in Stage 2, so she doesn't admit that he's right. Instead, she groans, dramatically sliding out of bed and puddling on the floor as if she's gone boneless overnight.

LIYAH SITS CROSS-LEGGED on the couch, wringing her hands. It's been a point of pride (though probably shouldn't be) that she's done well with quarterly appointments for the past two years. She hadn't hesitated on Sunday afternoon when she picked up the phone and asked for an emergency session, but now, sitting in this familiar office, she can't help but feel like she's failed by being here again after only a few weeks.

"I'm sorry, I'm working up to it," she says by way of explaining her extended quiet.

Her therapist, Maria, holds up her hand, a few gold bracelets sliding down her arm. "No need to apologize, take as long as you want."

As long as she wants turns out to be the time it takes to begin and abandon five different sentences and fall into seconds of thoroughly embarrassed silence.

"Do you remember why I first came to you?" Maria gives an encouraging nod. "I ran into him. At my museum—um, not mine, but like, it was at the holiday party that Daniel and I threw. Anyway, he showed up and was trying to talk to me and I panicked. So embarrassing, like it's ten years now? He had a wedding ring. He wanted to get drinks. Can you believe that? Drinks?"

Maria shakes her head. Liyah's been seeing her long enough to know that she's not going to speak until she needs to correct Liyah or she's sure Liyah's done, so she blazes onward.

"I'm probably not making a lot of sense. But he—Jerome"—the corners of her lips turn down; the name still leaves a bitter taste in her mouth—"Jerome was saying he 'regretted how we left things.' Like, what the fuck? I mean, I know what the fuck. He thinks I ended our friendship because I 'regret'"—she inserts air quotes for emphasis—"sleeping with him. Which, like, I do have regrets. Namely, getting drunk around him."

"You know this, Liyah, but I feel compelled to remind you here that it wasn't your fault."

Liyah nods. "Yeah, yeah. I know all that. It's—remember when I told you about him cornering me in the library? And he was going on about how he wanted to know if I felt badly about it or if there was something 'fucked up' about what happened, and I begged him to leave me alone? I wasn't ready to admit to myself what it was at that point, and I can't even totally remember the conversation. I don't know what I said. Maybe I told him it was all aboveboard and he had nothing to worry about, just to get him off my back."

"Sometimes we say things we don't mean to protect ourselves. That's okay, especially in those circumstances."

"Yeah, you told me so years ago. But I can't help but think he knew. Like he *knew* what he did to me, and I'm the one who excused it. And so now he believes he can come up to me and ask to hang out while he's in town. Why didn't I tell him to fuck off? I don't usually have a problem doing that. You know what's the really crazy part? What really gets me?" Liyah pauses to catch her breath. She looks down, and picks at a hangnail until it bleeds.

"What's that?"

"If you asked me how I would react to seeing him again, I would have been worried about having flashbacks to that night, or the next morning. But I can't stop thinking about that conversation in the library. That's what's been haunting me. That feeling of being trapped by myself at the corner table, trying to speak in hushed tones, having no idea how I was gonna get out of there."

Maria nods her head slowly. "I'm so sorry that happened to you." Liyah wonders if they teach that soothing voice in counseling programs or if it's a natural talent required to get into the field. "Is that how you felt when you saw him this Saturday?"

"Yes." Liyah rakes her teeth over her bottom lip as she considers it. "But only at first. Daniel was in line at the bar when he came up, and then he came back. It felt different then."

"Like you had someone in your corner?"

"Yeah, like that. He was so patient with me, even though . . ." Liyah trails off. The years of rapport she's built with Maria don't save her the shame of what she's about to admit. "Even when I drank most of a bottle of wine and tried to initiate sex, and then got mad at myself when he said no, and *then* asked him to cuddle me so I could feel better." She cringes, hearing it aloud. It feels like such a regression.

"You seem upset with yourself."

"Disappointed. Aren't you disappointed in me?"

Maria's brows knit together. "Why would I be disappointed in you?"

"Because this is what we worked on! Here I was thinking I'm doing better, and I'm just as bad as I've always been."

The corners of Maria's eyes crinkle as she grins. Liyah folds her arms over her chest. "Okay, let's check the facts: you had an unexpected run-in with someone who caused you a great deal of trauma, yes?" Liyah nods. "You reached first for an unhealthy coping mechanism you've relied on before, yes?" Liyah nods. "But ultimately, you switched course and asked for help when you needed it, from Daniel and then from me, yes?"

"Yeah, I guess that's true."

"Do you think that's how you would have handled it when you were twenty-three? Or might you have stuck with the less healthy option?"

Liyah snorts. "I probably would be telling you about the four different people I slept with that weekend, two of whom I wasn't that attracted to."

"Exactly. Your recovery isn't about you suddenly being perfect; it's about you getting better at making these difficult choices."

Liyah chews this over, then laughs. "God, that's good. Ever consider becoming a therapist?"

CHAPTER 22

"**YES,** deadly serious," Liyah says around a mouthful of mapo tofu.

"*She's the Man* is your favorite movie of all time?" Daniel clarifies yet again, putting down his bowl of General Tso's chicken so he can give her a full view of his duly incredulous expression. Her face reveals nothing, but part of him feels as though she's pulling his leg.

"It would be one of your favorite films, too, if you had any taste."

"*If* I had any taste?"

She narrows her eyes. "Yes. It's literally Shakespeare."

"It's also mid-2000s Amanda Bynes."

"I thought you were taking the negative argument? If you want me to debate against its merits, I'm gonna need to review my notes."

Daniel shakes his head and lifts his beer bottle to his lips, taking a generous swig. "Nope, still very much anti."

Liyah shifts on the couch so that she's facing Daniel and crosses her legs, knees bumping against the side of his thigh. His hand unconsciously falls to settle on her ankle, thumb stroking the only bare skin it can access. They've been doing this—whatever *this* is—for a few weeks now, but his fingertips have yet to get their fill. Liyah never seems to mind.

"Daniel. You're *missing the point*. It's the fact that it is Shakespeare *and* Amanda Bynes that makes it so special. There was one, like, ten-year period where Hollywood decided the world needed modern American teen remakes of British classic literature. And you know what? They were absolutely fucking right!"

"I had no idea you felt so strongly about this." Daniel smiles. She feels this strongly about everything, and he's only really saying it to get a rise out of her.

She holds up a hand and begins ticking off her fingers. "*Clueless—Emma. 10 Things I Hate About You—The Taming of the Shrew. Mean Girls—Julius Caesar. She's the Man—Twelfth Night.* All absolute bangers. The trend sort of fizzled—although *Fire Island* is officially the best version of *Pride and Prejudice,* so I'm keeping all my fingers and toes crossed that it'll kick off a decade of adult queer retellings."

"Okay, okay, fine." He rubs his free hand along his jaw and does not miss how Liyah's eyes briefly drift to follow along. "It just seems like *favorite ever* is a stretch." She glares. Daniel retraces his steps. "You work in a museum! I thought your favorite would be something a little more . . . I don't know. Acclaimed? I expected you to insist on something from Barry Jenkins or Aaron Sorkin."

Liyah scoffs, poking him in the chest. "That's because you've been brainwashed by mass media into believing intellectual women must reject traditionally feminine interests!" She fires back, barely stopping to breathe. "Because God forbid a teenage girl likes a movie about a—gasp—*teenage girl.* These movies got me through middle school *and* high school."

"How is it you never mentioned these to me at camp, then?"

"Would you even remember if I had?" she asks, one eyebrow raised. He takes another swig of his beer so he doesn't have to look at her as he nods. "Well, as a preteen, 'I'm not like other girls' really had me in a choke hold. But I have since realized that my shame was a construct of the patriarchy. If you wanted to hang out with someone who jerks off to Martin Scorsese, you should've asked one of your non-Jordan coworkers."

Daniel wants to kiss her. It'll piss her off, though, so he settles for glancing at the deep groove of her cupid's bow and letting his lips slide into an easy smile. "I didn't know I registered for Feminist Reading of Popular Media this semester, but I can't say I'm disappointed."

"It comes free, like the side of rice." She leans across him—brushing against his chest much more than is strictly necessary—to scoop more rice and tofu onto her plate. "Have you ever even seen the movie?"

Daniel shrugs. "With Kayla, maybe? It would've been forever ago."

"And you're judging already." Liyah sucks her teeth disapprovingly. "Now we *have* to watch."

Daniel laughs, no longer able to resist the urge to wrap his arm around to the small of her back. Instead of lowering his lips to hers, he veers left and lets them brush against her neck just below her ear. Liyah shivers, the same way she did the last time his breath touched this piece of skin, and the time before that. "I never said I didn't want to watch it."

"Could've fooled me," she says, voice a touch rougher than usual. He grins into her neck, and she pushes him flush against the sofa cushion and swings her leg over so she's straddling his lap. He trails his hands up her thighs and under her sweater until he gets to the soft skin of her rib cage. She sighs and leans into the touch, her hips rocking forward, eliciting a sharp inhale from Daniel. Noses brush as Liyah dips her head downward.

"You're so easy." She laughs softly. "Your eyes have gone dark already."

"I'm half-hard and it's my eyes that clue you in?" He leans in, but she tilts her head back at the last moment, evading his kiss. She cradles his jaw in her hand, gently angling his face so she can examine each iris.

"They're usually this deep chocolate brown, kinda golden in the light. It's the color of a beer bottle." She clocks his raised brows. "In a good way, I promise. Right now, your pupils have dilated so much they're mostly black." She unbuttons his shirt as she speaks, spreading the fabric aside to trace the planes of his torso. The outline of his tattoo is usually where she starts, and today is no different.

"No fair. Your eyes are always pitch-black. They never give away their secrets."

She pulls her sweater over her head, some of her mussed curls shielding her eyes from view as they fall, the rest landing against her bare shoulders. "Maybe I'm always turned on," she whispers mischievously, brushing her hair away from her face. "Or never."

"Never?" His fingers creep up from her ribs, pulling the lace cup of her bra aside and drawing circles around her already pinched nipple. A single brush of his thumb and it tightens further.

Her teeth sink deeply into her bottom lip, and she shrugs, feigning nonchalance. "Maybe." He draws her breast into his mouth, and her breath hitches. She doesn't give in yet. Her fingers find the button of his jeans and then she's unzipping and sliding her hand into his boxer briefs. He bites into her shoulder to avoid groaning.

Holding out, pretending to be unaffected until one of them can't take it anymore, is Daniel's new favorite game. Liyah is a formidable offensive player—she can get him so wound up that he thinks he might die if he doesn't get inside of her—but she lacks the necessary self-control to play defense. It's always a photo finish, but he wins every single time.

And that's the fun of it, finding that one last touch that will force her vocal cords to vibrate against one another. Usually a whimper, but once he got a delicious, strangled groan. Then the dam breaks.

Liyah's playing the best game of her life. They're both completely naked before she makes a single sound, and Daniel has let out a breath that is dangerously close to a moan one too many times. Surprisingly, he finds today's pressure points in rather innocuous locations: one of his hands at the small of her back, the other on the side of her face, his lips pressing a chaste kiss to her collarbone.

Her defeat comes with a soft, low whine followed quickly by a hissed "fuck you" and a grind of her hips that would have cost Daniel his win had it come ten seconds earlier.

"Gladly," he responds, gathering her in his arms so he can lay her against the emerald velvet of her couch, knocking off one of Laura or Lara's excellent throw pillows in the process.

"Thank God," she says. "Those things belong on the floor." She interrupts his laughter with a rough kiss. With great effort, he pulls back so that he can crawl down her torso, filling his mouth with her everywhere he wants to do so.

An untold number of minutes later, when he's lost in her, hands aiding in the hypnotic motion of her hips, upright chests pressed together, heavy breaths mingling, he's hit with a startling thought: *I love this woman so much.*

It's a mistake, drawn out by the feeling of her around him and above him. *I love* having sex with *this woman so much,* it should have been. Or maybe *like.* He meant to think *like.*

Liyah stills and leans back to surveil his face. "Is everything okay?"

Daniel smiles. "I'm great, actually." He kisses the moles

on her cheekbone. "Just thinking about how lucky I am to be here right now."

"Daniel. You can't say that."

"Why not?"

"Because it makes me want to . . ." She trails off, pouting. "I don't know! You just can't. You're so . . ." She huffs. The way her nose crinkles and her eyes squeeze shut tells him that whatever he's *so . . .* is a good thing.

His smile gives way to a grin. "Sorry."

"You should be," Liyah says before using a particularly luxurious roll of her hips to coax out twin moans.

THEY WATCH THE movie completely naked, Liyah draped over Daniel's body, her cheek pressed to his sternum. Half an hour passes before she realizes that he's the first she's done this with, had so much skin on skin when it's not a prelude to sex (at least not immediately; she hasn't written off a late-night round two). She's had exactly one relationship, and she and Spencer had been nervous sixteen-year-olds who couldn't get beyond half-clothed fumbling. Anybody else, she would've either felt self-conscious or altogether disinterested. Not with Daniel.

Besides, Daniel smells wonderfully earthy, and from this vantage point she can feel his warm chest shake with laughter and thus find new ways to say *I told you so.*

"You know, this is the first Friday night without SSC since August. Except the snowstorm," she marvels aloud.

Daniel *mm-hmm*s, and she feels it against the whole left side of her face. "Yeah. I'm glad you're still here, though. Chinese food and a movie on Christmas would be much less fun by myself."

She laughs. "You'll be eating your words at five tomorrow morning when you're driving me to the airport."

"I should not have agreed to that."

"Hey!" Liyah says, tilting her face so she can look Daniel in the eyes. "You can't back out now."

"I wouldn't dare." He kisses her forehead, and she rolls her eyes, earning a short chuckle. "Why this movie?"

"You're missing the carnival scene!"

Daniel feels around the coffee table for the clicker and hits pause. "Of all the ones you listed, why is *She's the Man* your favorite?"

"It's embarrassing. You're gonna think I'm dumb."

He cocks his head to the side, giving her an unimpressed look. "Liyah, come on."

"Fine," she says, turning so her cheek rests against his chest. She's not avoiding eye contact, she's simply enticed by the freeze-frame of Amanda Bynes removing her wig and sideburns in a Tilt-A-Whirl. "Neen and I used to watch it a lot. Like, objectively, it's an extremely straight movie. But if you squint just right, it's a bisexual guy falling in love with someone who's gender-fluid. We were obsessed before we even knew why. You take what you can get, I guess." Fingers run up and down her spine as she speaks, drawing out more words than she intends. She feels her muscles tense involuntarily.

"Damn, we've gotten to queer analysis and it's only the first semester! No wonder I'm hot for professor," Daniel jokes, and her body relaxes.

"Can we finish the movie now?"

"Thank you for sharing this with me, Liyah," he says, the earnestness in his voice making her stomach flip, then presses play before she has a chance to respond.

CHAPTER 23

DANIEL'S hand rests on Liyah's thigh as they cruise down the Kennedy Expressway, mostly empty at this hour. Her fingers, peeking out of her puffy winter coat, grip a thermos full of coffee from which she takes periodic sips. Daniel is jealous; he had to chug his cup before they hit the road.

She sighs into her dark roast, and he sneaks a look at her. Her hair is braided into four large cornrows—he helped her make sure the parts at the back of her head were straight last night—so he can take in her entire side profile at once. As beautiful as her hair is when she wears it out, framing her face in masses of curls, he loves it like this, too. Pulled back, her features unobstructed.

Liyah's eyes meet Daniel's. He swallows. "Are your headphones charged?"

"Yes, I double-checked," she replies, voice viscous and tired. "I need them to ward off chatty seatmates."

"So that you won't accuse them of a hate crime?"

She breathes out a quiet laugh through her nose. "I just don't have time in my schedule. The last time I *implied* the cute guy next to me might've said something ignorant, six months flew by, and I still haven't gotten rid of him."

Daniel cracks a smile. "So, you thought I was cute?"

Liyah rolls her eyes. "Glad that's your takeaway."

The departures lane arrives faster than Daniel expects. Once pulled over, he hits his hazards and unbuckles his seat belt. He knows how Liyah feels about kissing in public—very, *very* against it—but the short daylight hours this time of year have given him the cover of darkness. And technically, his car is private property.

As he leans across the center console, Liyah does the same. Liyah rakes through the hair at the back of his head while they kiss, as she often does, and Daniel's hand finds the spot where her neck meets her jaw.

Liyah gently nips at his bottom lip by way of parting, grinning as she scrambles out of the car, racing him to the trunk. She pulls out her suitcase and shuts the hood victoriously. "Ha! Beat you."

Daniel clutches his chest. "You wound me."

"You'd better get back in before the line monitor yells at you."

"Will do. Text me when you land?"

"Sure thing," Liyah calls, already wheeling her luggage toward the entrance, walking backward so that she still faces Daniel. "See you next year, Rosenberg!"

"Until then, Cohen-Jackson!"

I'll miss you, he wants to say, but he bites his tongue and climbs back into his car.

JACKIE COHEN AND Charlie Jackson wait on the other side of Seattle-Tacoma Airport security, Liyah's mother bouncing back and forth and waving her hands above her head, her father standing still with his arms crossed and a warm smile on his face. Two very different displays of roughly equivalent excitement. The last time she saw them was when they visited in late July. Once again, she's struck with the specific adult realization that her mental construction of her parents is out of date. The roots of her dad's chest-length locs are more salt than pepper, and her mom, still larger than life in her memories, barely reaches Liyah's earlobes.

After she hugs them both tightly (granting her mother's *me first* demand), her father wordlessly takes her suitcase from her. "Avi?" she inquires.

"Asleep." It appears that her father has not become more verbose in her absence.

"You know how teenage boys are. If he doesn't get ten hours, he's a total nightmare," her mom titters. "Unlike you at that age. You were a nightmare regardless. Worse if you hadn't eaten."

"Mom—"

"I'm just saying!" This is one of Jackie's favorite phrases. It's her version of putting "no offense, but" in front of something incredibly offensive. "It's normal for teenage girls. God knows your bubbe went through worse with me. Anyway, his college applications are due in a few days, I say let him have his rest."

"You'll help him with those?"

"Yes, Dad. I might have to throw his Chanukah gift at him so that he'll get up first, but I'll help, promise."

He squeezes her shoulder. "That's my girl."

Forty-five minutes later, Liyah finds her younger brother fast asleep, lying diagonally across his full-sized bed. He's slept this way since he was small, guaranteeing that Liyah would end up on the floor at least once during every family vacation. Now he's a pile of gangly, teenaged limbs, and his feet poke out from the left corner of his duvet. As promised, Liyah drops an artfully wrapped shoebox (a bit scuffed from travel, but the effort is obvious) on the center of his chest.

"Ow, what the fuck? *Aliyah*. That hurt." Avi brushes the box aside and sits up, rubbing the spot it hit. He groans in that very teenaged way where the *g* in *ugh* is over-enunciated. "You're the worst. This is why I'm Mom and Dad's favorite."

"Aww, *Avraham*, it's cute you still think that," Liyah coos as she backs out of the doorway. "I'll concede on Mom, but I've had Dad wrapped around my finger since birth."

"Get out of my room."

"Be ready in twenty minutes, or I'll make you ride in the back," Liyah says, shutting the door with a *thunk* behind her.

"Liyah, don't slam doors," her mom calls from downstairs.

Safely away from her mother's view, she rolls her eyes as she yells an apology. In her old bedroom (long scrubbed of music posters, Neen's art, and far too many cheetah-print items), Liyah changes from her airplane uniform of sweatshirt and leggings to a pair of wide-leg overalls and a cropped sweater. While Avi's filling their shared bathroom with the smell of Axe body wash and completely unnecessary aftershave, she heads to the one downstairs to wash her face and apply some makeup.

When she emerges, her mom looks up and exclaims, "You look so cute, honey!"

"Thanks, Mom."

"Famous early hominin, abbreviated as *Ar.* something. Seven letters, starts with *r*?"

Liyah smiles. It's been a while since her mom called her with an anthropological crossword clue, but she always does it like this, with no context or introduction. "*Ardipithecus ramidus*. R-A-M-I-D-U-S."

"Oh, it's so good to have you home. You really should visit more often. What kind of example are you setting for Avi? I'll be an empty nester soon, and then I'll have children I see three times a year."

Avi appears behind their mother's armchair. He's been taller than Liyah for two years, but every visit, the first time she sees him standing is unsettling. "I'll make sure to see you more than that, Mom." He bends down to give her a hug, turning to Liyah and mouthing *favorite*. She wrinkles her nose and jingles the car keys.

"Sweet kicks," she says as she unlocks the family SUV. She bought them on intel from Jordan; apparently, they're a very sought-after colorway of Nike Blazer Mid '77s, and she had to refresh her browser obsessively to nab them before they sold out. Not that she'd tell that to Avi.

Something about the way he replies, "Yeah, they're sick," makes her think he knows anyway. "Can I DJ?"

"If you play Brad Paisley to fuck with me again, I'm driving us into oncoming traffic."

"We're half white, Liyah. You gotta embrace our culture."

"I fully endorse all lesbian country songs and murder ballads about abusive husbands if you want to play those. It's the I-like-guns-and-women-and-beer-and-trucks stuff I can't stand. Here." She tosses her phone into his lap and buckles her seat belt. "Text Neen and tell them we're on our way."

At the coffee shop, Avi jiggles his leg impatiently and swipes fingerfuls of the whipped cream atop his drink. "Will you tell me what you think already?"

"It's well written," she says. "But it isn't funny."

Cue the infamous Avi pout. "So?"

"You're funny," she says. "This is not. It's kind of boring, actually."

He grumbles, spinning his laptop so that he can see the document, now marred with Liyah's comments and bright red edits. "I thought I had to be a serious person to get into college."

She folds her arms. "Your grades and varsity letters show you're a serious person. Your essay should show that you have a personality. That's hard for some people, but yours isn't awful, so you should be fine."

"*Ugh*, Liyah. How am I supposed to do that?"

"Try telling the story like you would tell me. We can edit it for professionalism later." The bell above the door sounds, alerting Liyah to Neen's entrance.

Liyah barely makes it out of her chair in time to catch Neen's running hug. "C-J!" they say, as if in disbelief of her presence, before pulling back and offering their ear. Liyah bumps it with hers.

"You guys are so fucking weird," Avi says.

"Aw, Avi, are we embarrassing you?" Neen croons, reaching over to pat his cheek (if they'd gone to ruffle the short locs atop his low fade, they might've lost a hand).

"Yes."

"Good," Liyah responds. "Now get to work on those edits."

"Okay, *Mom*."

Liyah ignores him and, spying a croissant in the pastry display case, joins Neen in line.

KAYLA'S BALCONY IS small but cozy, lit only by string lights, and has a beautiful view overlooking the city skyline. Daniel is drinking wine in silence with his sister, fuzzy blankets draped across their legs to keep warm, when his phone screen flashes with a text.

Liyah

[image of ball gown made
from tinsel] My New Year's
Eve look. Thoughts?

> **Daniel**
>
> you can't wear that

Liyah

Why not???

> **Daniel**
>
> i already bought it. you
> don't want to compete with
> me for who wore it best, i'll
> win
> what are you doing? house
> party?

Liyah

Nah, Neen and I will
probably go to a queer bar
with a dance floor. You?

Daniel doesn't actually know; when Kayla invited him to
New York for the long weekend, he didn't ask a lot of questions. "Noona, what are we doing for New Year's?"

His sister looks up from where her nose is buried in a Za-
die Smith novel and shrugs. "We can always go to a bar, and
a few people I know are having a party. We could even stay
here. So long as you don't ask me to go to Times Square, the
world is your oyster."

"I could be down for an apartment party," he says.

"Alright. Get ready to meet a ton of thirtysomethings in boring jobs who do shit like make homemade pickles on the side."

Daniel smirks. "Well, you know, now that you're a Brooklyn hipster, I expected as much."

Kayla responds with an exaggerated sigh. "Hi pot, I'm kettle. Nice to meet you. Go back to texting your girlfriend, I want to finish this chapter."

He laughs and returns to his phone.

> **Daniel**
>
> kayla's friend's party. excited to see what's in store for me after thirty

Liyah

Let me know your findings.
I'll add it to the exhibition

> **Daniel**
>
> i'll be sure to take notes

Daniel finishes the *New Yorker* article he was reading and makes it halfway through the following one before he realizes that he never corrected Kayla.

He clears his throat. "Liyah's not my girlfriend. We're, um, friends." The end of his sentence pitches up involuntarily. Kayla's lips curve. *Oh shit.*

"Wow, took you fifteen whole minutes to come up with that one, huh?" He opens his mouth to reply, but Kayla brings her finger to her lips. "Shh, I'm *reading.*"

CHAPTER 24

LIYAH is not in the head-to-toe tinsel number she suggested, but she hasn't exactly gone for subtlety in a short, silky, silver dress and sky-high chunky heels. She kept her hair off her face for dancing in a row of twists that open to her natural curls, and Neen decorated each part with silver glitter. Neen also insisted that they mix a shimmering body oil into their lotion, and now every bit of the two of them (collarbones, knees, elbows) glows opaline in the strobing lights. She'll be washing it all off for weeks.

Growing up in a white area of town, going to an Ashkenazi synagogue, and just generally wearing her hair natural and big, Liyah has spent a lifetime as the subject of public stares. Pair her with Neen, who accessorizes their androgyny with visible tattoos, piercings, and a wardrobe that employs the entire color wheel, and you get quite the head-turning duo. It's an inevitable fact that Liyah has become so accustomed to, she no longer notices (except in the few circumstances when she's looking for it).

Not here, though. Not in the center of this dance floor,

populated with the finest drag and sparkle that Seattle's young queer scene has to offer. She melts into the crowd, aware of her body only insofar as she can feel the bass pulse through her ribs and thighs. Less sure of her existence with each bump from an unfamiliar form against hers. The anonymity is more intoxicating than any liquor.

At this point in the night five years ago, Liyah would have been nearly naked in a bathroom stall with a stranger, leaving Neen to find her a sweaty mess around closing time. On occasion, Liyah misses the thrill of those adventures. She never longs for the depressive episodes that would follow.

"You good, C-J?" Neen asks as they wedge their way through neighboring bodies, the tassels hanging from their jumpsuit narrowly missing someone's drink.

"Yeah, I'm good," she shouts back over thumping speakers, accepting the plastic cup filled with vodka and tonic water.

"You have your thinking face on."

Neen's right. A lot of suppressed thoughts have floated to the surface in recent weeks. Telling Daniel has unlocked a lot of doors she likes to keep closed. None of her worst fears—that he would treat her differently, that he would see her as less than the person she worked so hard to become—have come to fruition. But that's almost worse than the alternative, because doesn't that mean she could have told someone sooner? That she could have let herself work through the thoughts that intrude in her most restless moments, and it wouldn't crack through every foundation she's ever built? Maybe crafting her life so the only person she lets see all the way through her lives thousands of miles away is less of a safety net and more of a way to ensure a certain level of loneliness.

It's New Year's Eve. Stop, she tells herself, and knocks back her drink in one go.

"Jesus, Liyah."

Liyah grimaces at the burn of the vodka. "No more thinking!"

Neen grins their best Cheshire cat smile and empties their own cup. "No more thinking!"

The night is a blur of music and movement and Liyah lets it fill her until she's floating outside herself, everywhere and nowhere at once. Sweat-slicked skin and cold liquor sliding down her throat. At midnight, silver and gold balloons fall from netting in the ceiling, and she and Neen share a peck of a New Year's kiss. She keeps her promise not to think, until she pulls her phone out on the way out of the bathroom.

Daniel

happy new year! Find anyone
to kiss? ;)

Is that a joke? It must be a joke. It would be too weird for him to earnestly ask. Still, she's discomfited by the question, even in jest.

Liyah

Yes, it was marvelous. Who
was your lucky lady?

Daniel

wait, you really kissed
someone?

Liyah

;)

Daniel's typing bubble appears and disappears. Three *separate* times. She squints at it to make sure her eyes aren't playing tricks, and there it goes again.

Daniel
have you been hooking up
with other people in chicago
too or is this just a new year's
thing?

Liyah blinks at her screen in disbelief. She was just going along with the bit. Was he not joking? What's with the winking face, then? Is he mad at her? She's too drunk for this. Also, what the *fuck*?

Suddenly aware of the crushing humidity in the bar, Liyah makes eye contact with Neen, points to the door, and mouths *I need air*. They nod and she rushes off, pushing into the chilly, damp night. The brick exterior of the building scratches against her shoulder blades; her jacket is still inside. Two vaguely masculine figures are practically dry humping twenty feet away and the smell of pot wafts from around the corner, but Liyah's alone in all the ways that matter.

That is, nobody is watching her type and delete messages for five minutes straight before giving up and pressing call.

"You wanna tell me what that was about?" she blurts as soon as the rings cut out, not giving him a chance to speak.

"I just . . . I didn't kiss anybody." The gruffness of Daniel's voice livens up winged insects somewhat like butterflies in her stomach. Liyah ignores them. They're probably moths, chewing holes in the emotions she keeps stored away for an appropriate season yet to come. "I haven't been sleeping with other people. I thought we should talk about it?"

"You thought you'd ask me over text? With an emoji?"

"Yeah, I guess that wasn't my best idea."

Liyah's snort is contemptuous. "You think?"

"I should have known you were. I mean, we're casual and everything. And we've been safe. You know, condoms and getting tested and all."

Liyah rubs at the furrow in her brow. When she lowers her hand, glitter streaks across the heel of her palm. "I'm pretty fucking drunk, Daniel."

"Yeah, me too. It's three thirty here. I don't know what I was thinking."

"Are you, like, mad at me?"

"No, I'm not." His voice still sounds off. Liyah assumes he's lying.

The "You have NO RIGHT to be" she declares loudly into her receiver earns a brief head turn from one of the dry humpers.

"I'm really not," he replies softly.

He sounds resigned, which only agitates her further. "I don't believe you. Why the fuck else would you send me that? At twelve thirty on *New Year's*. Fuck's sake."

"I hope I didn't ruin your night."

"You didn't ruin my night!" She feels her volume climbing and forces it back down. "I just want to know what's going on. I thought you were joking at first, but now it feels like I walked into a trap."

"It wasn't a trap—"

"Then what was it, Daniel? How was I supposed to respond?" Both dry humpers look this time. One of them calls something like *tell him, girl!* before reapplying lips to neck.

"I don't know!" Daniel shouts back. "I wasn't thinking. Really, I just wasn't thinking. Please don't—fuck, Liyah. I'm sorry." His voice breaks, and with it, Liyah's resolve.

"Neen, dummy," she mutters.

• • •

"WHAT?" DANIEL ASKS, lifting his head out of his free hand. He'd just finished brushing his teeth when Liyah called, and now he's sitting on the edge of his sister's guest bed in only his boxers, feeling like the stupidest person alive. If he ruins what they have over a drunk text . . .

No, he doesn't want to think about that. This isn't a grovel-proof fuckup. She's forgiven him before, and he's pretty sure he can Brownstein's Bagels his way out of this if need be.

"I kissed Neen. It was a peck, nothing we haven't done before."

"Oh. I thought . . ."

"I know what you thought. *I* thought we were joking, so I was going along with it."

His shoulders relax. "I'm just a dumbass?"

"Yeah, pretty much."

"So, nothing's changed from last year?"

His heart jumps when she laughs. "Guess not." They're silent for a moment, and Daniel feels the relief reach his extremities. "I would tell you if I were sleeping with other people, Daniel. If for no other reason, at least for safety."

Daniel is closer to the comedown of his night than Liyah is to hers, but it appears that some liquid courage remains. "I think I'd rather it just be us, if that's okay."

"That works for me." She giggles, and he's even more aware of her drunkenness. "Also, between work, SSC, and, y'know, fucking, you see me almost every day. Where would I find the time?"

"You're a determined individual when you want to be," he retorts with a smile. "Look, I'm sorry I messed up your night. I'll give you a ride home from the airport to make up for it."

"If I hadn't spent twenty minutes upset about this, it would've been something else. Don't worry about it."

"Is that a no to the ride?"

"No takesie-backsies. See you in forty-seven hours, sucker."

"Good night, Liyah."

"'Night, Daniel," she replies, and hangs up.

Flopping back onto the bed, Daniel lets out a long sigh. Drunken jealousy is not a good look and it's a worse feeling. He hadn't even seen it coming. That first text *had* been a joke. But his brain had gone from zero to *I don't want other people to touch her* in three-point-five.

He runs his hand through his hair, pulling the waves off his face. Is it toxically masculine to want to be the only one who gets to be that intimate with her? He's not about to go all caveman and try to smash someone's face in, so maybe House Rule #3 is still intact. If so, he must be breaking some other unspoken law.

A knock at the door jolts him upright. "Yes?" he calls, pulling his T-shirt over his head.

"Can I come in?"

"Sure."

Kayla pokes her head inside first, as if checking for signs of danger, before sliding the rest of her body through. Enough light slips through the crack in the door for him to make out her concerned expression. "I'm not going to pretend I heard all of that, but I'm also not going to pretend I heard none of that."

Daniel looks at her blankly. He shrugs. Kayla edges closer to the bed.

"Can I sit?"

"Sure."

She sits so slowly that he barely feels the mattress depressing. He has half a mind to check the floor for eggshells. "That was rough, Danny."

"Thanks."

"No—I mean, you *really* like her, don't you? You always have." He nods so slightly it would be imperceptible if Kayla's gaze weren't so perfectly fixed on him. "Have you thought about talking to her about it?"

"I don't know how she feels." He pauses, reconsidering. "No, I do. She's made it very clear that she's not into relationships. I don't want to ruin our friendship, or . . ." He trails off.

"Or stop sleeping together?"

"Noona!"

"What? I know you have sex, I'm pretty sure I saw you lose your virginity."

Daniel groans, running his hand down his face. "Don't remind me."

"I wish I hadn't reminded myself. It was traumatizing." She shudders in horror, then chuckles.

Daniel feels less amused. "There're some things you feel weird telling your older sister about, even if she's a therapist."

"As long as you spare the gory details, you can tell me about it. Especially if it's got you in one of your tailspins. I've got a whole three years of experience on you; I might be able to offer some advice."

"Are you gonna charge me?"

She shoves his shoulder. "No, jackass. This is strictly older sibling stuff." She inhales. "I've spent a lot of time falling quick and hard for people who didn't quite feel the same. Stuffing my feelings down never did me any good. It always seems to come out eventually. Usually, at the most inopportune moments."

He sifts her words through his mental sieve, but he can't find anything wrong with what she's said. That only means he'll need to run them through again. "I can keep myself in check for now."

"Okay. Just, you know, if you get to a point where it feels like you can't, try talking to her. If you plan out the gist of

what you're going to say beforehand, it'll be easier, trust me."
She pats him on the shoulder and stands up, opening the door
and widening the sliver of light streaming into the room once
again.

"Thanks, Kayla. I appreciate it."

"No problem." Right before the door clicks shut, she
swings it and sticks her head back through. "For what it's
worth, I've seen you and Liyah together, and I wouldn't be so
sure that you already know how she feels."

And then she shuts the door behind her.

SSC #16 MEETING NOTES

Secretary: Siobhan

- First of the new year!
- Hols check-in
  - That means holidays/vacations, for all ye yankees
  - Jordan had a cozy time in Raleigh, appreciated the less awful weather
    - Got laughed at when he tried to explain the concept of SSC to his cousins
  - Daniel visited his mom in Madison and spent New Year's in New York with Kayla
    - Kayla says hello to everyone
  - Liyah's little brother loved the shoes Jordan picked for him
    - Liyah is eternally grateful
    - It's weird how tall he's gotten; she misses when he was smaller than her
    - I didn't need to write that down, apparently
  - Siobhan had a lovely time in Dublin
    - Went out with friends that included ex-boyfriend, and it was totally normal and not terribly awkward at all! (sarcasm)
    - Liyah says I don't have to write that it was sarcasm, but I would like that here for posterity
- Work
  - A shame we have to go back, but the break was nice
- Dating
  - SIOBHAN FUCKED WILL!!!!! CONFETTI!!!! FIREWORKS!!!! APPLAUSE!!! (Liyah)
- Rule addition: 11. In the presence of Daniel and Jordan, Siobhan may not describe a penis she has seen sexually

CHAPTER 25

LIYAH twiddles her thumbs as they wait for their appetizers, trying not to look at her phone. The snow on the ground was expected this time, and the roads are plowed to perfection. Well, not quite to *perfection,* but to usable standards. Jeff granted her request for two coat check attendants. She has no reason to expect that her night will end anywhere but her own warm bed, except that none of the other events have gone as planned.

"I need you to take a deep breath," Daniel says.

"There's nothing wrong with my breathing," Liyah replies.

"Oh, is your chest moving rapidly because your heart is beating out of it? My bad."

"Why are you looking at my chest, Rosenberg? Is it your first time seeing breasts in the wild?"

The waiter comes with their samosas then, looking like he's ready to burst with laughter. It's the last of the events in their proposal (meaning the last event before Jeff makes up his mind on her promotion) and they decided to make a night of it and grab dinner at a bougie London-style Indian joint whose reviews promise tastes straight out of Southall. Liyah shoves a bite of samosa in her mouth the moment the waiter leaves, hoping to avoid the rest of the conversation.

She sighs, closing her eyes, forgetting the reason she'd taken the bite in the first place. Liyah has never been to Southall, but if it tastes like this, she will happily lick every surface of the neighborhood.

When she opens her eyes, Daniel is studying her, that unreadable look he sometimes gets overtaking his face. He clears his throat. "I know you're nervous, but it's going to be great. If attendance straddles the gap in rates for membership purchases from the holiday party and sleep-in, we'll surpass our original projections. The influx of revenue is already better than expected."

Liyah leans over the table, placing her hand over Daniel's. *"Influx of revenue,"* she purrs. "I love it when you talk dirty to me."

He matches her posture, his lips right up against her ear. "Wait until you hear me say *furcula*."

Liyah laughs and pulls away, warmth pooling in her abdomen.

After fifteen minutes of people watching at the Field (which goes about the same as the last wine night: Daniel reclining against a pillar and Liyah white-knuckling a plastic cup), Daniel convinces her to try participating instead of panicking on the sidelines.

They go from exhibition to exhibition, adding sloshes of wine and hunks of cheese to their already full bellies. It's not long before they're wine drunk and giddy, carefully reading the tasting notes as though they hadn't written them together a few months prior, ad-libbing some new ones on the spot.

"It has a large bouquet. But mostly baby's breath," Liyah says of a sauvignon blanc.

Daniel swirls a Bordeaux under his nose. "Notes of . . . gasoline. And patchouli."

Liyah knocks back a pinot grigio. "Honestly? Couldn't taste a thing," and they both erupt in laughter.

On their way to the L, Liyah checks the newsletter sign-up stats from her phone. There are 634 people from tonight alone, all of whom will receive a nudge about this year's membership benefits from Siobhan come Monday. Nothing's guaranteed, but she can't help but feel some of Daniel's infectious optimism. She shows the phone to him, and he wraps her up in a hug tight enough to lift her clear off the ground, spinning her around and nearly tripping over himself in the snow.

"Easy there, cowboy."

"Sorry, got a little excited." As he puts her down, Liyah raises her eyebrows. "Don't say it," Daniel says, shooting a glare that in milliseconds becomes a rosy-cheeked, crooked smile.

"You know," Liyah says, kicking a chunk of packed snow. "Tonight would've been a really good date, if I did that kind of thing. Or, y'know, if anybody ever wanted to do that kind of thing with me." She looks to her side, where Daniel has gone completely rigid. "No, no. Not like that." Her arms are out-of-sync windshield wipers trying to take back her words. "I know this is a work thing. I'm not saying . . . I mean, it's romantic, no? Dinner at a dimly lit restaurant, wine-tasting in a museum, sobering up enough on the ride home for fantastic sex. If you took a girl you liked out like this, she'd wake up the next morning completely smitten."

She watches Daniel swallow, blink slowly. "Liyah—" he starts, voice syrupy thick.

Liyah puts her hand on Daniel's shoulder, wanting to mollify but unsure how. He relaxes slightly under her touch, and her panic eases. "I'm sorry, I made it weird. I was trying to say what a nice time I've had tonight, and I had to go and say that someone could fall in love with you off this night alone. I need to learn how to give you a normal compliment."

"You think?" Daniel says.

"Yeah, I know, I'll work on it."

"No, I mean you think someone would fall—would be smitten with me off this night alone?" He's giving her that look again, the same one as when she was eating the samosa.

Liyah drops her hand. "I mean, if I was on a date with you and it went like it did tonight, I'd want you naked the second my apartment door closed."

Daniel laughs now. "That could be arranged."

Liyah laughs, too. Mostly in relief.

IT'S NOT QUITE the *second* her apartment door closes, but it's not much longer than that. They wash up and climb into bed, bone-tired. Daniel finds himself reaching for her once more, the words *fall in love with you off this night alone* ringing in his ears as he slides into her. They drift off to sleep sweaty and completely spent, Daniel resolving to tell Liyah how he feels in the morning.

A few hours of sleep and a mostly demolished plate of scrambled eggs and veggie sausages later, Liyah is scrolling through her phone, legs draped across Daniel's lap. He traces circles on her knee, convincing himself that he can't put it off anymore. *Liyah, I think I should tell you that I have feelings for you.* Or maybe, *In the interest of honesty, I want you to know that I like you as more than a fuck buddy.* Even just, *Hey, Liyah, I like you.*

Liyah mutters an expletive under her breath.

"What happened?" Daniel asks, unable to mask his concern.

Liyah waves her hand. "Oh no, nothing bad. I forgot that my mom is visiting next weekend. I'm gonna text the group chat and let everyone know I can't be at Survival Club on Friday."

Daniel's shoulders relax. "Ah, okay. You should invite her," he jokes.

"Ha. Never. SSC must remain a parent-free zone at all costs. Otherwise, they'll take the fact that none of us are well-adjusted adults as a personal affront."

Daniel plucks one of her curls and watches it spring back into place. Liyah side-eyes him. "Speak for yourself. I'm very well-adjusted. Siobhan, too. Not sure about Jordan. What time does your mother go to sleep?"

"She'll be back in her hotel by nine thirty, why?"

"Why don't you come by after? It's not like you've ever showed up on time before."

Liyah groans. "We always do sleepovers in her hotel room when she visits—please don't laugh at me, the tradition started when she sat down on my mattress in college and said it felt like cardboard and it just never stopped—and I don't want to have to explain every detail of where I was."

"What, you embarrassed of the club? On behalf of all of us, I'm wounded."

She shakes her head. "Nah, it's just that she'd ask who I was with, how I know them, etcetera. My mom can read me in an instant so there would be no hiding anything."

"She'd poke around your sex life too much for your liking?"

Her face puckers in disgust. "Worse, she'd find out who you are and immediately pick out the glass for you to break at our wedding."

The thud in his stomach is quick and painful, which is probably why the next words race out before he can think better of them: "And why is that so bad?"

Liyah pauses, eyes wide. "Why would I not want my mom marrying us off and trying to force us to pop out grandchildren? Let me check my notes." Daniel's frown doesn't waver. "You're being weird. Why are you being weird?"

"I'm not being weird. It just sounds like you're embarrassed to be sleeping with me," he mumbles. *Nice save, dumbass.*

"No, Daniel, nothing like that. You're an absolute catch, and when you eventually fall in love, you'll make someone an excellent husband. I just don't want my overzealous mother to ruin our friendship."

Fuck friendship, Liyah! I don't want to be your friend. I want to wake up next to you every morning. Is that not the most obvious thing in the world? He bites his tongue and scowls. *What a disaster,* he thinks. And then, *Maybe Kayla is right, I should've done this sooner.* But what could he possibly say now?

Liyah's hand finds his knee and squeezes. That look of worry he wishes he'd never had reason to become so familiar with is etched into her features. "Hey, I'm sorry. That came off super harsh, but I promise I didn't mean it that way. I'm not always great at thinking before I speak, and I feel terrible that I offended you."

Daniel forces a wry smile. "I thought you didn't care about offending me?"

LIYAH HAS OFFICIALLY put her foot in it twice in under twelve hours. Possibly a personal record. "I care about it in this way. I really am sorry," she says.

"We're good, Liyah. I'm sorry for being weird. I've been stressed about work stuff," he says, but something still seems off.

She nods. "Well, I'd invite you to go shopping with us to make up for it, but that would be a nightmare for absolutely everyone involved."

"Right," Daniel says.

Liyah furrows her brow, confused. Why can't she smooth

this over with humor? It's almost as though he *wants* to go with her and Jackie and witness the ease with which they weave from affectionate to bickering and back again.

Maybe it's that she's met his family, and he hasn't met hers. But that's completely different; Minji and Kayla were here before they started sleeping together. And, technically, Liyah had already met Kayla.

"I feel like I'm making this worse, but I'm grasping at straws, here."

"I told you, it's work stuff."

"Oh," she says. "Is something wrong with the CTA account?"

"No, they liked the campaign."

"Something I don't know about the Field? Do the numbers look bad, and you're afraid to tell me?" She feels her heart begin to race.

"No, Liyah. It's not that. Different account." Daniel's eyes are pointed in her direction, but Liyah gets the sense that he's looking straight through her.

"Okay, well. In case it *was* something I said, I'll pick up a new mind-mouth filter at the store today." The corner of his mouth only just turns upward. Liyah sighs. "Can we start the last ten minutes from the top?"

Daniel nods, his smile a little more certain. "Sure."

"Okay," she says, holding up three fingers. "Three, two, one: go!"

CHAPTER 26

DANIEL'S eyes have been on Alex for the past several minutes. His bartending is awe-inspiring, a choreographed dance in which the copper-colored cocktail shakers reflect spots of amber light onto the ceiling. It's not something Daniel's paid much attention to before, but that's probably because he's always watching Liyah. Not that he isn't engaged in the rest of the group—his gaze just regularly snares on something about her. Most any skill can be developed over time, and Daniel is becoming the world's foremost expert on listening intently to Jordan's and Siobhan's dating issues while also cataloging the way Liyah twirls a cherry stem or how the moles on her left cheek jump when she smiles.

She insisted that they soldier on without her, but everything feels slightly out of place. Their table has lost a leg—if they reassemble, they could get it to stand, but as is, it keeps tipping over. One Survival Club, and he's like this. There's a dull ache at the thought of what would happen if their friendship ended poorly.

"Are we not interesting enough for you?" Jordan asks, severing Daniel's line of thought.

"Sorry. Long week at work." A lackluster and overly relied-upon excuse.

Siobhan sighs. "No, be honest. It's weird without Liyah, isn't it? It feels like we're cheating on her."

Daniel laughs. "Yeah, something like that. It's not even hanging out with the two of you. It's the hanging out *here* that gets me. It feels like Prohibition is sacred."

Jordan leans in conspiratorially. "Y'all think Alex would be disappointed if we dipped?"

"I'll promise to clean the bathroom next time it's his turn if I have to."

Siobhan sets her empty glass on a wilting cocktail napkin. "There's a Lou Malnati's three blocks from here. What would it take for me to convince you lot to split a deep-dish pizza?"

"Not a damn thing," Jordan replies, already out of his seat.

Jordan's napkin is obliterated into microscopic shreds by the time the food arrives, but the waitress's disapproving scowl disappears when he flashes her his signature smile and wink. As soon as their server is gone, Daniel fans himself and Siobhan clutches her chest, letting out twin barks of laughter.

"I thought it was Liyah who was determined to shrink my ego."

Daniel swallows his bite of too-hot molten cheese and sauce, shaking his head. "Nah man, she's just the loudest."

"It's true," Siobhan adds, hand hovering in front of her partially full mouth. "Why do you think we're always laughing along with her?"

"I hate y'all," Jordan says, but he's grinning. "I came here under false pretenses."

"What's false about it? We promised pizza and good company, and that's exactly what you've got."

"Aite, moving on from Comedy Central's Roast of Jordan

Ames, can we get a Will update from Siobhan?" Jordan pauses just short of his first bite—Southern manners always remaining intact—to add: "Keeping in mind House Rule number eleven."

Siobhan's cheeks and chest pinken. "Listen! You asked me to keep the juicy bits to myself and I have since obliged. No Will updates, per se . . . but since we're not exclusive, I went on a date with a different bloke."

"Any good?" Daniel asks.

"Hardly. I made a joke about being a big girl—because the moment called for it and I am quite funny." It dawns on Daniel that Siobhan would not have complimented herself in that way in front of them a few months ago. He smiles brighter. "And he had the nerve to tell me, 'No, you're beautiful.'" She rolls her eyes, and Daniel and Jordan wince. "First of all, I *am* fat, I think I'd know. And second, when did I say I wasn't beautiful? I'd assume he thought as much since he asked to be on a date with me. I decided he wasn't so good-looking after all and ended up in Will's bed at the end of the night." She eyes Jordan. "End of story, so as not to scandalize you."

Jordan places his hands in prayer position and bows his head. "Much appreciated. And, on behalf of all men, I apologize."

"Tentatively accepted."

"That's shitty. At least you got rid of him," Daniel interjects.

Siobhan glances at Daniel and sighs into her beer. "If I've learned anything from Liyah, it's that there's plenty more shit men where he came from. If you don't think it's abdicating my Survival Club responsibilities to try new things and whatnot, I think I'll stick with Will for now."

"Dating unexclusively is overrated and exhausting. You do you," Jordan says.

"Especially if you already know you like one person best," Daniel finds himself adding.

Both pairs of eyes snap to him. "Speaking from personal experience?"

"*Current* personal experience, she means."

Daniel nods, quickly looking down at his pizza to conceal the gesture. Not his smoothest move.

"You and Liyah always avoid talking about relationships, and you've been seeing someone? Way to hold out on us, man."

Words cannot describe his relief that Jordan said *someone* and not *each other*. It seems Alex kept his promise. But Daniel still feels as if he's been caught by Kayla all over again. "*Seeing* is a strong word."

"But there is someone," Jordan confirms—a statement, not a question. "Alex wouldn't tell me anything, but I knew it!"

"Oooh," Siobhan squeals. "Can we see a picture of her?"

"No," Daniel says too quickly. "Just . . . gotta figure some shit out first."

Siobhan and Jordan exchange a look. "Okay, fine. Spoilsport," she adds before changing the subject.

On the way home, the deep dish sits poorly in his stomach. Daniel only has so many narrowly missed disasters left before something gives.

Sometime between the Damen L stop and his apartment, Daniel's phone vibrates in his pocket. He removes it from the depths of his winter coat and uses the trusted cold weather method of swiping with his nose. His screen fills with a picture of Liyah, and with it, his chest fills with warmth. She's in his UW Madison shirt, leaning back against a stack of hotel pillows. Her mother, from whom she has inherited much facial structure but few features, is fast asleep on her shoulder, jaw hanging open. The accompanying text message reads:

Liyah

Been stuck like this for two
hours, but afraid to wake the
momster by switching the
show. Can you OD on house
hunters? Please advise

Daniel stops in his tracks. *Done for* doesn't cover it. He's
in love with her. Not enamored. In *love*. Like, stupidly. It's
effervescent and fizzing painfully through his arteries from his
heart to his extremities, and he has to lean against a nearby
building so that he doesn't collapse with the weight of it all.

It's bare instinct that has him thumbing through his contact list and pressing call, and for a blissful half second, his
subconscious expects someone to answer.

Three ascending tones and a robotic voice brutally remind
him that there's nobody on the other end. For the first time in
his life, Daniel is in love, and his father will never know about
it. His mom or Kayla might pick up, but he can't bring himself to call. It would be tantamount to saying he's replaceable,
and Aaron Rosenberg is anything but.

Was anything but.

Past tense is so morbid.

Daniel inhales deeply, frigid air stinging his lungs. "I met a
girl," he says on his out breath.

Famous last words, his dad would reply. *What's she like?*

"Eomma and Kayla met her already, and they love her.
Her name is Liyah, short for Aliyah. She works at a museum
and loves skeletons and coffee and poking fun at me. Sweet
Potato—my cat, you don't know that I guess—might like her
even more than she likes me. She's got the quickest wit of
anyone I've ever met." This side street is dead at this time of
night, but Daniel presses his silent phone to his ear just in
case as he makes his way toward his building.

Your eomma was always smarter than me. It's what made me fall for her. Her face didn't hurt, either, Imaginary Dad says.

"Liyah's so completely beautiful, it's unreal. I love her, Dad. I wish you could meet her." Tears well as he walks, but he makes no move to wipe them away.

Does she feel the same way?

"Sometimes, she looks at me in this careful way and I think she might, but she always says she doesn't date and . . . I don't know. I should talk to her, but I can't figure out what to say. What do you think? What would you do?"

Imaginary Dad's answers can only go as far as Daniel's imagination. It's a quiet walk the rest of the way home.

LIYAH FELL ASLEEP in her mother's hotel room last night sometime during the fifth episode of *House Hunters*, never having made it out of the position she was stuck in. More importantly, never having made it *into* her hair wrap or so much as a scrunchie. Now, her mother is impatiently waiting on her couch as Liyah rushes through her morning routine.

"I don't see why you couldn't leave from the hotel. You're beautiful without any makeup. Six letters, a plant or hilly evidence of pre-Clovis Americans."

"Cactus. Cactus Hill is an archaeological site in Virginia." Liyah stuffs the front of her sweater into her high-waisted jeans. "And it's not about makeup, I needed to shower and do my hair. It was a mess after I slept with it out." She rolls on her wool socks and exits the bedroom.

"You could have put your hair up and nobody would notice. Then I'd get to see your shayna punim." A perennial complaint from Jackie Cohen: Liyah's hair blocks her pretty face. "I could have loaned you a hair tie if yours wasn't good enough."

Liyah rolls her eyes. "Yours have metal clasps! Would you like to cut it out of my hair?" She forces her feet into her snow boots and begins the tedious process of lacing them.

Her mom slips her crossword into her purse. "You're ready now, so it's neither here nor there. Breakfast?"

"Yes, please."

They walk arm in arm to a little waffle place in Wicker Park, her mother saying things like *Oh, it's so good to see you!* and *When will I see you next?* despite the two full days they have remaining.

"How long will your exhibit be running? Dad and I won't want to miss it," her mom asks the moment Liyah finishes complaining about Emiliano's antics and shovels a generous bite of waffle into her mouth.

She pouts, chews as quickly as she can, and swallows. "At least a year. You'll be able to see it, I promise. Just let me know when and I'll get your tickets." Liyah replaces the piece of waffle.

"Oh, we're so proud! I can't wait." Her mom reaches across the table to pat her wrist. "So, have you been seeing anybody special?"

Liyah shakes her head. "You know I don't really date, Mom."

Her mom tsks. "That's what you tell me. How am I to know? Maybe you don't want to keep your mother in the loop."

"You want to hear about my sex life that much?"

"So, there is someone!"

"Someone I'm sleeping with, Mom. Not dating."

"Who is he? She? They?"

"Mom," Liyah protests.

"Are they goyishe? Is that why you won't tell me? It would be hypocritical of me to judge, and you're a woman, after all. Your kids will be Jewish no matter what."

Liyah groans. "See, that's the issue. We're just sleeping together; I don't want to talk about kids." She takes a bite of eggs in the hopes that the conversation will end.

"You're friends?"

"Yes."

"Interesting. Good friends?"

"Yes." Liyah is surprised at her own lack of hesitation. She takes another bite of waffle.

Her mother taps her chin. "Your father and I were good friends, once."

Liyah rolls her eyes. "Yeah, but you probably always wanted more than that. You were the marriage kind, you know? That's not who I am." *Daniel is probably the marrying type,* she thinks. But whenever it happens, it will be with someone kind and normal. Who can say hello without making fun of him, who doesn't have meltdowns in synagogue on the High Holidays. Who hasn't dissolved into a puddle of tears while naked in his arms on more than one occasion. It would never be with her.

"Oh, sweetie, there's no such thing. People just get to a point in life when they're with someone they love and marriage feels like the right thing to do. I didn't grow up dreaming of a white wedding." And then: "You really should eat more slowly, it's not good for your digestion."

Liyah scrunches her nose. At the same time as her mother, she says, "Don't make that face, you wouldn't want it to freeze."

Jackie laughs. "Am I really that predictable?"

"Like a broken record," Liyah replies, and rudely places another forkful in her mouth.

CHAPTER 27

LIYAH arrives at Prohibition at the uncommonly early time of 9:13, ten minutes after the rest of the group has settled in.

She hangs her snow coat on the back of the chair next to Daniel's. "God, no matter how early I arrive, I always feel like I'm late."

Daniel exaggeratedly checks his watch. "That's because you are."

"I had hoped for a warmer welcome." She pouts her wind-chapped lips, the bottom one pinker than usual, and Daniel wonders if they'll feel rough against his later tonight. "Thought you all might have learned to appreciate me in my absence, but alas."

Daniel coughs into his fist to cover his laugh. He's seen her—a *lot* of her—every night since Tuesday. As she unwinds her scarf and slides into her seat, she eyes him like she's thinking something similar. The lingering gaze flicks away before it can be caught by their comrades, but it's enough to unleash that bubbling feeling in his chest.

"How was Momma Cohen-Jackson's visit?" Jordan asks.

"Just Momma Cohen. She always says that Jackie Jackson

would have sounded bad, but Jackie Cohen-Jackson would be even worse."

"That's a good reason to keep your name, I suppose," Siobhan says around her straw.

"She would have found another excuse, I'm sure of it. It was good, even if I had to dodge a few 'When will you give me a grandchild' questions. I'd have two IUDs in if I could."

Jordan holds up his hand. "Spare me the details, please."

"I said three letters. I didn't even mention where I'd place them. They'd go in my *uterus,* Jordan. The strings go through the cervical opening and into the vaginal canal, so that the device can be removed. Would you like to know how it works?"

"I'd like to not have to retake tenth-grade health." Jordan's grimace deepens.

"If you feel comfortable inserting your genitals into something you can't hear the name of without cringing, you probably should. Though I'm not sure it would help; sex ed in this country is abysmal."

"Liyah," Siobhan objects.

"Yeah, yeah, I will limit my doom spiraling in the interest of morale. Surprised you haven't made it a rule yet."

"House Rule number twelve: Liyah must limit her doom spiraling in the interest of morale. All in favor, say aye."

Daniel and Jordan chorus their agreement, and Liyah pretends to frown as she writes it down at the bottom of today's notes. Under the table, Daniel feels the gentle pressure of the side of Liyah's boot against his. It's like speaking in code; her mouth says, "Jordan, no matter what the house rules say, I'm getting you a book on human reproduction," but that bump of her knee says *it's good to see you.*

He knocks his elbow against hers like *good to see you, too.*

A couple drinks in, the toe of her boot trails up his calf: *excited to see you later.*

His hand subtly—and very briefly—falls to her thigh and squeezes: *can't wait.*

Their pinkies brush: *I'm thinking about your fingers.*

Knees: *you look so, so good tonight.*

When she leans away completely and squares her shoulders for a fight, it's because Jordan has brought up romance once again. Motherfucking idiot, worst friend of all time, torturer of souls, Jordan. Daniel could strangle him.

"Listen," Liyah says. "I am more than happy to talk about the rest of your guys' dating misadventures. Delighted, even. But love is not, and has never been, my thing."

Siobhan rolls her eyes. "I bet you tell Daniel."

"That's not true," Daniel interjects. "I promise she's just as guarded with me." Maybe not *just* as guarded. But her emotions are still so often such a black box, he wonders if she's hiding them from herself, too.

"Why would I tell Daniel and not you two?"

"You spend the most time with him." Jordan shrugs.

Liyah's eyes widen; she feels cornered. Not good. "How can you say that? I work with Siobhan! Nine hours every single day!"

"You also work with Daniel, love. And I think Jordan means outside of work, anyway," Siobhan points out. Her voice has softened, and she's looking to Daniel, equally aware of Liyah's agitation.

Jordan has no such social grace. "We're just saying that y'all have become really close friends."

"No, we haven't!" Liyah spits.

Daniel is unable to shield his wince, and all three pairs of eyes catch it.

"I, um. I didn't mean it like that," Liyah adds weakly. "The four of us are all close friends, not just me and Daniel. I really value the group we have." She inhales deeply. "Do you want to know why I really don't want to be talking about this? It's because I don't think that romantic love is real."

Jordan shakes his head. "You've said that before. I call bullshit."

Sometimes, Jordan's lack of tact comes in handy. Daniel and Siobhan exchange another look. They've all been thinking it. "Your parents are still together. And had maybe the best meet-cute of all time."

"I know, Daniel. But that's . . . I don't know. Attraction, at first. Lust, and friendship, and then they built a life together and it works. They're not outwardly lovey-dovey. It seems like they just pleasantly coexist, not that the light of a thousand suns can't burn brighter than one another's beauty."

"I don't think love has to be like that for it to be love," Siobhan says.

Jordan nods. "Also, even as their kid, you don't know what's happening behind closed doors. My parents were the most loving couple, but it turned out that they both had a nigga on the side." He takes a swig of his scotch, avoiding eye contact. Daniel's heard this story, but he knows it's the first time Jordan's told the rest of the group. "When they divorced, everybody was shocked, but they'd hated each other the whole time."

"Damn, that's . . ." Liyah gulps down the rest of her drink. "Okay, fine. Maybe my parents are blissfully in love, or at least more in love than I can see."

Jordan, ever insistent: "So, we have established that romantic love is, in fact, real."

"Could be," Liyah corrects.

"Would you like to share about your dating life now? You don't even have to give us names. Just one bit of information."

"No, I would not like to share."

"Why not, then?"

"Jordan—" Daniel warns, but gets waved off.

"No, because clearly there's some issue here. This is late-twenties group therapy, right? So, we're therapizing. Why not, Liyah?"

"Seriously, Jordan—" Siobhan starts, but Liyah cuts her off.

"Because I don't think it's real for me! For you all, maybe. Probably, actually. Not for me."

A sailor's knot forms in Daniel's chest. "You don't think you're capable of falling in love?"

The table is silent.

Liyah sighs. "No, it's—I'm kind of a mess, emotionally."

Siobhan touches Liyah's forearm. "We all are, sometimes."

"No, like, I've never met anyone as truly confident as Jordan. And Siobhan is so funny and caring and conscientious and artistic. And then Daniel . . ." She trails off, looking down at her napkin. Why can't she finish this sentence? What's wrong with him? After a breath, Liyah continues, voice small. "I'm not like that. I'm grouchy and have a big chip on my shoulder and a lot of issues that make me an incredibly difficult person to be around. I don't think anybody could ever fall in love with me."

Daniel is taken aback. "That's ridiculous."

"No, it's not." She says it firmly, like she's returning a tricky serve.

"Yes, it is!" he volleys, his heart hammering.

"It's really not," she pings back.

"Yes, it is!" he repeats dumbly.

"No! Why are you arguing this? How would you know?"

"Because I'm in love with you! Liyah, I promise you, it's so goddamn easy to be."

A collective gasp alerts Daniel to the fact that he's just said those words aloud. His head falls to his hands.

"No, you aren't. We work together. We're friends."

He lifts his head to make eye contact, dragging his hands down his face in the process. "Oh, don't give me that, Liyah. I think we've—I think I've had enough time to figure out how I feel about you."

Liyah's eyes flicker around the circle. "Why would you say this here, in front of everyone?" Her voice could cut a diamond.

Daniel lets out a hiss of a breath. "I didn't mean to, but I'm sure they could tell. I'm not very good at hiding it; I kinda thought you knew."

"Well, I didn't know! And how would they know? They didn't even know we're fucking!" Siobhan snorts, and Liyah practically breaks her neck snapping her attention that way. "*What?*"

"Liyah, love, come on. Do you think we're that thick? We're not."

Jordan winks. "Speak for yourself."

Siobhan gives him a withering look. "Not the time."

Daniel would very much like to crawl under their table. At this point, his height is all that's stopping him. He racks his brain, but short of one of them being immediately hit by a blue-line train, he cannot imagine this going any worse.

"You both *knew*? So, what was this, a setup? Get me wound up until I confirm your latest gossip? Some friends you are," Liyah accuses.

Siobhan and Jordan shake their heads. "Liyah, that's obviously not—"

Liyah looks to Daniel, eyes piercing right through him. "Did you tell them?" On the surface, she sounds angry, but Daniel knows better. She's hurt.

"No, I didn't. I swear. I wouldn't . . . I wouldn't break your trust like that," he says, trying to keep his voice gentle.

"Really? You wouldn't? Because breaking my trust is *exactly* why I stopped talking to you at summer camp."

His eyes go wide, volume dials up. "Are you kidding me,

Liyah? You're bringing up Maccabiah? I thought we put that to rest months ago!"

Liyah's hands ball into fists. "I thought I told *you* it wasn't just about color wars months ago! Need I remind you that while you were praised for making out with someone who wasn't your girlfriend, I was ridiculed for it."

"Wait, was the archery field—" Jordan starts.

Siobhan frowns, face going red. "What? You said you hardly talked to him at summer camp. I asked you, and you looked me in the eyes and said that."

"I didn't want to relive it, okay? His buddies found out, he got a few high fives and fist bumps, and I got humiliated."

"We've been over this. *I didn't tell them.* And yes, you're right, I should have warned you, but also, I was a thirteen-year-old boy. Are you going to hate me forever for acting like a child when I *was* one?"

"Here's the thing, Rosenberg," she hisses, cold as ice. "You can argue with me about the minutiae of that summer all you want, but none of that matters. *Maybe* I was dead wrong about you back then. But I can tell you right now that springing how you're supposedly 'in love'"—she uses air quotes—"with me in front of our friends who are not involved in our *private relationship* seems like a pretty fucking big breach of trust to me."

"Don't do those fucking air quotes at me, Liyah. I told you I'm in love with you and you're being patronizing? How unfeeling can you be? You're above that."

"Apparently, I'm not." Liyah rips her coat from the back of her chair and storms away, yanking out Daniel's heart and half his other vital organs in the process.

THE COLD AIR of the alleyway hits Liyah like a ton of bricks; in her rush to leave Prohibition, she barely got one arm through her parka. She hurriedly wraps her scarf around her neck, doing her best to stuff her hair into the faux fur–lined hood before she zips up. Her fingertips are purpling by the time they're tucked into her mittens.

To say she's unable to think about what just happened would be wholly untrue. No, she's a whirlpool of every possible thought and emotion and her poor brain can't seem to get them organized, confusion the only buoy in sight.

When Liyah reaches the train station, she doesn't board. Instead, she turns onto Milwaukee, walking alongside the barreling whirr of the train below. The wind whips at her cheeks, dries out her eyes. She pulls the scarf up over the bottom half of her face, wishing the pricks of water doing their damnedest to keep her eyes from shriveling wouldn't also blur her vision. Or feel so conspicuously close to crying.

The walk takes the better part of an hour, and when she strips off her outerwear inside her apartment, she can't tell whether she's shivering or trembling with frustration. In her bathroom, she seals the drain of her tub and runs the water as hot as she can stand. She uncaps a bottle of bubble bath and pours it under the stream, watching the foaming blooms. Liyah is a Victorian handmaid scorned, angrily drawing a bath. It's so ridiculous, she should laugh. Instead, lips pressed in a harsh line, she knots her hair atop her head and secures it with a scrunchie.

The water is bordering on scalding as she submerges herself, but the stinging skin soothes her. She swipes around her Spotify in search of a suitably calming playlist, only to give up and FaceTime Neen instead.

"Calling me from the bath, are you? Naughty girl."

Liyah rolls her eyes half-heartedly. "All the spicy bits are covered in bubbles."

Two different voices call *which girl is calling you from the bath?* and *can I see?* from off-screen. "It's my best friend.

And no, Dan, you cannot. Hold on C-J, I'm gonna step outside." A minor commotion follows, and then the screen is filled with Neen's face and what appears to be a considerably less frosty night than what Liyah trudged through. "What's up, babe?"

Liyah wipes bubbles from her nose with the back of her hand. "I don't even know where to start."

"How about the middle or the end, if the beginning isn't doing it for ya?"

"Daniel told me he loved me."

"Ah, okay." Neen nods. "We knew that already, didn't we?"

"No—like *in love* with me. Like romantically."

Neen furrows their brow. "I'm gathering that I should be shocked," they say before clearing their throat. "Wow! He's in love with you? That's crazy!"

"It *is* shocking," Liyah insists.

"Right, it's shocking. Is that why you're so upset? Because you didn't expect it?"

"He did it in the worst possible way, Neen. We were arguing about romantic love—no, don't groan at me, please. I'm hanging on by a thread here."

"Sorry."

She unloads everything until, at long last, Neen satisfies Liyah with an appropriately stunned expression. "Oof, okay. C-J, I just want to say, you are an extremely lovable person. And so deserving of love. I get frustrated when I hear you say things like that, so I imagine it was rough for Daniel to listen to you."

Liyah balks. "Are you seriously taking his side?"

"No, I don't think he handled the situation well at all. I am taking Jordan's and Siobhan's side, though. You owe them apologies."

"I know." Liyah sinks deeper into the bath until the foam tickles her chin. "I didn't really mean what I said. I was just . . ."

"Overwhelmed?" Liyah nods. "Yeah, I've seen you when you get that way; it's not pretty."

Liyah blows on a palmful of bubbles, watching them slowly drift back down to the tub instead of looking at Neen's face on her phone screen. "Thanks."

"You're very welcome." Their tone turns from sarcastic to concerned. "Have you given any thought to what he said?"

She shakes her head, frown deepening. "You're hearing all of my thoughts as they're coming to me."

"I mean whether you feel similarly."

"You mean like whether I'm in love with him?" Liyah's stomach knots. The last time she thought she was in love, she was sixteen. This feels *nothing* like that. "No, I haven't considered that! I don't even think he's in love with me! He's probably doing that mid-to-late-twenties thing where you assume that each new person you sleep with is the love of your life because you want to settle down so badly."

"Is Daniel really that desperate for a partner?"

"No, but . . ." Liyah trails off, her heart hammering.

"Can you give me a real reason why he can't possibly be in love with you? And don't say because nobody could."

But that's a perfectly good reason. She is not the love interest! She's the person you meet on the way to the love interest. The one you joke about having had great sex with in your twenties, the one who bummed you out for a month or so when she ended it. Who made you realize that you could move on to someone a little more sane and a lot less broken. And she would say this to Neen, but she doesn't want a lecture. She wants *help*. So instead, she says, "Well, we work together."

"Oh my God, only kind of! And isn't that almost over? Try again."

"This really sucks. I feel like someone's taken an ice cream scooper to my insides."

"I wonder why that is," Neen quips. "C-J, I love you. I also think that you're not in the right headspace to receive any feedback I can give. Why don't you finish your bath, go to bed, and we'll talk in the morning?"

Her breathing shallows. She shouldn't be alone right now. "Neen, no! I need you to help me sort through this."

"I am happy to be your sounding board after you're a bit more settled. I can't feel your feelings for you, though. No matter what, that job can never be outsourced."

She knows the resolution in Neen's voice. There isn't anything she can do to make them stay on the line. Liyah takes a deep breath, then forces a smile. "Can't you write a program for that?"

"I wish. Are you gonna survive if I let you go now?"

Liyah sighs, swirling her fingers through the warm water. "Barely."

"Okay. See ya, C-J."

"Bye, Neen."

They click off, and Liyah balances her phone on the wide lip of the tub.

The silence stretches.

In love with me. What a cruel joke. How dare he? In public! After everything I've told him, to call me unfeeling. That's not love. We had an agreement. We're friends! We were friends. He's the unfeeling one. No consideration for me at all.

Incensed. That's how she feels.

She inhales, then sinks even lower in, letting the water cover her head completely. How long can she stay this way? It's safe under here, all sense reduced to nothing but the heat of the water against her skin.

She cloaks herself until her lungs physically burn for air. And then some. She only comes up for a breath when she's sure she can't stand it a moment longer. Her ribs ache with her heaving. The screen of her phone flashes.

Call from Daniel Woo-jin Rosenberg.

Liyah holds down the side button until the screen goes black.

CHAPTER 28

NIGHTS go like this: Daniel gets home, laconically replies to an increasingly concerned Alex before he leaves for work, cooks dinner, has a beer, gets in bed, and watches Netflix until he can bear falling asleep. Sweet Potato trails him even more than usual, sits on his chest and purrs until his eyes close. Returns the moment they open again.

That conversation at Survival Club lasted mere minutes, and six months of friendship, gone.

He called three times. Once that night, once the next day, once the day after. Left voice mails. Four text messages, one each day since it became apparent that she wouldn't pick up his call. Asking for a chance to talk in person, at first, but by the last one he just wanted to confirm that if he sent her an email, she'd read it. Radio silence.

It's been a full week, and here he is, about to be late to work, deleting and retyping his fifth message.

Daniel

i don't expect you to
respond to this. i don't want
to make you uncomfortable,
so i'm letting the crew know
i won't be there tonight. if
you change your mind, you
know how to reach me.

Daniel to SSC

hey guys, i have so much
work to catch up on today,
so you should go ahead
without me.

It's a transparent out, but not technically untrue. Sweet Potato's purring on his chest intensifies. In his deep dive into cat behavior the day of her spontaneous adoption, Daniel learned that cats purr at a frequency that promotes healing. He scratches behind her ears. "Not sure it's gonna work for this one, but thanks anyway, Sweet P."

Daniel wishes, more than anything, that he could wish he hadn't met Liyah. It would be easier that way, to call the last few months a wash and move on. To tell himself that she was right, and he doesn't really love her after all. If only.

Days go like this: Daniel misjudges the timing of his train, arrives slightly late to work, thinks of Liyah telling him to stop blaming his Jewish internal clock on the CTA. Daniel works, or pretends to work. It's hard to tell the difference. Jordan pops in to "get his opinion on something" three times more than usual, ignores the dark circles under Daniel's eyes. They eat lunch. More work. Bus to L to home. Laconically replies to an increasingly concerned Alex before he leaves for work. Etcetera.

Today—slightly different. When they sit down in their fa-vorite Lebanese lunch spot, Jordan says, "I'm really, really sorry about last week. I shouldn't have kept pushing her like that, and it blew up on you."

Daniel swallows his bite of shawarma and takes a big gulp of water, deciding how to respond. He settles on, "It's not on you, man. I shouldn't have . . . it was not the right time. You couldn't know that it would go that way."

"No, Liyah was right." Jordan's voice catches on her name, as if he's worried about Daniel's reaction. "I wasn't tryna catch you in the act, but Siobhan and I guessed a while ago, so even telling her she didn't have to name names, I knew I was flying close to the sun. I didn't realize how bad you'd caught feelings, but it wasn't cool. So, I'm sorry."

"Thanks, I guess." Daniel chews. "This is something you and Siobhan talk about?"

Jordan shakes his head. "I know that's part of what upset Liyah, but it ain't even like that. We only had two conver-sations. One was about how we thought y'all were sleeping together—that was that first SSC back at Prohibition after the Chanukah party. And on the way home a few weeks be-fore that, I said I thought you were crushing mad hard, and Siobhan said she thought Liyah fancied you. It didn't go be-yond that, I promise."

"Wow," is all Daniel can think to say.

"Wow what?"

He shrugs. "You and Siobhan picked up on things pretty fast, is all. Guess we're not as sly as we thought."

They eat in silence for a few minutes, and Daniel won-ders if he's off the hook for the rest of the conversation. Fat chance, knowing Jordan, but he might as well enjoy his lunch staring blankly out the window while he can.

"Hey, man." Sure enough, Jordan comes back with his anxious-older-brother voice. "You sure you don't want to join us tonight? I'm sure work can wait," he adds, like they don't both know it was a limp excuse.

"She still hasn't spoken to me."

"At all?"

"Not a thing. I've thought about sending her an email, because I don't even know if she's been checking the texts . . ." Daniel shakes his head. "I don't want this to be the first time I see her."

Jordan rubs his hand over his chin. "Damn. Okay, I get it if you want to sit this one out. But I think Survival Club has been good for you. For all of us, man. I know it's fucking corny, but I love y'all. I really do. Siobhan's been dating, and Liyah delegated at work, and sometimes doesn't expect the worst to happen. I've spent some time single, and it's good. And you went to therapy!"

"Yeah."

When he says no more, Jordan frowns. "Look, man, I'm getting worried. I haven't seen you this bad since your dad passed."

Daniel sighs. "I meant what I told her. I knew the deal, that we were supposed to be friends. But some small part of me thought she might feel the same way. Or at least care about me enough not to ghost."

"Dude, she does care about you. You know Liyah, though. She think she too hard for feelings. She might just need a little bit of time."

"I don't know how much time I can give her."

"That's up to you to decide. But don't lose hope."

"A little tone deaf, don't you think?"

Jordan flashes his charming grin. "I can't help it. Too many romantic comedies and pornos, remember?"

Daniel can't muster the energy to pretend to laugh. He thinks he convinces the corners of his mouth to turn upward, but who's to say?

"Damn, not even a smile. Okay. You sure you can be on your own tonight? I could tell S and L that I'm on a last-minute project with you."

Daniel waves him off. "No, don't do that. I'll be . . ." Good? Definitely not. Fine would be a lie, too. "I can handle myself for one Friday night."

Jordan scans his entire face, as if looking for the single eyebrow hair or muscle twitch that'll tell him Daniel's about to crash. He finds none. "Okay, man. Hit me whenever and I'll be there."

Daniel mutters his appreciation, eats more shawarma, and then he's back at work.

Work goes well, it seems. Brett stops by to congratulate Daniel on a job well done with a firm handshake and a clap on the shoulder. Daniel knows that with Jordan, Brett eschews handshakes altogether and only offers awkward fist bumps. Another answer to the eternal question of Daniel's and Jordan's employment at Kinley: is it an age thing or a race thing?

Brett tells him that the CTA loved his digital work. He knew as much since they already had him convert some of the online promos for their social media profiles to physical ads, but it's a shock to Daniel that anyone at Kinley was paying attention. "They went up in a bunch of trains and buses last night."

Daniel plasters on his best phony smile—the kind that would fool all but three people in his life. Or two, now. "That's great news. It was a pleasure working with them; I'm so happy they liked it."

"It was good stuff, I told ya. 'Where you go on it,'" he misquotes. Daniel tries not to stare at the obscenely high, gelled, blond coif. "Genius, bro. Genius. I haven't heard back about final numbers for the Field, but they've seemed happy so far. I thought these accounts would be total duds, but you've made Kinley look good. We put some bullshit on the website about how we're invested in helping local public services—it's great marketing for us." Daniel smiles again, telling himself that he's okay with Brett using whatever rationale he sees fit. "Keep up the good work." Brett exits the office, shooting finger guns at Daniel as he leaves.

That *was* great news. Daniel should be elated. He's not, though. Obviously.

At five o'clock, Daniel makes his way to a coffee shop around the corner from his office, waiting there until he's sure he won't cross paths with Alex at home. He's acting like a melodramatic teenager. It might be cause for embarrassment in a few days, but right now, it feels necessary for survival.

Sweet Potato greets him at the door, extends her paw to pat his cheek. The little pink pads on the bottoms of her feet are the cutest in the world. *Have you checked?* Liyah would ask if she were here. *I don't have to, I just know,* he'd reply.

He heads to the fridge, pulling out a beer and a Tupperware of leftover pasta that he doesn't bother to reheat. Sweet Potato impatiently meows as he settles on the couch, then curls into her favorite position on his lap.

Eyes glued to a muted Chicago Sky game, Daniel alternates between his beer, food, and Sweet Potato. Sip, bite, pet, repeat. He hasn't once looked away from the screen, but if someone asked who was winning, he's not sure he could tell them.

The phone rings. *FaceTime from Kayla.* He considers letting it ring out, but he's done that twice this week. He attempts to fix his hair—which probably only makes him look more disheveled—before answering.

Instead of his sister's face, the screen fills with a pixelated image of her living room wall, a framed artwork he doesn't recognize taking up most of the space.

"Danny! What do you think?"

"I think you need to hold your phone still so that it can focus."

"Sorry! I'm just excited. I've been trying to show you all week." Kayla steadies her hand, and the image crystalizes: a vintage Coca-Cola advertisement, circa 1900. In beautiful hand lettering, it boasts being charming, healthful, the most refreshing drink in the world. Five cents at soda founts and carbonated in bottles. The ideal drink for discriminating people. "Is it cool or dumb? I saw it at a thrift store and loved it, but now I'm kinda worried that it's weird to have an ad for a pop I don't even drink in my living room."

"Very cool, Noona. We studied an ad like this in one of my classes in college."

"Okay, glad to have a seal of approval from the Rosenberg family ad expert. Where's my feline niece?" She switches the camera so her face comes into view. Her wavy hair is piled atop her head in one of those clawlike clips that Daniel loved playing with growing up. Dark eyebrows knit together and mauve painted lips frown, Kayla apparently having looked at Daniel's face on her screen for the first time. "Danny, what's wrong? I knew you were avoiding me! I told myself you were just busy, but I should've listened to my Spidey senses tingling."

Where to begin? "You were right."

"Of course I was. What about?"

"Liyah. I was gonna tell her, I swear. I waited too long, and it"—he borrows a phrase from Jordan—"blew up on me."

"Oh, Danny. I'm so sorry. She told you she didn't feel the same way? I have to say, I didn't really expect that, but I guess you never know." She could say *I told you so,* but she doesn't, and he's thankful.

Daniel rubs his temple. "I wish. She didn't tell me anything! She got mad at me for saying it and basically said I'm the same piece of shit I was at thirteen and stormed out—which, okay, I did say it in front of Jordan and Siobhan, so I get that." Kayla's eyebrows shoot up half an inch. "But she didn't answer my calls or respond to my texts asking for a chance to apologize and explain. I'm starting to think she might have me blocked."

"Do the messages say *delivered* underneath them?" Daniel checks the thread, trying not to visibly wince at the sea of uninterrupted blue that takes up the entire screen. Sure enough, there's a tiny *Delivered* printed under the final text bubble. He nods. "I don't think you're blocked, then."

Daniel sighs, nervously running his fingers through his hair. "She doesn't have read receipts, though. I still don't know whether she's seen them."

"Don't take this the wrong way, but have you *actually* explained and apologized? Or did you just ask for the chance?"

"The latter," Daniel grumbles. "But I asked if she'd read an email I sent, and she didn't respond. Besides, it's not like I'm the only one who has something to apologize for."

"I'm sure you aren't, but that doesn't mean you can't be the first to do it."

She's right. Of course she's right. But that doesn't mean he likes it. "Isn't that, like, harassment? I wasn't planning on sending any more texts. I don't think she wants to be contacted," he tries.

"I'm telling you to send her one email, Danny. You can let her contact you after that. Don't show up at her apartment in the middle of the night or at her office unannounced, and you're good."

Daniel is quiet for a long moment, working to accept the idea. "What if she never replies? What if she never speaks to me again?"

Kayla purses her lips. "What exactly did you say to her? Was it unforgivable?"

Daniel shakes his head. "It was more the way I said it than what I said." *Unfeeling.* Not his best choice of words. "Mostly. There was one thing . . . she was being condescending and it pissed me off, so I said she was above the way she was acting and asked why she was being so unfeeling, or something like that. Not great."

"Right, not great. Not exactly evil, either. You want my take?" She's clearly about to give it regardless. "If you send her something heartfelt and she never talks to you again, then she wasn't worthy of your friendship or your love in the first place."

Maybe that's somewhat true, but it can't totally be. Yom Kippur, the snowstorm, his dad's Jesa-Yahrzeit. Liyah *is* a friend to him. That doesn't just go away. "Okay," he says noncommittally.

"You'll write the email?"

"I will," he replies, unsure whether he's lying.

Kayla tells him that she loves him and to take care of himself, and he asks her a few more questions about where she got the advertisement and what she's doing this weekend, and then they hang up and he's alone in the stillness of his apartment once again.

He disturbs Sweet Potato to retrieve a second beer. Again, to find the clicker and unmute the game. The Sky win; blue and yellow confetti bursts across the screen. A game show starts. He switches to Netflix.

Clueless is suggested, an 82 percent match based on his watching history.

Fuck.

He extracts his laptop from his workbag and pulls up the browser tab permanently open to his email.

To: Aliyah Cohen-Jackson <a.cohen.jackson@fieldmuseum.org>
From: Daniel Rosenberg <dwrosenberg@kinley.com>
RE: write a subject before sending this

Dear Liyah,

Nope. Fuck, that feels weird and formal. He tries again:

To Liyah:

He's never addressed an email that way. He checks his
other email threads with Liyah. They usually don't address
each other at all. It feels wrong to just jump into this message,
though. He goes with:

Liyah—

I'm not sure if you'll read this, but I hope you do. It feels important
that I send it anyway.

A swig of his third beer gives him the courage to go onward. He types out three paragraphs of utter nonsense, then
does his best to mold it into something intelligible. After several reworkings and a few scrapped sentences, there's not
much more to do. Reading it aloud only takes him so far. As
if making sure it's perfectly free from typos will change her
mind.

He rewrites the subject line as *I'm Sorry* and checks his
watch. She'll be in the middle of Survival Club right now.
One o'clock on Saturday is an innocuous time; usually, they'd
be at a café ironing out logistics for their next event by then,
so she isn't likely to be in the middle of anything. He sched-
ules the send time and shuts his laptop before he can continue
his second-guessing.

Later, when he's in bed watching *Clueless,* he gets a text
from Jordan.

Jordan
I think you should write the
email.

A few of the last evaporating droplets of hope replenish as he drifts off to sleep.

CHAPTER 29

LIYAH feels like shit.

There's nothing left to do. Two days until the exhibition opens, and everything is double-, triple-, quadruple-checked and ready to go. Her biggest career accomplishment all but said and done, and Liyah, instead of basking in joy, feels like shit.

She told Neen as much. *I wonder why* they replied via text. They refused to explain further. Siobhan hasn't been much help, either. Monday morning, she graciously accepted Liyah's apology, but since then, her blue eyes go round if the conversation steers anywhere near the subject of The Incident. And last night's Survival Club only made her feel shittier.

Everything felt wrong. Nobody took notes. Jordan didn't bring up dating (for obvious reasons), which is tantamount to a forecasted blizzard in the Sahara. She ended up in bed by eleven, up eight hours later.

Now, she's been watching YouTube videos in her empty office for going on four hours, waiting for some work to materialize. It hasn't. Only an email from Jeff:

To: Aliyah Cohen-Jackson <a.cohen.jackson@fieldmuseum.org>
From: Jeff Chapman <jeff.chapman@fieldmuseum.org>
RE: Just got the membership numbers back and they looked really good. I hate

to email you on a Saturday but wanted to share that 25–35 is at a 150% increase in new membership rates as compared to last year. Good job. I'll get started on that promotion package.

Sent from my iPhone

The first read gave her a jolt of excitement, but duller than it should have been. On the second, third, and fourth times, she was only grasping at wisps of satisfaction. She's closer than ever to her dream, and still, here she is, feeling like shit.

Maybe it's time to give up.

She waits on the bus stop bench, leg jiggling from impatience and the creeping chill. The 146 shudders to a stop, kneeling over its front wheels to ease her ascent.

"We'll get you warm, sweetheart," the bus driver says as she flashes her pass, completely misreading Liyah's scowl.

"Thank you," she mumbles, pulling down her hood and unwinding her scarf. Liyah finds a seat midway between the front and back doors to avoid the inevitable blast of cool air from the next stop. The patterned pile fabric reminds her of one of Daniel's button-downs. It's hideous. It looks good on him.

There's a series of ads above the seats that Liyah hasn't seen on her commute before. The leftmost one shows a snorkeler swimming with a sea turtle and various tropical fish, the Shedd Aquarium logo on the breast of the wet suit in sharp focus. Next to it is an image of hanging replicas of Saturn and Jupiter from the Adler Planetarium. To its right: SUE, the iconic *Tyrannosaurus rex* fossil of the Field. The final pane reads *Museum Campus: The CTA is where it takes*

*you. Check us out on Twitter @cta, Instagram @chicagocta,
and facebook.com/thecta.*

Daniel's digital series, plastered all over her commute. She
didn't know they were making in-person ads out of it. They
must have gone up this week, or Daniel would have told her.

Liyah's chest fills with an unnamed dull ache. She presses
her fist to her sternum, trying to massage it out. It doesn't
budge.

With screeching brakes, the bus arrives at Washington, its
driver wishing the disembarking passengers quick arrivals to
somewhere safe and warm. Liyah descends the stairs to the
L platform, mind numbing alongside her body. It's good, the
blankness. Safe.

She boards, and there it is: another ad series. This time,
a picture of the rock wall at Maggie Daley Park, next to the
pretentiously titled *Cloud Gate* that locals and tourists alike
know as "The Bean," followed by the Jay Pritzker Pavilion.
Millennium Park: The CTA is where it takes you.

On another car, another train, another bus, there'll be
shots of the Lincoln Park Zoo, the rival baseball stadiums,
the Chicago Public Library, the Riverwalk, Lake Michigan.
The CTA is where it takes you.

If it were last week, she'd pull out her phone and text
Daniel a selfie, flattening her hair enough for him to make out
the ads in the background. But it's not, and their text thread
has been on Do Not Disturb since last Saturday morning. No
notifications because she doesn't want to know if he's texted
her. Or worse, if he hasn't.

The pain sharpens and oh! Here come the tears. They're
silent, and she's almost at her stop. If she's going to cry in
public, at least there's that.

The four-minute walk home feels incredibly long, on account of the whole crying-in-public thing. She can't help it,

though, the waterworks just keep coming. She'd probably feel humiliated, but there's no more room in her chest.

Inside, shivering and still crying, Liyah strips down to her sweater and her underpants, heading to her bedroom to roll on fresh fuzzy socks. She withdraws a throw blanket from the basket she keeps near the radiator (about seven inches away yields the perfect warmth) and wraps herself in it, hobbling over to the kitchen to start some herbal tea. When the kettle whistles, the tears are still falling. It's high time she texts Neen.

She nearly drops her phone and her mug of tea when she sees the email notification. Subject line: *I'm Sorry.*

No no no nope. Nope! I can't read that. Should I read that? Fuck.

Pacing across her living room, she FaceTimes Neen. Then, remembering the state of her appearance, she quickly hangs up.

She shouldn't have bothered. It's no surprise that her phone immediately lights up with a returned video call. They'll be suspicious if she tries to switch to audio only. *God, what a mess,* she thinks as she swipes to answer.

"Jesus Christ, C-J. We're at burrito blanket stage?"

"It's cold out," Liyah weakly protests, not bothering to wipe her eyes.

"You are crying in a burrito blanket. I didn't think you'd let it go this far."

"I don't even know what I'm feeling right now, Neen! You're so in touch with your feelings, and I just don't have any, until I do, and then I can't even figure out what they are."

"Not having feelings and ignoring the feelings you have are not the same thing."

Liyah shrugs. "It works for me."

"No, dummy, it doesn't." Liyah glares. Neen makes their

and what about it? face. "You're being a dummy; I'm gonna call you a dummy."

"I'm gonna hang up."

"And have a meltdown by yourself? Try again. Have a seat, and let's go through it."

Liyah waddles over to her couch (slowly, lest she spill scalding chamomile) and sets her phone on the coffee table so that she can warm both her hands with her tea. "Today I was at work, but I didn't do any work, and then I watched some videos, and I went to my bus stop."

Neen shows the palm of their hand. "No. Do not give me the BuzzFeed listicle version of your day. Use some emotion words."

"Stop acting like my parent," Liyah snaps.

"Happily, the second you stop acting like a child."

They're right. "God, *okay.*" Liyah shifts in her seat. "Well, I woke up early because Daniel didn't come to SSC and it ended early. I felt . . . restless. I usually work with him at a coffee shop on Saturdays." She hates how small her voice sounds when she says his name. "So, I went to the office instead and I felt . . ." She shakes her head. "I don't know the word for this one."

"Okay, continue, and we'll circle back if we need to."

Liyah nods. "I left, and when I got on the bus, the seat pattern . . ." No, that's too embarrassing to say. "Well, I sat down, and then I saw this series of ads that Daniel made. He did a lot of the work for it while sitting next to me, when I was doing stuff for the exhibit. It was all digital, I had no idea the CTA had made them physical. It must've happened since I last talked to him. It made my chest ache."

"You miss him."

"Yeah, I do." Liyah's mind hadn't quite stitched that one together. "Wow, I really do. I miss Sweet Potato, too. She'd sit on my chest and make me feel better, and then I wouldn't need you anymore."

Neen rolls their eyes. "Yeah, yeah. Go on."

"I got off the bus and onto the train and there were more ads he did. That's when I started crying. And now I can't stop."

"And you feel . . . ?"

Liyah pouts. "Shitty."

Neen laughs. "Not very specific, but it's a start, I guess. When you talked to him about what happened, what did he say?"

"Nothing. Or, rather, I didn't talk to him."

"C-J, what the fuck? Has he called? Texted you?"

"He called at first but stopped. I don't know if he texted." She averts her eyes, suddenly fascinated by the philodendron in the corner of the room.

"What do you mean you don't know?"

Liyah sinks into her blanket, letting it cover her chin and mouth. "I put him on Do Not Disturb."

"C-J, *what the fuck?*" Neen exclaims, aghast.

"He sent me an email. When I called you. I can't read it."

"Why not? Is it really that bad to see someone say they love you? I'm honestly getting tired of this, C-J."

"He doesn't love me!"

"Even you're not that fucking obtuse."

"I'm not obtuse! That's what we argued about. I said he wasn't in love with me. Because he's not. You know what the subject of the email was? 'I'm Sorry.' What do you think that means, huh?"

"It means that he's sorry for saying it in public. Anybody who knows you well would expect that to be shocking. Or maybe he's sorry for summer camp. Or both!"

"Or it means that he's sorry for saying it, period! It means he wants to take it back, as anyone in their right mind would, because in what world would he love me?"

"In this one, Aliyah! That's what you're afraid of? That's actually stupid."

"Don't call me stupid!" Liyah snaps.

"Then don't be stupid!" Neen snaps right back. "Have you decided why this is so scary for you? Because that's the one thing I can't do for you. As much as I may want to."

The ache in Liyah's chest expands and contracts, twists and turns, slowly morphing into something she might be able to name. "I don't think I can do this, Neen."

"You can, I promise."

"Can I call you back? I think I need to read what he sent me."

"If I don't hear from you in two hours, I'm calling your mom."

"You wouldn't dare—" Neen has already hung up.

Liyah stands, shedding her blanket cocoon. She can do this. If he says to forget it, that he doesn't love her and it was all a big mistake, she'll be fine. Right? Nothing she doesn't already know. All she needs to do is grab her phone. She reaches for it, only to draw back and flex her hands. Circles the coffee table once, twice. Draws the line at three times. She snatches the phone quickly and gingerly, as though it might burn her.

Her thumb heads to her mail app.

No, not yet. Maybe check if he's texted first, that's easier. But what if he hasn't?

She shifts her weight from leg to leg, taking a few deep breaths. Voice mail. He called first, that's where she'll start.

"Hey, Liyah."

The sound of his voice crackling through her phone speakers makes her heart thud.

"I get why you ran out; I know we both said some things . . . Can we talk tomorrow? We can meet somewhere, or I could come to you, or whatever works. I feel

*like it would be best to talk in person. I hope you sleep
well."*

*"Hey, Liyah. I know you didn't call back or text or
anything after my message last night, but I wanted to
let you know that I still want to talk. I know I need to
apologize, and all I'm asking for is the chance to do
it face-to-face. I'll be at Bee's Knees on Division and
Wolcott at one. It's around the corner from you. I can
stay as long as you need. If you want to meet anywhere
else, just let me know. I'm sure Sweet P. would love to
see you. Talk to you soon, bye."*

*"I hope you didn't come early and leave before I got
there. I stayed until closing but I didn't see you. If
you don't want to talk in person, that's okay. I just,
I . . . I care about you a whole lot. I don't want to lose
your friendship. Please let me apologize. Call me back
whenever. I took my phone off silent, so I'll hear it."*

That thing in her chest coagulates. She swipes through her
text message threads, finding the darkened one with the little
crescent moon icon. She clicks. Five messages, spread over
five days.

Daniel
hey, i thought i'd try text,
since i know you don't always
check your voice mail. just
want you to know that i'm still
available whenever to call or
link, lmk

would you want to talk
tonight? i'll buy you a coffee
or a beer or something. i
promise not to take too much
of your time. you can lay into
me if you want, i deserve it.

i'm sorry if that last message
sounded too glib. i'm not
exactly sure what to say here.
i messed up, and i really
hope you'll give me a chance
to explain over the phone.
like i said, my ringer is on, so
call whenever.

i get that you don't want
to talk to me, but i still owe
you an apology. if i sent you
an email explaining, would
you read it? you can like this
message to confirm, you
don't have to reply.

i don't expect you to respond
to this. i don't want to make
you uncomfortable, so i'm
letting the crew know i won't
be there tonight. if you
change your mind, you know
how to reach me.

The thing is gaining sentience and starting to rattle her rib cage. She rubs her chest and wipes her eyes. Oh my God, she misses him. Only the email now. Maybe she should just forward it to Neen, make them read it aloud so she doesn't have to look. *Ha.* They'll never go for it. Her teeth sink deeply into her bottom lip as she braces for impact.

To: Aliyah Cohen-Jackson <a.cohen.jackson@fieldmuseum.org>
From: Daniel Rosenberg <dwrosenberg@kinley.com>
RE: I'm Sorry

Liyah—

I'm not sure if you'll read this, but I hope you do. It feels important that I send it anyway. Maybe that isn't fair to you, but here goes.

I am so, so sorry for where, when, and how I told you. It wasn't right, and it wasn't thoughtful. I'm even more sorry that I said you were "unfeeling." I was so hurt by your response, and I spoke in anger. I know you try to conceal it, but you are one of the most fantastically empathetic people I've ever met. I'm also so sorry that I didn't find a way to warn you all those years ago. About Maccabiah, about all of it.

Other than that, what I said was true. I'm in love with you, Liyah. I probably should have told you earlier, and I definitely should have told you in private. That doesn't make it any less true. I love you, and I've been in love with you for what feels like a long time now. I can see your face reading that. Rehinge your jaw. It's true. I should never have pretended otherwise. You'd think I would have learned my lesson after telling you to forget about the kiss—I regretted that the second you told me you hadn't forgotten, by the way. I'll probably be kicking myself forever over losing those extra two weeks of kissing you.

I know you say that love isn't your thing, but I think some of that is because you don't believe someone could love you. I'm living proof that you're wrong. And I can say with certainty that even if you don't want love from me, you'll be able to get it from someone else. You're amazing in all the ways that matter, and in some of the ways that don't.

I want to stay in your life, if you'll have me. If you don't like me romantically, I'll respect that. I don't think I can handle us sleeping together if that's the case, but I promise I can still be your friend. It would be difficult at first, and I might need a little time, but you're more than worth it.

Love,

DW

It's grown arms and legs now, and it's trying to climb out of her chest. She's crying even harder, which she wouldn't have thought possible.

Oh my God. I love him.

"I'm in love with him," Liyah says aloud, and she is answered by the sound of a key turning in a lock.

Before she has a chance to react, Lara/Laura and her conservative parents are in the living room, greeted with a half-naked, full-sobbing Liyah. She sniffles.

"Oh, I—uh, didn't realize you would be here today."

Her fine-featured mother folds her arms across her chest. "Why wouldn't she be? This is her home, too."

La(u)ra quickly steps in. "I thought I told her I'd have to go into work next Saturday, and that you were visiting today. I must have mixed up the dates."

"Uh, yeah, or maybe I did. Sorry."

They stand there, coffee table between them, staring blankly until La/u/ra's father clears his throat.

"Right, yeah. I'm going to go take a shower. Enjoy Chicago, Mr. and Mrs. . . . ." *Fuck, what's their last name?*

"Filmore," her mother supplies, looking wide-eyed at L[a/au]ra.

"Yes, of course. Couldn't remember whether you had taken your husband's name or not."

"Why wouldn't I have taken his name? We're married!" Mrs. Filmore says, looking more horrified at the suggestion than any other part of the exchange.

"Right. I'll be going."

Liyah and her "roommate" mouth *sorry* at one another before she scurries off to the bathroom.

Daniel, she thinks as the water runs over her, the sounds of the Filmores' exit filtering through the door. *I love Daniel! Who would've thought?*

Literally everybody else, it seems, when Neen picks up the phone.

"Why are you acting like this is so obvious? It's a big discovery for me."

"C-J, I love you, and you're brilliant, but you can be really slow sometimes. I've known the whole time. I'd bet Jordan and Siobhan did, too."

"Surely not the *whole* time."

"Since you told me you two were having sex, I knew you were either in love or on your way there."

"I've told you about having good sex before!"

Neen clucks their tongue. "Yeah, but you've never waxed poetic about it. 'Oh, we were so connected, it's like we could communicate with just our bodies, blah blah blah.' You should've heard yourself. All that about a man, no less. I never thought I'd see the day."

Liyah buries her face in her hands. "I hate you so much."

"No, you don't, you love me. And you love Daniel."

She isn't good with words the way Daniel is, so she'd never be able to get out what she needs to say over email. There's something she can do, though, and she pulls out her laptop the second she gets off the phone with Neen. She's brimming with nervous excitement and love that's now a living, breathing thing in her chest.

That night, she barely sleeps. The next one's not much better.

CHAPTER 30

DANIEL cannot wait for the workday to end. This morning, he debated packing a change of clothes so he wouldn't show up in his work suit. By four thirty, he's glad he decided against it. He's bouncing out of his seat with impatience and the thought of staying here a second longer than he has to makes him want to stuff his head in his rarely used filing cabinet and close it. Repeatedly.

The seconds tick by even more slowly than they did last week. This burgeoning hope is bound to destroy him.

At a quarter to five, Jordan appears in his doorway. "It's gone take you twenty minutes to get there, just go."

"I feel weird leaving before five."

"It's one time, man. If anyone says anything, I got you," he replies, and Daniel's already standing up and sliding his laptop sleeve into his messenger bag. "You ready?"

Daniel shakes his head. "Oh God, not at all."

"Bring it in," Jordan says, arms outstretched. They hug tightly, and Jordan draws back, squeezing Daniel's shoulder. "You got this. She's been flirting with you since the moment you met, remember?"

"Antagonizing."

He grins. "Same difference."

Daniel drums his fingers on his knee the entire ride there. He'd probably do it on the walk from the bus stop, up the marble steps, and to the ticketing desk if it were anatomically possible. With only one hand free, he fumbles with his phone, trying to pull up the confirmation email.

"Would you like to put that down, honey?" the elderly woman at the kiosk asks, gesturing.

"Oh! Yeah, that would probably be easier." He manages to retrieve the message and present the barcode to be scanned. The woman—her name tag reads VIOLET—hands him a physical ticket and wishes him a good visit. "Thank you, Violet."

"Anything for you, sugar." She winks. His confidence levels shoot dangerously close to Jordan's as he makes his way out into the lobby.

It occurs to Daniel that he doesn't really know what to do. The email Liyah sent the ticket in was only two words long: *for you.* He's not even totally sure he interpreted it correctly. Maybe it's a consolation prize. *I don't love you, our friendship is over, but I feel like I owe you a ticket to the exhibit I wouldn't shut up about for the last six months. Sorry!* Liyah wouldn't do that, he doesn't think, but he also didn't think she'd ignore him for a week, so . . .

He heads toward the stairs. Should he look around first? Or go straight there? Maybe she expected him to meet her in her office. But then, why send the ticket? He should have texted her first. Except she *still* hasn't texted him, and sextuple texting with no response must be some sort of federal offense.

The original plan was to see Evolving Us, so that's what he'll do. He ascends two steps at a time, avoiding eye contact with the passing museumgoers. The stairwell opens across from the exhibit, and he takes the opportunity to study the façade as he circumvents the atrium. The logo is punchy and eye-catching but easy to read; Siobhan's done excellent work.

No sign of Liyah.

He pauses at the entrance, heart racing, unsure of his next move. Should he go in? Maybe she wants to talk to him after he's finished the exhibit. Or maybe she *does* want him to go to her office, after all. But again, why the ticket? He wasn't lying to Jordan. He's not ready for this.

The heat in the Field feels like it's set to maximum. He sets his bag and winter coat on the bench by the entrance and removes his suit jacket, rolling his shirtsleeves to his elbows. Resisting the urge to hang his head in his hands, he takes a seat and pulls out his phone. A minute passes.

"You're not going to go in?"

Liyah.

Her chest is rapidly rising and falling with her breath, like she ran. There's a gentle flush in her cheeks, a sheepish smile on her lips. The top half of her hair is pulled back in a puff of curls, giving him a full view of her deep, dark eyes and thick brows, the moles on her left cheek. So beautiful. All the blood in his body is replaced with pure adrenaline. He stands, hiding his hands behind his back.

"It's good to see you." God, is it good to see her. There's a moment of silence, and Daniel awkwardly laughs.

"I'm glad you came. I wasn't sure if you would." She averts her eyes briefly, they skate up his face as they return to his. He so badly wants to take her hand.

"Does the ticket mean what I think it means?"

She nods.

His cheeks split with a grin. "And that is . . . ?"

HE'S GOING TO make her spell it out, which she was prepared for. But now, it feels like there's an immovable lump in her throat. His gaze is so piercing, Liyah is surprised he's not able to read her thoughts.

She swallows. "It means a lot of things."

Daniel quirks his eyebrow. "Like what?"

Liyah takes a deep breath. "Like, I'm sorry. For bringing up summer camp. You're right, you had already apologized. That was petty. And I'm sorry for doing the air quotes, and for storming out, and for not reading your texts, and for not contacting you sooner."

"And? What else does it mean?"

"And I miss you. So much it's stupid. I miss you for me and I miss you for the rest of the club. I was really down the last few days." She says it to his neck.

"And?" Daniel's Adam's apple bobs.

She glances to the exhibit entrance, her every instinct telling her to escape. But she won't run. Daniel is worth more than that. At last, Liyah meets his eyes. "And I love you. I am fully in love with you. I'm very set in my opinions sometimes, but if there's anybody who could change my mind on this, it's you. I never thought I'd feel safe with someone like this, but it feels good to be cared for, and to care for you. I've felt this way for most of the time I've known you, but I was so sure I couldn't be in love, because I thought that love meant rejection. Maybe it still will, but that doesn't change the fact that I'm in love with you. I don't know how I thought I wasn't, but I'm glad I know now. If you'll have me, that is. If not, then I'm a little less glad, but I guess it's better than not knowing."

Daniel regards her carefully. "You're sure? You could have called me or met up any other day this week."

Liyah nods. "More than sure, Daniel. I finally realized on Saturday—"

"You could have told me this yesterday!?"

"I needed to figure out what I was going to say! This doesn't come easy to me, you know."

"I know. But you're sure?"

She flicks him on his exposed forearm. "Yes, Daniel Woo-jin Rosenberg, for the eightieth time, I'm sure."

"Thank God," he says, finding the small of her back to pull her in. Then: "Can I kiss you?"

She answers by rising up and pressing her lips to his. Not too much, she's technically at work, but enough for her to remember just how much she loves the feel of his lips against hers, her hand on his jaw, his fingers at the back of her neck, the smell of him. Old Spice Fiji and fresh laundry and the *just him* bit.

When they separate, he wears a dopey smile that must match her own. "I got you this," he says, inserting a small pot into the narrow space between them.

"You got me a cactus?"

"I thought about flowers, but then I thought you'd tell me that getting you a dead plant was wasteful. I wasn't sure how this was going to go, and I don't trust myself to grow anything more complicated."

Liyah laughs and kisses him again, not caring where they are. "I love it."

"As much as you love me?"

"Not even close." She wrinkles her nose. "Look at me, all mushy and gross. Don't get used to it."

"I wouldn't dream of it."

"You know, you haven't said you love me yet."

"I said it first!"

Liyah giggles. "In a bar with all our friends, and then over email! That doesn't count."

"Oh, my bad," he says, wrapping her up in a tight hug. She positively melts against him. "I love you, Liyah. So, so much."

She giggles again. (What is *wrong* with her?) "What now?"

"I think we're together now, for real."

"Daniel, I meant like what are we doing for the rest of the evening."

"Oh. Do you have any more work to do?"

"Nope. Spent the whole day celebrating, and Siobhan even convinced Jeff on Malnati's for lunch. Everyone else went home at like three; I stayed in my office trying not to hyperventilate until Violet told me you'd arrived."

Daniel shakes his head, then leans in to press a kiss to her forehead. "You know, you really could have just sent me a text. Would have saved us both a lot of stress."

Liyah steps back, just so he can see her roll her eyes. "Where's the spice in that? The flavor? Come on, you can drop your stuff in my office and then I'll show you the exhibition." She slings his bag over her shoulder, takes his hand, and leads him through a door labeled STAFF ONLY.

When the door to the office clicks shut, Daniel asks, "What convinced you that you loved me, in the end?"

"Aside from feeling generally miserable while we weren't talking—"

"While you weren't talking to me." He smiles, but it's tentative.

"Right, that was bad," Liyah replies softly. She reaches up to cup his cheek. "I promise not to do that again."

Daniel leans into her hand, his smile brightening several watts. "Thank you."

"*As I was saying,*" Liyah starts, dropping her hand to his shoulder. "Aside from general miserableness, I saw your ads on the train and started crying."

The hand that isn't holding his jacket finds its way to the small of Liyah's back. "Wow, I knew they were good, but I didn't think they were that good," he deadpans.

"I wasn't crying at the ads, I was crying because I missed you, you idiot."

A slow smile spreads across Daniel's face. "I know."

"I know you know. I just wanted to call you an idiot. Now, please put your shit down so you can really kiss me."

"What about the exhibit?" he asks, but he does what she says. This time, he kisses her long and slow, and she feels a shiver zip from her neck to her toes.

"It'll still be there in fifteen minutes," she says against his mouth.

"Hmm . . ."

"Just kissing, I promise. Siobhan works in this office, too."

"We're not gonna have sex in your office? I'm hurt." Daniel pouts, and Liyah wonders if there's a seed of truth in his feigned disappointment.

"Only because I explicitly promised Siobhan that we wouldn't." She brushes the stray strands of hair off his forehead, trailing her finger down, and cups his cheek once more. Her eyes linger on his lips. "Just kissing," she mutters, mostly reminding herself.

Daniel does her favorite crooked smile. The one she loves so, so much. "Give me twenty minutes and you've got a deal."

EPILOGUE

Three years (and some change) later

"**LI!** I'm home," Daniel calls, to no response. From the foyer, he spies a bowl of popcorn and two unopened beers on the table: one sour and one India pale ale. It's Monday, which means they're supposed to be watching twenty-five men attempt to seduce one woman—Liyah prefers this to the inverse, as she thinks the "fragile male egos" make for better drama. Having sampled both over the seasons, Daniel must agree.

He walks past the framed picture of their camp cohort. Third row on the end is a tiny Liyah making even tinier bunny ears behind Daniel's head. It was Kayla's birthday present to him this year—though he uses the word *present* loosely, given how unfortunate he looked at that age. It can't be good for your mental health to stare at a picture of thirteen-year-old you, mid-blink and metal mouthed, over coffee every morning.

Two beers, but no Liyah. The bathroom is empty, as is the bedroom, where he drops his gym bag.

Come to think of it, Sweet Potato didn't greet him at the door. It's not a strange occurrence on nights when Liyah gets home first; the cat learned that he'll come to wherever she is soon enough.

The last room to check is the office/library/indoor jungle that once belonged to Lora—*who the fuck spells Laura that way? You go by Leah, spelled L-I-Y-A-H! Shut it, DW.*

The door is slightly ajar, and when Daniel pushes it open, he's greeted with an excellent view of Liyah's ass in his favorite jean cutoffs of hers. As it turns out, they *were* made—or at least tailored on Neen's sewing machine—specifically for her. She's kneeling on the fire escape, presumably holding their cat just beyond his view.

"Drop it, Sweep, I'm begging you." Liyah decided about a month into their official relationship that Sweet P. didn't roll off the tongue easily enough and began calling her Sweepy instead. That bastardization was eventually converted to Sweep, which has evolved into the occasional Bristles, Broomstick, or once even Mop Bucket. Liyah rule number 32: do not point out that those names are syllabically identical to or longer than Sweet P.

"What's she got?" Daniel asks, leaning on the doorframe.

Liyah yelps and whips around, stopping just short of slamming her head into the half-open window she'd climbed through. "God, Daniel. You scared me."

"Sorry."

"She has a dead mouse in her mouth. It's so big I thought it was a rat."

"I hope you thanked her for her pest control services."

"She tried to drop it in my lap, Daniel. *My lap*." She dips her head and whispers, "Thank you, Sweet Potato," anyway. It's one of those moments that makes Daniel fall in love with her all over again.

"Here, let me try." Daniel folds himself through the window, joining Liyah on the steel grate. Sweet Potato blinks up at him, pupils round and innocent, a mouse the size of her head dead and bloodied between her jaws. "Hold her over the railing a little more, but don't drop her."

"I'm not going to drop her!"

He reaches his hand under Sweet Potato's neck, careful to avoid the rodent carcass, and gives it a soft tickle. Sure enough, she drops her prey, and Daniel and Liyah watch as it sails to the empty sidewalk below.

"I swear I tried that three times already," Liyah grumbles, finally ushering the cat back inside. "You just have magic fingers. Also, hi. You smell good."

"I'm all sweaty from climbing."

"Yeah, that's what I said."

Daniel grins. "You loooove me," he sings.

"That I do," she replies, and slips back through the window. He's glad, otherwise that ring box he hid in the pocket of his suitcase for this year's trip to San Francisco will be a horrible waste.

When they're both firmly on solid ground, she pulls on the chest of his dry fit shirt, drawing him into a sweet kiss *hello*.

"Shower quickly, I need to know what happens between Matt S. and Matt C."

He does as he's told, mixing in a dollop of Liyah's lavender conditioner to his own. Her hair products are heavily moisturizing and leave his hair weighed-down and greasy—he learned from experience—but he loves the scent so much that he found a way. They never talked about it, but at some point, Liyah stopped buying her aloe deodorant and started using his Old Spice instead. He likes the thought of them carrying little bits of each other around each day, a pleasant reminder whenever he frustratedly runs his fingers through his hair at work. He supposes that means she's reminded of him when she stress-sweats, but he tries not to think about that too hard. It's cute. It's definitely a cute couple thing.

There's a lot he loves about living with Liyah. Perhaps his favorite is waking up next to her every morning, no matter how grumpy she is. He loves that she pokes fun at him, always keeping him on his toes, but is so nonjudgmental about the things that matter. The first time she caught him talking to his dad, she introduced herself, kissed Daniel on the cheek, and left the room. He loves that he can be there to hold her, skin to skin, coaching her through deep breaths when a nightmare wakes her. He loves that she's always willing to talk or listen when he needs it, how she never rushes him to figure out his emotions. He loves how much she loves his cat.

There are hard things, too. Like when he pushes her away on bad days and she snaps at him, or how she sometimes goes silent instead of asking for the love she wants. But they're always trying, and the good far outweighs the bad.

"Dee-Dubs, your beer is getting warm!"

DANIEL EMERGES FROM the shower, hair wild from his always aggressive towel drying, in naught but a pair of boxer briefs. Liyah had to acclimate herself to his propensity for walking around shirtless when he moved in. How he doesn't freeze under the air-conditioning, she'll never know, but rain or shine, he's half-naked at the first opportunity. She's come to see the rolled shirtsleeves as an incredible exercise of self-restraint rather than self-indulgence.

She's come to see a lot of things about Daniel differently. All of them make her love him even more. It's amazing how long you can spend getting to know someone; she'd always assumed that once a relationship was counted in years instead of months, there would be little left to discover. For the first time in her life, she's happy to admit that she was wrong. She'd like to keep learning about Daniel indefinitely, if he'll have her. Maybe one day, she'll make Neen her Theyd of Honor (the name is a work in progress, bear with her). Shockingly, she wouldn't mind if it were soon.

"Which Matt are we rooting for, again? C.?" Daniel asks as he takes his usual spot on the sofa, leaning against one of Lora's atrocious throw pillows. Or Daniel's, now, as he spent fifteen whole dollars to keep them when Lora moved out. Liyah wishes he had withdrawn the money in cash and set it on fire instead.

"No, S.! C.'s the one who started it." His hand falls to her thigh; she fiddles with the friendship bracelet Avi made him during his freshman orientation at Northwestern.

"I still couldn't tell half these white guys apart if there was a gun to my head."

"Maybe that's secretly the producers' intent. If they all look the same, then it's the one with the best emotional connection that wins out."

"Yes, it's truly about the depth and complexity of human relationships, that's why they're expected to get engaged after approximately twenty-two hours together," he deadpans.

There's no real argument there, so Liyah glares at him and presses play. She loves these Monday nights, when the workweek has yet to render either of them too tired for extended conversation, and they can flirt and banter and yell at the TV, Sweepy periodically switching between their laps and the cat tree that's nearly Daniel's height. They usually rush to their shared bedroom the moment the episode ends, but often they don't make it off the couch, Daniel having traced too many tantalizing circles on Liyah's skin for her to resist. On occasion, they make it halfway, ending up on the floor or against a wall.

Together, they're still worthy of poetry and prose.

Tonight is a couch night. Afterward, having decided that

popcorn was not, in fact, a suitable dinner, they stand naked in the kitchen eating cold pizza straight from the refrigerator. A clump of cheese falls from Daniel's slice. Sweet Potato races toward it but he scoops her up before she can get there, holding her unnecessarily high above his head. In a panicked voice, he asks Liyah to pick it up before it can upset his baby's tummy. Liyah laughs hysterically, and it's one of those moments that makes her fall in love with him all over again.

ACKNOWLEDGMENTS

The very first person I need to thank is Betsy, without whom I can truly say this book would not exist, period. Thank you for your support, gushing emails, FaceTimes when I had no idea where to go next, and undying love for Daniel and Liyah. You are an incredible friend and invaluable beta (and alpha!) reader.

Thank you to Claire, the Liyah to my Neen, the Neen to my Liyah. Love you oodles, babe.

All my friends who read a draft or offered support in any form (in particular, Alex, Anj, Chapla, Isabella): that meant the world to me. Thank you to Karen Kong Wilson for loving Daniel and Liyah even in their earliest draft. Your love of romance novels is the gift that keeps on giving.

Thank you, Mom, for your unconditional love. And for reading the very first draft and giving me feedback, despite the embarrassment the 1.5 sex scenes may have caused you. Thank you, Dad, for reading the draft that eventually sold, even though you had to read those scenes with one eye closed. I will forever be flattered that you both read a romance novel for me. Thank you to the rest of my family, who I'm sure will have bought a copy, even if you never choose to read it. I promise it's okay if you don't (see aforementioned 1.5 sex scenes).

To my emotional support 2022 debut authors, Ava Wilder and Sam Markum: thank you for your kindness, your friendship, your guidance, and for always providing a space to vent. Sam, there is absolutely no way I could have survived querying without you, and it was your comment about how Daniel and Liyah always thank each other when they're vulnerable that sparked the idea for this title. Ava, you kept me sane through that first revision process, and your openness about your publishing journey made the anxiety of my debut year so much less awful. Mostly, you have contributed to and elevated so many of my crying cat [positive] moments. I can't thank either of you enough. Reader, if you haven't already (I literally cannot imagine that, but just in case), go check out their books. I am lucky to call such fabulous authors my friends.

Jessica Mileo, "the call" with you was the highlight of my 2021. You are an absolute dream of an agent. Thank you for your professional support, phone calls, and always giving me the sense that you have complete faith in me. It goes without saying that this book wouldn't be in anybody's hands without you, but I'll say it anyway. I am so fortunate to have you on my team with your editorial eye and agenting expertise.

Vicki Lame, I am still a bit starstruck that I get to work with you. From that very first call, I could tell that you understood this story, these characters, and my writing in general, and I couldn't wait to work with you. Thank you especially to Vanessa Aguirre. To everyone from the editorial, publishing, design, and marketing teams at SMPG (Rivka Holler, Brant Janeway, Lauren Ablondi-Olivo, Kelly Too, Olga Grlic, Soleil Paz, Jeremy Haiting, Susannah Noel, Chrisinda Lynch, NaNá Stoelzle, and Anne Marie Tallberg), thank you so much for putting your time and effort into making this book something real that readers can hold in their hands. Thank you to Poppy Magda, the incredible cover artist.

Finally, thank you to the individuals who sat with me

doing their own thing while I drafted (or, on occasion, tried to "help" me type), Patrick and Essi. Essi, thank you for sitting on my lap/on my chest/by my side through the difficult parts. Patrick, thank you so much for letting me read aloud random bits I was proud of or stuck on. You heard this story all out of order to the point where it was nonsensical, but you were so patient with me. And thank you for the advice about how men talk to each other when no women are present. I took most of it, and Daniel and Jordan are all the more real for it. Thank you for loving me. I love you both so much that it hurts.

ABOUT THE AUTHOR

Patrick Wilson

RACHEL RUNYA KATZ is a contemporary romance writer currently living in Durham, North Carolina, with her partner, her cat, and far too many houseplants. Her books center queer Jews of color and their layered lives of joy, sadness, and love.